GOOD WITCHES DON'T CURSE

Academy of Shadowed Magic - Year Three

S.W. CLARKE

Cover: Covers by Juan

Proofreading: Kathy Waghorn

FREE SHORT STORY: Liara Youngblood and Lucian the demon prince clash in the prequel story *The Fae and the Demon.*

Join S.W. Clarke's reader newsletter and get *The Fae and the Demon* for FREE only at subscribepage.io/swclarke.

CHAPTER ONE

My flames cut through the August air with a hiss, the London humidity parting in a straight line toward Aidan North's chest.

He hadn't expected that. His brown eyes followed the flames with almost scientific fascination, his glasses flickering with the reflection.

"Gotta move, North," I called out.

That seemed to awaken him. He threw himself out of the way as he always did. But where I expected him to land with an inglorious thump on the grass, this time he managed to return fire as he did.

Blue everflame blossomed from his hand, sprayed out from his fingertips in five directions. Three of them were on course to hit me.

Well done, Aidan, I had time to think before I dropped, hitting the grass chest-first, fingers tented as the flames rushed overtop me.

He and I stared at one another from opposite ends of the lawn, his chest moving fast.

I smiled. "About time."

He shrugged one shoulder, adjusted his glasses. "I guess sheer repetition can overcome even the worst depth perception."

I pushed myself up to a crouch. "Show me how you did that, with your fingers."

"Oh, you mean the Five-Finger Flick?" He blew on his not-flaming fingers with irritating smugness. "It's patented. You'll have to pay for use."

I stood. "One, you need to rebrand that. Two, if you don't show me in the next five minutes, I will absolutely not hesitate to double-team you with Loki."

From the patio, Loki gave a loud, portentous meow, his tail flicking.

Aidan's eyes shifted between us. "You wouldn't."

"I'm a fire witch, North." I took a step forward, my left hand igniting. "Don't put anything beneath me."

For a moment, his eyes widened with something like concern. He studied my face from his seat on the grass, and I could tell for a split second he was searching for some sign I was joking.

It lanced me through the chest. He hadn't ever doubted me before the incident earlier in the summer. But ever since that day, he'd never quite gotten back to trusting me completely. And no matter what I did or said, that moment of trepidation always appeared when my dark humor came out.

So I bared my teeth at him like a feral cat, scrunching my nose.

A second later his fear was gone, replaced by a small smile. "Maybe I'll teach you... if you can win the next round."

I nodded, lifting my other hand. Flames hissed to life. "You know I will."

He stood, blue flames appearing in both hands. "I don't know, Cole. You don't win them all anymore."

And it was true. We'd practiced every day this summer, and I really didn't win them all. The majority, but not all.

Sometimes, of course, the everflame got the better of him. On those days we called it a draw.

Aidan had a unique fighting style. You wouldn't expect it, but he was all offense. He came at me fast and hard, sending out a wave of flame to obscure his movements until he burst through it like water.

The thing about Aidan's everflame: I couldn't dissipate it like regular fire. It burned hotter, longer, and didn't obey anyone but Aidan.

So all I could do was backpedal, fists at the ready.

He came out the other side of the flames airborne, leaping with a yell that made Loki jump. I would have laughed if Aidan hadn't been coming straight at me with five blue knuckles of righteous fury.

He'd gotten quicker. I hadn't expected him to be this quick.

I only had one choice.

I swung my upper body left, threw out my hand to grip his forearm and send him past me. Of course, the everflame extended up his arms, too—and it caught on my hands the moment I touched it.

That was the other thing about Aidan's gift: it spread mindlessly, grasping whatever it could touch. Which in this case happened to be my hand.

Thank god for his parents' anti-burning enchantment on this property. Otherwise the whole place would have been incinerated on the first day of summer.

Unfortunately, my *body* wasn't included in that enchantment.

The blue flames consumed my red ones, streaking up my hand and arm with a wildfire's speed. There was only one way to get rid of them.

I spun, pitched toward the patio's edge where the deceiver's rod lay. In a second I'd gripped it, felt its power rush through me. Felt the blue flames dissipate under the heat of my own.

I had long ago discovered just one means to overcome everflame: the weapon. The key and the rod, swimming with their own power. That was all we had managed to figure out about it over the summer— the sheer power of the key and rod combined were immense, and that I preferred to wield it like a baseball bat.

So much for great epiphanies.

"Bloody hell, don't use it like that," Aidan said from behind me.

I swept around, pointing the rod at him. "If it works, it works."

His eyebrow went up. "You're seriously going to point that weapon at me?"

I stood, still pointing it at him. "It's only half of a weapon."

"Don't underestimate it, Clementine."

I rose, coming forward and jabbing it at him like a sword. "I'm its master, North. It only does what I ask of it."

Before he could reply, I swung around with a roundhouse kick I knew he would dodge. But he wouldn't expect the rod whistling through the air as I came back around; I threw out my arm, caught him lightly in the side with it. "Gotcha," I breathed. "How's that for a new trick?"

His arms went across his midsection, mouth opening. "You just hit me with a five-hundred-year-old weapon."

I straightened. "I'd call that 'lightly batted.' Anyway, I win."

The house's back door began to open, and Aidan and I exchanged a quick glance. The moment we did, I dropped the rod into the nearby shrubbery.

When Charlotte North's face appeared, she folded her arms and leaned against the doorway just the way Aidan would do. No question he was her child. But I wondered if she was as perceptive as him; she showed no sign of having seen the rod. "Who won the second Battle of the Ages?"

Loki stood, trotting over to her with a meow. He loved that woman's cooking.

Aidan jerked a thumb at me. "Clementine."

"To the victor goes the largest slice of minced pie," Charlotte said in a sing-song. "Come on for the last supper."

The last supper before we left for the academy.

Aidan started toward the house, but I remained where I was. "I'll be just a second," I called out. Aidan knew why; he didn't stop to ask.

When the two of them had left, I picked the rod out of the bushes. Stared down at it, considering Aidan's fear of it. Of *me*.

Nothing would happen if my anger didn't appear. If the Spitfire didn't appear. And I'd only been truly angry once this summer. Just one time, and I hadn't even been holding the rod.

But I wondered what would have happened if I had been.

I gripped it, started toward the patio where my cloak lay. *Just don't get mad, Clementine*, I thought. The moment I stepped onto the stone, a voice sounded from the yard.

It was my name, high and breathy.

When I spun, I caught a glimpse of red hair disappearing behind a far tree.

I blinked, staring.

A moment later, a cardinal flew around from the other side. Swept up onto a branch and perched there, staring back at me.

Not my red hair. Just a bird's tail feathers.

I stood a minute longer staring at the bird—watching, listening. Nothing else happened. Nothing except the soft uptick of wind as an English rain blew in.

Aidan and I sat opposite Charlotte and Tom North, a minced pie being passed around the dinner table for our last meal. Loki sat at the head of the table with his own plate, as he did every night.

That cat would never accept anything less again.

With Aidan's family, I had begun to feel normal. For three months, I'd felt like someone's daughter.

It was different with the Norths than with Eva's family. The Norths were human, like me. They were about the same age as my parents would be. They had given me a bedroom to sleep in, my own place for a few months.

And like me, Charlotte North was a fire mage.

"Back to the academy tomorrow," Charlotte said, eyeing us both. She had the warmest green eyes I'd ever seen. "The both of you third-year scholars. And you a guardian, Clementine."

I took a large bite of pie, occupying my mouth. That way I only had to nod. All summer I'd been avoiding thoughts of—and sometimes re-remembering—what lay before me.

I was going to be a guardian.

And every time the thought returned, a strange swirl of feelings twisted inside my chest. Thrill lay in there, but it twined tight with dread.

"Hey, what do scholars eat when they're hungry?" Tom asked, already chuckling at the thought of the punchline to come.

Charlotte rolled her eyes toward him. "Not that. Please."

"Dad," Aidan said. "It's not fun—"

"*Academia* nuts."

I snorted into my pie. Meanwhile, the rest of the table groaned.

Not long into my stay, I'd decided Aidan's dad was the kind of man I would have liked to have for a father. He didn't make me uncomfortable like some men had done. He didn't look at me longer than he should. He loved and appreciated the people around him with a rare keenness, the kind you didn't often see after so many years of having a family.

I liked his dad jokes. He had earned them.

"Tom and I will take you three to the leyline in the morning," Charlotte said. "You know, just in case."

Aidan raised a hand. "No, Mum. It'll be fine."

"We heard about what happened at my mother's home," Charlotte said. Once again, she surprised me with her maternal care, given she was Farina North's daughter. She must have gone through a real gauntlet to become the woman she was today. "If you're leaving the property, it's best Clementine is escorted by one or both of us."

"Nothing's happened," Aidan said. "Nothing all summer."

And it was true. The few times we'd been into town, no one had bothered us. It was almost as though, for one gilded summer, the formalists didn't exist. The Shade didn't exist.

But life had taught me that such things never really disappeared. They only stayed out of sight for a while.

What Charlotte and Tom didn't know was that Aidan and I had come to a conclusion in June. Maeve Umbra had made me a guardian. She knew almost everything at play, and we figured she had come to one conclusion:

The only way to defeat the darkness was to face it.

Prudently, of course. With weapons and horses and whatever magic you had at your disposal. But face it all the same.

The one thing Umbra didn't know was about the prophecy. I was supposed to defeat the Shade, and there was only one way to become powerful enough to do so.

I had to fend off her army, the shards of her power. I had to defeat them again and again until I could take the queen herself. Only through a trial by fire would I ever be strong enough to win.

So I couldn't hide myself away from the world. Not entirely. And going alone with Aidan to the leyline near their home wasn't a reckless thing.

I had the enchanted moonstone from my mother. I had Loki and the weapon. And I had my fire.

"We'll be fine," I said to his parents. "The formalists don't know I'm here. And if something does happen, Aidan and I will send up smoke signals." I raised an eyebrow at Aidan's dad.

He pointed at me and nodded. "Nicely done."

From his seat, Loki meowed. Then, to me, "Must we leave?"

I half-smiled at him. "You want to live here forever?"

"It isn't that I don't enjoy Vickery's conjurations, but you don't encounter minced pie like this twice in a lifetime."

I turned my attention to Charlotte, jerked a thumb at Loki. "He's wondering if you could adopt him. Not because he loves you, but because he loves your pie."

Charlotte, who'd always been charmed by Loki, shot him her most indulgent smile. "Absolutely, my love. Gods, what I wouldn't give to have been born a witch with a familiar. He's such a sweetheart, that one."

Of course, she only thought he was a sweetheart because I filtered out most of his snark.

Loki turned self-satisfied green eyes on me, licked his lips. "Now that's the kind of treatment I expect."

Later that night, as I stood in my bedroom packing everything into my tangibly manipulated cloak, I lifted out the deceiver's rod. Ran my fingers down the cool length of it.

I'd been holding this rod when I had heard my name on the wind. When I thought I'd seen that red hair in the yard.

That was a first.

When Aidan and I returned to the academy, we would delve into the prophecy again. The only book we'd ever found that discussed it remained tucked away in the Room of the Ancients, and Aidan had never properly translated the Faerish for the last two parts of the weapon described in the prophecy.

The cursed chain, and the thief's blade.

They were still out there in the world, somewhere.

"Is that your precious now?" Loki asked from his recline atop the bed's duvet, tail flicking.

"Would you be jealous if it were?"

"Never. It's an object. I'm a living, highly intelligent being."

I sat down on the bed with it. Some part of me wanted to tell Loki what I'd seen in the yard, and another part of me hesitated. I felt a little crazy. What I'd seen reminded me of the apparition in the center of the Boundless Labyrinth. She'd looked just like me. She'd sounded like me. She *was* me.

And I still didn't understand how she'd come to be.

Seeing things. Hearing voices. Maybe I was just now manifesting schizophrenia.

Or maybe—even worse—the fire magic itself was beginning to affect me. I had already lost control of the Spitfire once this summer, on Aidan of all people. That should never have happened.

But when I considered my other choices, I didn't see that I had any. It was only to grow in power, to assemble the weapon, to defeat the Shade. That was my path.

So I set the rod into my cloak and put it all aside.

Tomorrow, we had to be up early. After a long summer, we were finally returning to Shadow's End and the prophecy.

CHAPTER TWO

Aidan's mother must have hugged us each three times. She tearily pressed a wrapped pie into Aidan's arms, pushed his hair back to kiss his forehead. She even picked Loki up, held him like a swaddled baby (to which he didn't object; that cat loved her). Meanwhile, Tom slid a hand over his wife's shoulders, gave us each one-armed hugs.

"Goodbye, scholars," he called after us.

It was just a fifteen-minute walk to the leyline, which ran through a little-used field not far from their home. Passing down the lane and all the pushed-together houses, I shook my head. "I still can't believe Farina disowned your mother."

"Can't you, though?" Aidan said to me. "You met my grandmother."

I'd done more than met Aidan's grandmother—I'd set her hair aflame. Still no regrets. "Yeah, and the disowning should go the *other* way around."

"Anyway, Mum and Dad have done fine for themselves," Aidan said. "They're happier than my grandmother ever was or will be, hoard of wealth or no."

I'd never met my own grandparents. My mother always said they'd died long before I was born, but that they were good people. I wondered now how true that was; after all, Charlotte North hadn't once badmouthed her own mother in my presence.

I guess it was a reflection of what kind of people my mother and Charlotte were, that they only spoke well of people who couldn't answer for themselves.

"You're going to be a guardian," Aidan said as we walked. "How're you feeling about that?"

I joshed him with my elbow. "That's how I feel about that."

"It's something to be proud of, Clementine."

"Does that mean you're going to embrace your gift and become a guardian?"

He avoided my eyes, his attention on a cat in someone's garden. "I haven't decided. I quite prefer reading old books and drinking tea to burning people alive."

As we passed by, Loki came to the gate to sniff. In the garden, the white cat sent up a ferocious hiss.

Loki strafed away, blinked up at me as shocked as he'd ever been. "I'll tell you what: that cat is no familiar."

I bent over, swept a comforting hand over his head and back. "But you've got much better control of the everflame," I said to Aidan. "Way better than that one afternoon…"

"Can we please not talk about the afternoon we went to visit my grandmother?" Aidan said with pleading eyes on me. "I'd much rather pretend it was a dream."

"Fine by me." We reached the cross-street, turned. "Anyway, North, the point is this: I've only got Liara Youngblood and a bunch of strangers to watch my back. It would be real nice having you there on missions."

"I'll think about it," he said with the kind of finality I knew meant Aidan was done with the conversation. More than done. Pressing him would only make things worse.

Soon we struck into the field, high-stepping through the unmown grass toward the spot where the leyline ran under the ground. Aidan was most familiar with it; he'd come and gone by this spot his whole childhood.

Me? You could have set me in the center of that field and I would have spent the next two weeks trying to find the right damn spot.

We hadn't gotten very far in when Loki stopped, black tail upright like a signpost sticking out of the grass. "I smell magic," he said in his low, serious voice.

Aidan hadn't noticed; I had to get his attention. Then I nodded at Loki. "Someone's around."

And by someone, I meant a mage.

Aidan went stiff, staring around the wide field to the lanes beyond, the houses and their curtains totally still. A car passed down one road, a breeze tickled the grass, a cloud passed over the sun.

The world darkened, chilled, my skin goosepimpling.

"Where are they?" I asked Loki.

"I don't know," Loki said. "It's strange, but I can't figure out a direction. It's powerful, though."

I'd had a similar experience to this in the fae market in Vienna, standing with Nissa Whitewillow. Someone with powerful magic had been watching me then. Someone with ill intent.

"I don't see anyone," Aidan said, turning a circle.

"Loki can't tell where it's coming from," I said.

Aidan and I met eyes. This summer had put us more or less on the same page; we had gotten very good at telling each other's thoughts from one gesture, from a single expression. In a second, we had come to the same conclusion: We should move.

I started forward, faster than before. "We're going, Loki."

My familiar didn't object. Loki fell into a trot beside me as Aidan took my hand, and the three of us struck across the field toward the leyline.

When we arrived at the spot, the ground began rumbling from the far side of the field.

I turned, staring. I couldn't see any difference except the swaying grass and the nearing sound of the earth shifting. It carried toward us with lightning speed, vibrating under our feet and then just as quickly passing onward to the other end of the field.

And like that, the world went as still and regular as it had been before. Except the cloud still remained over the sun.

I spun in a slow circle, expecting an earth mage and seeing no one. "What was that?"

Aidan had also turned a circle, hands up. "It was the leyline, I think. Whatever that rumbling was, it followed the leyline's path."

"What does that mean? Like a fault line?"

He shook his head. "Seems that way." When he turned, he raised his finger to cut the air. "But we need to leave this place, get to the academy."

Loki pressed close to my leg. "I agree."

Aidan made a swift incision in the veil, not sparing any time for straight lines. Without pause, he nodded at me. "Go on. I'll follow."

I didn't hesitate. I pressed the veil aside, ducked through. But when I stood up on the other side, we weren't in the forest outside the academy.

We weren't in a forest at all.

I stared with wide eyes at an enormous, half-frozen lake and the barren tundra beyond. Here and there, snow streaked across the land. The air felt fifty degrees colder. And the sun lay low on the horizon.

This wasn't the academy.

"Aidan—" When I turned, Aidan had already come through and straightened behind me. In his wake, the veil was already reseaming itself. Not that I wanted to go back to where we had been.

Aidan's eyebrows rose high above his glasses as he took the place in. His quick breath crystallized in the air. "This…"

"Isn't Shadow's End," Loki finished for him.

I swept a hand out. "Why did you take us here?"

"I didn't." Aidan pulled his cloak tight. "The leyline must have."

"That's possible?" I asked.

Aidan took a few steps over the hard ground toward the lake, staring out. "I've read it's possible. Never had it happen to me before."

I turned after him. "And why would a leyline take us somewhere else than where we wanted to go?"

He shook his head. "I don't know, Clem." He glanced back at me. "But you heard what happened right before we went through."

Of course I'd heard it. Every creature in a mile's radius had heard it—and probably felt it. Including Aidan's parents.

"I heard it." I paused. "We should go back for your family."

"No." Aidan's voice was as adamant as it ever got. "My parents are under an enchantment. They're experienced mages—more than us. And most of all, they wouldn't want us to go back. Not right now."

"And you're just willing to accept they're all right on faith?"

Aidan pulled his cellphone out of his cloak, waved it in the air. "I can use technology, you know."

"Oh, that." My arms had gone across my body for warmth, and I turned back to the leyline. "I'll part the veil this time, take us back to the academy."

Aidan's eyes wandered the landscape, not quite focusing on me. "If the leyline will let us." But he didn't move; the wind caught his hair, blowing it wild.

Loki leapt onto my cloak, crawled up to my shoulder. He perched close to my neck for warmth. "Just an FYI: I'm ready for someplace that isn't a cold, barren wasteland."

I set a hand on Loki, but kept studying Aidan. He was deep in thought. "You're wondering why we ended up here, aren't you?"

Aidan's eyes snapped to me. "There's got to be a reason." He glanced down at his phone, began tapping the screen.

"What are you doing?"

"Getting coordinates." A few seconds later, he replaced his phone back in his pocket. "Just in case."

I turned toward the spot we'd stepped through. "Let's hope this try doesn't drop us into lava."

Aidan stepped up to my side. "Here's trusting the fire witch."

I raised a finger, poising it in the air. It had been a few months since I'd cut the veil, but for the first time, I felt the humming power before me as my hand went out toward the leyline.

This was a place of power.

I couldn't yet see a leyline, but I could sense it like the faintest radio signal. And there it was, the proof I'd been seeking all summer: I was growing. I was becoming more powerful.

I drew my finger down, slicing through the veil toward the ground as I imagined the forest outside the academy. This time I pressed it aside before stepping through; on the other side, I recognized a familiar set of trees.

When I glanced back at Loki, he stepped closer, sniffed. "Smells vaguely like horse dung. This is the place."

I gestured for Aidan to come through. "Loki's given his toe-bean stamp of approval."

"Good enough for me." Aidan ducked, passed through to the other side. Loki followed.

I remained crouched with the veil pressed aside, hesitating.

When I looked over my shoulder, the wide, sunset expanse of the lake and the tundra greeted me again. What a beautiful, barren part of the world. It felt untouched, completely natural.

There was a reason the leyline had brought us to this place.

"Clementine?" Loki said from the other side.

I refocused on my familiar and Aidan, both waiting for me. When I came through the veil and stood, Aidan was on his phone again, fingers tapping away.

A second later, he gave an enormous relieved sigh. Looked up at me. "Mum and Dad are fine. They heard a rumble, but nothing else."

We started through the forest. "Did they have any idea what it was?"

"Mum supposed earth magic, but she couldn't know for sure. Apparently a mage of any sort can touch the ground and imbue it with their magic."

"Interesting," Loki said from beside me. "They thought it was mage-made."

"So it wasn't the leyline itself," I said to Aidan.

He shrugged. "Hard to say. Best we get to the academy first, talk later."

Minutes later we passed through Umbra's enchantment around the academy grounds; for the first time in three months, a weight I'd grown used to lifted from my chest, allowed my lungs to fill.

I had never realized how safe I felt here. I had never realized how badly a childlike, primal part of me *wanted* to feel safe.

When we came to the campus and I saw my first set of fae wings, I was already looking for Eva's face. But she wasn't attached to them.

Only about half the student body had arrived. We were early—Aidan was early to everything, and as a result, so was I—for a school year that wouldn't start until tomorrow.

"We should tell—" Aidan began, but I had already struck a hard left and was jogging toward the stables, Loki following me at a jog.

Yes, we should tell Umbra about what had happened.

Yes, we should be responsible young adults.

But as I came to the stables and opened the half-door and saw Noir's handsome face appear over his stall door, I knew I'd made the right choice.

"Someone's been eating well," Loki murmured.

I came up to Noir and set my hands under his velvety chin. He inhaled my scent with wide nostrils, and here in this simple place with my cat and my horse, I'd found home.

"Oh," a sharp voice cut into my moment. "You again."

CHAPTER THREE

Quartermistress Farrow stood with folded arms, her body lit from behind in the open-air aisleway, that whiplike braid over one shoulder. She scrutinized me with the same hard eyes as the first time we'd met.

I half-turned, ran a hand over the side of Noir's face. "Missed me that much?" I asked her.

Faint humor appeared at one side of her mouth. That was as much as anyone ever got from her. "I'll tell you one thing, I've missed you cleaning stalls. That one in particular makes an awful lot of shit."

I scratched under his jaw, observing the inside of his stall and spotting a flake of prized alfalfa. "I think he charmed you, Farrow."

"Please." She came to my side, observing Noir. "His idea of charm is banging the stall door when he's peckish. Or wants to be scratched. Or he's bored."

"So, all the time."

"All the time."

Loki hopped up onto the stall door in front of Farrow, perched there and meowed at her.

She obliged by petting him. "This year you'll be riding Noir through the veil."

My gut cinched. She was referring, of course, to guardian missions. "You think he's ready?"

Farrow went on petting Loki. "You saved his life. That horse will go anywhere and do anything you ask of him."

I hadn't heard that kind of sentimental talk from her before. "You think horses can feel gratitude."

"The first guardian trial showed me all I needed to see." She sighed as if caught in memory. "I don't know if I've ever seen a stallion move like that. You're suited to him, too."

Those were the nicest words Farrow had ever offered me. I didn't know how to respond, so I only said, "I'll be back to mucking stalls tomorrow morning."

"Oh no." Farrow almost chuckled. "You're a guardian now. That's it's own job."

"But she excels at shoveling poop." Loki's eyes taunted me. "I would know."

I snorted. "What if I want to keep my job here?" I said to her.

Farrow set a weighty hand on my shoulder. "Trust me, Clementine, you'll have your hands entirely full. Your head, too."

"She has no idea how dirty that sounds," Loki whispered.

I grinned at him. Then, to her, "Were you a guardian?"

She shifted her eyes off me, around the stable's interior. "No, but I've seen the guardians come and go on the horses. I've seen for twenty-three years how it affects them—the stress of it, the adrenaline." She paused, meeting my eyes. "It's a sacrifice you make, every time. I won't have you cleaning these stalls."

That sounded final. I tilted my head with the smallest smile. "Who'll ever be able to replace me?"

Farrow flicked a hand through the air, turned toward the stall opposite Noir's. "Come meet the new mare. A two-year-old paint, lovely little thing for the right rider."

I followed Farrow to the stall, found a horse around fifteen hands staring back at me from under long lashes. She nickered when she saw me, came forward to sniff my hand. "What's her name?" I asked.

"Minibar."

I laughed. "I knew there was a reason I hung around you, Farrow."

A half-hour later, I left the stables for the dorm Eva and I shared. When I came to the room, I found it empty and musty. If Eva had gotten back—regardless of whether she'd cleaned at all—it would smell of vanilla and freshness.

Loki came in, stepping with high paws. "Ugh."

I pressed a layer of film off my desk. "Forgive me, Lord. I don't have any fae dust to sprinkle."

"Let's be honest, you've never lifted a finger in the name of cleaning." He hopped onto my bed, and regular old dust lifted visibly into the air. "But I tolerate you anyway."

I stepped over to Eva's full-length mirror, rubbed it clean with the hem of my cloak. "Thank you, Your Graciousness."

I'd heard from Aidan that Eva and Torsten were arriving this evening from Iceland. Until then, Loki would have to live in squalor.

Meanwhile, I had responsibilities. One in particular.

When I came down from our dorm and crossed the clearing toward Umbra's office, the big double doors opened, and Aidan stepped out.

"Did you already tell her?" I asked him.

"I told her."

Well, at least I didn't have to bother. She'd probably offer me marmalade and more half-truths. "And?"

"She asked if my parents were all right."

"*And?*"

"I told her they were all right."

"The leyline, Aidan. What did she say about the leyline?"

He shrugged. "Like she'd tell me. She just grabbed a tome from her bookcase and shooed me out."

"Ah." I twirled a finger toward Umbra's double doors. "Welcome to the Academy of Shadowed Magic, where there are more shadows than light." I threw an arm around his shoulders, redirected him toward the library. "You know what they say."

He groaned. "This is going to be another thing that only you say, isn't it?"

I ignored him; this punchline had simmered for a whole ten

seconds. "If you can't get your answers from unreasonable professors, you can occasionally get them after hours of scouring old books."

His pace increased. "I am itching to get back into the Room of the Ancients."

"And after we do this, we duel." I dug a finger into his side, pulled him close when he tried to wriggle away. "Because six hours of sitting in a library makes me itchy to light fires."

Aidan laughed, shoved me off. "Fine, we'll fight. For every two hours in the library, we duel for one hour."

We had agreed over the summer that we would learn all we could about the last two pieces of the weapon. And so we went into the empty library—where not one other person wanted to be right now, even Milonakis—and spent the next four hours studying leylines.

Finally, I looked at Aidan overtop my book. My fingers were getting twitchy. "It's time."

He adjusted his glasses, clearly disappointed to go. "I haven't found anything useful."

"Neither have I." I clapped my book shut. "But if we sit here any longer, we risk blood clots."

We got up to head toward Spark's common room for our duel. On the way out, I nudged him. "We'll be back to your moth-riddled tomes before you know it. We've still got a prophecy to research."

He didn't smile. "Every day, until we know."

That had been our agreement over the summer: back at the academy, we would research in the library every day until we knew exactly where to find the third piece of the weapon.

I extended a hand. "Let's meet in the mornings. You bring the tea and biscotti, I'll bring a night owl's grumpiness."

He accepted it. "Deal."

———

When we came into the empty common room, I had a moment. I'd expected to see Callum Rathmore standing against the sofa, dark eyes staring back at me.

This was where he had brought the Spitfire out. This was where he had taught me to control it.

It had taken a year, and I thought I'd hated him for most of that year. In truth, I hadn't hated him at all; sometimes during the summer I brought out the page he'd ripped from *Jane Eyre* and given to me, stared at the underlined sentence.

I am not an angel, and I will not be one till I die. I will be myself.

I hadn't seen him since the night of the first guardian trial in May. The last time we'd spoken, his hand had been on my wrist. He had told me he had to leave, that he'd taught me all I needed to know, and one other thing.

I shouldn't trust Professor Ora Frostwish.

That wouldn't be a problem; she was an air fae, Eva's professor. I'd barely seen her in two years except in passing.

When Aidan set his bag down, he pulled out two pieces of paper. Handed one to me. "Oh, here's your schedule."

"We don't get these until tomorrow."

He raised one shoulder. "We're early, and when I saw Umbra she thought we'd like to have them early. I certainly do."

The paper in my hand listed three classes:

MOUNTED COMBAT II

ADVANCED FIRE MAGIC

HEXES

"Huh." Aidan tapped his own sheet. "I'm in advanced fire magic. Apparently Umbra's not worried about me everflaming the academy to the ground."

My eyes had fixed on the last class. *Hexes.* That was a word I hadn't heard used here.

I dragged my attention to Aidan. "You can quench the everflame when you want."

"Yeah"—his mouth worked—"unless I can't."

He'd never gotten over what had happened at Farina North's home. The day he'd lost control.

I forked my fingers, directed them between my eyes and his. "I'm in that class, and I'll be watching."

He made a face. "Was that supposed to be comforting?"

"Yeah, but you're talking to a fire witch." I shrugged off my cloak, set my schedule aside. "You want comforting, you go to Eva. You want threats and dark looks? You come to me."

He shook his head with a small smile, removed his own cloak and we both stepped toward the center of the common room, our hands lighting with fire.

We dueled for the next half hour. I bested him three times, and he got me once. Generally we finished when our hands were too slick from sweat to gain any purchase on the floor, which didn't take long— everflame burned hot. At least Umbra's enchantment over the academy was strong enough to keep it from scalding me.

We both slumped to a seat against opposite walls, breathing hard. After a time, Aidan asked, "What are your other classes?"

"The usual. Except for one."

His sweaty forehead wrinkled, eyebrows rising.

I tapped the schedule next to me. "Ever heard of a class called 'Hexes?'"

Aidan's tired face shifted to full intrigue. He crossed his legs, sitting forward. "You're joking."

I extended the sheet to him. "Look for yourself."

He did. Then he shook his head. "Gods, Umbra's going to have you learn hexes."

"Care to share the obviously negative implications with the rest of the class, North?"

He raised a finger, began chewing on the nail in what seemed like an anxious childhood habit. "I don't see how it's possible, though. You're a fire witch."

"How what's possible?"

He went to lean against the sofa's back, stared down at the sheet. Looked up at me. "Didn't you read about hexes in *The Witching World?*"

"No. Because the book didn't talk about hexes. It did talk about *curses.*"

His eyes went wide, and the chewing on his nail continued. "That must have been before..."

I sighed through my nose. "You're worse than the opening credits to an old movie."

He stopped chewing. "What's that supposed to mean?"

"It means you're taking too long to get to the good part."

He stood. "You're learning curses, Clementine."

Now I stood, too. My brain sifted back through two years to recall everything Raven Murkwood had written about curses.

Sensing this, Aidan said, "Back when witches still lived—well, more of them than just you—they could curse people. You know, like in children's stories."

The chapter was coming back to me now. "But Murkwood always talked about curses in theory. They weren't actually a thing."

"Well, they became a thing. Except I'd always thought it was an art belonging to air witches. You know, because they had to *speak* hexes."

I nodded slowly. "And speaking uses air."

"Right."

Now I had the strange inclination to chew on my nail. "But all the air witches are gone. There's none left to teach me hexes."

"I suppose you'll find out the answer to that puzzle tomorrow." He handed the paper over to me. "When you show up for class."

He wasn't wrong.

A buzzing started in Aidan's bag, and he pulled his phone out. "Eva's here. She says she bears gifts."

I tucked the sheet into my pocket, my brain unwilling to shift into the social gear. But as we came out of the common room and toward the clearing, I realized as she flew toward me that I'd missed that girlish, ecstatic way she had of throwing her arms around you with a cry. As a teenager, I'd always been derisive and envious of girls who did that.

Yes, I'd missed it all. Her sense of organization. Her anxiousness. Her grace.

She hugged me tight, then held me at arm's length, hands seated on my shoulders as she met my eyes. Her fluttering wings blew her lavender hair up until it floated over her shoulders. "Clementine, you're doused in sweat."

I jerked a thumb at Aidan. "Blame the everflame."

With a half-smile, she twirled a finger, sent a small vortex of air between the two of us like the spout of air at the end of a car wash.

"Thanks," Aidan said. "Now I'm covered in dried sweat."

"You bet." She eyed him. "Does that mean you're using your magic now, Aidan?"

"Every day," I said. "Unwillingly for the first month, and then only a little argumentative in the last two."

"Excellent. Oh!" Eva drew her small backpack around, unclipped it. "I've got loads of gifts from my parents."

By the time she'd finished handing me gifts, I must have had a whole new wardrobe in my arms. And on the top she set a primly folded dress. "This," she said, "is for your initiation tomorrow. Mama wore it when she became a guardian, and she tangibly manipulated it to your size. And then I manipulated it to accommodate the *orichalcum*."

It was too much. "But Eva, this should be for you."

"Of course it is." She tapped the dress. "When I become a guardian, I'll tangibly manipulate it to my size."

No one had ever been more thoughtful toward me. I just stood there under my pile of clothes. "You know I'm not good at things like this."

"I know." She winked. "Which is why you don't have to thank me."

CHAPTER FOUR

Tomorrow, my world would change again.

Classes would start, and in the evening I would be initiated as a guardian. It had to happen quickly, of course; the Shade's army didn't wait for pomp and circumstance and bureaucracy.

Everything was happening faster now. I was already a third-year and in possession of one half of a weapon that had once been used to dominate the world. And here I was, feeling like the same nineteen-year-old who'd walked barefoot onto the grounds in her pajamas.

I could only think of one solution to the issue of time: I convinced Eva to take a long walk around the meadow with me. Whenever we took our long walks, time slowed.

We each talked about our summer—mine near London, hers in Reykjavik. The whole time, she gushed with pinked cheeks.

Torsten's family had predictably loved Eva from the moment she'd floated across the threshold of their home. The couple had driven the ring road around Iceland more than once. She'd flown down the length of a waterfall when no one was looking.

"Oh, and the ponies." She squeezed my arm, linked with hers. "Gods, you'd have died for those ponies."

"There's only one horse I'd die for, and he's no pony."

"Trust me," she said. "You'd lie down in the middle of a road if it meant saving an Icelandic pony."

I hip-checked her. "I don't want to hear about ponies. Tell me what happened under the waterfall."

"You're terrible." She shook her head, staring out into the trees. "Like I said, it was a magical summer..."

That trailing off sounded ominous. "And?"

She kept her eyes averted. "And at the end, Torsten and I realized we didn't work together."

I stopped us. "You ended it?"

"We did. We both decided."

"Hey." I stepped around to see her eyes.

Her head swiveled toward me, strangely mechanical. Her mouth puckered into a facsimile of a smile. That wasn't the face of a woman who'd made a decision she was entirely happy with.

"Why?" I asked. "You said it was magical."

She shrugged in a simple, helpless way. "I wasn't lying. But the magic was around us, not between us."

I sighed, hugged her. "Ain't that a bitch."

She laughed into my shoulder, that amused and surprised noise she always made when I said something crass. "You sound like you've experienced it."

"Have I." I pulled back with a wry smile. "I've been there more than once. It sucked every time."

She wiped at a tear at the outer corner of her eye, like a tiny diamond. "Anyway, I need to focus this year. I'm not going to let you go three years as a guardian without me."

We resumed walking. "You would have made it last May," I said, "if you hadn't thrown yourself at Frostwish during the first trial. Still feel bad about that one, by the way."

I could still hear the sounds of the two fae crashing into one another, their limbs like slender tree branches. All so that I could pass.

"I forbid you to feel bad." She flew up to the low branch of a tree, plucked an untouched leaf. When she landed beside me, she twirled it between her fingers. "I made my choices with open eyes, Clem."

That made me wonder how many choices I'd made in life with my eyes closed.

Lots, really.

"We're going to need to tangibly manipulate all your clothes," she said. "Unless you want to explain to everyone why you're carrying an orichalcum rod everywhere."

"I was thinking I'd just wear my cloak all the time."

"Totally inconspicuous." She waved her leaf in an arc through the blue sky. "Especially in August."

I elbowed her. "Leave some good points for the rest of us." Then, "You know what this means though, don't you?"

She turned curious eyes on me. "I hope you aren't going to make me do all the manipulations. That'll take months."

"No, Eva. I'm talking about the trials." I circled my finger around the meadow. "We'll start with lots and lots of jogging. And what if you fight me in the second trial? Gotta be prepared for a fire witch."

She gasped, one hand touching her open mouth. "Gods, I never thought of that. Oh, I don't mind you. It's Liara who scares me."

I set a hand over my heart. "In the words of every millennial when dissed: ouch."

Her familiar smile appeared. "Of everyone, I know you best of all. I'm not scared of fighting you, Clementine. On the contrary."

I shook my head, bending over. "Excuse me while I pluck my reputation from the grass."

She laughed. "I'd say I'm sorry, but I'm not." When I straightened, my eyes caught on her wings. And a thought occurred to me. "Eva, you know Professor Frostwish."

"Of course. She's a marvel at air magic."

"How long has she been at the academy?"

Her head tilted. "I suppose she started the same year as us." She paused. "Why?"

Curious. A coincidence, maybe, that she'd started at the same time? And yet I couldn't stop seeing Rathmore's face when he'd told me not to trust her. He'd been as grave as I'd ever seen him.

We kept walking. I was veering us toward the pond, the place where Mariella the guardian had taught me to fight water mages. The place where I had taken Noir during the first trial.

It was a secluded place. Safe. We'd be unobserved.

"She's my professor," I said.

"Really? But she only teaches air magic."

"She's teaching me air magic. Ever heard of hexes?"

Eva stopped hard, dropping her leaf. "Of course. Hexes are a large part of why witches were killed off."

Now I stopped, turned. Waited for her to go on.

"A hex is a curse on someone, Clementine." Her eyes were unswerving on mine, like I might curse her right there. "It hurts them. That's all it does—it debilitates your enemy. And that's why the formalists declared it a forbidden art."

A forbidden art.

I won't pretend my heart didn't spike with anxiety. But I also won't pretend a thread of anticipation didn't wind itself in there, too.

When you're a fire witch, you've got enemies aplenty.

That night, Eva and I did a bang-up job manipulating the skirt of my uniform to hold the deceiver's rod. It wasn't clean, but it would do the trick—and it only took us eight hours. Which meant we got about three hours of sleep, the two of us.

When we woke, we got ourselves up and dressed with lidded eyes, staggered to the dining hall while Loki slept on.

Inside the hall, the world seemed to exist in technicolor, and in unique decibels of sound. Over a hundred students had come for breakfast, a whole cluster of them at the food table, others mustering laughter that sounded to my sleep-addled brain like cackling.

The new crop of first-years must have been larger this year. Or—as I glanced at the clock—I realized we'd hit the dining hall at the worst hour.

Eight o'clock. It was always a traffic jam in here at that hour.

Eva went for a plate and started filling it up. I struck for a coffee carafe, poured myself a straight black brew.

I was one of those worst-case coffee drinkers. By which I mean, I only went for it when I was in the worst possible way. But at least my rod hadn't fallen out of my skirt yet. If I'd mentioned that to Loki, he would have snickered.

I idled in front of the carafe, unable to move before caffeinating. This was going to be a very long day—three classes, and capped off with a certain initiation with everyone's favorite headmistress.

"Hello, Clementine."

I turned with a splash of coffee. She stood before me as regal as ever, her staff in one hand. "Headmistress."

Her head tilted, eyes straying to the spilled coffee and then up to me. "You look dire."

New goal: become as blunt as Umbra by the time I reach her age. "I was up late."

"Hm. I suppose you aren't a guardian yet." She moved around me to pour her own cup from the carafe.

I turned with her. "What's that mean?"

"You'll learn all this evening." She straightened with her cup. "No need to say now what I'll tell you and Liara later."

Fair enough.

"Headmistress," I began.

Her eyebrows rose as she waited.

"You enrolled me in hexes."

"Yes, I did."

I shrugged. "Eva told me it's a forbidden art. That it's dark. Not that I mind a little darkness here and there, but..."

"It is forbidden by the formalists. But we aren't formalists here, are we?" She paused. "And as to its darkness, I suppose that depends on the moral fiber of the witch herself."

I straightened like my posture had some bearing on my character. "That magic belongs to air witches, doesn't it?"

Another student appeared at Umbra's side—a redhead, her green eyes wide with wonder. "Excuse me, Headmistress."

A first-year, most likely.

Umbra set a hand on the fae's shoulder, kept her eyes fixed on me as she said, "Professor Frostwish will tell you all. She's studied the art with some keenness."

A non-witch had studied a dead, dark art. That didn't exactly add any weight to the "Trust Frostwish" side of the scale.

When Umbra turned to the redhead, the girl went on to introduce herself with twinkling eyes, her hands clasped at her chest.

I left Umbra with her starry-eyed first-year, lifted a blueberry muffin off a platter and found Eva seated with a group of other unfamiliar, new faces. Somehow she'd rallied and looked as awake as ever. Such was the social grace of my roommate.

I sensed eyes on me. Across the room, Liara Youngblood sat with two Whisper friends—hair like a black abyss down her back, eyes flinty. When I focused on her, she averted her attention to them.

After our time in the Boundless Labyrinth, something had changed between us. It was possible she no longer hated me.

And maybe there was a small possibility she and I could be friends. I'm a cat person; we're most compelled by creatures whose trust isn't so easy to earn.

When I dropped to a seat at Liara's table, all three fae turned dinner-plate eyes on me. I knew I'd violated a rule of requesting to sit before actually sitting, but I didn't care. I plucked a blueberry from my muffin, popped it into my mouth. "What's happening, girls?"

The other two fae waited for Liara to speak. They were either aware of our history or sensed the tension like a palpable thing in the air.

Liara's spoon hovered above her yogurt, her face unreadable. Then, after a few seconds, she dipped it in. "You'll need more than a muffin and coffee to eat."

The tension dissipated, and the other two fae relaxed.

"Maybe she's an intermittent faster, Liara," the green-haired fae offered.

"That's right," I said, though I had no idea what that meant. "Maybe I am."

"Intermittent fasting means you don't eat during certain windows. She's eating," the pink-haired fae pointed out.

Liara shook her head. "Anyway, Sebille, you were in the middle of your story."

I sat forward as the green-haired fae went on to describe her summer romance with a water mage who was "entirely too wishy-washy" for her.

I snorted into my coffee.

The others looked at me.

"Wishy-washy," I said. "And he's a water mage. It was clever."

I had spent too much time with Aidan's dad this summer.

The vaguest smile appeared on Sebille's face. I considered that a victory. She went on with her story, and as she did, more new students filled in the empty spots at the table around us.

The one who'd sat down next to me tapped my shoulder.

When I turned, a fellow ginger stared back. She was skinny and all coltish limbs and covered in freckles. Her hair was short and straight. "You're the fire witch," she said. It wasn't a question.

This was the first-year who had introduced herself to Umbra.

I set my cup on the table, breezing past the question of how she knew that. "Sure am. Need someone offed? I'm your girl."

She smiled. "You're funnier than I'd expected."

My eyebrow went up. "You'd expected things?"

"Yeah. What happened to you in London last year was in the news."

I lowered my chin. "Seriously? Are you..."

"A formalist?" She shook her head. "Gods no. But you have to pretend to be one if you're going to live in Edinburgh."

So I had been in the news. The magical world knew about the fire witch, which wasn't great for me. The formalists had no doubt painted me as, well, a *witch*.

"I tend to like anything the formalists hate," she went on. "Which includes witches."

I was fond of this kid already, and not just because she was a redhead. I extended my hand. "Clementine, but you probably know that already."

She took it. "Saoirse. And I do."

CHAPTER FIVE

When I came into the stables for my first mounted combat lesson, Noir was banging a hoof against his stall door. He rumbled when he saw me, extended his head for scratching under the jaw.

"That's right," I said as I obliged him. "We're back in business, my man."

Mounted Combat II was mostly composed of fourth- and fifth-years. Actually, I was the only third-year of the eight of us standing beside our horses in the ring.

Farrow stood at the center, explaining the class. The concept was simple: we were to learn to use magic while we rode.

I had a head start on that—Rathmore had taught me the fundamentals of fire riding—which I guessed was why I had been entered into this class as a third-year. Farrow knew as much.

What she didn't know was how spectacularly I'd failed at fire riding in the first guardian trial.

When Farrow had finished her introduction, she led us out into the larger pasture where the horses were sometimes left to graze. "Trust me," she said to the question in my head, "you'll want the space."

Thirty minutes later, I understood why.

A plume of water rained through the air at one end of the pasture. The air whipped to a frenzy in another, sending one of the new horses into nervous dancing, his mane and tail blowing wild. The earth rumbled in another corner.

And in my little part of the pasture?

No fire at all.

I rode Noir at a trot to warm him up, then a canter. Around we went, Rathmore's voice echoing through my head. I had to let go of his mane; fire riding took both hands. I had to allow the fire to consume me, to give the Spitfire some portion of control, but not too much.

And my flames had to take Noir, too. That was the difference between me and those fourth- and fifth-years: their horses wouldn't be encompassed by their element.

Truth was, three months without riding—or even visiting—had put a certain distance between Noir and me. I wasn't the same rider on his back as I'd been in May, and he wasn't the same horse under me.

We'd have to reconnect before I could give myself over to fire riding, and before he'd trust the Spitfire.

Apparently Farrow had noticed. Of course; she missed nothing. At the end of the lesson, as I wiped Noir down in his stall, she appeared at the half-door. "You did well."

I ran the towel over his flank. "I didn't even get to the fire part."

"That doesn't mean you didn't do well."

I paused. "Everyone has higher expectations for guardians."

"Well, Clementine"—she leaned closer—"that's the thing about high expectations. It's in our nature to rise to meet them. Speaking of which, aren't you in the advanced fire magic class this year?"

I dropped the towel. "I'm going to be late."

She tapped a finger on the door, turning away. "High expectations."

I guess it didn't matter that I couldn't shower after the stables. As I ran to Spark's common room, I knew I'd be covered in sweat the rest of the morning, anyway.

I was the last one into the common room. A class of eight or ten people stood near the entry. When Professor Goodbarrel spotted me from the center, he clapped his hands. "Clementine Cole. I knew you'd make it."

I staggered through the entry, wiping my forehead. God bless that man.

Aidan was there, hands clasped behind his back, looking especially uncomfortable. When I bumped him with my shoulder, he didn't even feign a smile.

This was going to be a long year for him.

You wouldn't expect it, but Goodbarrel was more of a theorist than Rathmore. If Rathmore had been all action, Goodbarrel loved to get into the minutiae of technique. And the first technique he wanted to teach us was splitting the stream of our fire.

"Now this is where you'll truly level up." He leaned against the couch with his hand lifted to chest-height, his fingers splayed. "When you can ignite fire on each fingertip."

One by one, each of his fingers lit like candles. He smiled behind his hand, invited us to ask why that was such a crucial skill.

"Control," someone said.

"Sure," Goodbarrel shot back. "Let's hear more about that."

"Control allows for precision," said Maise, the only fourth-year I really knew. "It's helpful to be precise with fire."

"Yes! More." Goodbarrel gestured us on. "What else?"

"A smaller flame can sometimes be more deadly," the boy next to me said. "It burns hotter, like lightning."

Goodbarrel nodded. "Indeed it does. But why have I set each of my fingers separately alight?"

Aidan's face appeared in memory, the moment five blue flames had appeared on his hand in his parents' yard. "You've got five shots on one hand," I said. "Five chances."

"Yes, Clementine." Goodbarrel's whole hand lit. "And I'll show you why five chances are better than one."

He swept his hand knifelike through the air, a horizontal sweep that sent fire out in an arc toward the entire class.

About half of us—and me—ducked. It had the instant effect of bringing me straight into my body.

Two people dissipated the fire. The other three didn't react in time.

Every face must have been wide open, because Goodbarrel clapped his thigh, burst into laughter. "I just love doing that on the first day. Really wakes you young folk up." When Goodbarrel stood, his face went serious. He raised his hand again, all five fingertips igniting. "It took me months to learn to do this, but it's perhaps the most important skill I can teach you. Here's why."

His fingers curled toward his thumb, and when he flicked his hand open, fire shot from his four fingers, raced faster than my eyes could track into four of us with almost instant hisses.

I glanced down at the fire dissipating harmlessly on my shirt, thanks to Umbra's fire-dampening enchantment.

Goodbarrel's flames had moved faster than I'd thought possible.

When I looked back up, he was grinning, cheeks rosy above his red-gold beard. "And I'm not even that fast anymore."

The next forty-five minutes were spent seated, cross-legged, Aidan and I next to one another as we both stared at our upraised hand and attempted to set our fingertips on fire.

Turned out, I was really good at turning my whole arm into a torch. Not much good at anything else. Which wasn't surprising; "control" and "precision" were my two least-favorite words.

Beside me, Aidan had managed to do two fingertips by the end of class. I kept grousing, looking on enviously. Even when Goodbarrel adjourned us, I didn't move.

Maise came by and slapped me on the back when class was done, stood over me with brown eyes gleaming. "Come on, fire witch. Nobody's going to die because you can't do Goodbarrel's trick on the first day."

If only she knew.

When I stepped into the meadow, the sun had already fallen halfway to the horizon, slanting through the trees.

And no one else was around.

I clenched the apple I'd brought from the dining hall, bit into it with all the pent-up ferociousness I'd brought to this first meeting with Ora Frostwish.

Of course she would keep me waiting. That definitely seemed like something untrustworthy people would do.

My mind had already latched shut. I didn't know how I'd learn from her when I couldn't trust her, but I couldn't change the fact of my enrollment in this class. So here I was.

Alone, apparently.

"You eat that apple like you hate it," a voice murmured from above.

When I glanced up, she gazed back down at me from her crouch on a tree branch. Her hands hung between her legs, elbows resting on her thighs, eyes fixed on me, waiting.

One of my eyebrows popped. "That's how you've got to eat an apple. Otherwise it'll get the best of you."

She straightened, dropped to the ground in a flutter. She landed with cropped blue hair afloat; she'd gotten a haircut this summer. And dammit, it suited her. As did the dark professor's robes she wore, the golden cinch at her waist. "Do you know where we are?" she asked.

That question was too obvious. I rolled my eyes skyward. "I'm guessing Romania. Maybe Bulgaria. But no one's ever bothered to tell me."

A faint smile appeared. "Really? That was an oversight. It's Romania, Clementine." She paused. "But that wasn't what I meant."

I didn't answer. This was beneath me, but I was doing my best ice queen impression: pursed lips, folded arms, tilted head.

Okay, this wasn't all to do with Rathmore's warning. It was also to do with all the times I'd seen Frostwish whispering into his ear at dinners, dancing with him at the winter gala. The way he called her "Ora."

Call me petty, but I blamed my heart. I could never control the damn thing.

Frostwish pointed into the trees. "That's where you escaped me during the guardian trial in May." She fixed keen eyes on me. "That was when I knew Callum was right."

Now my petty heart beat overlarge. "'Callum was right?'"

"He thought you were one of the most promising students he'd ever seen."

"Because of my fire magic?"

"No, Clementine." Frostwish stepped closer. "I didn't even see you use your fire. I think he referred to that as 'good enough.'"

He would say that. I gave the apple another hard bite, ripping the flesh out to the core.

"I see your ego written all over you." Frostwish's eyes flicked to my abused apple. "And yet you should feel complimented. Do you know what it means to show great promise without great talent?"

"A lifetime full of disappointment?"

She smiled prettily, which I found difficult to reconcile with my need to distrust her. Fae made themselves so hard to dislike. "It means you have incredible drive. Callum described you as unputdownable."

She kept saying his name. That last time, my throat got thick. My eyes closed for a moment longer than they should.

I'd never known he'd thought well of me.

Not like this.

Frostwish's hand fell on my shoulder, and my eyes opened. "You may think you were assigned this course by the headmistress. But it wasn't Umbra who asked me to instruct you in hexes—it was I who asked her."

"Why? I'm no air witch."

"Ah, but aren't you?" Her eyes remained fast on mine. "Every fire witch has a little air witch inside them."

"If that's true, then every fire mage should be able to use air magic."

"No." She shook her head. "A fire mage isn't born of an air mage. Fire passes down through the line, as does air."

My brow furrowed. "But a fire witch is always born of an air witch?"

In the pause that followed, I scrutinized Frostwish's face. She didn't answer with the same quickness as before, and the smile that appeared wasn't so natural. But she said, after a beat, "The fire witch is such a rarity that she has only ever been born to an air witch. And that gives you a special duality. One that will allow you to cast hexes."

"You're sure of that?"

Frostwish's head tilted. "If history is to be believed."

I swallowed. "What history are you referring to?"

"If only you could see the mages' library in Edinburgh, Clementine." She turned away, swept a hand through the air. "The main room is the size of this entire meadow. There's even a section devoted to witches." When she glanced at me over her shoulder, dimples appeared. Of course she had dimples. "The smallest section at the library contains twelve thousand books."

"The formalists would arrest me in Edinburgh." I paused. "Are you a formalist, Professor?"

She laughed. "Join with those squares? Gods no. They're perfectly dull, unimaginative. But I did grow up in the city. Shame it's been overrun with rubes. Every time I visit my old mentor in Inverness, that's the word he uses. I happen to agree."

She hadn't answered my first question. "And you said I wouldn't be the first fire witch to use a hex."

Frostwish turned back to me. "Far from it. That is, of course, provided you're willing to learn."

I one-shoulder shrugged. "Do I have a choice?"

"Always." She clasped her hands. "You can part the veil, Clementine. You're already powerful enough to travel the world, to escape whenever and to wherever you wish."

She was being pedantic. "But if I choose to stay at the academy, then I have to participate in your class."

"You're never going to learn to hex properly if you don't want it." She paused. "Do you want it?"

"I don't even know what *it* is."

Her chin lowered, eyes large on me. "Shall I show you?"

"Absolutely."

"On you."

My eyebrows rose. "What?"

"You're the only other soul present for me to hex." A small smile appeared. "It won't hurt. At least, this one won't."

I paused, fully distrustful. But I figured if anything happened, Umbra would spidey-sense it. "All right."

Frostwish's perfect lips parted, and her mouth began to shape whispered words. Her eyes hardened, boring into my skull as a soft breeze washed over me.

As it did, every muscle in my body flexed, and I went completely rigid. Stiff. Immobile.

She had paralyzed me.

CHAPTER SIX

Eva leaned forward with enormous eyes, hands on knees as her bed creaked beneath her. "And how long did she paralyze you for?"

I flopped back on my bed, rubbing my fingers together to enjoy the feeling of control over them. "I don't know. Maybe ten seconds, maybe ten minutes."

"How don't you know?"

"It was the worst feeling I've ever experienced."

"But you said it didn't hurt."

"It didn't." I stared at the soft lamp hanging from the ceiling, the magical flame burning inside. "But for those ten seconds or minutes, she had complete control over me. She could have done anything she wanted. I never want to feel that again."

"So you told her you don't want to learn hexes?"

I lifted my head. "Are you kidding? I'm all in."

"But why? If it was the worst feeling, you wouldn't want to inflict it on anyone else, would you?"

"I *would* want to inflict it on the Shade's army. I probably wouldn't mind inflicting it on any formalist bastards who try to capture me. The more I practice it, the stronger my mind will grow against anyone else trying to hex me. So why wouldn't I want to learn it?"

A pause. Then, "I'm surprised Umbra approved it."

I rose to my elbows. "What does that mean?"

"It's putting incredible power in the hands of a twenty-one-year-old. Devastating power in..."

"In the hands of a fire witch," I finished. "That's what you mean, isn't it?"

"Fire is a corrupting element, Clementine," Eva said softly.

Now I understood what this was about. "Aidan told you what happened between us this summer, didn't he?"

Her eyes dropped elsewhere; she began tugging at her bed's duvet. "He mentioned it."

"We were dueling, and he got too aggressive." I sat up fully. "Yes, I got angry with him. Yes, I lost control for a second."

Eva's eyes drifted up to mine. "He said you were like a different person."

That had been the Spitfire. He'd seen the Spitfire emerge—but Aidan had also tackled me, held me down even after I told him to get off.

I hated being held down. Controlled. That was my anger, too. It wasn't just the fire's influence.

Right?

I pressed down the old feelings about myself. I was better than this —I had to be better than every fire witch in history. They were going to make me into a guardian tonight, for god's sake.

"You trust me, Eva." I paused. "Don't you?"

Her lips pressed together. She nodded.

Loki cracked an eye open from atop my pillow at the head of the bed. "Can you just do a few trust falls so the cat can sleep undisturbed?"

I ran a hand over his back. Glanced over at Eva. "Umbra believes I can do this. She must, or else she wouldn't have let Frostwish teach me."

And yet you haven't told Eva what Rathmore said.

Don't trust Frostwish.

Truth was, I had planned to try dropping out of the class some way or another. Play hooky, plead my case with Umbra.

That is, until Frostwish had hexed me in the meadow.

I wanted that power. I needed it. And it was about more than just hexing my enemies.

"Eva," I went on. "Remember the part of the prophecy about the chain?"

Her eyes unfocused. "Something about tethering…"

"'A hex will tether the cursed chain,'" I recited. "A hex, Eva."

"Oh my gods." She set a hand to her mouth, whispering between her fingers. "And you think this is that hex?"

"What else can it be?"

"It makes total sense. But doesn't it all line up too easily?"

I nodded. "I was thinking the same thing. Just after I get the deceiver's rod—and now need to find the cursed chain—I'm enrolled in Frostwish's class to learn hexes."

It's too perfect. I wondered if Frostwish knew more than she should.

"Rathmore told me not to trust Ora Frostwish," I said.

"Callum Rathmore told you that? When?"

"The night he left the academy back in May."

One of her eyebrows rose. "And you didn't think to tell me?"

"I didn't really think about it. It didn't matter until now." My fingers tightened on the duvet. "Why would he tell me that, Eva?"

"I don't know. Frostwish is a wonderful professor. There's nothing she's ever done to make me wonder."

"I can smell your nervousness," Loki groused from his pillow. "Would you please take a shower before you smoke us all out of here?"

"And when was the last time you bathed yourself?" I said. "I'm not the only one being initiated tonight."

"Ten minutes ago." He gave me a withering look. "I'm a cat."

Eva glanced between Loki and me, looking for a translation.

I stood. "He says I'm sweating from nerves."

"About the prophecy?" Her eyes flicked to the clock on her desk. "Oh, you have to go, Clem. You'll be late."

I was already crossing to the bathroom. "I've got four hours to put on one dress," I said. "But I know how you feel about lateness. We'll reconvene to gossip about Frostwish later. At the end of class she told me she's going to visit her dear old mentor, who thinks the formalists are rubes. Wonder who this edgy mentor is."

"Mentor, you say?" A glint had entered Eva's eyes. "Where?"

"I think he was in Inverness."

"Four hours *is* quite a bit of time."

I stopped, faced her. "Evanora Whitewillow, are you suggesting we do something underhanded?"

"Rathmore said we can't trust Frostwish, right?" Eva leaned forward. "Let's see for ourselves."

I pointed at the clock on her desk. "You were just telling me I'll be late."

She flipped the clock onto its face. "There's a priority to things, Clem. Getting fresh is lowest on the list. Somehow you can do that in ten minutes—I've clocked you."

I just stared at her. This was a new Eva.

"Loki?" I said. "Do you want to go to Inverness?"

He cracked an eye. "I want *you* to go to Inverness so I can sleep."

Eva understood that well enough. "So?" she said. "Do you want to find out more about Ora Frostwish, or don't you?"

I did. I absolutely did.

———

Ora Frostwish walked with the kind of feline smoothness that made me wonder if she had joints at all. In fact, she didn't walk—she pooled toward the leyline outside the academy grounds.

A minute earlier, she'd flown from the landing of her home, high up in a tree—which Eva and I had been hiding at the base of—and off into the forest. We'd followed her blue hair as fast and soundlessly as we could, but hadn't caught sight of her until she'd landed.

That was when she'd pooled. She moved bonelessly.

She made a picture of a fashionista as she stopped in front of the spot where the leyline crossed invisibly under the ground outside the academy: blue-black bob without a hair out of place, the fine lines of her neck exposed down to a loose linen powder-blue jacket, which she wore over a knee-length dress and heels.

She was certainly dressed to see someone important to her.

Frostwish cut an unsurprisingly perfect line in the veil from her head to the forest floor as Eva and I crouched behind a far-off tree. We glimpsed a street streaked with sunset pinks and oranges as Frostwish stepped through.

"That's the high street," Eva said to me. "I've been there."

"You've been to Inverness?"

"When your parents can part the veil, why wouldn't you visit every country in the world?"

I had no good answer to that. "You've been to every country?"

"My parents wanted me to be able to get anywhere I needed to go in the world." She started forward to the spot where Frostwish had stood. "We have to be quick, or else we'll lose her."

Eva made an unsteady cut in the veil, but it did its job. When she pulled it aside, the sunset poured over the high street and through the opening. Its beams even touched the forest floor on our side.

Frostwish had taken to the sidewalk, her heels clicking.

I turned to Eva. "Are my curls showing?"

She tucked a stray hair into my hood, which had been pulled up over my head. "You're good."

"I have to say, I do like this Evanora." I started through the veil and felt her close behind.

"I've always been the same Evanora." She came to my side once we were on the high street, and the two of us crossed onto the sidewalk behind Frostwish. "I trust you, and you trust Rathmore. If he told you not to trust Frostwish, then we need to investigate."

We kept our distance, always keeping Frostwish in sight but never coming too close. She turned a corner, then another. Soon enough we were headed into a residential section. "Who do you think her mentor is?" Eva asked.

"She was into hexes as a student in Edinburgh, right? So I'd guess a professor." But we certainly weren't in Edinburgh, or headed toward a university. Then it hit me. "Her mentor's probably old and retired. We're not going to any school..."

Eva got it. "We're going to a *house*."

We hit an upscale street brimming with elegant houses with yards. I knew by now that space—a yard especially—was a sign of wealth here. No better sign of money than owning things whose only purpose was aesthetic. Time with Aidan's family in London had taught me all sorts of things.

The sun had finally fallen below the horizon, which made following Frostwish easier. In the blue hour we were hardly visible, especially as we avoided the streetlamps. On and on she went, deep and deeper into the neighborhood.

"She sure can walk in heels." I stopped to swivel one ankle. "My feet hurt in these sneakers."

"Oh, Clementine." She leaned close. "Do not underestimate the art of walking in pumps."

I gave a silent laugh, then went stiff. "She's stopped."

We stopped, too. Up ahead, Frostwish stood before an iron gate, pressing a buzzing button. Faint words were exchanged, and then she opened the gate and passed through into the yard of a very fancy old two-story home.

We crept closer as Frostwish passed toward the front door. A rectangle of light appeared, and a dark figure stood there to greet her. A moment later she had gone inside, and the door shut.

Eva and I exchanged a look.

"Sneak over the wall?" she offered.

We couldn't be stopped by a bunch of bricks stacked on top of each other. Not when one of us had wings and the other had a sketchy record from childhood. "Sneak over the wall."

I managed to climb it with ease. Eva flew up and crouched atop it, pulling me up until I'd crested it. We dropped into the grass on the other side, snuck toward the dimly lit window of the house.

We stood at either side of the window, pressed to the side of the house, and I turned my face to glance in.

Inside, a beautiful marble-countered kitchen lay clean and empty and only faintly lit.

I nodded at Eva and gestured for her to follow. We moved around the side of the house toward the back, where another window glowed like a beacon.

Again we pressed to the side of the house, and when I peeked through the glass, I glimpsed a stately sofa and armchairs. Bookcases lined the high walls, filled from end to end. A fireplace announced itself against one wall, not burning but promising an enormous fire if the occasion were to call.

And sitting in one of the armchairs was Ora Frostwish. She faced mostly away from me, but I'd recognize that geometric bob anywhere.

I didn't know the older man sitting in the armchair opposite her, but a vague familiarity registered in my brain. Something about the shape of his jaw, his brow, the scrutinizing dark eyes.

Their lips moved through the glass, but I could only make out muffled half-words.

I whispered to Eva, "Can you hear?"

"Yes." She ducked beneath the window to my side. "Ora keeps calling him 'Tristan.' Who do you suppose that is?"

I glanced in through the window again, intending to take another look at his face, but my eyes wandered. And they fixed on a family crest over the wooden mantel. Black and red, with two crossed swords at the center.

Beneath them, an engraved name I recognized:

RATHMORE.

CHAPTER SEVEN

I ducked back, leaning hard against the outer wall as much for support as to keep myself hidden.

Tristan Rathmore sat inside that room.

Callum's father.

"What is it?" Eva mouthed to me.

"Look above the mantel," I said without moving. "The family crest."

When she had done so, she turned back to me with gray eyes like small moons. "Professor Rathmore's father is Ora Frostwish's mentor. What does that mean?"

I shook my head; I didn't know.

Rathmore's profile in *Witches & Wizards* returned to mind. His father had been a professor at the University of Edinburgh and on the Mages' Council there. He must have retired to Inverness, or maybe this was his vacation home.

This I knew: Tristan Rathmore was a powerful man. And yet Callum had disappeared for years, forsaking his seat on the council. There must have been a rift between them. Bad blood.

This connection also explained how Ora and Callum knew each

other. If she was his father's mentee, no doubt their relationship—whatever it was—had existed before he'd come to Shadow's End.

But he didn't trust her.

Eva had gone back to listening, her ear next to the glass but still just out of sight. After a time, she squeezed my hand. "They're talking about you, I think," she whispered. "I heard mention of the 'new witch.' Then they said your name."

The new? But I was the only. I was the last.

I still couldn't hear a thing; curse her sensitive fae ears. Well, not *curse* curse.

Eva listened a time longer, then nestled closer to me. "They're getting up," she said, pressed tightly out of view. "They're walking out."

I squeezed her shoulder. "Tell me everything."

"Once we're out of here." She glanced at me, eyes wild with intensity. "They said some strange things, Clem."

The front door of the house opened, and Frostwish's heels clicked on the front stoop. Words were exchanged, pleasantries, and then she clicked her way down the front walk toward the gate.

We waited until she had gone down the road and her heels were fully out of range of Eva's hearing before we snuck back over the wall. When I crested the top, I sat there for a moment, staring back through the window into the kitchen.

Tristan Rathmore stood at the counter, buttering a crumpet and brewing himself tea. He was tall like Callum, his hair fully white but nicely combed. Except, even from here, I could see the hard set to his mouth.

I'd bet money he had spent a lifetime making sure his lips folded that way—downturned. Severe. Maybe even cruel.

He knew about me. He'd said my name, and I suspected not in a nice way. Was he a formalist? If he was on the Mages' Council, I had almost no doubt.

Tristan Rathmore didn't seem like a good man.

But there he was, making himself an evening snack in his late sixties. That was the way of the world sometimes: bad men took what they wanted, afforded themselves nice homes and security. Self-sacrificing good men often didn't end up as fortunate.

"Clem," Eva called up. "What are you doing up there?"

I dropped down to the sidewalk without answering her question. There, we deliberated.

"We should head back," Eva said. "You have your initiation."

"We've still got two hours." I didn't move. "If I'm late, they'll wait for me. At this point Umbra can't rescind it, can she?"

"She's the headmistress. She can do anything she wants."

"She won't." There weren't many guardians, and they needed all the qualified people they could get. "We need to go somewhere secluded and sit until you tell me everything you heard."

"Fine." Eva turned a half-circle, then pointed toward the high street. "This way. There's a pub my parents took me to that should still be open."

We arrived at Wetherspoons after a ten-minute walk. It was mostly empty, just a couple of unconcerned young men seated at the counter, watching rugby with their pints.

It was perfect.

We took a table in the back corner, the two of us sitting in armchairs with sodas. Eva kept sipping, her eyes going unfocused, until I leaned forward. "So tell me."

She glanced up at me. "A lot was said I didn't understand. I definitely heard your name, then 'new witch.' They talked about hexes and what kind of progress Frostwish was making. Frostwish said something like, 'I doubt she could ever become as capable as Murkwood.' Who's Murkwood?"

I set my soda down with a clink of ice. "Raven Murkwood?"

"They didn't say."

"The full name is Raven Murkwood. She was a witch in the sixteenth century who wrote *The Witching World*. It's the only book the academy has on witches. She was powerful."

Eva gasped. "The sixteenth century? But..."

My eyebrows went up, waiting for her to finish.

"They kept talking about Murkwood like she was alive," Eva finally said. "They were talking about Murkwood's plans, and what she'd last said, and when they would see her again."

"Maybe they meant another Murkwood," I murmured, though I felt doubtful. "Or a descendant."

But that wouldn't make any sense; Murkwood's descendant would be a witch, and I was the only witch. At least, that was the story I'd been given.

On the other hand, Raven Murkwood still being alive after so many centuries made even less sense.

Unless she's the Shade. That was a possibility. But it was one I really didn't want to consider, seeing as how I'd read *The Witching World* more than once.

"Anything else?" I said.

"Rathmore talked about a ripple." Her brow furrowed. "That he thought Callum had caused a ripple, and he wasn't sure about his loyalties. It remained to be seen where he would land."

A tremor. I sipped my drink; Umbra had talked about ripples of magic when it came to abductions. I didn't quite understand about ripples, but I did understand about loyalties. And I knew I agreed with Callum: I had no loyalty to Ora Frostwish.

We returned to the academy with just enough time for me to get into the shower for the initiation. Even then, the getting-ready process took a little direction from Eva.

"Don't forget to wear the dress from Mama," she called as the bathroom door closed behind me.

The dress from Nissa Whitewillow was a deep purple and had been altered to fit me with stunning exactness. The sleeves came right to the caps of my wrists, the shoulders not even a degree outsized, the neckline demure and the length—just past the knees—perfectly suited for an initiation.

When I put it on in the bathroom and tied my hair away from my face, I stared at myself in the mirror.

I was about to be Clementine Cole, guardian.

If only my pervy boss at Corner Mart Grocery could see me now... Actually, never mind that.

When I came out, Eva sighed with gleaming eyes, came over to hug me. "You deserve this," she said as we separated. "I know you doubt that. Please don't."

She knew exactly what had been written on my face. I pulled on my cloak and put on my best smile. "Down, doubt. Down."

"Are you talking to your feelings like a dog?" Loki trotted over to my legs, staring up at me in obvious judgment. "I don't know whether to laugh or be appalled."

I scooped him up. "Why not both?" I made toward the door, waving goodbye to Eva. "See you."

She followed me to the door, sent me off into the evening like a nervous mother. "You'll do great!"

As I walked to Umbra's office, I fell into a grave silence. I'd do great or I'd do terrible—for someone like me, there was no in between.

I pushed open the grand double doors leading into Umbra's antechamber. Inside, eight robed students stood around the head-mistress. Among them, I recognized Liara Youngblood.

Above the group, an ever-changing blue light twinkled over the space like water. The will-o-wisps, floating high up near the ceiling, the only light in the room. The previous bearers of the liar's key.

Umbra turned to face me, her face shadowed. "Welcome, Clementine. You're the last to join us."

I set Loki down, and he stayed by my legs as I came forward, passing over the illustration of the Battle of the Ages covering the circular floor of the antechamber. "Had to take a shower. My cat said I smelled."

A flicker of amusement passed over Umbra's face. Her hand went out. "Please, stand beside Liara at the center."

As Loki and I approached Liara, who stood flanked by the seven guardians, she kept her eyes strictly ahead. Under this swimming blue light, she looked unearthly—black hair gleaming, dark eyes proud and spreading wings taller than her head.

Despite how much she'd loathed me from the beginning of our time at the academy, she and I shared a connection.

We had gotten through the third trial—the labyrinth—together.

We were the only two from our year to join the guardians.

To top it all: she was tough as nails, brimming with lightning, all hard edges. I liked the hell out of her. And as a guardian? There weren't many I'd choose over her to fight by my side.

If nothing else, I hoped she'd come to respect me.

I came to stand beside her.

And to my surprise, she leaned over to talk to me. It'd been a while since she'd initiated a conversation. That was progress. "Your cat's touching me," she rasped.

I glanced down at Loki, who stood between the two of us, his tail curling around Liara's leg. Held back a smile. "He likes you."

"Make him stop."

I shoulder-bumped her. "He's chosen you. No greater compliment."

She was about to bite back when Umbra took a step forward, her staff tapping on the floor. "Guardians and guardian initiates, welcome. I'm fortunate to be looking at nine of the bravest, most capable souls the academy has to offer, though I suspect not everyone here has been acquainted. Guardians, please step forward and introduce yourselves."

Umbra nodded to the student on the far left to start.

The tall girl on the end took a step forward, hands clasped behind her back. She'd cropped her white-blonde hair to her ears; a muscle in her jaw feathered as she glanced over at us. "I'm Fi Waters, a fifth-year from House Gaia."

When she stepped back, the student next to her stepped from the line. He ran a hand over his shaved head, a nervous tic I recognized as something I used to do in front of groups. He had enviously white, straight teeth. "Akelan Phiri, fourth-year from House Gaia."

The third student to come forward was small and black-haired, her braid almost to her waist. She had a high, breathy voice. "Welcome, guardian initiates. My name is Mishka Reddy, and I am a fourth-year from House Crest."

Four more guardians remained, all of them fae who stood on our right side.

Next came a fifth-year, her hair and eyes a marvelous sapphire blue. She introduced herself as Circe Petalfleck, of House Whisper (as all fae were).

I recognized the fourth-year next to her—a fae named Keene

who'd been in my combat class when I'd first arrived. He had the enviable ability to disappear and reappear six feet from where he'd been standing a second earlier. He'd been a real pain to fight in that class, and I'd never gotten the best of him in our duels.

The last two I could have guessed were related. They did, after all, look absolutely identical—tall, muscled for fae, arms crossed beneath their shocks of silver hair. And they also stepped forward at the exact same time.

"We're Elijah and Isaiah," the one on the left said, knuckling his twin in the shoulder. "And we're fourth-years."

Last of all, Umbra nodded to me and Liara. "Guardian initiates, please step forward to be inducted."

Without even glancing my way, Liara came forward to stand in front of Umbra.

I sucked in a breath. Came forward to Liara's side, glancing back at Loki for him to join me. He trotted to my side at the center of the room.

Umbra straightened, as did everyone else. "Please state your name and house, guardian initiates."

Beside me, Liara bore all the regality of a princess. The light shimmered over her black hair, a canvas of water. "Liara Youngblood, third-year of House Whisper."

"Clementine Cole," I said, then gestured to my familiar. "And this is Loki Cole. We're third-years in House Spark."

"The three of you have passed a series of increasingly difficult trials to become guardians of the magical world. Do you understand the gravity of the mantle you seek to wear, the importance of the undertaking you will embark on for the next three years?"

"Yes," Liara said at once. "I want nothing more than to send the Shade's army back to the underworld and to destroy her. To do that, we must protect the lives of our fellow mages."

Umbra nodded. "Well said, child." Then her gaze shifted to me, rocky and unyielding.

The gravity. The mantle. Did I understand the importance of the undertaking?

I understood that the Shade would never be defeated until

someone descended into the underworld to end her. I understood that the person to do that must be me.

And until I retrieved the rest of her weapon, the very best I could do would be to burn the hell out of a few of her minions.

"Loki and I know what we need to do," I said, jaw stony. "And we're prepared to do it."

Umbra stared at me a moment longer, her eyes shifting between mine. Searching, maybe. Seeking. For what? Truthfulness? Sincerity? I didn't know.

But I knew I felt what I'd said, even if my path to get to this point hadn't been conventional. I wanted to be the person Eva and Aidan thought I was.

I wanted to do this.

So I stared back at her, my mouth a straight line.

Finally, she seemed to find what she was looking for. Her eyes warmed. "Very well. Then, with this gesture, you three shall join us."

When Umbra stepped to Liara, she raised her thumb, pressed it into the center of Liara's forehead. A white light grew there as Liara's eyes closed, diminished a moment later.

I hadn't known about this part.

The headmistress stepped to me. Her thumb rose, and when she pressed it to my forehead, I found my eyes closing automatically as a voice entered my mind.

Welcome, child, Umbra whispered into my head, *to the circle of guardians at Shadow's End Academy*.

CHAPTER EIGHT

When Umbra's thumb lowered from my forehead, my eyes snapped open, anger flaring.

She'd penetrated my mind. No one had mentioned she would do that.

"It's done," Umbra announced, tapping her staff on the ground once more. "The guardian initiates have become guardians, and now there are nine of you."

That was all well and good. Meanwhile...

"You didn't warn me about the part where you can read my mind," I blurted into what felt like a religious silence.

Beside me, Liara gave an overlarge sigh. "I doubt she'd have any interest in reading your mind, anyway."

At my feet, Loki snickered.

Umbra's head tilted, eyebrows rising. "I can only speak into your mind. It helps to facilitate the rescues."

I gestured straight up, to where I suspected that massive horn sat amongst the branches above us—the one that sounded every time the guardians had to scramble. "Your mega-horn seems to do the trick."

"She gives us details as we prepare," Fi said from behind me. "Where we're going, how large the magical disturbance was."

"If it comforts you, once you've passed through the veil, our connection will be broken," Umbra said. "It's only when you're nearby I can speak into your head."

That was a strange comfort. My brain was only big enough for the Spitfire and Rational Clem—I didn't think I could handle a third voice piping up all the time without breaking.

Of course, I had never told Umbra about the Spitfire and Rational Clem. No one knew about my duality except Callum Rathmore.

"From here on, you must be prepared at all times to answer the call," she said to the three of us. "Day or night, no matter where you are or what you do. You must answer the call as quickly as you can, for a person's life and death may depend on your haste. Do you understand?"

"Yes," Liara said.

"Yes," I echoed. At my feet, Loki gave an emphatic meow, and I jerked my thumb at him. "He does, too."

Umbra smiled down at him, then returned her attention to the two of us. "Thank you," she said, "Liara, Clementine, and Loki, for the sacrifices you will make."

That didn't sound foreboding at all.

The twins came to either side of Liara and me, each slinging an arm around our respective shoulders. "Come on, guardians," Isaiah said. And, on the other side, Elijah added, "We've got our own initiation in the dining hall."

Liara's shoulders dropped. "Is this a requirement?"

Umbra stepped aside, a softness to her face I wasn't expecting. "It's a long tradition."

I glanced past Elijah's arm to Umbra. "What about training? You know, to fight the forces of darkness and all that."

Umbra nodded toward the guardians all ushering us out of the antechamber. "They're your trainers. Good ones, at that."

Out we went into the night, the twins hooting as all of us paraded toward the dining hall. A few people had come out to watch, standing on the landing of their dorms, cheering for us.

"I hear you're a fire witch," Elijah said, his arm still slung around my shoulder. "Who'd have thought?"

"Who'd have thought I'm a fire witch? Basically anyone who's seen my fire."

He pointed up into the trees. "No—who'd have thought people would be *cheering* for a fire witch."

"I won't let my head get too big—they'll be back to throwing things at it by next week."

Inside the dining hall, two tables had been pushed together to form a long banquet table, brimming with food I recognized as Chef Vickery's creations. At the end stood a huge bowl of grape drink; I could smell its alcoholic spice from here.

I raised an eyebrow up at Elijah. "Training, huh?"

He smirked at me. "Can't train well without strong bonds, Clementine."

"Goddamn right." Isaiah slapped my other shoulder as he passed us, headed for the food. "It's all about trust."

"Bonding over spiked grape juice?" Loki muttered from my feet, even as all the other guardians filtered around us. "Sounds hedonistic and nauseating. Count me out."

A second later, Circe set a bowl of milk in front of him, and his face disappeared into the center of it.

I laughed, accepted a drink from Akelan, who shook my hand in a strangely formal, endearing way. "I suggest drinking at least three of these before we start," he said with a small smile.

"Start?"

He didn't answer that. He was already being pulled aside by Keene, who wanted to talk earth magic. Meanwhile, Liara was being chatted up beside a plate of cookies by Fi, who pretended to shoot lightning from her hands.

Fingers fell on my arm, and I found Mishka beside me, her dark eyes staring up into mine. "Clementine. I regret we haven't met before."

"I'd guess you've been busy," I said. "How long have you been a guardian?"

"This will be my second year. To be honest, I didn't think I'd make it through the first."

"You thought you'd drop out?"

"Never." She smiled, gently shook her head. "It's darker than that, I'm afraid. I'll tell you some time—ideally after a mission." She raised her plate, brimming with a flaky dessert. "Baklava? I just love them."

I took one, bit into it. "Do you enjoy it, though? Being a guardian."

"I enjoy this." She gestured around. "And I enjoy the thought that we'll be successful someday."

I paused before I took a second bite. "Someday?"

Her head tilted. "That we'll rescue someone someday."

I stood there with baklava hovering in front of my mouth. "You've never been successful?"

"Not last year. The last successful rescue was two years ago, last fall."

That was before I'd even arrived at the academy. No wonder Jericho had been so depressed half the time.

"All right, everyone," Elijah called out from a circle of chairs set at one end of the hall. "We're starting."

We all took a chair, seated facing one another.

Isaiah stood in the center of the circle. "Anyone had less than two drinks? If not, get another. We'll wait."

I stood, crept over to the bowl and poured myself another drink. By the time I sat back down, Isaiah was explaining the game by demonstration.

"Human." He tapped Circe on the shoulder as he walked around the edge of the group. "Human." He tapped Liara on the shoulder. On he went, repeating, "Human," as he tapped every shoulder. Until he arrived at Isaiah.

"Werewolf!" he bellowed, and took off flying around the group.

Isaiah leapt up, chasing Elijah. He didn't catch him before Elijah dropped into his seat, breathing fast.

"And that's the basics," Elijah said, cheeks ruddy.

I gestured around the circle with my drink. "We're literally just playing Duck Duck Goose."

Beside me, Keene grinned. "The witch thinks we're playing a human game."

Across the circle, Isaiah's wings fluttered as he conjured a tiny, drunkenly wavering tornado in his palm. A maniacal expression slid onto his face. "Ever played Duck Duck Goose with magic, Cole?"

That night, I drank more than three glasses of grape wine. And as I walked with my arm over Mishka's shoulders back toward my dorm, I asked, "Are werewolves real, anyway?"

"As real as unicorns," she said with surprising sobriety.

I shifted an uncertain gaze down to her. "I'm not sure if that's a yes or a no."

She laughed, a ringing sound in the dead of night. It must have been after midnight. Around the time Akelan tripped Liara by making the floor rise up to encase her foot, I'd lost count of how many rounds of Human Human Werewolf we'd played.

A lot.

"It's a no," Mishka said. "Demons, though? Real. Maybe we ought to call it Human Human Demon."

I stared at her. "How do you... make words right now?"

She held me tighter as I swayed. "You mean, why aren't I slurring them like you?"

"Yeah."

"I diluted my wine with water," she whispered.

"Because you're a water mage," I exclaimed into the night. "That's genius."

She smiled as we passed through the clearing. "Kind of you to say so."

"I thought we would be training tonight." I mimed driving a sword into an invisible torso. "You know, practicing missions. Planning. Serious things."

"Instead of having a frat party?"

"Uh-huh."

She let out a breath. "That's the thing you quickly realize about guardianship, Clementine: all you have when you're out there is one another. You can plan and strategize and train all you want, but if you don't trust the person next to you, you're at a disadvantage."

I raised an eyebrow at her. "And that's why we get smashed and play Human Human Werewolf?"

She met my eyes with her own, complete sincerity on her face. "That's why we get smashed and play Human Human Werewolf."

There was actually some logic to that. I absolutely wouldn't have been slung over Mishka, heading back with her at this time of night like she was my designated driver without what came before.

"Trust me," she said as we came to the steps up to my dorm. "There'll be training. Lots of it. Do you need help getting up?"

I glanced at the steps, which extended for miles in my wavering vision. Turned back to her. "I'm good."

She smiled at me. "I think you'll fit in well, Clementine. Just remember, we're here for each other. My door's always open."

When she'd gone, I just gazed after her, blinking into the night. I didn't even know where her door was.

Part of me contemplated the absolute travesty it was going to be getting up those stairs. And the other part of me felt warm. Maybe that was the grape wine, and maybe it was the strange feeling of being a part of something.

Bonds. Trust. Those weren't in my old vocabulary.

By the time I got to the top of the stairs, I was crawling and nauseous. And then, reaching the landing, I heard a meow and stared back the way I'd come.

I had forgotten my damn cat.

His eyes appeared first, and then he padded his way up beside me to stand on the landing. Stared at me a second. "You going to open the door or not?"

I stood. "Can we pretend like you didn't witness me crawl my way up here?"

His tail flicked. "I have no idea what you're talking about."

I gave him a thumbs-up as I opened the door and we came into the dorm to find a sleeping Eva. Together, we climbed into bed—I didn't even bother to undress—and I slept. Oh, did I sleep.

It felt like only a moment had passed before I opened my eyes to Eva's voice.

"Clementine?" Her face loomed over me.

"Yeah?" I croaked through a veil of hair.

Paper crinkled in her hand. "Aidan left this note for you. He writes, on account of your guardian celebration, you can meet at seven-thirty this morning."

I took the note, but my vision was too blurry to read it. "What time is it?"

"Seven-twenty."

"You're a liar—it's the middle of the night," I groaned half into my pillow.

At my head, Loki grumbled and stretched.

"It's seven-twenty in the morning." Eva grabbed her satchel from her chair. "And I suggest you at least brush your teeth before you go."

"Is it that bad?" I called after her as she went out the door, a blinding rectangle of daylight searing into my vision. All at once, a banging headache formed.

"Yes," she said, and then the door shut.

Evanora Whitewillow was maybe the only person in the world who could be that blamelessly blunt with me. And the worst part—I breathed into my hand, sniffed—was that she was always right about these things.

My breath was rank.

Twenty minutes later, I came into the library with a minty mouth, wild hair, and lidded eyes.

"Clementine Cole," Professor Milonakis said from the circulation desk, lowering her spectacles to wind up for some passive aggression, most likely. "Congratulations."

I stopped in front of her desk, my head throbbing with the suddenness of it. "What have I done wrong?"

Her eyebrows pulled together. "I'm not aware of what you've done wrong, though I imagine there is *something*. I was congratulating you on your induction."

As a guardian. I was a guardian now.

She was being sincere.

"Well, I, uh... Thanks."

Her spectacles dropped another degree. "No books from the Room of the Ancients may leave the library."

There was the Milonakis I knew.

"Right." I passed on through. "I remember."

She was reciting another rule when I came into the library proper. Inside, only a few students occupied tables on the first and second stories. We'd always met at this time of morning; it was easier to talk about illicit things, which it seemed like was all we ever talked about nowadays.

Aidan had taken our usual table on the second story, a trail of steam coming from the teapot on the table. When I took the seat across from him, he pressed a plate of biscotti toward me. "You played Human Human Werewolf, didn't you?" he said without preamble.

I bit into a biscotti. "You've heard of it?"

"I'm a mage. Of course I've heard of it."

"How'd you know we played?"

He half-smiled. "I've heard it's a guardian tradition."

"Not like I can remember much of it." I poured myself a careful cup of tea, gripping that mofo like it was his mom's finest china. "Though I do have a vague recollection of someone's shirt getting blown off."

His arms folded. "Male or female?"

"Don't be a dude." I set the teapot down. "Let's talk prophecies."

"There's another order of business. Drink your tea; I don't want that hangover I know you've got at present interfering with this."

I did so. When I'd finished the cup, Aidan tapped the screen of his phone. "Remember when I recorded the GPS coordinates after we passed through the leyline into that tundra?"

"Of course."

"I looked them up." He leaned closer. "We were in Siberia, Clementine. Near the Arctic Circle."

CHAPTER NINE

I sat back, which set my head into fresh pounding. "No kidding. Now I can take Russia off my bucket list."

Aidan raised one eyebrow. "That's all you've got to say?"

I plucked another biscotti from the tray. "I know you've got some theory as to why the leyline brought us there." I dipped it into my tea, waited.

At first, he didn't speak. And then, with a sigh, "Yes, I have a theory."

I took a bite. Kept watching him.

He patted one of several books on the table. "I was reading about leylines. Seems if you're a powerful enough mage, you can manipulate them. Infuse them with your magic."

"So that noise we heard before we passed through. You think someone was manipulating the leyline."

"I think so."

"To bring us to Siberia."

He nodded.

I set my cup down. Snapped my fingers, conjuring a plate of steaming fae rolls. "And now the question is who."

Aidan pulled one fae roll apart from the others, took a bite. "These are good. Better than last year by a long sight."

"God knows I practiced," I murmured, picking at a piece of roll. "Any theories as to who it was?"

"None as yet."

I bit into a raisin, considering. "What if we come at it from a different angle—*why* this mage wanted us to end up in Siberia. What's in Siberia?"

"Practically nothing," Aidan said. "It's one of the least inhabited places on the planet, besides maybe Namibia and the poles."

"That could be relevant."

"The lack of habitation?"

"Sure. We humans are so human-centric. What if it had nothing at all to do with *who* was there?"

A slender hand reached between us, yanked off a roll from the plate. "Every fae mother would be so proud." Circe Petalfleck leaned against the table as she bit into the roll. "Delicious."

Aidan sat back, our brainstorming session interrupted.

When we broke eye contact, Circe was beaming down at me, blue eyes shining. "Hello, Clementine. Care to come with me?"

I gestured to Aidan. "This is my friend. Aidan North."

Circe whipped around, extended a hand. "Circe Petalfleck. Fifth-year guardian."

"I know who you are," Aidan said. "You've come to get her for training, haven't you?"

Circe gave a deep nod. She was the most theatrical fae I'd met. "Unless what you've got going here takes precedence." She circled a finger over our spread of tea and goodies.

"Actually—" I began.

"It doesn't," Aidan cut in. "Guardianship always takes precedence. But think about what we talked about, Clem. All right? And meet back here tomorrow at seven."

Circe had already picked up my satchel. "I'll carry this for you."

I stood, eyes still on Aidan. "Tomorrow." Then I grabbed one of the books on leylines. The cover read, *Fae Customs and Culture*, which sounded like something I ought to read now that I was taking a class with Frostwish. "Can I borrow this?"

He gestured for me to have it.

Circe's strong hand took mine, and she led me toward the staircase. "Toodaloo, Aidan North."

It was rare I allowed myself to be led like a child. Only in moments of extreme discombobulation. Like right now.

When we arrived at the staircase, I slid my hand out from hers. "I won't call that rude, but I won't call that polite, either."

Circe glanced back at me as she floated the rest of the way down. "What, taking a roll? I'll conjure up ten more if you like. Hotter and spicier."

She'd known what I meant. "Brushing off Aidan."

"He's a mage—he knows about these guardian things."

I followed her down to the first floor and through the maze of tables. "We could schedule a training, you know."

"All right." Circe handed me my satchel. "How about seven-thirty on Tuesday mornings?"

"Aidan and I meet in the library at seven. Like we were just doing."

We came through the circulation room, and Circe clicked her tongue and made finger guns at Milonakis.

And in the biggest shock of my life, Milonakis just smiled back at her. "Good morning, Ms. Petalfleck."

As we came out of the library, I gestured over my shoulder. "Did Milonakis get body-snatched?"

"Nah. She just adores guardians. There's a reason she teaches rescue. Dreamed of being a guardian herself back in the day, but never passed the trials."

My eyes widened. "That explains her obsession with tests."

Milonakis had once wanted to be a guardian. That must have been around the time the Shade's army began to emerge, started snatching people from their homes at night. No wonder she'd become mingy and shrink-wrapped—she'd never achieved her goal.

I both pitied and respected her more.

Circe laughed. "Good observation, witch."

Meanwhile, Circe was guiding us toward a part of the grounds I'd rarely thought to head toward. This was mostly faculty housing, but there was one particularly fat tree I'd always wondered about, and that was the one we were headed toward.

Beside me, her blue hair shone with almost glaring brilliance under the sunlight. She walked with a smile I couldn't quite explain; maybe that was always present.

"What's this training for, anyway?" I asked.

"We're getting you on the right page with protocol. What to do when the horn sounds or when Umbra talks in our heads." She twirled a finger through the air. "You know, to make a tight unit. You'll be part of the mounted unit, of course."

"Mounted unit?"

"Sure. I saw you riding that big stallion in the first trial—I don't imagine after all that time practicing on him you want to go and learn to ride a broom."

"Noir," I said. "His name's Noir."

"He's a hellbeast is what he is. And he's perfect."

We came to the enormous tree in the midst of the faculty housing, and Circe led me around to the far side. "You see a door here?"

It looked like an unbroken trunk. I shook my head.

She tilted her head. "So you don't believe you're a proper guardian, then."

Oh, it was one of those things.

"I believe it," I said with more insistence than necessary.

"Sure. Except you still don't see it." She shrugged. "So we're going to have to wait out here until you can convince your brain otherwise." She folded her arms, staring at me.

I set a hand to the trunk, ran my fingers over it. No door. But she was telling me one existed, and I believed her.

I *did* believe I was a guardian. Didn't I?

Except guardians and good witches don't cheat to pass the third trial, that small voice whispered.

"Listen, Clementine—" she began.

She was cut off by the sound of the horn, low in the distance, rising in pitch as our eyes met. A moment later, it reached an unmistakable crescendo, bellowing through the grounds.

Umbra was calling on the guardians. All of us.

Circe's smile dropped. "It's too soon."

"I'll get Loki—"

She set both hands on my shoulders. "No time. Get your horse, meet me by the leyline outside the grounds. The others won't wait for you, but I will. Stay with me during this mission, all right?"

A tremor ran up the length of my body, her sapphire eyes like gems gleaming back at me. Full of anticipation. Uncertainty.

This was what I had signed up for. This was my job.

My fingers curled to fists. I nodded.

She whirled around, took off into the air. A moment later she had disappeared into the canopy, and I was alone.

I took off at a run toward the stables. The quartermistress would have fed Noir his first meal an hour ago, which couldn't be better timing. He wouldn't be full or sluggish, and he wouldn't be peckish yet.

I didn't have to saddle him. I didn't have to bridle him.

I only had to get him and go.

When I came to the half-door of the stables, I nearly ran into a first-year hauling a saddle. "Sorry!" she exclaimed as she wheeled around to catch the swinging stirrups.

I half-turned, waved a hand, completing my turn as I reached Noir's door. He was idling in the corner of his stall, his head at half-height.

Quartermistress Farrow's voice rang down the aisleway. "Clear it out! Guardians massing."

I glanced in her direction. So far, I was the only one who had arrived—and just when another class was starting.

That was a good thing for Fi and Akelan. They needed saddled horses.

"Go on, then," Farrow said to me as she strode past, entering one of the other stalls. "Time's of the essence, Clementine."

I flashed her a smile. When I undid the latch, Noir's head jerked up. "Hey, buddy," I murmured, followed by a click of the tongue. I only clicked at him when it was go-time. "I've got a surprise for you this morning. We're going out into the world."

He nickered as I approached him, running one hand down the length of his muscled, silky neck. With my hand at his shoulder, I urged him through the door and into the aisle.

He trotted onto the cement with a flick of the tail, turned toward the open back of the stables toward the paddock.

By now, Fi, Mishka, and Akelan had come in through the half-door. None of them even acknowledged me, if they'd noticed me at all. Their eyes were glazed, all business.

"Got the stirrups at your length, Waters," I heard Farrow say from one of the stalls. "Siren's ready for you."

I came into the aisle, and with a click, Noir followed me out into the back paddock. Out there on the hardpack, I took hold of his mane halfway up his neck and at his withers. With two steps and a jump, I threw my leg up, hooked it over his back.

By the time I was mounted and turning Noir back toward the stables, I could already hear the sounds of Fi, Mishka, and Akelan's horses leaving their stalls, their hooves clicking over the cement aisle.

They were impossibly fast. How were they so fast?

Out they came—Fi on Siren, Mishka on Minibar, and Akelan on the gelding quarter horse—one horse's nose nearly on the other's rump. That was how close they rode as they tore past me and out through the gate, which Farrow had jogged to open.

I spun Noir toward the gate, and Farrow threw a hand out. "Well, what are you waiting for? A mailed invitation?"

I grabbed up Noir's mane at the withers, pressed my thighs into his rib cage. He fell into a trot, and then a canter through the gate.

That was when I heard Umbra's voice in my head.

Chiang Mai. One girl, seventeen. They're headed north to the river.

And in a blossoming explosion at the center of my vision, I saw the place. Three-forty-five in the morning, the neighborhood street quiet and dim, the moon a great lantern in the sky.

I blinked, and the vision was gone.

So that was how the guardians knew where to go. When Umbra

felt the magical disturbance, she could tap into it with her vision. Maeve Umbra was a far more powerful wizard than I'd ever known.

Noir and I passed the stables, cutting past the clearing and the amphitheater. I caught a glimpse of the central grounds, where all activity had stopped. Fae hovered in the air, students stood with bags held tight.

I had stood that way more than once. I had watched the guardians ride.

The horn had that effect. On it went, long and low and insistent.

By the time we hit the path, I couldn't see Fi and Akelan through the trees. They'd pulled away, disappeared.

But Circe had said she would wait. That remained to be seen.

I pressed Noir into a gallop, and we left the academy grounds, thundered toward the leyline in the woods. What would be a twenty-minute walk became a two-minute ride.

The trees kept appearing in front of me, but no Circe to be seen.

When I arrived at the leyline, we came to a hard stop. I spun in a circle on Noir, found myself alone.

"You were too slow," a voice said from above. Circe flew to the ground, eyes flicking over the two of us. "Everyone's already through. I nearly left you here."

It wasn't worth the breath it would take to make excuses. I only nodded.

Circe flew up to the height of Noir's head, began cutting the veil straight to the earth. "When I open this, you go straight through. I'll be just behind you. You heard Umbra's directions, right?"

"One girl being taken north to the river."

"Right. When you're through, you'll be on the street Umbra showed us. Head to the river—it's possible we can catch up." She stepped aside, pulling the veil open. "Good luck, Clementine."

CHAPTER TEN

Before us lay a large triangle of darkness, warm air wafting over my face.

I pressed Noir through the veil, and though I expected some resistance from him, he didn't hesitate. He walked us straight into the night, into the humid warmth of northern Thailand.

Around me lay the same street I had seen in my mind, the moon the only light above, cars and tuktuks parked alongside.

North. We had to head north.

I stared up into the sky, seeking out the brightest star. I used to imagine, not long after I'd lost my family and I still believed in magic, that my mother and sister had merged with the North Star. Like my mom, it was a constant in the sky, a source of guidance.

Those things were still true.

I spotted it east of me, overtop a row of two-story homes. I spun Noir toward it, pressing my heels into his sides.

It was only when I used my heels he knew I meant business.

With a snort, he started into a canter, then a gallop. We headed down a cross-street directly toward the North Star, toward where I assumed the river lay. Noir's hooves clattered across the asphalt, the noise breaking the silent peace of the night.

Of course, that peace was an illusion. This was the witching hour.

Chilly recognition clawed up my spine. I hadn't been outside the safety of the academy during the witching hour in years.

We'd gone one block when a voice sounded above and to my left. "How'd you know this way was north?" Circe asked, flying alongside me.

"The North Star," I called back, low over Noir's neck.

"Well done, newbie." She pulled ahead a few paces. "I can hear Fi's and Akelan's horses. They've got about a quarter mile on us, and they're moving fast in pursuit."

I listened, but heard nothing over Noir's hooves and the bellows of his lungs. "How can you tell?"

Circe tapped the side of her head. "We fae have better hearing than you. Keep your wits up, Cole—this is the witching hour. You never know what could happen, or who could pop out of the darkness."

She was so nonchalant. A seventeen-year-old girl was being kidnapped the same way I had been that winter night not so long ago, and to Circe it could have been any other night out. It could have been a game of Human Human Werewolf.

Which told me one of two things: she was either taking this less seriously than she should, or she'd become desensitized to the emotional overwhelm of a situation like this.

Probably the latter. My heart was beating too fast right now to do this more than twice in my life unless I got a hold on my emotions.

I squeezed my eyes shut. *Keep your wits up.*

"They've slowed," Circe said. "We'll be catching up to them soon."

We raced forward, Noir and me and the blue-haired fae, passing through streets I didn't recognize, under a sky I'd never seen from this part of the Earth.

The only things I recognized were the moon and the North Star. They were enough.

Ahead, finally, I did hear noise.

Yelling.

Circe put a hand out, and I slowed Noir to a canter as we came to the end of the next block, the street opening up to what looked like a marketplace.

At the center of the marketplace, blue lightning lit up the sky.

Liara.

That was followed by the rumbling of earth magic; the vibrations passed up through Noir and into my body.

Circe came to a stop in midair, staring over the scene. I stopped with her, sitting back on Noir.

All we'd seen was the light show of Liara's magic, but no guardians. None of the Shade's army. No kidnapped girl.

"Wait here," Circe said. "I'm going to get a better view."

Before I could say anything, she'd disappeared into the darkness, leaving Noir and me standing alone.

He gave an impatient stomp of the forehoof, and I ran a hand down his hot neck. His breathing came quick under me; he still wasn't recovered from the run. "It's all right," I whispered. "You'll get to run again. Trust me."

Silence fell around us. No lightning, no earth magic, no Circe.

It was as though the whole world had enclosed to Noir and me, the two of us standing alone in the middle of a dead street. The hot air pressed in tight, thick in my throat.

And then it all happened quickly.

The darkness moved.

It moved through the open marketplace faster than my eyes could track, like a shadow following light. But no light had appeared—just the moving blackness.

Noir had seen it, too. His head jerked up, his breathing short and intense.

A deluge of water poured after it, and Siren burst through the water in a gray streak, Fi low over her neck. That was followed by Akelan on the quarter horse.

I'd just seen one of the Shade's minions.

Noir and I burst into motion in the same moment Circe's voice rang out—"Clem, there!"—and we took a hard right after the creature, nearly skidding on the asphalt before we corrected.

Ahead, Fi and Akelan shot off bursts of magic in the creature's wake. Somewhere I imagined the other fae tracked above us. That was confirmed when the space ahead of me distorted, a vortex of air forming out of nowhere.

But the air magic wasn't quick enough. The creature was already past, and Fi and Akelan had to swerve their horses around the vortex.

I remembered now how fast the creatures had moved when they'd kidnapped me. Ten, twelve miles an hour with ease. This thing moved faster than any of us.

But I hadn't properly tested Noir's gallop against it.

I pressed my heels into his sides and he let himself out, his neck stretching to almost a straight line as it had done during the first trial in the meadow.

I had no training as a guardian, but I did have training for this. If nothing else, we could run.

We came up on the other horses' flanks in seconds, broke through a fresh rainstorm—probably courtesy of Mishka—and passed them up.

Ahead, I could see it now. The creature was slower than Noir, pressing away light as it ran. It was darkness incarnate.

And it was carrying the girl.

I could take it out with my fire. The only risk would be hitting the girl, and I hadn't had enough experience with control and precision in Goodbarrel's class to fully trust myself.

"It's closing in on the river," a voice called from overhead. Either Elijah or Isaiah. "We need to end it now."

I didn't have time to get closer. If I struck the girl, we could heal her—as long as I didn't hit her in the head or the heart.

My hand shot out, flames bursting to life over my entire arm. I took a moment to steady my arm over Noir's movement, and then I curled my wrist, flicked my hand to send a stream of flame toward its head.

The flame swept out from my hand on a course with its head. A second later, it made contact—

"Bullseye," I whispered.

—and the flame passed right through it.

The creature kept on running, the girl still over its shoulder.

I had hit it. My flames had skewered its head. But it'd had no effect.

"Akelan, coordinate with me," one of the twins called from above. "Ready?"

"Ready," Akelan called from my flank, pulling closer. By now Noir had slowed, half-exhausted.

Akelan's quarter horse nosed beyond Noir; as he passed me, I spotted one of his hands out in preparation.

"On my mark," the twin called. When I glanced up into the sky, several fae flew just ahead of us, nearly above the creature.

My attention flicked between Akelan and the fae and back again. A coordinated attack—but why?

The creature reached the bank of the river, slowed for the first time since I'd spotted him. I thought I saw one of his ghastly arms go up—was he parting the veil?

"Now!" the twin yelled.

An arrow of wind sliced through the sky, headed straight for the creature below. In very nearly the same moment, the earth burst to life beneath it, though its arm didn't stop moving.

The ground swelled, rose to encompass the creature's legs.

The arrow pierced its head, sliced it into two shadowy parts.

But the arm didn't stop moving. It dragged straight to the ground at the river's edge.

It *was* parting the veil.

"Get her," Circe cried. "Grab her now."

Together, fae and horses descended on the spot. Noir and I did, too.

But the headless creature's body still had arms. It lifted the girl off its shoulder, threw her through the partition. In a moment, she disappeared.

We skidded to a halt as the veil reseamed, the creature's body dissolving into nothing but smoke.

All that remained was us, breathing hard. The horses heaving. The river rushing by.

And Fi, who climbed off her horse, stood at the river's edge, and let out a yell with balled fists.

Circe dropped to the ground next to her, set a hand on her shoulder.

"We had it," Fi said with what sounded like nettles in her throat.

"We did," Circe said.

Akelan rode up next to me, patted me on the back. "That was a good attempt you made there."

"I hit it," I said, still staring at the spot where the creature had died and the girl had disappeared. "It wasn't an attempt."

"I saw."

I dragged my eyes to him. "But it had no effect."

He gave a slow nod. "Circe didn't get a chance to tell you before this all kicked off."

"Tell me what?"

Elijah flew to the rail of the bridge near us, stood atop it. "We should go back. It's still the witching hour."

"Right." Mishka urged Minibar toward Elijah. "You'll do the honors?"

Elijah had already raised his hand, was cutting the veil.

"Tell me what, Akelan?" I repeated, staring him down.

Akelan had already started toward Elijah. He glanced back at me. "It takes two types of magic to bring down one of the creatures."

"Two types," Liara said from the riverbank. It was the first time she'd spoken; I had almost forgotten she was with us. She stood there, rigid, her face a mask. I'd known her for over two years now; I could see the disappointment written over her, even in this darkness.

Circe pointed at her. "We'll get to you. As soon as we're back, we're discussing everything before that godsdamn horn has another chance to blow."

Elijah and Isaiah ushered us through the veil one by one. We came back into daylight, the forest outside the academy, where birds chirped, a squirrel squawked at us from a nearby tree.

I squinted into the canopy, the sunlight almost blistering.

It wasn't even nine here yet.

"We had her." Fi walked beside Siren, holding her reins lightly. Her blonde hair gleamed above her slender neck. "We did."

Circe walked beside her. "It was too close to the river. We've got to head them off sooner next time—but by then we'll have the other two chasers..."

After that, her voice had faded away.

I waited atop Noir for Elijah and Isaiah to come through.

When the veil had closed behind them, one of the twins ran a hand through his shock of hair. "So, Clementine," he offered when he saw me waiting, "would you say we work the day shift, or the night shift?"

It seemed so irreverent; a girl had been lost to the Shade.

But I was beginning to understand.

Mishka had told me they'd never had a successful rescue. Not for two years. If every failure devastated you, all your hair would fall out in six months. You wouldn't eat for stress. You'd be a shell.

"Both," I murmured, turning Noir toward the academy.

"See, Elijah says night shift," Isaiah said. "Because no matter what, your sleep schedule is going to hell."

"How often do these rescues take place?" I asked.

"Maybe once a week," one of the twins said as they flew beside me. "Sometimes less, sometimes more."

"This was the worst timing," the other twin said. "Really unlucky."

Unlucky. If that wasn't the story of my life.

But it didn't have to be. Another life didn't have to be lost on my watch.

I pressed Noir into a canter straight toward the academy.

CHAPTER ELEVEN

After I'd gotten Noir back to the stables, wiped him down, and given him an extra helping of alfalfa and oats, I returned to the spot where Circe had told me a door existed.

I still didn't see a door.

So I did what I'd done when I had first come to the academy. I sat down in front of the tree, crossed my legs, and waited.

"Oh, Clem," Circe said when she found me there ten minutes later, "go get some breakfast before the dining hall closes until lunch. You've earned it, for gods' sake."

I didn't avert my eyes. "Not hungry."

She came to stand over me. "You're in shock. You need food in you."

"I'm not in shock. I want to get to our training."

Circe sat down beside me. She snapped her fingers, and a plate appeared before me. Six purple fruits lay on it, each steaming.

I nodded at it. "What's that?"

"Food. It's good—better by far than anything you've had."

"Fae food, then."

She picked up one of the fruits, handed it to me. "Fae food. It'll help."

I didn't move to take it. "I told you I'm not in shock, Circe."

She angled her face to meet my eyes. "Don't make me pull rank on you."

"You don't have any rank on me."

Her blue eyebrows rose. "Don't I? I'm two years above you and a year your senior as a guardian. Not that anyone's counting."

My eyes flicked between the fruit and her. "What happens if I don't do as you say? Pushups? Flogging with a paddle?"

A small smile appeared. "This isn't a frat, but now you're giving me ideas." The fruit remained aloft; it was almost painfully fragrant and smelled delicious.

I plucked it from her hand, took a bite. When I did, my eyes closed.

"We call these pluma," Circe said. "They calm the spirit. Ease tension."

"I can see why." It was soft, sweet, and like the rolls, contained some trace spice I had only encountered in fae food. It was addictive, and I took another bite.

When I opened my eyes, Circe's smile had grown mischievous.

"What?" I said.

"They have a staining quality. Just so you know, purple lipstick would suit you."

I gave an overlarge smile. "If that's their worst feature, I'm eating a plate of these every day."

Her hand fell on my knee. Circe was a toucher, for sure. "I saw what you did out there, Clem. It was a really good shot, and I know you thought you'd saved her."

I chewed. Beyond my questions about *why* my magic hadn't worked and the mechanics of my failure, something else was broiling. For some reason, my chest had clenched. "That girl's gone forever."

Circe's face went solemn, and she didn't speak. Her sapphire eyes said all I needed to know.

I swallowed, lowered the fruit. Part of me had known it was true the moment she had passed through the veil, and part of me hadn't believed it. "Fuck."

"The Shade's army is powerful."

"And what happens to these people? The girl who passed through the veil—where did she go?"

Circe's eyes lowered to the grass. Her palm went flat atop it. "Below. The witching hour is the only time the magic between the above world and the underworld is weak enough for them to emerge. The hour only occurs in darkness."

I stared at her hand. "How do you do it?"

She knew exactly what I meant. "One day at a time. Sometimes I cry. Sometimes I drink too much wine. Once I slept with Elijah after I drank."

The ghost of a grin touched my lips. "Are you sure it wasn't Isaiah?"

"Positive. He'll never let me live it down, especially when I'm sober."

I gripped the fruit until my fingers sank into the warm skin. Met her eyes. "This year is going to be different."

Circe fixed me with a half-interested, half-amused look. "Is it now?"

"Yes, it is." I set the fruit on the plate, stood. "You've got Liara."

She stood with me. "Not Clementine?"

I examined the spot on the trunk where the door ought to be, running my fingers over it. "I'm fast, but Liara combines two types of magic. She's a wizard, isn't she? Like Umbra."

"Very smart, Clementine."

I paused, feeling a groove in the tree. I had found it, through sheer anger and determination, I had found my belief. As I traced the groove, the door became obvious.

I pulled the knob, glanced back at Circe. "Smart is as smart does."

Inside, the room spread wide with ornaments and portraits and knickknacks from what I assumed were years of guardians. Lots of weapons, too; there was even a weapons' rack in one corner, chock-full of every lethal blade you could imagine.

A staircase wound around the edge of the room toward a second story, and then a third. Whatever was up there, I couldn't see it past the railing.

It was a common room for guardians.

Mishka sat on one of two cozy sofas, staring into a fireplace that wasn't even burning. Her eyes were red-rimmed. Mishka's gaze trailed to me. So she'd opted for crying. "Hello, Clementine."

As soon as she spoke, Loki's head popped up from Mishka's lap. "You left me behind."

I threw my hands out. "You could get in here, but I couldn't?"

He hopped down, crossed toward me. "I've always believed in my catness. My prowess. My superiority."

"Of course you have."

Circe stepped up to my side. "Welcome to the guardians' space. This place is open to you twenty-four hours a day."

I crossed to the center of the oriental rug laid over the floor, turned a circle, eyes trailing up. "Bigger than my house's common room."

Elijah and Isaiah appeared through the doorway, followed by the other guardians. Liara was among them. "Has to fit a lot. Training space, bedrooms, a kitchen."

"And of course the best room of all," Isaiah added, pointing straight up. "The view of the world."

The other guardians led Loki and me up the stairs, passing several rooms on the second story. Bedrooms, a communal kitchen, a combat training space. When we came to the third story, the landing had you facing into what looked like a strategy room. A large circular table with chairs, a chalkboard on one wall.

"Here it is," Isaiah said, passing around the other side of the walkway.

When I turned, I knew I was looking at the room he'd called "the view of the world."

A double-sized doorway opened into an expansive space with a semi-transparent globe the size of me floating at the center. Slender golden lines crisscrossed the entirety of it like wrapped tinsel.

I came around the walkway and into the room, approaching the globe and raising one finger. "Tell me now if I shouldn't touch it."

"Touch away." Elijah came to stand next to me, arms folded. "That's its purpose."

When I set a finger over Greenland, the globe recognized my touch with a blossoming flash of white. Four red markers appeared, two each over towns called Nuuk and Sisimiut.

I glanced at Elijah.

"Red markers are rescues," he said. "Attempted ones, at least." He reached out, flicked a finger over the globe and sent it spinning. "They're on every continent."

"What about successful rescues?"

"Fewer of those," Fi said from the doorway. "Yours is on there."

I stopped the globe, slowly turned it to the United States. There, partway up the East Coast, sat my green marker.

Maeve Umbra had come for me that night.

I wondered if the people standing around me would have been so successful, or if I would have been lost like the Thai girl.

"How is it," I said, "that no one except Maeve Umbra noticed me being kidnapped in the middle of a major city?"

"The creatures aren't visible to regular human eyes," Circe said. "To them, they're shadows. Their sounds are just the wind."

My eyes flitted over the rest of my country. So many red markers; so few green.

I slowly circled the globe. "What kind of magic is this?"

"Umbra's, of course." Liara came forward. "Some of these rescues are a decade or more old, aren't they?"

"That's right," Circe said. "This globe is the guardians' equivalent of a journal, among other things."

"And the golden lines—leylines?" I asked, my finger hovering down the length of one running straight through my old home. All my life, and I'd never known a leyline ran through my city. I'd probably walked over it thousands of times.

Elijah nodded at me through the transparent globe. "Lots of them, aren't there?"

More than I'd ever imagined.

And it was in that moment—taking in the armchairs in the

corners, the bookcases, the chessboard set up at one end of the room —I knew I would spend some time in this room.

If I could, I would memorize all the leylines. I didn't know if I was capable, but then again, I'd spent most of my life not knowing my real capabilities.

I was only beginning to understand how much more lay inside me.

"We'll need to add one over Chiang Mai," Fi said, jaw clenched. "Does one of you two want to do it?"

Liara and I met eyes. She nodded.

When she stepped forward, Elijah said, "Pinch the globe to bring the view into the city. Just press your finger to the spot near the river. Hold it down for five seconds."

When she had done so, a silence fell as the red marker appeared.

I stared at the globe in the moment that followed, my eyes flitting over the leylines to memorize them, when Circe leaned toward me. "Come on. Don't want to be out on your ass for the next mission, too."

I had noticed one odd thing: leylines didn't move in straight lines. Sometimes they curved, and sometimes they angled.

In the room across the way, the guardians were taking seats around the circular table. Circe and I sat down at opposite ends of the table.

Fi was the only one to remain standing. She leaned forward, both hands on the table, surveying us. "We were meant to be training Liara and Clementine right now. Instead, we ended up on another failed rescue. Let's make this training quick and decisive so we don't get hung out to dry again. Sound good?"

Well, if I had any questions as to guardian leadership, they'd been answered.

"We have a mounted unit"—Fi gestured between me, Akelan, Mishka, and herself—"and we have the air unit." She nodded at the fae around the table. "You don't want to leave the others if you can help it. No heroes here. At the very least, you want one other guardian around. Never go anywhere alone on a rescue."

"Yeah, Keene." Elijah punched the other fae's shoulder.

Keene just gave a lopsided smile. "My bad."

"You say that every time," Mishka murmured.

Fi ignored them. "Ideally, one member of the mounted unit and one member of the air unit will coordinate an attack. That's what you saw Akelan and Isaiah pull off this morning. That assures you'll always have two types of magic working together."

My eyes tracked to Liara, who sat silent, watching Fi.

Fi noticed. "Except, of course, for Liara. She's a wizard who combines two types of magic—air and fire—and she could take down one of them alone. Which leads me to roles." She crossed to the chalkboard, began writing in caps.

WATCHER

GUARD

CHASER

She tapped her chalk against the board by the first word. "Watchers are the fae. They've got an aerial view and can keep those of us on the ground abreast of everything going on."

Her chalk moved down to the second word. "Guards are a mix of humans and fae. The watchers will tell them where to move to hem in the Shade's minions, to slow them down. Akelan, Elijah, Isaiah, and I are guards."

Finally, she moved the chalk to the last word. "Chasers are the fastest among us. They'll be the ones in pursuit and generally coordinating their attacks. Circe, Keene, Mishka, Clementine, and Liara are the chasers. Each brings separate specialties that make them uniquely suited to the role. Clem and Liara, you'll need to train with the other chasers to ensure smooth attacks."

I sat back. I was a chaser. Fi had pegged me; that was exactly what I'd done the moment they'd released Noir and me into the world. I'd given chase. It was my instinct, and it was my horse's, too.

"Now pay close attention," Fi said to me and Liara. "In two hours, you'll know exactly where to go, what to do, and how to survive the witching hour."

CHAPTER TWELVE

Fi wasn't wrong. The next time the horn blew I would know exactly how to respond, even if she'd had to drill the basics into my head.

At midday, I came into the dining hall and found Aidan tapping into a crème brûlée, the rest of his meal done. He had an open book next to him, of course. And I realized for the first time that Aidan North was particular about the people in his life.

He wasn't a loner. He wasn't unintentionally friendless. He just preferred to be alone and reading much of the time. I respected that; he'd certainly enlightened me with that reading on more than one occasion.

I sat down across from him with a salad and salmon, lifted my fork. "Where were we before we were so rudely interrupted? Oh, right—in a different building entirely."

His head jerked up, eyes struggling to focus.

I pointed my fork at him. "You've been reading all morning, haven't you?"

"You expected any less?" He closed his book. "What happened, Cole? I heard the horn."

I began stabbing at lettuce. "Let's talk about anything else right now." I paused. "The guardians have a cool treehouse."

"So I've heard." He studied me. "You just came from training, didn't you?"

I pressed a forkful of food into my mouth, nodded. "Watchers, chasers, guards. Mounted units, airborne. We're like a militia."

"Aren't you, though?"

My eyebrows rose. "I thought it would be more of a fellowship of the ring."

"Two of the fellowship died—if you count Gandalf—and one went mad and lost a finger."

I sighed. "I was thinking more of the beginning part than the ending."

"There is another reason, you know, why I was reluctant to be a guardian." Aidan pointed to my shaking fork hand.

I lowered it to the table, met his eyes. "You have the luxury of not having to fulfill a five-hundred-year-old prophecy."

He winced, and an uncomfortable silence fell between us in which I studied my food. "I'm sorry," he finally said. "You had no choice but to go into the labyrinth."

I resumed eating; I didn't want this weirdness between us. "Any thoughts on Siberia?"

"Apparently when leylines cross, it amplifies their power." He paused. "I guess that doesn't really have anything to do with Siberia."

"Au contraire. Did you know"—I drew a triangle with my finger on the table—"that leylines can form right angles?"

His eyebrows pulled together. "No. How do *you* know that?"

"The guardians. They have a big old globe in their treehouse with leylines drawn all over it." Then, "You said we were near the Arctic Circle, right?"

He sucked in air. "Right."

"Guess where two leylines form a triangle."

He exhaled hard, sitting back with both hands going over his hair. "We were at the crux of two lines. That's a massive point of power."

I stood with only half my meal eaten. "Let that simmer a while."

"Where are you going?" he asked. "We're onto something."

"Class. Can't save the world without skills."

"Tomorrow in the library at seven?" he asked from behind me. "I'll bring tea and chocolate cookies."

I grinned over my shoulder as I left. "Chocolate cookies? You're upping your game."

But the moment I was alone with myself outside the dining hall, my smile disappeared. This heaviness—was this what every guardian carried all the time? Or was it just the newness of it all?

Death. It was the shock and grief of death.

In Goodbarrel's class, I couldn't stop seeing her, the girl. The helpless way she'd lay over his shoulder, exactly as I'd lain when I'd been kidnapped. Their touch sapped all the warmth and energy from you, left you unable to move.

Nobody noticed as I went through the motions of summoning fire; Goodbarrel's class was big enough to blend in and unfocus.

It was only when I came into the meadow and Ora Frostwish stood scrutinizing me with folded arms that I knew the gig was up. "I heard the horn," she said as an opener.

"So did I." I came to within a few feet of her. "But I'd rather just focus on whispering angry words at each other, if you don't mind."

Her lips began to move, soft noises coming from between them. And two seconds later, I couldn't move to itch my nose.

Well, she'd given me what I'd asked for.

Frostwish began a slow pacing around me. I couldn't follow her movement with anything but my eyes. "Can you move at all, Clementine?"

"No," I breathed through unmoving lips. As I said it I realized that wasn't true; I could move my eyes, my tongue, pass the air in and out of my lungs to form slurred words.

"And how long do you imagine I could keep you this way?"

"Forever," I threw out.

She laughed, appearing in front of me. "Kind of you to say so, but no. My ability to keep you where you are depends on two factors: you, and me." She paused in front of me. "Your strength, and my strength."

"What kind of strength?" I slurred.

"Well, we could discuss the basics of your power as a witch and mine as a fae, about fire and air, but I'm going to tell you the truth of it: I'm talking about the ephemeral kind." Her head tilted as she observed me. "It doesn't require great fire magic to escape my hold, Clementine. There's an X factor that's the real key—you could call it force of will or inner strength. It's its own magic in the alchemical mix."

I just stared. "I don't exactly know what you're talking about."

"I suspect if it were a matter of life and death, you would get it quite quickly." She drew in a breath, blinked once, and I was released. "If you've got any inner strength, you'll develop a resistance to the hexes I cast on you. That remains to be seen."

I sagged halfway to the ground before I caught myself, all my muscles sapped. "Hey, Professor," I breathed.

"Yes, Clementine?"

After what Eva and I had seen the evening of my initiation, I had resolved to be as uncooperative as possible with Frostwish. It was easy enough to tap into my frustrations when I screwed up, to pout and stomp around the meadow as I would have done when I was a perpetually angry teenager.

Eventually I knew Frostwish would lose her temper, and then the two of us would end up in an argument.

I lifted my face, my lip curling against my will. "When do I get a chance to do that to you?"

Her eyes glinted. "I was waiting for you to ask." She took two steps forward. "The language is fae, so you must know the words well. *Pairilis síoraí.*"

As much as I wanted to pick her apart—to discover her neuroses through arguing—the pull of learning the paralysis hex was strong.

"*Pairilis síoraí,*" I echoed. "Now do I get to circle *your* paralyzed body?"

A vague smile appeared, as though I'd mangled the words. Actually, I knew I had. "Not quite yet. Say them, and say them again until you know them as well as your own name."

I repeated the words. *Pairilis síoraí.* Repeated and repeated, all while Ora Frostwish looked on, correcting me now and again. Her face had an almost terrifying precision about it, all the features too regular. She had control over every muscle in it.

"These words," I said finally. "They mean nothing without air magic."

"That's correct."

"And how do I tap into that magic?"

She drew her fingers through the air like she was tugging on an invisible harp's strings. "Have you heard of synesthesia, Clementine?"

That evening, the Summer's End Feast would mark the start of the school year. Eva and I went together, her arm hooked through mine.

"Air magic is visible to your eyes," I said again as we walked down the path toward the meadow, Loki trotting alongside. "All this time, and you never thought to tell me."

Beside me, she adjusted the drape of her yellow dress. "Would you bother to inform me that your hair is red?"

"But you can see for yourself that it is."

"It's the same with air magic. We who use it can see it as well as I can see your hair."

"I'll need your help, Eva." I glanced over at her. "Between classes and guardian missions..."

She raised a hand. "Say no more." As we came into the meadow, the spread of tables and golden lights stopped us both. "Gods, I'll never get over how beautiful that is."

Loki, on the other hand, trotted on. He was always first to a party.

"And there's the cursed chain," I went on as we walked. "Which can only be gotten with a hex. I should be in the Room of the Ancients researching it, not—"

Eva stopped me, set both hands on my shoulders. "Clementine."

"What is it?"

"The book is in Faerish. You can't even read Faerish."

"I could translate it word by word..."

She shook her head. "You're not in Frostwish's class. You're not in the Room of the Ancients. You're here. Be here while you can."

She was right. Before I'd arrived at the academy—before I'd found out about prophecies—I had always prided myself on being a creature of the moment.

That Clem had become a girl of the past.

I nodded. "I'm here. Mostly."

"Good." She started us walking again. "Because I need you to be my wingwoman."

"Wingwoman? You want me to help you pick someone up at the feast?"

"Actually, the word has a different meaning for fae." She paused. "Basically, it's the opposite."

I laughed. "So what you're saying is fae women are so attractive, you actually need a friend to keep the men at bay."

She flashed me a glance. "The way you put it makes it sound so self-aggrandizing."

"But who—" I began, and then I realized.

Her breakup with Torsten hadn't been mutual.

Not entirely.

"It's Torsten, isn't it?"

She sighed. "He wasn't exactly appreciative of how I broke up with him."

"Be blunt, please."

"I may or may not have ended our relationship while we were touring the penis museum in Reykjavik. Apparently that's unforgivable."

I suppressed a childish snort, instead offering a one-shoulder shrug. "He probably took the visit for foreplay. May have been a shock."

"Yeah. So I discovered."

We came to the feast, already in full swing with faculty and students, the long food table brimming with good smells. "Got it. Fae wingwoman—I can do that." I didn't see Torsten. Maybe he hadn't come, anyway.

"Clementine!" a voice called. Elijah, waving me over to a table already packed with the other guardians. "Come on. Saved you a seat."

"That's new." I kept my arm hooked in Eva's. I hadn't ever been the saved-you-a-seat friend. "You want to join them?"

"There's only one seat," Eva said.

"So we'll pull a chair over. I'm your wingwoman, remember?"

We got ourselves goblets of honey mead, came over to the guardians' table. They all met my eyes, raised glasses. All except Liara, who just nodded at me—which was a definite improvement in our relationship.

I yanked a free chair over from the next table, and Eva and I scooted in.

Isaiah leaned forward when Eva sat, obviously intrigued. "Evanora Whitewillow. Precocious third-year who's entered the guardian trials twice and been eliminated during the first trial both times. Planning to enter again this year?"

"I wouldn't have passed the first trial if she hadn't saved me," I cut in. "She would be a guardian right now. Believe me."

"Not true," Eva said with pink cheeks.

Isaiah's eyebrows went up. "Interesting. Capable and humble."

Circe slapped his shoulder. "Don't be creepy."

"But I will be entering again this year," Eva said. "And I intend to pass."

"Let's hope you aren't matched up against Liara in the second trial," Akelan said. "Lightning will pierce right through those wings."

Fi shook her head, rolled her eyes overtop the rim of her goblet. "This is supposed to be a pleasant evening."

"And lightning trumps air every time," Keene said. "Getting her would be a death sentence."

"Except Clementine defeated Mariella in her trial," Liara said, dark eyes on me. "Fire defeated its opposite element, and no one saw that coming, did they?"

Unexpected, but I'd take it. I raised my goblet.

"Speaking of fire." Circe set her elbows on the table, leaned forward conspiratorially. "Did you folks read the gossip section of this week's *Witches & Wizards*?"

Mishka waved a hand. "You'll rot your brain with that junk."

As they spoke, my mind wandered back to one thing. I hadn't expected this—that at every moment I would be waiting for the sound of it.

I was listening for the horn. As though my life began and ended with that noise.

When the horn was silent, my life could go on. When it was not, everything changed.

Circe leaned closer. "Turns out one former Shadow's End professor has caused quite the stir in Edinburgh."

My attention sharpened on her. "Who?"

Circe's eyes flicked to me. "Callum Rathmore. Who else?"

"What did he do?" Eva asked.

"Disowned himself from his family," Circe said. "Which really means he's rejected his father. Apparently Professor Rathmore's not a Rathmore anymore."

Now the whole table was intrigued. And me? My stomach was trying to squeeze its contents back up my esophagus.

"But why?" Elijah said. "He would have been set for life."

Circe jogged her eyebrows. "That's the question, isn't it? Rejecting the Rathmore fortune, the honorary seat on the Mages' Council. It's a delicious disgrace."

My hand went into my skirt pocket, felt the folded page from *Jane Eyre*. I knew the lines Rathmore had highlighted carried as much weight with him as they did with me.

I am not an angel, and I will not be one till I die. I will be myself.

I had always suspected we were alike. That feeling only deepened.

And I wondered now where he was, and when I would ever see him again.

"Hello, Evanora," a voice said from behind us. When I lifted my head, Torsten stood there like a beautiful, sad statue.

It was time to play the wingwoman.

CHAPTER THIRTEEN

The next morning, Aidan stabbed the open book. "It's indecipherable."

Around us, the library had that lovely morning emptiness I could only appreciate twelve minutes after I'd arrived. I knew now, after many mornings spent this way, for certain: twelve minutes into our sessions was exactly how long it took me to properly wake up.

And after the Summer's End Feast, having to distract Torsten when he'd approached Eva later that night, and then how late she and I had stayed up talking about relationships...

I lowered my mug of tea. "But you deciphered the parts about the key and the rod."

"Well, with Eva's help." He gestured at the page. "But this. This part doesn't make any sense. Any of it."

"Read me the line."

He cleared his throat, formal and annoyed. "'The chain cannot move. It cannot see. And as the summer solstice nears, the world becomes light.'"

"The prophet said this?"

"See what I mean?" He threw off his glasses. "Indecipherable."

"It's a riddle."

"And I hate riddles," he said.

"Really? I thought you'd love them."

"I like knowing things, Clementine. You know this about me. And that's exactly why I hate riddles—they keep me up at night."

"So until you figure this riddle out, you won't be sleeping."

"Exactly." He folded his arms. "So we need to figure out what it means before we leave this library."

I tapped a finger on the table as we sat in contemplative silence. "I don't know. I have to let it incubate."

"Incubate?"

"You know, swirl around in my head a while as I do other things."

His jaw shifted. "That's the opposite of what I asked for."

"Well, the riddle makes one thing clear."

"And what's that?"

"We've got time."

"And what makes you think that?"

I lifted a chocolate chip cookie. It was still warm, still soft—just perfect. "The prophet mentions the summer solstice. That's my best guess for when we can retrieve the chain. June, right?"

"Huh." He tilted his head. "I was so fixated on figuring out where it was, I hadn't even thought about that."

I bit into the cookie. "That's why you have me to point out the easy parts. But Aidan, why a riddle at all?"

He sat back, gazing at me. "As opposed to how the prophet simply told us where the rod was?"

"Right."

"The rod had been hidden in the labyrinth. You don't think that was a riddle in its own right?"

Touché. God knew figuring out where that damned rod was had been the greatest riddle of my life. "All right, then. So two riddles—but my question still stands. Why?"

"The pieces shouldn't be easy for just anyone to find," Aidan said. "If they were, the weapon would have been reassembled at once."

True. And yet... "The wisps had the key. Without the key, I

wouldn't have been able to find the rod. And the wisps would only give the key to another fire witch."

Aidan's eyes narrowed. "And a fire witch only comes along once in a great while."

"Exactly." I finished the cookie. "So whoever hid the pieces designed these riddles not to keep the weapon inaccessible to the world, but to make it difficult for the fire witch with the key to assemble the other pieces. Hidden in difficult-to-reach places, only retrievable during the witching hour. Because a fire witch with the Backbiter could simply choose to take over the world herself, right?"

We gazed at one another.

"But I wouldn't," I said. "Just so we're clear, I wouldn't take over the world."

Aidan didn't speak at first. Then, behind him, the clock tolled eight.

"I have to go." I started gathering my things. "But we've covered ground."

He watched me with obvious disappointment. "What do you have at eight? Not class."

"Guardian training. Supposed to meet Fi and Loki at the stables."

Aidan sat silent, his cup of tea gone cold in front of him. I could tell the riddle was plaguing him.

I tapped my knuckles on the table. "What do you say we duel at nights? I know a good spot where we won't be bothered."

He glanced up. "Are you saying that for me, or for you? You know you're the one who loves to duel."

"You got me. But your everflame is my only excuse to bring out the weapon. Well, aside from petting it like Gollum with the ring."

He snorted. "That makes it so appealing."

"So tonight at ten?"

"That's late, Cole…"

I pulled my satchel over my shoulder. "We both know you won't be sleeping—the riddle's still unsolved. I'll see you at ten."

When I came out of the library, I stopped, staring up at the spot in Umbra's great tree where I knew the horn sat nestled.

Waiting. Waiting.

A life like this could make a compulsive out of me.

———

Fi nodded at Loki, who sat with his tail wrapped around his feet as he sat atop a fencepost. "Has he ever ridden Noir?"

I ran a hand down the horse's neck; he stood uncommonly docile and quiet beside me in the paddock. "Not yet. I don't even know how the horse or the cat would react."

"Not well," Loki groused. "Not well at all."

"We'll find out today, won't we?" Fi said. "You'll need to bring Loki with you on missions. Umbra's told us your familiar will be a great asset."

Loki flicked his tail. "Is it my stunningly silken fur?"

I smiled, swung up onto Noir's back. "Must be." Then, to Fi, "He's wondering what he'll be needed for."

"A witch's familiar can scent magic." She raised her eyebrows at Loki. "And I've heard black magic smells particularly pungent."

Loki's green eyes shifted to me. "Smells like shit."

I tilted my head. "Does it? You never told me that."

"Why would I want to talk about what smells of shit? I don't hear you talking about litter boxes."

Fi folded her arms. "Your familiar sounds…"

"Like he's talking back to me?" I said down to her.

"I wasn't going to put it that way."

"Please, put it that way. He was like this even when I thought he was just a regular cat."

Fi's austere expression opened up in a new way. "I always forget. You grew up as a human, didn't you?"

"For nineteen naïve years."

She let out the softest sigh. "If only my greatest worry was nuclear war and not the Shade. How blissful that would be."

"Yeah, it was total bliss." I rubbed the horse's withers as he shifted under me. "Noir is getting antsy. Loki, you coming aboard or what?"

Loki didn't move. "I'd prefer to run ahead."

"You'll never keep up. Now get on."

"Fine. But there's no way I'm sinking my claws into that animal unless you want another episode of leaping fences and emergency dismounts."

I patted my cloak. "Do it, then."

With the simplest leap like water through air, Loki landed in a perch on my shoulder. He remained there, pressed to the side of my head and securing his hold.

"Is that where you're going to sit?" I asked.

"There isn't exactly a sidecar on this ride."

"Fair enough." I glanced down at Fi. "We're all boarded."

"Start around the paddock at a walk, and when you're ready, up the gait—a trot, and even a canter if you feel up to it today. Go at your pace."

Loki swayed at first as we set into a walk, passing around the fence line. Noir kept trying to stop to rip at patches of succulent grass, and every time I had to redirect him. Each time, Loki and I leaned forward in an awkward distribution of weight.

But after our first pass around the paddock, he'd settled into the horse's gait. We migrated into the larger ring to start trotting, the jerkiest one of all.

"Oh gods," Loki said when we hadn't gone twenty feet. "I'm going to be sick. And not hairball sick. *Legit* sick."

"We won't be trotting when we're out there."

"Then why are we doing so now?"

"Good point. You want to canter, then?"

"I want to get off, but I'll take cantering over this hell."

So we cantered. And that was, surprisingly, the easiest gait for us to synchronize in. And soon enough Loki sat firm, staring out, as much a part of this unit as Noir and I had become.

When we'd finished and I brought Noir back to the stables, Fi hung over the door as I wiped him down. "You and your familiar have a kinship," she observed. "It was obvious when you were on the horse."

"She sees how well I tolerate you," Loki said from the rafters, peering up into a sparrow's nest.

I ran a brush down Noir's dusty legs. "Funny enough, our relationship didn't even change after I learned he could talk two years ago."

"What was it like, being a human?" Fi asked.

I moved the brush over Noir's back. "It was a lot like it is being a witch. Except I had to use a lighter to make things burn."

She laughed—the first time I'd heard her do so. "But you weren't a fire witch then. You weren't any different than other people. Don't you miss that?"

"Not one bit. I was always different, just in other ways. Worse ways."

Lonelier ways. I had more—and better—friends as a fire witch than I'd ever had as a human.

I only missed one thing. My family.

"Different?" Fi asked.

"Oh, you know." I straightened, exchanging the brush for a hoof pick. "I was moody. Hard to know. Why are you so interested, anyway?"

She examined her hands. "I've spent my whole life hearing stories of the Shade. My parents raised me in fear of her—and now that I'm a guardian, I understand why."

"She's as bad as your parents' stories?" I lifted one of Noir's back hooves.

"Worse. From what I hear, the guardians outside the academy aren't having much more luck than we are. Sometimes this thing we do feels hopeless. And yet I'm the leader here—I have to be the one with the most hope."

Eva's parents were guardians, but they didn't seem to lack hope. Maybe they were better at hiding it.

"How many guardians are there?" I asked. "Outside the academy."

"Hard to say exactly. Maybe a thousand across the world? We aren't exactly organized like the formalists."

A thousand. Just a thousand.

I was almost afraid to ask my next question.

When I straightened, I gripped the pick like a weapon. "And how large is the Shade's army?"

"That's an impossible question," Loki said from above us.

"We can't see the whole of it to know," Fi said with a lowered voice, as though we were being observed. "To answer that question, we would have to descend into Hell itself. That's a move we can't make."

Can't see. Can't move.

In a flash, the answer to a different question came to me.

I set the pick on the rack. "Fi, thank you. I have to go."

CHAPTER FOURTEEN

I'd planned to find Aidan. But the moment I stepped out of the stables, I found myself face-to-face with Maeve Umbra.

The old wizard always wore the same face: unreadable, maybe noble or maybe a little arrogant, the finest hint of a smile.

She would have been a terrific poker player.

"Hello, Clementine." She nodded me toward the path leading around the outskirts of the grounds. "Do you have a moment?"

It wasn't a question. When the headmistress asked you if you had a moment, you did. Not that she would tell me anything useful.

"Of course."

We fell into a walk along the path, her staff tapping over the grass. "I heard from Fi about the events of your first rescue."

My stomach tightened. "You heard we failed?"

"I wouldn't call it a failure."

"Oh?" I glanced at her. "What would you call us losing that girl forever, then?"

She returned my glance, held it. "I would call it a tragedy. But my understanding from her is that you rode boldly."

"Failure, tragedy—whatever you want to call it, my 'bold' riding didn't stop anything."

In that moment, she looked at me with almost aching empathy. Her hand went up as though to touch my shoulder, but retreated back to her side. We went on walking. "You punish yourself too easily. It will be your undoing, if you allow it."

I didn't want to think about my undoing. Not right now. "Is this what you wanted to talk about?"

"No, it isn't. Aidan told me about the incident that occurred a few days ago in London."

"With the leyline."

"Yes. The leyline. I don't expect you know what any of that was about, do you?"

"Do you?"

"I might do, actually. You know, Clementine, that when a magical disturbance occurs in the world, I can feel it. It's how I know where to send the guardians."

"I remember."

"So you will not be surprised to know I felt the disturbance along the leyline at Mr. North's parents' home outside London."

I turned to her as we walked. "Was it the Shade?"

"Oh, no. She grows in power each day, but as far as I know she still cannot traverse the world outside the witching hour." Her lips drew together. "But nonetheless, I do believe a mage infused the leyline with the power you encountered."

"When Aidan and I went through the veil…"

"You ended up elsewhere," Umbra finished as we came alongside the meadow. "He told me."

"And you think the two events were connected."

Her eyebrows rose. "Oh yes, I very well do. Unless Aidan has somehow been to the place he described, and he assured me he had not."

So someone had wanted us to end up there. In the middle of Siberia.

"Why?" I asked. "It was a barren place."

Her eyes gleamed as she gazed out over the meadow. "Unlike here. I do so love the grounds in August—the lush and bloom of this place never grows old."

I tried to catch her eye. "Right. Do you have any idea who it was who sent us there?"

"A powerful mage indeed." She gave a flourish of the hand as though to indicate such power. "To infuse a leyline with your magic requires intense concentration. And to redirect the course of your travel, the both of you? Even more difficult."

"They must have been watching us. Waiting for us."

"Perhaps so. Though there are other ways besides a simple stakeout up a tree." She tapped her staff against a trunk as we passed. "I know certain fae are fond of that."

I tucked away that detail for later. "What ways?"

"You once asked me about Lucian the prince. Do you know what a demon is capable of?"

Lucian the prince. I hadn't thought about him in months. But his image was still burned into my mind—that one night in the spring of my first year when I'd ended up outside the gates of Hell.

Was she implying that he was the one who'd infused the leyline?

"You told me Lucian the prince serves the Shade," I said. "Her army can't leave Hell except at night."

"Ah, perhaps so for the foot soldiers. But the Shade has grown her tendrils into the world above—into *people* in the world above. And in the magical world, Clementine, a demon is no underworld-dweller."

This was more than Umbra had ever shared with me. Maybe because I was a guardian now. Maybe because I'd earned some portion of her trust.

"You think it was this demon prince," I said. "You think he was the one who touched the leyline."

"Perhaps. You see, once a demon has touched you, he has your scent for the rest of time. There is no place you can go without his knowledge, even this academy. If he wants to find you, he will."

Had Lucian the prince touched me that night?

I squeezed my eyes shut past the chill in my spine. I couldn't remember. I only remembered the sight of him. His voice.

Was *he* the dark presence I'd felt at the fae market that one winter night?

I shook my head. "But it doesn't make any sense."

She gave a light laugh. "And why not?"

"He serves the Shade. He could kill me at any moment if he can find me at any moment."

Now she stopped, so I stopped. She turned to me. "If all else I've said were true, then what is the logical conclusion?"

I went silent a moment, considering the other options after the most obvious one. But I knew which one she expected. "He doesn't want to kill me."

After Umbra and I parted ways, I didn't seek Aidan out. He could wait until our moonlit duel. The one thing that couldn't wait was my racing brain.

Back when I'd been alone in the system, I had always found a corner when things got to be too much. Too overwhelming. A place I could sit and bring all my thoughts to heel.

I didn't have that here. So I stalked deep into the woods surrounding the academy, to where the thought of the horn wouldn't plague me. Or not so much, at least. I walked a section of the forest I hadn't passed through before.

When I found a green, dappled break in the trees, I sat down in the sunlight and crossed my legs. I removed the deceiver's rod from the tangibly manipulated pocket sewn into my skirt and I held it in both hands before me.

With its power at my fingertips, I always felt more capable. Anything felt possible.

I considered Umbra's words.

If all else were true, Lucian the prince didn't want to kill me.

I had told Umbra it didn't make any sense. If he served the Shade, that should be his only goal.

He appeared in my mind's eye like a wraith. The heavy armor, the long sword, the sound of his voice when he called me "the sister."

I had once thought he and Callum Rathmore were the same person. They resembled one another. But Lucian the prince was immortal, or something close to it, and Callum Rathmore aged.

Aidan and I had seen pictures of him as a boy from some twenty years ago.

The last time Aidan and I had talked, we'd considered why someone would want to send us to Siberia. Now, Umbra had presented Lucian as the one who'd done it.

So why did Lucian send us to that empty place? I had a theory, one I would share with Aidan when he and I talked.

Which left the more immediate question: why had Umbra seemed so sure it was Lucian who touched the leyline?

The answer came at once: *Because she knows it was him.*

How? I thought.

He's maybe the only person in the world capable of following you anywhere —and she knows about things like this. It's a logical deduction.

"But why," I said aloud, "wouldn't he just talk to me outright?"

I had no answer for that. The birds might, if only I could understand their songs.

So the facts were these:

1. I had to locate the cursed chain before the summer solstice.

2. To get the chain, I had to cast a hex.

3. To cast a hex, I had to learn to hex properly.

4. To learn to hex properly, I had to tap into air magic.

5. To tap into air magic, I had to give myself over to Frostwish's teaching.

And in the midst of all that, if Umbra were right, a demon who served the Shade had my scent. He could follow me anywhere.

Fear and powerlessness lanced my chest. My fingers tightened around the rod, its power—real or imagined—like an electric thing coursing through me, pressing away the uncertainty.

"Clementine," a voice whispered.

I jolted, my eyes opening. Beyond the searing sun, I glimpsed red hair disappearing behind a tree.

In a moment I was up, the rod in one hand and my feet already moving. I'd seen that red hair in Aidan's garden. Twice, though I had completely written off the first time. And the second time I'd wondered about my mental health.

But not today.

That voice had been as real as mine.

I passed through the grove, came into shadows with the rod before me. "Come out."

No one came out.

When I approached the tree I'd seen her move behind, I paused, then jerked around the edge with a thrust of the rod.

Nothing. No one.

"It's a deception," a familiar voice said from above me.

Ora Frostwish.

My body went stiff as my eyes lifted. The rod dropped vertical to my side, tight against my thigh.

There she sat on a tree branch, her legs dangling. Umbra's words came back to mind: *A stakeout.* "You've found my favorite spot on the grounds."

"This grove?"

She nodded. "It's a good place for thinking. And reading." She tapped the book by her leg.

Not a stakeout, then.

"Sorry to interrupt." Inch by inch I moved the rod behind me, out of her view. "Did you... Did you see someone out here besides me?"

"I saw a deception," she repeated. "Not a very long one—maybe three seconds. But it was definitely you."

"The deception was me?"

She half-smiled. "Unless you know someone else at the academy with wild hair and that smoky voice."

I just stared at her, uncomprehending. Was she flirting with me?

"It's a kind of hex," she explained. "Different from the paralysis I showed you. The hex you used is called a 'likeness deception.' I'm sure you can put together what that means."

My mind had already returned to the Boundless Labyrinth, when I had finally found the rod. And there, in the room where it lay, I had seen myself.

My likeness.

"I created an illusion," I said, nodded over my shoulder. "An illusion that looked and sounded like me."

"Except in this case," Frostwish said, humored, "you hexed yourself."

If I'd hexed myself, it was the rod. It was all because of the rod.

And Frostwish might have seen it. I couldn't tell. I resolved to prod her the next time I was in her class, to force her to reveal her secrets. Her intentions. Or as much of them as I could drag from her.

I took a step back. "I'll leave you to your reading."

She didn't move. Didn't take her eyes off me. "Clementine."

"Yes?"

Her head tilted. "The likeness deception is an extremely advanced hex. Did you know, only a few witches in history have been able to use it? And only one ever mastered it."

I swallowed. "I didn't know."

"Where did you learn of it?"

I felt pinned. But if there was one thing I was good at from years in the foster system, it was weaving a tale when I was in a corner. "A book I read in the Room of the Ancients."

"Oh? What's it called?"

"I can't remember the name right now." I took another step back. "I'll tell you when I do."

She scrutinized me. The line between our eyes felt unbreakable, solid. For a moment, I wondered if she had hexed me right now.

And then, with a shrug, she pulled her feet up onto the tree branch and leaned against the trunk. "Please do. I should like to read it."

CHAPTER FIFTEEN

The duel wasn't meant to be for talking about riddles or hexes or untrustworthy professors. It was never meant to be for talking.

When Aidan and I met near the pond under the moonlight, I resolved to tell him everything after we'd pummeled each other with fire. And we did—pummel each other, that is. Blue flame met red flame over and over, the two of us sieging one another until the other hit the grass.

I got the best of him twice. He got me once.

The thing I liked most about dueling with Aidan was his sheer unputdownability. You wouldn't expect it, but he never lay down and gave up. Not once since we'd started our duels in the summer.

He'd gotten better with his magic through sheer diligence. If there was one thing I appreciated most in the people in my life, it was that.

Consistent, unsexy effort. Day in and day out.

Both he and Eva had that quality. Maybe that was why we'd been drawn to one another. We didn't have a whole lot else in common.

While we were sweating and exhausted and all we could do was sit there and look out over the water and talk, I started in.

"I've figured out the riddle," I said.

He'd leaned back on his hands, his breathing fast. "That fast?"

"I wasn't sure before I saw Umbra. Now I'm surer."

"Go on, then."

"The chain is in Siberia. Under the ground."

"Huh. Because it cannot move or see?" When I nodded, he contemplated this a little while as the frogs croaked around us. Then, wiping sweat from his forehead, "It might be. And what happened when you saw Umbra?"

"She suspects I'm being followed. And the person following me sent us to that place."

"By whom?"

I glanced at him. "Lucian the prince."

His eyes narrowed. "The Shade's lieutenant?"

"I think he pulled me up off the ground that night."

Aidan sucked in a breath. "Once a demon touches you, he has your scent forever."

"So says Umbra."

He rubbed his face. "But why wouldn't he have killed you already?"

"That, North, is an excellent question."

"And," he went on, "why would he send us to the place where the chain is hidden?"

"That's what I've been debating most of all." I picked up a stone, flicked it over the water. It hopped once and sank. "If it was this demon prince who did it, then it wasn't a coincidence."

"Why do it in such a roundabout way?" he went on, his voice gaining that distant quality when he'd been drawn into the annals of his own mind. At least I wasn't the only one who would spend brain power contemplating that question now.

I gave him a minute, and then, "Something else happened today."

He refocused on me. "Gods, what else?"

"I went into the forest around the academy to think on everything I've just told you. I found a break in the trees—it was a beautiful, empty grove."

"The Contemplator's Copse?"

"There's names for the groves here?"

"That one, at least, has a name." He nodded in that direction. "Just like you described. East, right?"

"Yeah."

"It's a perennial favorite of the introverts. So what happened at the copse?"

I closed my eyes. "When I held the deceiver's rod, I heard my name. Then I saw... an illusion that looked like me." Aidan began to speak, but I went on. "Ora Frostwish was there, too. Sitting on a tree branch." I cringed, even with my eyes shut. I didn't want to see Aidan's reaction.

But I heard it.

He sucked air between his teeth. "You think she saw the rod?"

"She didn't mention it, if she did. It only looks like another weapon, you know. How could she know what it really is?"

"Did she see the illusion?"

"She said it was a high-level hex. That I had created it."

He let out a low, slow breath. "And I take it she never showed you this hex in class."

"God no. We're still on the part where she hazes me like I'm rushing a sorority. I spend most of the class in her paralysis hex."

He shifted in the grass. When I opened my eyes, he had turned to me in full. "You think this hex has to do with the rod?"

"I know it does. She called it a 'likeness deception.' A deception created by the deceiver's rod. I saw the same thing back when I discovered it in the labyrinth—I saw myself."

"You never told me that."

"God knows why, but I didn't think it mattered. I thought it was some magical trap set on the thing."

Aidan nodded. "So if the key enhances your power, and the rod provides the ability to create a deception. Each piece affects your magic."

Aidan was right.

Each piece of the weapon enhanced my power. Which meant I would have to test the possibilities of this likeness deception. And there were only two people I could trust enough to show it to: him and Eva.

"Seems that way," I said.

"Well?" He clapped his hands. "You can't just tell and not show."

Fair enough. I brought out the rod, folded my legs. "Except I don't know how to make the deception occur."

"What were you doing the other time it happened?"

"Just holding it. Thinking with my eyes shut."

"So do that. Retrace your thoughts."

I did. Back in the copse, I had been contemplating what Umbra had said about Lucian the prince. I had been considering the riddle, and why he would send us to the barren place where the chain lay hidden.

And I remembered a feeling of distinct worry. Fear. Powerlessness.

That was when I'd tightened my grip. Relied on the power of the weapon to bring me confidence.

A twig cracked, and my eyes flitted open. Aidan and I both stared as, twenty feet away, my very own red curls vanished into the shadows of the forest. That was me—it was the likeness deception.

"Bloody hell," Aidan breathed, eyes flicking between the forest and me and back again.

Now I understood.

My magic depended on my state of being. Umbra had once told me it would come in fits and starts as I grew as a witch.

And so it followed that it wasn't my thoughts that created the deception. It wasn't the contemplation of a riddle—it was my feelings. It was the power of my need.

I knew what I had to do with the rod. It was just like anything else I'd learned—

I had to master the likeness deception.

Aidan didn't like my idea. Not one bit. I could tell by the way he worried his lip. "I don't understand why you need to master this hex."

"Only a hex can 'tether the chain,'" I said. "And what do you suppose that hex is most likely to be?"

"The one associated with the weapon itself." He sighed. "I've never broken into a library in my life, Clementine."

"But you're friends with me. You must have assumed it would happen eventually."

He eyed me. "Maybe I shouldn't be."

"That's where you draw the line? After everything we've done, your limit is breaking into a library. *You love books.* This should be your wet dream."

"It isn't just the library we're breaking into, Cole. It's their restricted room. Imagine what we have at the academy's Room of the Ancients, but so much bigger. Many of the books are probably the only ones in existence."

Aidan had told me only two libraries in the world could possibly have books on hexes: the Great Mages' Library in Edinburgh, or the Kowloon Library in Singapore.

And we definitely couldn't go to Edinburgh. Which left only one option.

I pulled up my knees, set my chin atop them. "I'm imagining."

"And what will we even do once we get inside?" He stared out over the pond. "Are you going to memorize a whole book?"

"No. We're going to use your phone to take pictures of the relevant parts."

"Digital simulacrums? Sacrilege." He sighed, still refusing to meet eyes. "You're a guardian, Clem. You can't just go running off to Singapore."

"Umbra hasn't bound us to the grounds. I think she knows if she did, our mental health wouldn't fare well. Besides, we'd only be gone an hour. Tops."

"Tops, huh? I've heard that before." Still, the corner of his lips twitched; my point was taken. So he moved on to his next argument. "I don't know the first thing about the Kowloon Library."

"Do you know anyone from Singapore?"

He began to shake his head, then stopped. His eyes tracked back to me, grew delighted. Aidan only ever gained that look when he was about to eat his mother's minced pie, or...

I pointed at him. "Don't look at me that way."

His expression didn't change. "Why not?"

"Because it means you've found a way out of my plan."

He smoothed his pants leg. "I may know someone from Singapore."

I wasn't sure if I wanted to know the answer. In fact, I was pretty sure of it. So I kept my mouth clamped.

His eyebrows rose. "Well?"

I stood, brushed off my skirt. "It can't possibly be that hard to get into the library's restricted room."

"You don't even want to know who could help you?"

"Not with that look on your face." I turned away. "See you in the morning."

As I walked away, Aidan called the name after me. And it was about as bad as I'd expected. "Liara Youngblood," he said. "She grew up there."

The fae whose parents had been killed by a fire witch.

I stopped. "You might as well have said your grandmother's name. She'd be as likely to help us."

"You'd be surprised at how people can grow, Cole. I suggest talking to Liara again."

I glanced over my shoulder. "I'd have to tell her the truth. Would you trust her that much?"

His mouth set in a grim line. "She is a guardian. Anyway, do we have a choice?"

No. No and no and no. We didn't. But I still needed time to mull the idea over.

CHAPTER SIXTEEN

Two days later, Farrow approached me in the stables before Mounted Combat. She cleared her throat, arms folded. I could tell by her stance she felt uncomfortable.

I came to the half-door of Noir's stall, leaning out as Noir's head pushed me to one side. The two of us gazed at the quartermistress. "You've got 'about to ask me a favor' written all over your face."

Farrow's eyebrows rose. "Do I?"

"Yep."

She worked her lips together, then, "I wondered if I might interest you in sharing afternoon tea with me."

I shrugged with a dirty hoof pick in hand. "Do I look like the kind of girl who would turn down tea over mucking out my stallion's stall?"

As I sat down in Farrow's home fifteen minutes later, I sensed that favor still waiting in the wings. Asking me to tea had been a prelude, a way of sweetening me up.

"So," said Farrow as she poured tea into my cup and sat down in her armchair, "you weren't able to fire ride during the guardian trials."

I upturned the pitcher of milk into the tea before me; it swirled in a vortex, turning black liquid to brown. "That's right."

"And you still can't." She paused, eyes unfocusing. "In class, you can summon the fire when you're atop the horse, but you can't make the flame do what you want it to do."

I lifted the teacup. "Did you invite me over just to let me know I'm going to fail your class?"

Farrow's unreadable face folded when she smiled. "Hardly. You could pass the class tomorrow—but you're not aiming simply to pass."

"No." I took a sip. "Rathmore taught me to fire ride. I'll never be satisfied until I've done it."

She set her spoon in her tea, swirled as she studied me. "And do you know why you can't do it?"

"He told me I had everything I needed. But…" I shrugged. She didn't know about the Spitfire and the challenge of giving control over to it, and I wasn't prepared to reveal its existence to her.

"My young fire witch." She set her cup down, leaning forward. "I suspect Professor Rathmore came to know you better than I do, but I also have a feeling I understand something of your nature as well."

"And what's that?"

A wistful look entered her eyes. "You've known pain. A great deal of it."

I busied myself with picking up a sugar cookie, dipping it into my tea. "Haven't we all."

"I'm no master of fire riding," she went on, "but I do know this: it's a painful art. It's painful because you must *tap into* your pain—your anger, whatever thorns still pierce your heart—in order to do it. You must dredge it up fully, bring it into the light. Are you prepared to do that, Clementine?"

I raised my eyes to her, tea in one hand and sugar cookie in the other.

Could I fully tap into that pain without bringing on another panic attack? Could I do so without giving myself over to the Spitfire completely and losing Rational Clem in the process?

I didn't know. But I knew I had to try.

So what I said was, "Pain? Sure. I'll just think of mucking Noir's stall every morning."

Farrow understood my uncertainty; I could see it in the glint in her eye. "That should do it, then. And as to your original thought, I do have a favor to ask of you. You're welcome to refuse, but I thought I'd ask."

I bit into the cookie. "I'm listening."

"I wonder if you would be interested in teaching a class."

I lowered my chin to properly meet eyes. "What now?"

"After seeing you ride in the first trial last spring, Professor Fernwhirl came to me with an idea. A good one, I think."

Professor Fernwhirl hated me. On top of which, she'd tried her damndest to dismount me during that trial.

I waited for Farrow to continue.

"She thought you were a marvelous bareback rider," Farrow said. "She suggested other students might benefit from the same."

I laughed. "Farrow, I never knew you to lie. Fernwhirl wouldn't say that on her deathbed. Besides, the only reason I do it is because Noir won't take a saddle and bit."

"She's certainly not dying, and I daresay I know the fae a little better than you to know when she's lying." Her shrewd look had returned. "Even so, I have to agree with her. As a guardian, you're eventually going to eclipse Akelan, Fi, and Mishka in rescues. They have to saddle up—you don't."

"Are you asking me to teach the other guardians?"

"No—they're already set in their ways. I'm asking you to teach a class of first-years."

This sounded to me like something more institutional. "You want to change the way the students here ride, don't you?"

Farrow leaned to within a confidential distance, even though we were alone. "We need more guardians. I'm sure you can see that now. And we need them to be the best at whatever it is they do."

"You think I'm qualified to teach them. I can't even fire ride."

"No one in the world can fire ride, Clementine, but perhaps one or two men. *Men.* And yet I don't think anyone here is more qualified than you are. You're the best rider I've seen come through this academy in twenty-five years."

Farrow wasn't a woman for compliments. If she gave one, it was lightning in a bottle; I knew she'd meant it.

All the same, this wasn't my thing. It wasn't at all like me. I didn't stand in front of groups and give instructions and tell them their weaknesses and strengths...

"Okay," I said before I could think on it further.

Why had I said that?

And yet the rational part of me knew at once: nothing was about me anymore. It didn't matter what my "thing" was. It didn't matter what made me uncomfortable.

What mattered was defeating the Shade. What mattered was stopping her army from taking anyone else.

Watching that Thai girl disappear through the veil had changed me.

Sitting now in front of Farrow, I finally understood what the feeling I'd carried around for the past week had been.

It was grief, yes. But it was also fundamental change.

"Okay?" Farrow sounded surprised.

"Tell me when to be here, and I'll teach them."

"Wednesdays at three?"

I bit into one of her sugar cookies. "Wednesdays at three."

That was three days from now.

I had gone from delinquent to student to teacher in what felt like a blink—I guess it had been a few years—and suddenly, on Wednesday afternoon, I stood in the center of the riding ring with six first-years staring back at me.

I wasn't a born teacher. If I was going to do this, I had to do it my way.

"Well," I said, "quit gawking and show me how you all ride."

They didn't move.

"Don't you want to know our names first?" a blonde girl said from where she stood next to Siren.

"I want to know how you ride," I said. "I'll learn your names when you screw up and I have to tell you about it. Until then, you're going by your horses' names."

A brown-haired boy made a face.

I smiled at him. "Hey, Minibar, we all screw up. I do it every day. Now I'd like to see you start screwing up by trying to mount your horse."

"But I haven't got a saddle or stirrups."

"Aside from the fact of that being the *point* of this class..." I stepped up to Noir. "Neither does he, and he's a hell of a lot bigger than that one." With the one-two hop, I leveraged myself up onto his back.

It was at that moment, sitting atop the enormous stallion, I became a god to them. They all began struggling to mount their horses in the same way I'd done, though not one of them actually succeeded. Some even fell in the dirt.

But like I've said: I do respect consistent, unsexy effort more than just about anything else.

At the end of the first class, I found Mishka standing at the fence line, watching.

I dismissed all my dusty recruits, led Noir over to where Mishka stood. "Hello, Crest."

"Hello, Spark." A faint smile appeared. "Your horse might be more than twice my height."

"He's nothing to fear."

"Oh, I'm not afraid." She stepped closer, reached out an open palm with oats in it; Noir stuck his face right into the handful. "Makes him all the better for chasing."

I had forgotten—Mishka was a chaser.

"Did you come to ride?" I asked.

"In a manner of speaking." Her eyes shifted to me as her empty hand lowered. "You're a chaser now, Clementine. Would you like me to show you what that means?"

"I thought I knew what it meant."

"You can't defeat one of them without another element at your side." She set one hand on the fence, stepped close. "If we're to defeat the creatures, the chasers must work together like an oiled instrument."

Except the other chasers were missing. "Is it just you and me today, then?"

She nodded. "We must have our own synchrony. Our own way of

coordinating. As you must with each other guardian, chaser or no. You never know whom you'll end up with."

Mishka couldn't have been much more than five feet tall. She was also, I felt certain as she gazed up at me, a powerhouse.

And that was confirmed when we were atop our horses.

An hour later, she galloped Minibar through the forest ahead of me with her black braid flicking through the air like a whip. "Alongside me, Clementine!" she called back.

I navigated Noir past trees, swerving him to catch up to her. "That's not as easy as it sounds," I called back.

"We're coming up on the creature in ten seconds." She pointed through the forest. "If you aren't with me by then, we'll miss our chance."

What choice did I have? I pressed my heels into Noir's side and left the navigating to him. A moment later, I ducked hard to avoid a low tree branch that would have taken off my head.

If I survived training with Mishka Reddy, I knew I could survive anything.

CHAPTER SEVENTEEN

As she and Minibar galloped alongside me, one of Mishka's hands left her reins. "I'll freeze the creature. When I have, you spear it with fire through the chest. Understood?" Her voice passed close then far away, shifting as trees swept between us, branches and leaves.

But I had caught her instructions.

Spear it with fire. I had never practiced spearing anything.

This seemed to me where Goodbarrel's precision and control came in. A shame I couldn't light up more than two of my fingers.

It didn't matter now; the practice dummy we had set up in the woods had come into view.

In an almost cinematic moment of elegance, Mishka sat up, both hands leaving the reins. She reached into the air, drawing water from nothing but the atmosphere. With one hand twining the water into a spin, she sent it rushing toward the dummy, now only a few hundred feet away.

It surged at him with a spearheaded tip, lashed itself around his body. With a jerk of her arm against her side, Mishka froze the water like ropes around his chest.

"Now," she yelled.

Now. The time was now.

That was when I reverted to using my lizard brain. It was a stuffed dummy we were capturing, but the note in Mishka's voice carried such intensity, I just acted.

My hand went overtop Noir's head, palm flat, and I sent a jet of fire soaring, expanding through the air in the dummy's direction.

When we passed the dummy, only smoke surrounded it. Leaves burned. A large, flaming tree branch had fallen. The chest hadn't even been touched.

Mishka yanked her water free. It flowed back around her as we slowed our pace, if only for the horses' sake. They breathed hard beneath us, Noir shaking his head as we came to a trot.

"So," I said. "Better than last time."

Mishka had regained her reins. "Yes, better than last time. This time you managed to shoot before we reached the dummy."

I'd wanted to forget that first try. "Timing isn't my forte."

"It wasn't your timing." Mishka slowed Minibar to a walk, and I did the same. "I asked for a spear of fire, and you gave me a plume."

"I haven't practiced spears much."

"How much have you practiced them?"

No use in lying to her. "Not at all."

Her eyebrows went up as she glanced at me. "But you're a third-year. You should have been taught a simple spear throw in primary school. And at the very latest, you should have learned it last year."

"My fire magic professor last year was... different. I have a feeling we weren't learning the usual stuff."

Rathmore had taught me about the Spitfire. About overcoming my worst emotions. About controlling the creature inside me.

It had taken a year, and I still wasn't sure if I had a handle on it.

"You learned with Callum Rathmore, did you not?" Mishka asked.

I nodded.

"I did always find him strange." She sighed. "Well, so be it. Clementine, it's crucially important you learn acute control of your magic. These creatures move fast, and they aren't much larger than humans. You can't simply incinerate them in a ball of flame."

"Can't I?"

She jerked Minibar to a halt. "Not unless you're prepared to take the life of a kidnapped mage in the process."

I stopped, turning Noir to face her. "It was a bad joke."

That seemed to soften her. "Until you're better with your flame, you and I will practice a special coordination. You're the fastest among us on your horse, and so you'll be able to get the closest."

I liked where this was going. "So I'll get close enough that I can't miss."

"Precisely." She turned Minibar around. "This time, you'll pull ahead of me. I'll direct the water from behind, and I'll time it to freeze the creature in the moment you're about to pass it by."

"Works for me."

She didn't set off just yet. "You need this kind of coordination with the other chasers. Ideally you'll have an understanding with all the guardians, but the chasers especially."

"Of course," I said.

"Soon," she pressed. "You never know when the next rescue will come. We're already overdue for one."

As if feeling Mishka's intensity, Noir stamped beneath me.

My fingers tightened in his mane. "I promise I will."

She gave a single nod, turned Minibar back toward the dummy. "Let's go, then."

I set off after her, my eyes again on her braid as she pressed the horse to a gallop. Mishka couldn't have been more than twenty-one or two, but she wore this mantle effortlessly. It was obvious she cared. Perfection and precision mattered to her, because getting it right meant saving a life.

The Clementine of two years ago—the nineteen-year-old who'd been kidnapped that night—would have been grateful for how seriously a woman like Mishka took this job, even if the Clementine of two years ago was directionless, angry, impulsive, and imprecise.

It was *because* I was so impulsive and imprecise. That was why a person like Mishka mattered in my life.

In one moment, chasing after that whipping braid, she became a role model to me. Just like Eva and her thoughtfulness. Just like Aidan and his studiousness.

Her voice ripped me out of my head. "For gods' sake, it won't work if you don't pass me!"

I leaned close to Noir's neck. "You heard the woman," I murmured down to him, squeezing my heels into his sides.

He had. His neck stretched out, and we pulled past Minibar within a few seconds.

"Good," she called from behind. "Now be ready to decapitate the creature on my call."

The dummy had come into view. One of my hands left Noir's mane, lighting with flames.

Wait. Wait on it.

Noir and I were only a couple dozen feet from the dummy, but I had to wait for her call. I had to tamp down my impulsiveness.

I had to trust her.

Just in time, the water shot past me and whipped around the dummy. It was as precise as Mishka herself.

This was the moment.

It was also when she said, "Now!"

I whipped the flames out toward the dummy's head as we sailed by. A thump sounded in our wake, and when I glanced over my shoulder, the straw-stuffed head rolled on the forest floor.

Farther behind, Mishka smiled.

After Inverness, Eva had been pestering me to poke at Frostwish. To get her irritable enough to reveal her inner feelings, maybe even her secrets.

And of course, I'd just stared at her. Swung a finger between us. "Did you and I switch bodies?" I was the one who was supposed to goad other people into making bad decisions.

All the same, Eva was right. After Frostwish had potentially seen the deceiver's rod, I needed now more than ever to know more about her.

In my next class with Frostwish, I did my best to draw her in, to embroil her. To pierce her cool veneer. Of course, the fae held up well

—I knew after Inverness how good she was at holding her secrets tight to her chest.

It was during that class that I finally managed a tiny crack in her shell.

We'd been going back and forth about hexes as a dark art, and I threw out, "I've begun to wonder if hexes shouldn't have died with the rest of my kind."

Ora Frostwish was normally a quick reply. This made her pause. "Your kind?"

"Witches," I said. "Both air and fire."

"Why would you say that?"

"My roommate, Eva." I chose my next words with care. "She told me hexing is a dark, corrupting art. That it's only meant to hurt people."

Frostwish's face darkened. "Evanora Whitewillow said this?"

I nodded.

"And what would the lavender-haired fae know about hexes?"

"I—"

"Nothing," she cut in. "She has a formalist's understanding of them. A modern understanding, simple and uncomplicated. That's how fae these days prefer things."

Now we'd gotten fully away from my practice and into Frostwish's mind, which was exactly where I wanted to be. "And you aren't a modern fae?"

She flicked a dismissive hand. "Attempt the paralysis hex again."

"Sure." I lowered my chin as though to hex her. "Before I do, where would you say this particular hex falls on the scale of corruption?"

"Gods." Frostwish's wings fluttered; now I knew I'd properly annoyed her. "It isn't the *art* that's corrupting. It's the desensitization to suffering that might occur as a result of practicing it."

I resisted a victorious smile. We were getting somewhere. "What's the difference?"

She raised her fingers as though to pinch the air between us. "The art itself is pure. It's the lips—and by extension, the mind—presenting the problem. This was the early understanding with which it was pioneered."

"Pioneered by whom, Professor?"

Her eyes widened. Now I'd caught her in a tight spot: she'd neglected to tell me about the history of the art, which was a fairly crucial bit of information for any professor to impart on, say, day one.

Her lips pursed. Then, "Her name was Raven Murkwood."

Raven Murkwood. The same name I'd heard invoked in Tristan Rathmore's home that night back in the fall. The witch who'd written *The Witching World.*

I hadn't expected Ora Frostwish to name her so easily.

"Oh, her." I nodded. "I found her book in the Room of the Ancients during my first year. Fascinating witch. Lived in the sixteenth century, right?"

"Fifteen forty-nine to sixteen-oh-four," she said in a clipped voice. "The greatest witch of the past millennia. She lived during the magical renaissance, of great discovery, before the formalists. Before witches were hunted. It was a better time."

And yet that wasn't how she and Tristan Rathmore had discussed Murkwood in secret. They'd talked of her as if she were still alive.

I tilted my head as though silently counting. "If Raven Murkwood only lived fifty-five years, then how did she die, Professor?"

Frostwish's lips moved, the words registering in my brain in the same moment she paralyzed me.

And just like every other time, this felt equally unnerving. I would never get used to being hexed by her.

"You think she was corrupted by the art, don't you? That it killed her before her time." She approached me slowly, eyes on mine. "No, fire witch. The art was pure, and it still is. It was humanity that was not. After all she contributed to the magical world, she was killed during the Battle of the Ages, may she rest in peace."

I couldn't move, couldn't speak. But my brain could still process at the same speed, and I could still keep my eyes on Frostwish.

She was agitated, upset. But more than that, she was wistful.

She was a fae who wished she'd been born in another age—namely, five hundred years ago. The modern world didn't suit her, and it was obvious she revered a long-dead witch.

Raven Murkwood, the pioneer of the art of hexing.

As I stared into Ora Frostwish's eyes, I wondered how much the "pure art" had afflicted her. How much it had addled her brain.

One thing had become clear over the past school year: she carried darkness in her, wore it over her like an invisible cloak. I trusted her less now than ever, and I knew I needed someone besides Ora Frostwish to help me with hexes.

I needed Liara Youngblood.

CHAPTER EIGHTEEN

On Monday morning I came upon Liara Youngblood at eight-thirty, precisely where she always was at that time: in the dining hall. Over the years, I'd also observed that she always ate a bowl of muesli with blueberries on top and drank a mug of coffee with cream.

This morning, at least, she was alone.

Maybe Aidan was right. Maybe she had grown.

I set down my own bowl and mug across from her, took a seat. "Morning, Youngblood."

That black hair, a silken waterfall over her shoulders, practically reflected my own shadow back at me. Her dark eyes lifted, a small line marring the flawless creamy space between her eyebrows. "Morning."

Common decency wasn't beyond her now. At least, not when it came to me.

She nodded at my bowl of muesli with blueberries on top and my mug of coffee with cream. "Good pick."

A smile touched my lips. "Seems to work for you."

She didn't return the smile. "You want something. It's written all over you."

She wasn't wrong. "We're both chasers, both guardians. Maybe I want to spend time with you. Get to know you."

She plunged her spoon into the bowl until it clinked on the bottom. "Maybe, but you don't."

"We'll have to work together, you and me. Practicing for rescues."

She nodded. "We will. But that isn't why you're here." She was too goddamn perceptive for me to avoid the truth. Not if I was going to receive her help.

So I opted for truth.

I spread my hands. "Do you still hate me?"

Her eyes narrowed, wings trembling like an overstimulated cat's tail. "What's this the preamble to?"

I took a deep breath. Before I could begin—

"I don't hate you, by the way," she said. "If that makes this any easier."

It did, actually.

I glanced around us. We were unobserved by the other students. "I need to break into the Kowloon Library."

She set her spoon down. Leaned closer. "You know I grew up in Singapore, don't you?"

"I've heard as much."

"It has one of the oldest collections of magical texts in the world."

I nodded. "So I'm told. I hear the restricted room is even better."

One elbow found the table's edge as she leaned even closer. "And do you know how strong the protective enchantments are around that room?"

"I was hoping you could tell me."

"Stronger than Umbra's enchantment around this academy."

"So... is there a way into the restricted room?"

She nodded once. "Yes. But only one way."

"And what's that?"

Her eyes glinted like onyx. "A fae has to escort you."

Liara had agreed to help me. She didn't ask why; she just asked when.

And when I'd said right away, she had nodded. "Fine. We'll go and be back before class."

This was too easy.

When she grabbed her satchel, slung it over one shoulder, and stood up with her bowl and mug, I stood with her. "You think we can be back before class."

"Did I stutter?" She brought the dishes to the discard tray, and I grabbed my bag and followed.

"Anyway," she went on, "we have to be quick. Guardians can't leave the grounds for long."

She had a point. "Do you have a phone?" I asked.

She reached into her pocket and fished out an iPhone in one gesture. "Will this do?"

"If I can borrow it while we're in the restricted room, then sure."

"I don't want witch fingerprints on it." She turned toward the doors, left me standing there with my bowl and mug still in hand. "What do you need it for, anyway?"

I set them on the tray, went after her. As we came into the sunlight, I said, "To take pictures of a book."

"Fine. I'll do it myself."

Well, if she was going to be so amenable... "I'd like to bring my friend."

"Only you can come." She didn't look in my direction. "Those are the rules."

"How about me and one cat?"

Now her eyes did flash at me as we walked. "Absolutely not."

So it would just be me and Liara. And she was headed toward the leyline that we would use to get to the library.

This fae was all business. And way too eager to help me.

As we walked, I looked over at her. "Why are you doing this for me?"

"It should be obvious."

"It isn't."

She gave a sharp exhale through her nose. "I owe you. I don't feel comfortable with outstanding debts. It's a fae cultural thing."

I paused. *Outstanding debts?* Then, "You mean what happened in the labyrinth?"

"Yes, in the labyrinth. Even though I know it was you who angered the boggans, I still wouldn't have made it through without your cat."

We passed the amphitheater at the center of the academy grounds, headed down the path toward the forest.

"You don't owe me," I said. "I don't consider you indebted."

She swiped that aside with one hand. "Please. You know as well as I do that debts aren't about the person to whom they're owed."

I did know.

It was about the unevenness you felt when someone had done you a favor, the lack of equal footing. It was all in the head, but it was as real as anything. Especially if that favor meant becoming a guardian.

I set my satchel strap over my opposite shoulder so it sat cross-body. "So you aren't going to ask why I want this."

"I'll admit I'm curious, but you can keep your secrets. I'm just here to repay the debt."

But I sensed it was more than that. Was it possible Liara was actually warming to me?

As we passed toward the leyline, I considered telling her some portion of the truth, maybe all of it. Aidan was right: she was, after all, a guardian.

But she also hated witches, and probably everything we stood for. Hexes were sure to be problematic.

So I kept my mouth shut.

We came in silence to the leyline, and she raised a hand. Glanced back at me. "Be ready. We're going to come out on a busy street near the library."

I nodded.

Liara Youngblood proceeded to cut the veil in a way I'd never seen done. She drew her finger through the air in a simple, effortless motion, and at the same time she passed through the opening she'd made.

It wasn't cut and then go.

It was cut and go at the same time.

Parting the veil wasn't simple or easy. Even as a third-year, I still had to place all my focus on the act, and I certainly couldn't move any other body parts as I did it.

From the other side, she glanced back at me; greenery and the sounds of a well-used street offered themselves from behind her. Her wings were already hidden from view. "Well?"

I came through, stepping onto a sidewalk. The faint smell of ocean touched my nose, and a humid breeze caught my hair. It was nighttime here, the street lit up and down its length by headlights and buildings. Far off, what looked like a six-story mall towered over the road.

"The restricted room will close soon," Liara said. "We have to be quick." Within minutes, she'd led me to a grand building with huge pillars as a facade.

I stopped on the stairs. "This is the National Museum of Singapore."

Liara tracked back, took hold of my arm and led me forward. "I don't have time to explain the magical world to you right now. You need to trust that I know my home."

Together, we passed under the arches, through the grand double-front doors of the building, and into a large lobby. An information desk was occupied by a smiling woman who greeted us with a brochure in hand.

"Bathroom," Liara explained to her, veering us right as soon as we'd come in.

We passed down a side hallway toward what was, in fact, the women's bathroom. Just as we reached the door, she turned to me. "What you need to know now is that there isn't a bathroom behind this door."

My eyes flicked to the ladies' sign, back to her. "Would you bet money on that?"

"Depends on what you believe." She glared at me, lips pressing together. "Do you believe it's a ladies' room, or the entrance to the Kowloon Library?"

I knew immediately what she was really asking: *Are you a human, or are you a witch?*

This was seeing the academy itself. This was the fae market. This was the inn in Abridge.

My chest tightened. That glare was a throwback; it was the same look she'd given me every time we met eyes during our first two years. Then, lifting my chin, "I believe there's a library."

"Then I wouldn't bet money, because you'd be right."

I nodded. "Let's go."

Liara pulled on the handle, stepped through the door without holding it open for me. It closed behind her, which left me to open it myself.

I set my fingers to the brass handle. *Not a bathroom. Not a bathroom.* When I pulled it open, a fluorescent brightness nearly blinded me.

CHAPTER NINETEEN

I t wasn't a bathroom.

"Good evening!" a voice called from somewhere across the room. As my eyes adjusted, I made out pale orange wings—and attached to them, hair so orange and so well-groomed the man's head might have been a fruit if he didn't have eyes and a mouth.

He waved at me from behind his desk like he would to a child. "Oh, a non-fae. It's been some time."

Liara, who already stood at the desk, glanced back at me. "She's harmless. A friend from school."

As the room came into relief, so did stacks of books on carts and bookcases lined with them, filling four of four walls. On the far wall, a massive etched wooden door sat firmly shut.

It was a circulation room, with two major differences:

The lighting was white-bright, like we had just entered heaven.

Some of the books were flying.

"Watch your head now," the orange-haired fae called out to me.

Before I could react, a book clipped me on the side of the head as it came up from behind. The obstacle—my head, that is—set it off course, and it veered, pages flapping, until it redirected course and made for a chute on the far side of the room.

When it dropped inside, it disappeared entirely.

Other books moved around the room in the same way, some flying to shelves, some lifting off them and disappearing down the same chute.

I set a hand to my stinging scalp. "Apparently the books aren't harmless."

The orange-haired fae exchanged a glance with Liara. Then, to me, "A newer mage, are you?"

Liara gave me a severe look, the meaning of which was obvious at once: stick to being harmless.

"Yes," I said with a laugh. "Just found out I was a mage recently, and Liara took me under her wing at school. Go House Gaia."

"Gaia. Isn't that sweet. Come stand over here, child, so you don't get concussed."

I did so—carefully. When I arrived in front of the desk, the fae clasped his hands atop it, faced Liara. "And I take it you'd like to bring her in as your guest."

Liara nodded.

"You do realize the library closes in thirty minutes."

"I realize. We'll be quick."

"So be it." With a twirl of his fingers, an equally orange quill lifted from an inkwell and dropped to a notepad. It began scribbling in large cursive; I assumed it was Faerish.

Liara's hands found the edge of the desk. "And I have one other request."

The librarian's eyebrows rose. "Yes?"

"We'd like to enter the restricted room with the section on witches."

There are multiple restricted rooms?

He smiled, wings trembling with affront. "Oh no no no. Absolutely not. All the books are in Faerish, anyway."

"I'd just like to give her a peek." Liara tilted her head. "Please. My mother always spoke so highly of you, Mr. Rosewort, and how open-minded you were to humans."

I'd never heard Liara say the word *please*. I'd never heard that tone in her voice.

I couldn't see her face, but it must have been equally plaintive. Because Mr. Rosewort's features softened, and he sighed. "Just a peek?"

"I swear it."

"Very well. Not like the girl could accomplish much in a room full of ancient Faerish tomes." He nodded to me. "What is your name, earth mage?"

My name. What was my name?

"Terra... Loam."

He eyed me a moment, and then raised his quill and set it to paper. "You earth mages and your odd naming conventions." He ripped the paper from the sheet. "Take care you carry this note with you into the room, lest the earth mage be booked in."

Booked in.

After taking a book to the head, I wasn't sure I wanted to know what that phrase meant.

"Of course." Liara put out her hand, and Mr. Rosewort set the note in her palm.

I hovered at the desk. "Do I get a note, too?"

Liara hissed out a breath in my direction.

Mr. Rosewort's eyes flicked to me, the softness tightening. "Remember, Ms. Loam, this is a fae library, and you may only enter as Ms. Youngblood's guest. She carries the single note, so please do stick close to her."

We passed toward the large wooden door, and as we went through, Liara whispered to me, "Terra Loam?"

"It worked, didn't it?"

"Barely."

As the door closed behind us, I stopped. Stared.

Above me, a whirlwind of books rose high toward a five-story ceiling. Some flew off to different directions, and some entered, but always the vortex remained. And around it spread a library three times the size of the one at the academy. So many stories up, so many books. So many beautiful gilded railings.

So many wings.

At tables around us, fae heads lifted from their study. Perfectly shaped eyes watched us.

If I'd known I was entering a room full of former Miss Universes, I would have put on my clean uniform.

In this room, a natural light shone. The sunset beamed through a glass ceiling spanning the whole of the place, casting beautiful shades of orange and red over everyone and everything.

Liara stood with me. For once, she didn't seem impatient. Maybe she knew I needed this moment. "It's the oldest library in the world," she said.

"How can that be? Singapore wasn't a city-state until…"

"You're thinking in human terms. Think in fae terms."

My attention sharpened on her. "Eva once told me about a portal between the fae world and this one. Are you saying it was originally on this island?"

"As far as we know." Liara nodded me forward. "It was easier when humans weren't so plentiful here."

She threaded us past watching fae, right beneath the vortex of books.

I couldn't help but look up. When we were directly under it, I could see straight up through to the orange sky.

"How do the books move?" I asked her.

She kept walking ahead of me. "How do you think they move?"

"An air enchantment is my guess."

"Well done, Cole—you've made the connection between fae and air magic." She brought us to a second large wooden door, pulling the handle. "Don't talk on the other side."

When we passed through, we came into a hallway with alcoves broken off at either side. Here it was dead quiet, the fae huddled behind stacks of books completely still.

Apparently even fae needed study rooms.

When we came to the end of that hallway, Liara stopped us at an empty doorway with a gold-leaf engraving curved over the top. It was clearly words in Faerish.

What lay beyond, I couldn't tell. Only darkness greeted me.

She turned to me, lifted the note. "When I set this to the door, you pass through ahead of me. I can't remove it until we're both inside."

"Liara…"

Her eyes hardened. "Are you really going to argue with me about whether there's a door?"

"Actually, I wasn't." I raised a hand, plucked a piece of white fuzz from her black hair. Flicked it away. "I was just going to tell you you had stuff in your hair."

Which we both knew wasn't true; I was going to talk about the door.

But now I could smirk. "Shall I go through?"

She rolled her eyes, lifted the note to the doorway. When she set it flat to the empty air, the piece of paper glowed gold. In the same moment, a whoosh of cool air pressed our hair back, and another room came into view.

The restricted room.

I passed through the doorway into the room. Here, the air was practically frigid. My arms came together over my chest as I stared down the length of a line of bookcases into darkness.

The restricted room felt small, enclosed, chilly. The walls here were dark stone, and even the few tables a darker wood than the ones in the main library. The only light came from the stained windows set high up on the walls.

Liara stepped up to my side, the note still in her hand. "We're short on time. Follow me." She struck off, headed three rows down, and disappeared from sight.

I remained where I was for a second, absorbing. The books in here didn't float or fly. They didn't move at all. And the smell—everything had the scent of age.

"Hey, fire witch," Liara's voice called. "Come on."

I found her at the end of a row, crouching to inspect a book. "You said you wanted to read a book on hexes, right?" She looked up at me.

I came to crouch beside her. "They've got some?"

She tapped the spine of a particularly fat tome. "Just one, it seems. Right here."

I went to slip it from the bookcase, but it didn't move. Not an inch.

"They're protected by air magic." She waved a hand, drawing whatever magic surrounded the book away from it. She lifted the book, handed it to me. "A final precaution against fire witches who manage to sneak their way into the restricted room."

The thing was heavy; I had to use both hands to hold it. "They don't like witches here either, huh?"

She stared at me. "Nobody likes witches anywhere."

I took a deep breath, stood up, and brought the book over to a nearby table. "I'm going to need your help finding a particular hex. I can't read Faerish except the curse words I made Eva teach me."

She came beside me, flipped open the book. "Learn the rest of it. It's maybe the most important language in the magical world."

"So I'm gathering." I paused. "If hexes were a witching art, then why would the fae have a book on them?"

"Because hexes are a bastardization of fae magic," she murmured, turning ancient, yellowed pages filled with script. "The Shade learned from the fae, and she warped what was good into something destructive."

"The Shade created hexes?"

Liara sighed. "Are you surprised? She created practically all the evil that now exists in the world."

Ora Frostwish had told me Raven Murkwood had created hexes. Now Liara was telling me it was the Shade.

More and more, I suspected the two were one and the same.

She kept turning pages, stopping when she reached a certain part of the book. "What hex are you looking for?"

"One called the likeness deception."

Her eyebrows rose. "That's an advanced hex."

"It's what I need to see."

She turned a whole sheaf of pages until she arrived at a section near the back. Her finger flitted across the page until she arrived at one particular section. Then she leaned close. "There's very little on the likeness deception. Only a few paragraphs." She lifted her phone from her satchel, took a picture of the section.

"Send Eva the image," I said. "I'm guessing you have her number."

"Because all fae have one another's numbers?"

I knew why Liara was the way she was, but all the same, I was getting bored of her snark. "Because you're both in Whisper."

"Fine." She thumbed the phone, hit a button and showed it to me. "Sent."

I glanced at the book. "Before we go, will you tell me how the hex works?"

She replaced the phone in her satchel and stared down at the writing for a few seconds, her eyes flicking over the words. "It requires a specific phrase." Her finger underlined a short passage set off from the rest of the writing. "*Mealladh coltas*."

The moment the words came out of her mouth, a thud sounded somewhere outside the restricted room.

Liara whirled to me. "*As ucht Dé*."

I didn't know those words, but I did know the tone in which she'd said them. Whatever that noise was, neither of us would be happy about it.

Her eyes darted away, to where a second thud had sounded. We rushed down the rows, found the magical doorway now partially blocked.

A row of books had flown to the bottom of the doorway, pressing themselves flat in a row. Then a second row of books flew to sit atop those, and a third, and a fourth...

By the time we started running for the doorway, I already knew it was too late.

And I understood what Mr. Rosewort meant by "booked in."

CHAPTER TWENTY

Within ten seconds, we'd been fully booked into the restricted room. What had formerly been an empty doorway was now wholly blocked by books.

Liara pulled her hands through her hair and let out a groan. "We're screwed."

I pointed at the wall of books. "Hey, it's all good. What are those to a fire witch except kindling?"

She grabbed my arm. "Don't even light one finger. If you use your magic in here, we won't just be screwed. We'll be dead."

"Because we're surrounded by paper?"

"Because it's strictly against fae law to use fire magic in this library. It's one of our most sacred institutions."

I turned a slow circle. "So, what? We're just in here forever?"

She leaned against a bookcase. "Might as well be. We're in here until Rosewort decides to undo the magic barrier and has thoroughly interrogated us."

"That doesn't sound so awful."

Her eyes, hard as stone, shifted to me. "If they find out you're a fire witch, you and I will be in a different world of problems."

"As opposed to a regular witch?"

"That's right." She slumped to a seat against the bookcase. "Regular witches are trouble. Fire witches destroy civilizations."

I slid down across from her. "And where do the fae stand when it comes to the formalists?"

"We're uninvolved in their affairs. We serve only good, only the light."

I leaned my head against the row of books. "So you're uninvolved, but you and the formalists just both happen to hate fire witches."

She folded her arms. "Like I said: everyone hates witches. Now I need to think."

"About?"

"How we're going to get out of this mess."

"Mr. Rosewort doesn't think I'm a witch. He just thinks I'm an innocuous earth mage."

She waved an exasperated hand. "It isn't just that. Our magical prints are on that book we took off the shelf. We'll have to explain why I pulled out a book on witches for an earth mage. And further, we'll have to explain why I triggered the barrier."

"Why *did* you trigger the barrier?"

"I spoke the words to a hex." She studied the doorway. "Even if I wasn't capable of casting it, when those words were spoken, the library's defensive enchantment responded automatically to seal us in."

Now I understood. "The library interpreted your words as an attack."

We sat across from each other in a moment of silence, the two of us gazing at the stone floor between us. Once again, we were stuck together—except Liara had herself to blame this time.

She shook her head. "I never should have gone anywhere with you."

"It's not the worst. So we'll be questioned by Mr. Rosewort, we'll tell him I got curious and asked you to read from a book, and he'll let us go."

Her eyes on me were searing. "An earth mage interested in the ancient, dark art of hexes?"

"So we'll say I lied about being an earth mage. That I'm actually an air mage."

"And once he knows we've lied, he won't trust our word." She rubbed her thumbs together atop her knees. "He'll have to investigate the truth of it further."

"There's no way he could figure out what I am."

Her lip curled. "Don't underestimate a determined fae."

"Well, when will he come?" I paused. "And is there a bathroom here?"

She groaned, leaning her head back. "I'm about to be permanently banned from the Kowloon Library, and you're worried about your bladder."

"What can I say? I'm driven by biological imperatives."

"Oh, no. You're much worse than that. You're a biological creature with biological imperatives who also possesses the ability to destroy entire families. Cities. Nations."

The Shade. She must have been referring to the Shade.

I hadn't known she'd destroyed nations during the Battle of the Ages. But then, why else would the war be called that?

"Liara," I said, "I would never do that."

She didn't lower her face; she kept on staring at a spot far above my head. "No one can make that promise. We never know what's in our hearts until we're truly tested."

"You don't think I've been tested?"

She scoffed. "Three guardian trials isn't a test."

"I'm not referring to the trials." I crossed my legs, sat up straight. "I'm referring to everything that came before the academy."

"Please, don't talk to me about your oh-so-sad childhood. We've all got a story."

I tilted my head, observing her. "You're better at that than I ever was."

"At what?"

"Covering over your feelings with a hard shell. If mine was made of concrete, yours is forged from pure chitin."

She laughed, lowered her chin to meet my eyes. "Don't patronize me like you've grown up. You're still as fucked up as ever—take it from a fucked-up fae."

I'll admit it: Liara did get to me. Over time her words burned through my veins, made me want to lash out at her with the fire just waiting inside me.

But we were alike. And so I knew lashing out would only be giving her what she wanted. I knew it because that was how I used to operate with just about everyone except Loki.

And I knew one other thing: the angrier she got, the closer I was to penetrating that shell.

I took a deep breath as we gazed at one another. "What's your story?"

She shook her head. "I see what you're trying to do. You're never going to make me like you."

"So don't like me. I have enough friends." I held her gaze. "But since we're both guardians now—both chasers—we're going to be in each other's lives. And I just want you to know: I know pain. Maybe not your pain, but I've undergone a lot of it. And I'm not afraid of your pain."

She stared at me, eyes tracking between mine. Her fingers clenched above her knees, and a thought as apparent as a cloud in the sky moved across her face. Unspoken words—which she didn't voice.

In that moment, the wall of books began to disassemble from the doorway.

Liara's eyes flashed. *Don't tell him*, she mouthed.

I knew, of course, what she didn't want me to tell: that I was a fire witch.

We both stood. When the doorway cleared, Mr. Rosewort stepped through with hands clasped behind his back. His orange hair turned dark as he passed from the lit hallway into the dimly lit restricted room, his wings clouding everything behind him.

He wore a semi-severe, semi-devious cat-caught-the-mouse expression.

He was, after all, a librarian. It was probably one of the more exciting moments of his year.

"Well." He passed down the row to stand before the both of us. "Well well."

Liara turned to him. "It was a mistake."

Mr. Rosewort raised a hand, and with a whoosh of magic, a book flew over the bookcases and into his waiting palms.

It was the book on hexes.

He observed it, turning pages and inspecting the front and back covers. "Which part, Ms. Youngblood? Was it that you took out a book, or that you managed to speak a hex from it?"

So he knew Liara had spoken the hex. Of course; between the two of us, he thought she was the only one capable of manipulating air magic.

Liara swallowed. "Both. I apologize—"

Mr. Rosewort raised a hand. "And where have you learned of hexes, Ms. Youngblood?"

She paused. Hesitated. In the realm of lying, a pause like that was death. "A professor at the academy..."

"Which?"

"Ah—"

"Ora Frostwish," I offered.

Mr. Rosewort's attention shifted to me. "Interesting thing. It isn't just your prints on this book, Ms. Youngblood." He nodded at me. "It's hers as well."

"She was curious," Liara said. "I let her touch it."

Mr. Rosewort stepped closer to me, eyes flicking over my face and hair. "What kind of mage did you say you were?"

I cleared my throat. "Earth."

"Earth." He raised a finger. "The two of you wait here. Move at your peril." He strode down the row, disappeared as he took a right.

What's he doing? I mouthed to Liara.

Investigating, she mouthed back. Uncommon worry marred her features, which meant his leaving us there was bad.

I just didn't yet know exactly why, or how bad.

When Mr. Rosewort's footfalls approached, he rounded the corner with a new expression—a homeowner who'd finally found the mold behind his walls that gave him his allergies.

He plucked the note he'd written from Liara's hand, examined it as though he had forgotten my name since we'd last seen him. "Terra Loam." His eyes lifted to me. "You might be the first earth mage interested in the art of hexing."

"It's for a report," I said. "On, well, hexes."

"And how much more curious that makes the whole affair. An earth professor assigning a project on the ancient, dead art of hexes." Mr. Rosewort gestured to us both. "Come with me. If you veer away or attempt to escape, the library shall restrict your movement and you will be returned to me by force. Do you understand?"

We both indicated we did.

And so we followed him out of the restricted room, down the quiet hallway—now empty, since the library had closed—and to the opposite end of the hallway, where he pushed open a door.

Inside were more bookcases, but these weren't filled with books. They were filled with files. Thousands and thousands of files set upright in bookcases ten rows tall.

"What is this room?" I whispered to Liara, who stood beside me.

"It is the registry of magical births," Mr. Rosewort answered. He had already taken to the air, searching through the files on a high row.

"A birth registry?" I said.

"How else are we to keep track of the world's mages?" he snapped down at me. "Simply by remembering?"

After a time, he paused. "There's no file for Terra Loam. None at all."

I shrugged. "Oh well. Must be a—"

"There are no mistakes in the birth registry," he snapped down at me. "*We have every birth on record.* So who are you, girl?"

Liara and I exchanged a look. I couldn't read her expression, except that she was full of anxiety.

"If you lie to me again," Mr. Rosewort went on, "I shall quickly find out. We have our ways, girl, from upside-down tickling with our wings, to a modification on the Chinese water torture method in which we use drafts of air, to—"

I raised a hand for him to stop. "Clementine Cole."

His chin lowered. "This is the truth?"

"There have been times I haven't wanted it to be," I said, "but yes, it is. My name is Clementine Cole."

He flew off, disappearing around a corner.

It never occurred to me that I would have anything other than a human birth certificate. I had no idea what it would say.

Beside me, Liara gripped my wrist. "This is the worst outcome," she hissed into my ear.

"Why?" I whispered back.

"Your magical birth certificate lists what your parents are. What you are."

"A human?"

"No." Her eyes grew large on me, loaded with meaning.

And then I understood.

My magical birth certificate listed my mother as a witch. And so it must list me as a witch.

A fire witch.

"Ah." Mr. Rosewort flew into view with a file tucked under his arm. "Here we are. Clementine Cole."

He flew down to us, landed silently, the file already opened. His eyes moved over the document within, tracking down the page.

When he gasped, I knew he'd found it.

He lifted his face, eyes wide on me. "A witch," he whispered.

"Sir," Liara began. "You must understand. She's not like the fire witches of—"

"Of old?" He tapped the page. "Of course not. A fire witch has not been seen in decades, and thank the gods for that. She is simply a witch, Ms. Youngblood."

Not a fire witch?

"May I see that?" I said, my voice hoarse.

He turned the file around, stabbed the spot with his finger. There, listed beneath *Magical Qualification*, were two words:

Air witch.

CHAPTER TWENTY-ONE

When we came out of the library, night had descended on Singapore. Around us, the city twinkled with motion and lights.

I turned to her. "Liara, I'm sorry—"

But Liara had taken a sharp right toward the six-story mall.

I followed after in silence. She had been banned from the Kowloon Library for three major infractions: first, lying about her guest's nature. Second, bringing a witch into the library. Third, for attempting to cast a hex in the restricted room on behalf of a witch.

She was pissed. I wouldn't stop her from feeling her feelings.

We came to a smoothie stand outside the mall with an enormous orange set atop it with a straw stuck in. An Orange Julius. We had these in the United States, too.

I gestured to the smoothie joint. "Is this a point of power I didn't know about?"

"I need one before we go back to the academy." Liara stepped up to the counter, began ordering. When she had received two enormous smoothies, she extended one to me.

My eyebrows went up.

"Well?" She thrust the smoothie almost to my chest. "What, you don't like orange?"

I accepted it. "Orange is fine."

We went to sit at an outdoor table as mall visitors passed in and out of the enormous lit-up glass structure. Both of us knew we needed to get back to the academy. We were guardians. But neither of us were willing to say so.

Liara crossed her legs, sipped, and sighed. "I used to drink these with my mother as a girl."

"Not your dad?"

"No. Just my mom—it was a special thing between us."

"That was kind of her."

She shook her head, gazed toward the mall. "She wasn't a great mother. Whenever she showed me the slightest bit of attention, I leapt to it like a dog."

I took a long sip of the drink, absorbing her words. I sensed this wasn't the right time for me to talk; she just needed to say what she'd said. If I tried to comfort her, she would reject it. If I made a joke, she would scoff.

Silence was better until she was ready to talk again.

She turned her attention back to me. "So, you're an air witch."

"You don't seem so mad anymore."

"Oh, I am. But right now I'm drowning it in sugar and milk."

She'd said she was mad, but this was different. This wasn't the Liara who'd been so stony and closed off.

"According to my birth certificate, I am." I set the drink down. I sounded much calmer than I felt. "But it must be wrong. You've seen me use fire."

"I don't think it is." She paused, staring at me. "Do you know why I can use lightning magic, Clementine?"

I shook my head.

She leaned forward. "It's something that happens when you're attacked by a fire witch. If you're young enough, you absorb some of that magic."

I jerked back. "But when were you..."

She glowered, willing me to finish the question. The answer lay in her eyes. Her angry, agonized eyes. Her parents were killed by a fire witch when she was a child. She had been present for their murder, but somehow she had avoided death.

And so, at the greatest cost of all, Liara had gained the ability to channel lightning.

A jag of empathy lanced my chest. "I understand."

She took another sip, waiting for me to speak again.

So I did. "You're saying I was attacked by a fire witch?"

"I can't see another answer. Magical birth certificates are never wrong."

Here in the middle of Singapore, another piece of my past had been unlocked. And another question raised, too.

I hadn't been born a fire witch. I was an air witch like my mother.

But at some point—if Liara was right—a fire witch had attacked us.

"Drink your smoothie," Liara said. "You're looking pale."

I obeyed, taking a long sip. Eyes unfocused. Heart hammering so hard my fingers tingled.

"But," I said, "if that's true, I should be like you. I should be channeling lightning."

She nodded. "You should. But you're different. Don't ask me why."

Silence fell, the two of us contemplating the consequences of all that had happened. What we had encountered in the library. The fallout of our actions.

Lightning was the consequence of a fire witch attacking a child who used air magic. Which meant...

I sat up straight. "Umbra."

Liara nodded slowly. "Umbra."

Maeve Umbra had introduced herself to me with lightning from the sky. She'd called herself a wizard, but now I wondered if that was just a designation for an air mage who had been attacked by a fire witch.

At some point during her childhood, the same thing had happened to her.

"Liara," I whispered, "I need to apologize. For the lie, for getting you banned—"

"You want my forgiveness?" she cut in. "Then answer my question."

"What's your question?"

"Why did you have me bring you here?" She swept a hand out. "Why the likeness deception?"

This was the inevitable moment. I'd expected it sooner, really. After all she'd gone through for me, she would want to know why. She deserved it.

Aidan had told me to tell her the truth. That she might have grown. She had, after all, bought me a drink.

I surveyed the area around us. We were unobserved, about as alone as we could be. "Will you swear to me, as a guardian, to keep anything I tell you after this moment to yourself?"

Liara's eyes narrowed. "Maybe."

I made a face. "Maybe?"

"I only keep secrets if there's a good reason to do so."

"You want a good reason? You're a guardian—you've sworn to protect the world from the Shade. And if this secret gets out, our chances at that may be ruined."

Her eyes narrowed. "All right."

"What I'm about to tell you will endanger two lives." I scooted closer. "But I don't think you'll mind which ones."

"Whose?"

"The lives of two fire witches." I lowered my voice. "Mine, and the Shade's."

Never had I so completely held her attention.

"You're right," she said. "I won't mind."

After I told her about the prophecy and the weapon, she folded her arms as she studied me. "If everything you've said is true, I want to see the weapon for myself."

I gestured around. "Here?"

"We're effectively alone. Just a bunch of regular humans out shopping for blouses and crockpots."

"Why do you want to see it?"

"Because I need to know you're not full of bullshit about this prophecy."

I stared at her. It was a fair enough request, given everything she'd done for me today. Everything she'd sacrificed.

I needed to trust her. I needed her to trust me.

"Fine." I reached into the tangibly manipulated pocket in my skirt, lifted out the rod. It gleamed ebony and radiated power under my fingertips, even here in this shopping center.

When it came out under the artificial light, Liara drew in a breath. "Where did you get it?" she whispered as I held it before her.

"At the center of the Boundless Labyrinth."

Her eyes flicked up to me. "That's why you took the other path. Why you left me and Loki."

I nodded. "The key led me to it."

"This is why the boggans were angry." She clicked her tongue. "I knew it was you."

I half-shrugged. "All's well that ends well, right?"

"Little ends well in life, fire witch. You should know that." Her eyes flicked down. "So this is the Shade's weapon."

I glanced around. We weren't noticed. "Half of it. It's missing the chain and blade."

"May I hold it?"

My hands jerked a few inches back. "No."

She tilted her head with raised, skeptical eyebrows. "After everything, you think I'll steal it from you?"

The truth was, I didn't. But still...

"After the past two years, do you blame me for being wary?"

"Fair." She raised one finger. "A compromise, then? Just one touch."

I sighed. "One touch."

Her fingertip lowered to the deceiver's rod. When skin met metal, her lungs filled to the brim. She looked up at me, shock and a thread of fear clouding her face.

"Do you feel it?"

She nodded once. Her hand returned to her side. "I've never felt power like that."

When we returned to the academy, Liara stayed mum as we walked down the forest path toward the grounds.

I had shown her the deceiver's rod and the liar's key. I had told her about the weapon and the prophecy. And a strange recognition had shone in her eyes as she observed them both and listened to me recite the prophecy itself.

When I was finished, she had sworn not to tell anyone else.

And I believed her.

Some part of me remembered her as the teenager who tried bullying me. Who'd shunned me for two years. Who hated me for being a witch.

And another part of me knew I could hold her to that promise.

It wasn't just because she'd sworn as a guardian. It wasn't just because she had a moral code. It was because she and I were more connected than we'd ever known.

At some point, the two of us had encountered a fire witch's flames, and it had forever changed us.

She had gained lightning. I had gained fire.

And, after all, we had one other thing in common: a hatred of a witch called the Shade. Mutual hatred of a thing, I had long ago discovered, was pretty binding.

When we came to the clearing, a hard-faced Fi struck toward us. Her expression smoldered with anger. "You've been gone for hours."

"We just went—" Liara began.

Fi's lips curled. "Hours."

I glimpsed someone being carried into the infirmary. It might have been Mishka; that black braid looked awfully familiar.

I looked back at Fi. "No."

"Yes." Her hands had formed fists, like she really wanted to commit violence. "We were sent out, and two of our chasers had vanished without any word. We were only seven."

I felt so small. So witheringly awful. "Were you successful?"

Fi scoffed, turned away. "Gods no. It was the worst rescue we've done since I was inducted."

"And Mishka?"

Fi was already walking away. "Go see for yourself. More than anyone, she deserves your explanation for why you two traipsed off this morning."

Liara and I exchanged a look. Her cheeks were red, her face barely a semblance of composure. When she lifted her phone, she found a series of missed calls. She groaned. "No reception in the library. It's blocked by the magic there."

Together, we went to the infirmary. Outside the door, I could swear I spotted blood on the ground.

When we came inside, a scream resounded from one of the closed-off beds.

Mishka.

"Oh gods." Nurse Neverwink flew past us into the storage closet, came out with all sorts of magical things. A small blue pot, a red pot, a capped syringe with a green liquid inside. "You two stay out of the way," she snapped at us.

She was always flustered, but I had never seen her like this.

Liara fell into a seat in the waiting area, her face going into her hands. Her hair formed a veil over her head. She rocked a little.

I stared at the curtain surrounding the bed, which jostled as Mishka cried. And without realizing, I came step by step closer. I could almost see around the edge of the curtain, which had been halfway pulled aside by Mishka's thrashing.

And when I came around and glimpsed her, I had to find steadiness with my hands. I gripped the edge of the opposite bed while Elijah and Isaiah held Mishka down.

Meanwhile, Nurse Neverwink injected her with the green fluid in the syringe. Not in her arm, because Mishka no longer had arms.

The injection went into her thigh.

So much blood everywhere. Her eyes wide as silver dollars, unseeing and frantic.

"Hold her!" Neverwink shouted. "I need to stop the hemorrhaging."

The nurse uncapped the blue pot, began applying an ointment from inside as best she could to each of Mishka's shoulders. As she did, the bleeding seemed to stop.

Mishka seemed to calm, or at least her thrashing tapered off. As did the screaming.

"The medicine's taken hold," Neverwink said with a sigh. "You can let her go."

Elijah and Isaiah, both with blood on their clothes, released her. One of them glanced at me, lean-sitting on the bed. The same anger Fi had held entered his eyes, and just as quickly dissipated at the sight of the tears down to my neck.

He came over to me. "She'll regrow the limbs."

I shook my head, wordless. "I..."

"She'll be okay, Clementine. She's tough."

Okay was such a relative term. Could you ever really be okay after losing both your arms, even if you regrew them?

In the waiting room, the chair squeaked as Liara kept on with her soundless rocking.

When we'd returned to the academy, I thought we might be questioned. I thought our excuse was fine. Good enough.

Now I knew no excuse was good enough.

We had been irresponsible. I had chosen not to inform Fi or the others because I knew they would ask questions. I knew it would raise curiosity, and I had thought my mission was more important than theirs.

Maybe it was in the grand scheme of things. But what did the grand scheme matter when you were the one who had to lose your arms?

It didn't matter at all.

Neverwink spotted me. Pointed at the door. "Out! Gods, didn't I tell you to keep out of the way?"

I turned, numb, and passed into the sitting room.

One of the twins helped Liara up, and the two of us left the infirmary. Outside, the sun felt too kind. Too warm for what we deserved.

The twin with blood on his face glanced at me. "Where were you both?"

"Singapore," I whispered. Not that it really mattered. "I asked to visit Liara's home for an hour."

"A visit." His voice was laden with wistful sadness. "But you were gone for much longer."

I leaned against the tree trunk. "I know."

Liara had slid down the trunk, sat with her knees up. This had affected her in a way I'd never seen.

As I stared at the ground, I realized I had never had any real expectations placed on me in my life. Not ones that mattered. So I had no idea how to handle those expectations. Those consequential responsibilities.

And I made a resolution.

I would never again think of myself first in this way. What mattered were the lives around me.

I raised my eyes to the twin. "This won't happen again."

The other twin shook his head. "For all our sakes, I hope not."

After I left the infirmary, I booked it for Hexes.

Of course, I was still late.

When I came to the meadow, Ora Frostwish was displeased. Though she only showed it in her posture—crossed arms, her mouth the size of a raspberry. Or maybe it had nothing to do with my lateness, and everything to do with our arguments during class.

Maybe she wasn't displeased at all. Crossed arms and pursed lips could just be her way of being. Truth was, I still didn't know Frostwish at all. She was a rare enigma to me.

It helped to be emotionally drained and numb; in this state, I couldn't be properly anxious about what she would do or say. I could only go through the motions.

I came jogging through the meadow. "Sorry, Teach. Was indisposed."

"Indisposed?"

"Guardian things."

Frostwish's lips unpursed. "Is that right?"

"Afraid so."

She surveyed me, head to toe and back. "I thought we would start today on a different note."

"Whatever you want. Though I'm fully prepared for another hour of being unable to move."

Her lips curled. "The likeness deception. I want you to show me."

She really did know how to cut through the chaff. But I knew this would come up again eventually. "I don't know how I did it. That day was a fluke."

"Flukes can be recreated." Her arms lowered. "You read about it in a book. You know the basics. Attempt it again for me."

Well, she didn't know she *was* actually right about the reading-it-in-a-book part, as of a few hours ago.

"Professor..."

"Please." She gestured toward the nearest tree. "Conjure your likeness over there. Just try."

I turned toward the tree, fingers rubbing against my palms. In my periphery, I could sense her watching me with absolute attention. It was obvious: she was onto me.

I still remembered the words I'd mouthed in the library. They were all I had right now; I couldn't very well bring out the weapon.

"I'll try," I said, and closed my eyes.

The best I could do was everything I had done before.

"*Mealladh coltas,*" I whispered into the air. When I opened my eyes, nothing had changed. Nothing at all.

I glanced at Frostwish. "So you know the words," she murmured. "And you pronounce them like a fae."

"I just read them in the book."

She stepped closer. "Do you speak Faerish, Clementine?"

"Not well. I've heard my roommate speak it, and studied it some..." Which wasn't entirely true, but how else could I explain my pronunciation?

"Your enunciation was perfect." She gestured through the air. "But I didn't see the words."

Neither had I, of course; my eyes had been shut. "Should you have?"

"Yes, if the hex has been properly cast." She nodded once. "Again."

I wanted to master this hex. I needed to master it.

But, in the most backward experience of my life, I didn't want to do it with the help of the only fae who could best assist me. The closer I got to casting the hex in Frostwish's presence, the more questions it would raise in her mind.

And I wondered now if it hadn't worked this time because the rod hadn't been in my hands. That was out of the question, of course.

So I tried again. I pronounced the words and nothing at all happened.

Frostwish crossed her arms once more. "Was something different the other day, when I saw you cast it?"

"No," I said too quickly.

Her head tilted. "Were you holding something? I could have sworn I saw a weapon in your hand."

Shit.

"A baton," I said at once, holding her gaze. "Lent to me by Torsten. He's teaching me blunt weapons."

"And why did you have the weapon out?"

"I was practicing with it."

"Really? I never heard any movement until you ran past me."

We stood in a standoff, the conversation becoming rapid-fire. "Well, I was." *It isn't my fault you were too deaf to hear me.*

"How did you end up casting the likeness deception while practicing with one of Torsten's blunt weapons?"

"I decided to incorporate it into my practice."

It was amazing how fast I could fabricate a story when I was annoyed. I had forgotten about my ability to weave untruths; I used to do it all the time as a teenager. Counselors hated me, fellow foster kids (temporarily) loved me for it.

I'd talked my way out of so much trouble. Problem is, when you can always talk your way out, you don't know the power of consequences.

Another problem: people stop believing you.

When nothing's your fault, everything's your fault.

I could tell in the ensuing pause that Frostwish had been backed into a corner. She had no other routes to pursue.

And that familiar old feeling came over me. Smug victory. It was particularly delicious when the person you were lying to didn't have your best interests at heart.

"Very well." Frostwish clapped her hands, a jarring noise. "Let's return to the paralysis hex. We'll focus on the synesthesia to start."

I nodded. "Let's."

CHAPTER TWENTY-TWO

Afterward, I gathered my bag and spotted a certain fae standing near the path leading back to the academy's center.

I approached her slowly. "Hey, roomie."

Eva looked at me like I was a homeless, malnourished cat. "I heard about what happened with Mishka."

As much as I knew Eva meant well, I couldn't take any more today. Mishka's screams had reentered my head without my consent throughout the past hour. Not to mention Frostwish's unrelenting push for the past half hour to get me seeing the air magic.

Which I still couldn't.

"Eva, I can't talk about it right now. It's too raw."

"I figured. You want to sleep, right?"

"Mostly I want unconsciousness."

We began walking back together. "What do you say," she began, "to dinner in the dorm tonight?"

I eyed her. "So we're eating fae rolls for the main course and dessert? The last time we did that we both nearly died."

"You think that's the only food I can conjure?"

"To be fair, I haven't seen you conjure anything else."

"Well, I can." We came to the dorm steps, began our ascent. "Lots of things—human food, even. Spaghetti, pizza, calzone. I'm just not as practiced."

"So by 'human food,' you mean Italian."

She glanced back at me. "I took a strong interest in conjurations when I was a teenager. So flame me for liking noodles and cheese and bread."

I laughed. It was the first time I'd laughed all day. "So even fae are dangerously obsessed with Italian food."

Thirty minutes later I was freshly showered, in my pajamas, and surrounded by conjured Italian food and one nosy cat.

I nudged Loki away from my slice of pizza. "Look, there's a whole pie over there. Why do you want mine?"

He stared at me, nose half an inch from my slice. "Because it's tastier when you want it."

Eva grinned from her bed, observing the two of us. "I can conjure milk for you, Loki."

"Do so," he said without taking his eyes off my pizza. "And whatever else you can that involves dairy. Now."

"He wants milk," I translated for Eva. "Anything you've got with milk, *please.*"

She snapped her fingers, and a cat-sized dish of milk appeared on my desk. That distracted Loki well enough for me to eat in peace.

"You're almost as good as Vickery," I said through a full mouth.

Eva twined her spaghetti around a fork. "Far from it. But I'll accept the compliment."

As I watched her, it occurred to me how much I'd needed this. We hadn't spent as much time together since the school year started. "Tell me about your life," I said.

Loki groaned, padded over to the door with droplets of milk on his whiskers. "Someone open this slab of wood so I can be free of girl talk. I'm a creature of the night."

I got up, allowed Loki out. When I closed the door, I knew he was disappointed in me. He was usually disdainful, but he didn't normally mind spending time around me.

Now I had let *him* down. I hadn't been present for a rescue, and that mattered to him, too. He was supposed to go with me on the rescues, after all.

I slouched back over to the bed. "Anyway."

Eva set a hand over her mouth as she chewed. "My life... it's classes, preparing for the trials, picking at my face. The usual." Then, "And you?"

I shook my head, folding my slice of pizza. "When I came to this place, everything was unusual. I didn't realize how much this had become my regular life until it all got turned on its head."

"You mean when you became a guardian." A wistful look came over her, and she nodded once. Went on eating. "It's a massive responsibility."

One I knew she was more than ready for.

God, I had so many things to tell her from today. From the past few weeks—

"I heard you and Liara went off the grounds today," she said. "That you two missed the rescue."

She hadn't asked me any questions because probing wasn't her way when she didn't feel entitled to know, but she might as well have.

For Eva, that was asking.

"We went to the Kowloon Library in Singapore." I set my slice of pizza down on the plate as Eva's eyes shot up to me. "I asked for Liara's help getting in."

"Why?"

I realized now I hadn't shared my theory about the chain with Eva. That felt negligent; she was as much a part of this as anyone. "There's a hex called the likeness deception. Have you heard of it?"

She shook her head.

"It's advanced. It allows you to create an illusion that looks like you —and somehow I've been able to cast it more than once."

She dropped her fork onto her plate. "How?"

"When I was holding the deceiver's rod, the hex happened twice over the summer. Then once here at the academy."

Her eyes darted in thought. "You think that's part of its power?"

"I think so. And I asked Liara to help me learn more about it in the library's restricted room."

I went on to tell her everything that had happened from the time we'd entered to the moment we'd been booked in, to entering the magical birth registry. Eva gasped half a dozen times throughout the story.

But we hadn't even gotten to the most gasp-worthy part.

"And what did you do when he read 'fire witch' on your birth certificate?" she asked.

"Well, he didn't read that."

"He skipped that section?"

"No—he definitely read the section. But it didn't say fire witch."

She set her plate aside. Licked her fingers off in preparation for whatever was about to come, as though clean fingers were a necessary part of being ready.

"It said air witch," I murmured, meeting her eyes. "I was listed as an air witch, just like my mother."

It wasn't often I heard Eva curse. And mostly she just said "gods," which was a questionable curse. But this time she let it fly in English. "Holy shit."

I laughed, went immediately somber. "Yeah, that about sums it up."

"You're an air witch?"

"Except for, you know, this." I raised my hand, set it aflame.

The two of us gazed at the flames, and then I doused them by closing my hand. "Eva, do you know how Liara and Umbra came to channel lightning?"

She shook her head.

"A fire witch," I said. "A fire witch attacked them both as children. Some of that magic rubbed off on them."

That elicited the loudest gasp of all. And Eva whispered, "So you must have been attacked."

"I don't remember being attacked. And I can't use lightning."

"Then it happened early—before you could form memories. And maybe more of the fire witch's power seeped into you than them."

She was on to something—in large part because of the creature I knew resided in me. The Spitfire had been there for as long as I could remember.

Sitting there with her, I remembered why Eva was my closest confidant. Why I told her everything.

She was smart. She asked good questions. But most of all, she cared. She cared about me, which meant she was tireless in getting to the bottom of things.

And that was when I finally told her about the Spitfire.

Eva didn't have the reaction to the Spitfire I'd imagined. I had thought she would be stunned, appalled, think differently of me. Find me suddenly questionable and untrustworthy.

None of those things were true. She was only curious and kind and full of questions.

She always surprised me with her constancy.

So I went on to tell her about Liara. How Liara now knew everything.

"And how did she react?" Eva asked.

"She was... hard to read."

"What does that mean?"

"It means she just nodded. When I asked her not to reveal any of this, she nodded again."

"Interesting." Eva's eyes narrowed, unfocused.

"What is it?" I said.

She shook her head. "Nothing."

But over the next week, she arranged a meeting between the five of us: her, me, Aidan, Loki, and Liara. We met in the secret room behind the unused storage room, and as soon as Eva had conjured some rolls on the table by way of hospitality, she leaned across it toward Liara.

"What are your intentions with Clementine?"

I jerked back. "Woah, she's not my date."

Liara's arms folded. "That depends. Are we talking right now? Because my intention in this moment is to sit as far from her as possible."

"I share those intentions," Loki said from atop the table. "Most of the time."

"Wow." I swept a hand out. "Anyone else care to roast me? I'm not crispy yet."

Eva swept a graceful, dismissive hand out. "I mean with regard to the prophecy. The weapon."

"I won't tell anyone about your secrets," Liara said. "If that's what you mean."

Aidan turned to her. "But will you help us?"

"I took her to the library, didn't I? Got banned for it, too."

"She needs your help with air magic," Eva said. "You're better with synesthesia than I am. Way better."

"Oh gods." Liara rolled her eyes. "Now I'm going to be her tutor? You couldn't pay me enough. Besides, you have Frostwish."

"Frostwish isn't trustworthy," I said.

Liara's eyebrows rose as she turned to me. She had a smug deviousness on her face, as though she'd predicted my words. "Oh?"

"Rathmore told me before he left."

"Rathmore told you?" Liara settled into her seat. "Now that's interesting. I wonder why a fae who's dabbled in hexes would be untrustworthy."

Eva straightened. "And Clem and I may have... followed her to Inverness once."

Liara's hands clasped atop the table as she looked between us. "I would have expected as much from the fire witch, but you've surprised me, Whitewillow."

I ignored the newest slight. "She met with Tristan Rathmore."

"Callum Rathmore's father," Liara said at once. "The head of the Mages' Council. He's famous."

"And Frostwish's mentor from her studies," Eva said. "They were talking about Clementine. Calling her the 'new' witch. And they mentioned Raven Murkwood."

"And who is Raven Murkwood?" Liara asked.

"I think she's the Shade," I said, and everyone went still. Even Loki's tail stopped moving atop the table. "I think Raven Murkwood is her. Or was her."

Liara turned an arched brow on me. "Now this is getting interesting."

When I explained why I thought they were one and the same, no one seemed doubtful about my theory. The discussion circled back around to Frostwish and her class.

"She's been tainted by dark magic," Liara said. "Can you ever make a glass of water clear again after one drop of dye?"

Loki's tail flicked. "Doubtful."

"I feel like she's studying me in class," I said. "Scrutinizing me. Waiting for something to happen."

"Isn't that what professors do?" Liara asked. I knew she was playing the devil's advocate.

"There's Goodbarrel scrutiny, and then there's Frostwish. They come from very different places."

Liara lifted a macadamia-nut cookie, turned it. "So you don't feel comfortable learning with her."

"Not when it comes to the likeness deception," I said.

"But I don't know the likeness deception."

"You could learn it," Eva said. "Faster than me."

"And how's that, Whitewillow?" Liara shot back. "Remember, I've been banned from the library?"

"So get unbanned." Eva's eyes held a challenge. "You're a Youngblood. You want Clem to take down the Shade? Get back into that restricted room and read that book."

Damn, Eva. She was doing the hardest work for me.

Liara's eyes flashed, but she only said, "I could."

I was beginning to understand the tone in Liara's voice. The teasing. She wasn't closed off to the idea of teaching me—but she wanted something.

"What is it?" I said. "Tell me what I need to give you to get your help."

She lowered the cookie. "This prophecy. You claim you want power to defeat the Shade, but few people who obtain power aren't corrupted by it."

"I won't be—" I began.

"You can't know." Her elegant throat bobbed as she swallowed, her eyes faraway. "You just can't know."

"So?"

"So I'll help you on one condition."

"Whatever you want."

Her eyes flicked to me, hard and flinty as ever. "If you fail in any way—if you turn to darkness, or you aren't able to defeat the Shade—you'll give me my revenge for my parents' death."

My stomach coiled like a snake. "And how can I do that?"

"One witch's life for my mother and father's." Her chin lifted. "Seems more than fair, doesn't it?"

"Well, this took a turn," Loki murmured.

The coiling grew tighter. "If I turn to darkness, I'm not likely to keep that promise anyway."

"But you'll know why I'm coming for you," she whispered. "You'll know I helped you in good faith, and you'll know you failed to achieve what you'd promised. The world won't mourn the loss of the last witch."

Now I understood what she was asking of me.

It wasn't a request. It was a threat.

If I failed and didn't die by the Shade's hand, I would die by hers. It was Liara Youngblood's twisted way of keeping me on the straight and narrow.

And given the ice crystallizing in my veins, it was effective.

"Clem—" Eva began, setting a hand on my shoulder.

I put my hand over hers, squeezed it. Didn't break eye contact with Liara. "That's fine," I said. "Because I won't fail. You'll have to live out your revenge fantasies when I take down the Shade."

Liara studied me for a few seconds. Then, with a decisive nod, she stood. "Meet me at the boggan's cave tomorrow after dinner."

"The boggan's cave?" Aidan and I said together.

The last time I'd been in there, I had nearly been drowned by the boggan itself. And then there was the incident in the labyrinth...

As a rule, I avoided boggans.

"You want me to help you?" Liara made for the door. "Meet me there."

CHAPTER TWENTY-THREE

"What did Eva mean about you being a Youngblood?" I asked as Liara and I stood at the mouth of the boggan's cave.

She shrugged, staring into the pitch blackness. "We have a reputation in Singapore."

"For what?"

"Connections. Power." She paused. "We've always carried influence, though I imagine that's changed now."

"Why?"

"A twenty-one-year-old is the heir to the Youngblood name after her parents' murder? Doesn't scream influence."

I looked over at her. "You've got influence. I saw the way you handled that librarian."

She snorted. "Mr. Rosewort loved my parents. I'm riding their coattails even now."

An inkling of understanding seeped into me about why Liara was the way she was. It wasn't just about me being a fire witch. "Do you have any sisters? Brothers?"

Now she met my eyes. "One little sister."

"So did I, once upon a time. If she was still around, I would have done anything to protect her. Even if it meant pretending to be a cold-hearted bitch to preserve the family name."

Her eyes narrowed. I thought she would say something cutting, but she only asked, "What happened to her?"

I faced the cave again. "Disappeared with my mom. It happened so long ago now, sometimes I wonder if they ever existed at all."

A wind blew into the cave's mouth, tugging at our hair.

"You don't have to be afraid," Liara said. "The boggan only hibernates here in winter."

My fingers clenched. "Did it ever try to drown you?"

"No"—her lips curled—"but two did try to kill me in a labyrinth."

Touché.

"Why did it pick this place, though?" I asked.

"Inside there is a place of minor power," she said. "That's why the boggan is attracted to it."

"Tell me we don't have to come back here more than once."

She sighed, started forward. "I won't lie to you. We'll be back." She disappeared into the mouth of the cave, and her disembodied voice called, "A light, please?"

Sucking in air, I followed, raising one hand and igniting it. The glow set us both into relief, shadows dancing on the cave wall.

Ahead of me, Liara stared back with eyes like black marbles. "See? Just us."

We started walking. "Such a comfort to be here alone with you."

For the first time, she gave a breathy laugh in my presence. "Likewise, fire witch." As we came to the back of the cave, she said, "I can see why Rathmore had a thing for you."

I stopped hard. Started walking again. "A what?"

She didn't notice. "He was into you. It was obvious."

"How could you possibly tell that? Unless you're excellent at reading scowls."

She turned down the passage, her hand going to the wall and trailing along. "He scowled longer and harder at you."

My first instinct was to press the implications away. I didn't want Liara hearing my heart thumping against my rib cage. "It's weird. He's a professor."

She came into the main chamber of the cave with the small pool, turned back to me. "In the ancient world, before the fae portal was closed, our kind lived for hundreds of years. A five-year age gap was negligible."

"I wasn't referring to the age gap. I was referring to the student-teacher gap."

"So he never acted on it. And now he's gone." She rolled her eyes, taking a few steps back from me. "Don't pretend like you wouldn't enjoy the student-teacher thing, anyway."

I smirked at her. "So Liara Youngblood enjoys speculation and gossip. Color me shocked."

"Douse your flame, fire witch," she said. "It's time for us to train."

"Douse it?"

"Are you just going to repeat after me now?"

I hesitated, then closed my fingers to a fist. The flame hissed away, enshrouding us in complete darkness. In a flash, I saw the boggan's face in my mind—the teeth, the eyes, the claws. I saw it pushing me into the pool just a few feet from where I was now standing.

I had hoped to never come back to this place.

"What's the point of this?"

"To master the likeness deception, you have to master synesthesia. One of the first things we're taught in Whisper is how to see magic. One of our first-year classes spends the whole year in the dark."

"How does it help me to see anything if we're in darkness?"

"Because it makes you desperate to see. Especially a place like this, where I've heard you had a very bad time."

She was right about desperation. Since I'd doused the flame, my fingers had been itching to relight it. My eyes had been darting all over, seeking anything to latch on to.

"And the more desperate you are to see," she went on, "the more likely you are to see the magic."

I let out a long breath, trying to slow my heart. It wasn't working. "I need to master the deception by the end of the year. Can you get me there?"

"Maybe. That depends on your commitment."

Which meant returning to the place—this cave—where I felt desperate to see, again and again.

"Fine," I said. "What happens when the boggan returns to hibernate for the winter?"

"That'll just make you extra desperate, won't it?"

"There's no goddamn way I'm coming in here with that thing."

"How committed are you, Cole?"

"Completely."

"Really? I'm not so sure about that."

"Liara—"

She shushed me. "Enough with excuses. Either you follow my lead and master the hex, or you're screwed. What'll it be?"

I ground my teeth together. I hated being shushed. "Let's start already."

"I've already started. The magic is in the air—don't you see it?"

My eyes tracked the space around me. I saw nothing. "No."

Footsteps sounded over the stone, approaching me. A second later, a hand fell on my shoulder, jolting me even though I knew it was Liara. "Look harder." And then she murmured familiar words at me.

The likeness deception. *Mealladh coltas.*

And her breath was purple. The darkest shade of blue, but I could see it moving in my direction for a split second.

I went rigid under her grip.

"You saw it," she murmured.

"I saw something." I paused. "That wasn't lightning."

"Congratulations—that's how it starts." Her hand fell away. "And the lightning comes from my fingers, genius. What I just did was attempt to hex you. Didn't work, obviously."

I didn't even have a typical comeback. No snark. Just silent, heart-thumping nerves.

When she spoke, I nearly flinched. "This cave really did a number on you, didn't it?"

I took a long breath. "You don't know the half of it."

We returned to the cave the next day, and the day after that. Liara was painfully diligent about making sure I mastered the synesthesia before we moved on to anything else.

Days turned into weeks, and Liara managed to get her ban at the library overturned. Now she could return to the restricted room and study the art of hexes herself. She'd promised Eva to do so; the fae had, after all, invoked the Youngblood name.

Meanwhile, life went on at the academy in a strange, frenetic stasis. Mornings I met up with Aidan in the library. Grabbed food at the dining hall. Then I attended my classes—Mounted Combat, Fire Magic, Hexes, and the first-year class I taught—with perfect regularity, never late, never missing. In the evenings, Liara and I trained in the cave. Grabbed dinner. Then Aidan and I dueled by the pond.

It was exhausting. It was the only way I knew to distract myself.

Because as the leaves turned, things got strange.

The guardians had expected to embark on a rescue once a week. That was how it had been the previous year. But Mishka's arms had long since healed, and still no horn, no rescue.

No missions.

By mid-October, we hadn't had a mission in over a month. It was an odd quietude, a held-breath sort of existence, and it made me uncomfortable in a way I'd never known.

I began to desperately wish the horn would sound just so I could have the satisfaction of breathing out.

During weekly guardian meetings, we speculated as to why. Maybe the Shade was diminishing in power. Maybe she'd kidnapped enough mages for her army. Or maybe, most terrifying of all, she was planning something big.

"The human saying exists for a reason, after all," Keene said during our meeting. "'The stillness before the storm,' isn't it?"

"It's 'calm,'" Akelan said, stone-faced. "But stillness feels more appropriate."

It did feel more appropriate. This wasn't calm. Not at all.

Fi told us to remain vigilant—as if I could get any more vigilant. I'd already trained with the other chasers: Keene, Liara, Mishka. In fact,

I'd trained with all the guardians one-on-one, just to know their fighting styles.

Elijah and Isaiah were quick on the draw, kept on top of the action. They stuck together.

Keene liked to blink from rooftop to rooftop, appearing and disappearing without using his wings.

Liara was a straight arrow of intensity. Once she'd locked on to her target, she was faster than her lightning.

Circe was a coordinator in the sky. She yelled directions, kept everyone where they needed to be.

Akelan was coolheaded. He kept us well-guarded on the sides.

Mishka waited for her moment, and then she absolutely speared the shit out of things with ice.

Fi was the strategist on the ground. She played the role she needed to—whether guard or chaser.

I studied them all. I practiced with them all.

Because of everything happening, Eva and I had begun Sunday night sleepovers, which really just constituted lots of summoned food in our pajamas. She was the only one I could reveal it all to: my fears, my sadness, my anxiety, my anger.

She took it all in, and she gave me empathy back. And in turn, we commiserated over her training for the trials, her awkwardness with Torsten, the challenges of planning the Winter Solstice Ball.

I came to rely on those Sunday night sleepovers.

Sometimes I brought out the page from *Jane Eyre* Rathmore had left me, ran my thumb over the symbol he'd drawn in the corner like a talisman. If I were superstitious, I would have imagined it brought me good luck. Not the shape of it—the three interlocked triangles—but the fact that he had drawn it for me. It was the intention.

I thought of him more often when I began to lose my way.

He'd been the first person to learn about the Spitfire. He'd been the first one to accept me for it.

October lapsed into mid-November. By now I could see air magic as well as the leaves on a tree—though Liara's magic was always varying shades of blue.

Some of her hexes were navy. Some were royal blue. Some were the color of a robin's egg.

They depended on the ferocity with which she spoke them, the intensity of feeling she inhabited as she sent her magic into the world. She hadn't been able to properly cast a hex yet—apparently that was wildly harder for a fae than for a witch—but that didn't make her less of a teacher. She was, to both of our surprise, excellent.

She challenged me, and she knew exactly how to explain concepts and when to move on to the next one. I'd rather have her as my professor over Frostwish.

All the while, I had been keeping track of when the boggan would return. It was soon.

So I told her one night as we stood in the cave. A wisp of her magic swept past me, and I said, "Azure. Also, I won't be here when it's here."

She went still in the dark. "It?"

"The boggan."

"Oh, Clementine..."

"Listen, we've done what we need to do in here. I can see the magic."

"This class normally lasts a *year*."

I shrugged. "Test me. Give me my final exam, Teacher."

She huffed. With a scrape of her shoe across the stone and my hair whipping around my face, she said, "Identify this."

The smallest whisper resounded through the cave, and with it, a tiny stream of magic.

"Lapis," I said at once.

"And this?" She bit the words out this time, dark with her intensity. The plume of her magic grew to encompass the space between us until it filled my vision.

"Denim—with a hint of indigo for spice."

The vortex slowed to a stop, and her footsteps passed through the cave toward me. "Mr. Rosewort had something right about you, Clementine."

"That I'm a liar?"

She gave a low laugh. "Two things right, then."

"Do tell."

"You're an air witch."

That wasn't at all what I'd expected. "Right, because that information was on my infallible birth certificate."

"You're still an air witch. Nobody who doesn't have a proficiency with air magic learns synesthesia in two months. Nobody."

I crossed my arms in a protective way, fully expecting the boggan to appear. "Does that mean I've graduated?"

"Yeah." She stepped past me, toward the passage out. "To the daytime."

I turned, followed her. "The daytime?"

As we came to the cave's mouth, she glanced back at me in the moonlight. "You can see the magic in this cave you so desperately want to leave. Seeing it during the day is your next challenge."

As we walked down the path toward the academy, the gratitude of leaving that place forever sloughed off me. I left it behind, in the cave.

"Liara," I said.

"Yeah?"

"We haven't had a mission in two months."

She blew out a breath. "Yeah." She paused. "Sometimes I can't sleep at night."

"Me either."

CHAPTER TWENTY-FOUR

December came, and with it, preparations for the Winter Solstice Ball.

I knew all about those, because Eva had become the head of the Winter Solstice Ball committee. It was composed of five women—all volunteers—three of whom were fae, and two of whom were overeager first-years.

Nights I came home to decorations strewn around the dorm. Sparkling pom-poms, Eva said, would hang from fixtures above the tables. Drawings of centerpieces. Swatches of color placed against one another for the "aesthetic scheme of the thing," as she called it.

Other times, I found her reading a book on evasive flying for fae. I would spot her practicing with another student in the meadow, dueling until she couldn't stand properly. This year, she was as serious about the dance as she was about becoming a guardian.

She gained an almost vibrating frequency, as though she were a tight ball of energy. This whole thing made her anxious in a way I couldn't quite explain, as though if she succeeded at planning the ball it was proof she could succeed at anything.

Some nights she hated the ball. Some nights she loved it.

I'd told her she had weeks. She'd told me she had half as much time as she needed for it to be a proper event.

I pretended not to care about any of it. And I didn't care about whether I was there or not, whether I danced with anyone. I didn't have anyone in particular I wanted to dance with; we'd only danced once, but Rathmore had ruined me for all that.

Amidst everything else, coming home to Eva's holiday cheer, to the sparkling things and the color and the charming disarray, heartened and distracted me. In a funny way, it made me feel the world was warmer, less chaotic than I imagined. The perfectly square swatches, the round poms, the elegant drawings of flowers.

Meanwhile, I began to see the colors of air magic in the daytime. Slowly, very slowly. But I was making progress.

December slid by in this way—daily preparations for the ball, classes, practice, and no rescues. Eventually the guardians met with Umbra in our meeting room, which was supposed to be a highly uncommon event.

This time it wasn't Fi standing before us. It was our headmistress.

She leaned her staff against the table, surveyed all ten of us (if you included Loki). "I've come here today to speak to you about the two-and-a-half-month interlude after that last disastrous mission."

I folded my arms tight to my body, didn't meet Mishka's eyes. Not long after she'd been released from the infirmary, I had spotted her in the dining hall and taken a furtive glance at her arms.

They'd looked exactly the same as before. They picked up a knife and fork with ease. She laughed as she chatted with another student, cut a piece of meat and set it in her mouth in the same way she would have before she'd lost her arms.

But I knew it wasn't the same.

The experience would never, never leave her.

I had apologized to her a few days afterward. She'd been strong, pretended I had nothing to apologize for except my absence. Still, things between me and Mishka would never be the same. I knew in a small, irrational way, she would always blame me for missing that rescue. Sometimes life went that way.

"This is strange," Umbra said. "I'll admit it now—it is odd. The last time this long a space elapsed between attacks was over a decade ago."

"So you're not feeling disturbances in the magic?" Fi asked.

Umbra shook her head. "No. Not a one. And I've looked into whether the issue stems from my magical awareness. It doesn't."

"So they've just stopped," I said.

"No." Umbra cut a hand through the air. "No, the Shade never stops. She may pause for a time, but until she extricates herself from the underworld or dies, she will never give in."

"Then what?" Circe said. "What's she up to?"

"I would most certainly tell you if I knew," Umbra said. "Her actions have always been unreadable for me."

Keene's wings trembled. "I can't stay in this holding pattern. I'm losing my hair."

Akelan snorted as the fae pulled at his hair to demonstrate. "That may not be due to stress."

Keene turned wide eyes on him. "Fae do not go bald."

"Guardians," Umbra said, "I recognize the immense amount of stress this places you under. That's why I've made a decision I intend to implement at this meeting."

All eyes shifted to her.

"Until things normalize, I will place you on shifts." She raised her fingers. "Five on, four off. There must always be at least one guard, one watcher, and one chaser among those five. The groups should be evenly balanced for the greatest possibility of success."

Fi sat up straight. "But that seems a dereliction..."

"Of your duties?" Umbra gestured to Keene. "I recognize your dedication, Ms. Waters. But I also would like to note the first case of fae balding, no doubt by consequence of the situation you're in."

Savage.

Keene looked like he wanted to blink out of existence and never reappear.

"Each of you will spend three and a half days on, and the same amount of time off-duty." Umbra nodded at Fi. "When you've decided on who will occupy each shift, please inform me."

Fi's face went serious; she was already contemplating the teams. "Yes, Headmistress."

Once Umbra had left, everyone broke into chatter.

Meanwhile, Fi rose, walked over to where Umbra had stood. Paced, staring in turn at each of us, then at the floor.

Around me, Elijah and Isaiah made the argument for never being split up. Circe was joyous to have half a week off. Mishka and Akelan sat together, whispering. Keene went on about his hair.

I glanced over at Liara, an unexpected lightness filling my chest. I would have more than three days each week to just... be.

And I realized that of anyone here, she and I knew each other the best. How had that come to be? It was all the training together. I knew the color and sound of her magic, her movements.

If the size of our group on a mission was going to be halved, sticking together gave us a greater chance of success.

She met my gaze. "We need to be on the same shift."

I nodded. "Great minds think alike."

Once Umbra had left, Fi placed both sets of knuckles atop the table, leaning forward. "All right, it's clear who should be on which team."

"Is it, though?" Elijah gestured between himself and Isaiah. "If you split us up, it won't be so clear to us."

Fi rolled her eyes. "As if I would do that. You two would never stop whining."

Isaiah smirked. "It's Elijah who does the whining. I have manly complaints."

Elijah punched him in the shoulder, eliciting an "Ouch."

Fi walked over to the chalkboard, began writing names in a vertical list.

In the first list:

Liara

Elijah

Isaiah

Fi

. . .

And in the second list:
   Mishka
   Clem/Loki
   Keene
   Circe
   Akelan

She tapped the board with her chalk. "I've split up our magic and our roles in terms of power balance. Any objections?"

Of course, nearly everyone objected.

When I managed to get a word in, I said, "You haven't taken into account who works best together."

Fi's eyebrows went up. "Oh?"

"Clementine and I have trained together," Liara said. "Extensively."

Akelan shook his head. "You're our two fastest chasers. Putting you together would hamstring the other team. No offense, Mishka."

Mishka, who'd at some point conjured a plate of baklava, shrugged and went on eating. "None taken."

I pointed down at my lap. "But you're forgetting one thing. Loki makes six members of the first team."

"He's like, half a member," Circe said. Loki and I must have both shot her a look, because she raised both palms. "Don't scratch my eyes out, you two."

Fi looked thoughtful. "Well, I can't split you and your familiar, so it is a fair point. Actually, it enhances the power of the first team—makes it unbalanced."

I sighed. "Just rotate us. Loki and I will be on both teams."

On my lap, Loki's claws dug through my skirt. "We'll what?"

Everyone turned surprised eyes on me.

"Rotate you?" Elijah said. "You're going to lose your hair faster than Keene."

Keene groaned. "Can we please drop that joke?"

I shrugged at Elijah. "I've dealt with worse stress. Besides, you need your two fastest chasers as often as possible."

These past few months had been awful on me, but I was telling the truth. I *had* lived through worse stress.

Besides, I owed it to Mishka.

"I'll rotate, too," Liara said into the silence that followed.

I glanced over at her, found her jaw set. She was totally committed to this line. She would be on duty every day without a second thought.

Mishka's injury must have also affected her more deeply than I'd realized.

Across the room, Fi folded her arms. "That's a major sacrifice for both of you."

Loki stared up at me. "Request a couple days off a month. Do it now."

I glanced down at him. "Since when did you become the master of negotiations?"

"Now's your best chance. And godsdamn, I'm not going to be roped into this without a few concessions."

I lifted my eyes. "Loki would like two days off a month."

"Fine," Fi said. "Clem, Liara, and Loki will rotate with two floating days off a month. Are we all happy with these teams?"

The others couldn't really complain. Mishka went on eating her baklava.

"Good. The first team will be on duty for the next three days." Fi pointed at the list. "We'll swap to the second team at noon on Thursday. Meeting adjourned."

As everyone left—even Loki, who went in search of food—Liara and I remained at the table.

"You're an idiot," she said once we were alone.

I smirked. "Takes one to know one." I stood to leave. "See you—"

"I need to know something," Liara said to my back.

I turned. "What is it?"

"Since I'm allowed back into the restricted room, I'll take one of my floating days and go this weekend to study hexes."

My eyebrows went up. "Really? And what do you need to know?"

She stood, turned to me. "I need to know that everything I'm about to do for you will pay off. I need to know you'll fulfill this prophecy."

"I will," I said at once. "Hell, you've already told me you'll kill me if I don't."

She raised a finger. "I'm going back into the restricted room. I'm going to learn the dark art of hexes. I'll share everything I learn with you. And when you recover this cursed chain, I'm going with you."

"Liara..."

"I can't let you fail, Clementine. Not at this. You know I'm more powerful than anyone else you could bring. You're better off with me there."

She wasn't wrong.

"And," she said, "after you've gotten the chain, I'll be there when you retrieve the blade."

"I don't even know where the blade is yet."

"But you will. After you've gotten this piece, you and Aidan will figure out where the last piece is located. It has to go in that order, based on the prophecy—one piece at a time."

I studied her. "Did you read this prophecy yourself?"

"Yes," she said without hesitation. "After you told me about it in Singapore, I went into the Room of the Ancients and found what I needed to."

Of course she had.

"I'll have to think about it." I began to turn away again, but her hand shot out, gripped my wrist. I tried to yank it away, but she had a vise grip.

"You have to understand," she said. "I was ten when my mother and father were murdered in their sleep. The witch tried to kill me, too."

I stopped trying to jerk away. Her fingernails were digging in, making grooves. But I gave her my attention.

Liara's eyes glistened with old horror and hatred. "My mother managed to scream before she died. That was what woke me. From her bedroom, she screamed, 'Liara, save Vivi.' That was all. And already the house was on fire, and I didn't know what to do. I just flew straight to Vivi's room, and I grabbed her."

I didn't open my mouth to say anything. I just listened.

"When I opened the window," she went on, "something blasted me in the legs. My pants caught on fire—gods, it hurt—and when I looked back, she was there. The fire witch."

"What did you do?" I whispered.

"I screamed." She blinked a tear free. "I was so scared. She glowed with insanity. Her eyes were like bonfires. I leapt out of the window and I flew."

So that was how Liara had gained her lightning. The fire witch had burned her legs.

Liara let go of my wrist, knelt. She'd always been one of the few students to wear tights under her skirt, no matter the season. And now I knew why. She ripped her black tights to reveal scarred and mottled skin at the calf and knee. Then the other leg.

"But why didn't you..." I began.

"Heal it?" She stared up at me.

And I knew. I already knew why.

Her hand ran over the burned skin. "Because I never want to forget exactly how it felt."

CHAPTER TWENTY-FIVE

The morning of the Solstice Ball, Aidan and I met, as per usual, in the library. Through the steam rising from the teapot between us, I nodded at him. "You were right."

He sat back from his reading, forearms resting on the arms of his chair. "There are so many things I'm right about."

"About Liara."

"She's grown?"

"That, and..." I swirled my spoon in my mug, trying to figure out the right words. "She's going to help us. When the time comes to retrieve the other two pieces, she'll be there."

"You trust her?"

I glanced up. "Not as much as I trust you or Eva, but more than I trust anyone else at the academy."

He gave an impressed nod. "That's quite a lot. How'd she earn it?"

"She's helped me in ways she hasn't needed to. But it's about more than that—she really, really wants to destroy the Shade."

"Why, besides the obvious reasons?"

"I'm not at liberty to share. But, you know—fire witches."

He nodded, his hair gleaming in the light as he did. And then it hit me—

I set my spoon down. "You styled your hair this morning."

His cheeks tinged. "I style it every morning."

I swirled a hand atop my head. "But you went extra fancy." My eyebrows rose. "You've got a date tonight."

He groaned. "Please don't make me regret it."

"That depends. Who is it?"

He shook his head.

"Is it a first-year?"

"Maybe."

"Cradle-robber."

He made a face. "And what are you doing tonight, Cole?"

"I'm on duty. Can't rescue anybody in a taffeta gown and heels." I wouldn't pretend I wasn't secretly happy about having to miss the dancing. It had about broken Eva's heart, but I had still promised to show up—I'd just be on the periphery.

"I still can't believe you volunteered to rotate."

"Can't you? I'd have thought you would understand about nobility and self-sacrifice and all that."

"I do." He eyed me. "But—sorry, Cole—nobility and self-sacrifice aren't what drive you."

My hand flew to my heart as though he'd pierced me. And in some ways, he had. Mostly because he was right.

Mishka's arms and her blood were what drove me. And beneath that, guilt and shame were what drove me, but that hadn't changed in a decade, anyway.

I needed to veer this conversation back to uncomfortable ground. "Tell me who your date is."

He tapped the book in front of him. "We still have the issue of the riddle, and where exactly under the ground in Siberia we'll find this chain. Have you forgotten about that?"

We hadn't made any progress on either of those things in months. It had become almost perfunctory to open books and lay out our notes but to accomplish nothing else on the subject.

"I haven't forgotten," I said. "But I have nothing new to offer."

Aidan accidentally broke off a biscotti he'd been dipping too long in his tea. "Maybe we're not trying hard enough."

I eyed the broken biscotti. "Or maybe we're trying too hard."

So we agreed that until we made any progress, we would focus on what we could control.

Later that morning in Mounted Combat, I let go of Noir's mane with both hands as he cantered around the ring. I focused on what Rathmore had taught me about fire riding—allowing the flame to consume me without letting the Spitfire take control—and managed, for the first time all year, to ride the edge of control as the flame sputtered its way up my body, encompassing my arms, chest, head.

"Good, Clementine," Farrow's voice said from some faraway place, though I knew she couldn't be more than thirty feet away. "Keep at it just that way."

And then the Spitfire raised its eyes. It expanded in my chest, on the verge of unleashing.

I had to let the flame go. The Spitfire couldn't come out; I wouldn't let it—not here with these people. Not when I still had so much trouble reining it in.

It was progress, but it wasn't fast enough.

In Goodbarrel's class, I finally managed to light all my fingers. I raised ten flames like candles toward the ceiling, and Goodbarrel clapped. "Well done, Clementine!" He pointed at the far wall, where ten circular, two-foot-radius targets had been hung. "Now hit all of those at once with your separate flames."

Half the class had already mastered the targets. The other half, including me, could maybe nail three at once.

Aidan couldn't even attack the targets; his everflame would eat them up before he quenched it. As a solution, Goodbarrel had conjured fat marshmallows and set them in a line at one empty end of the common room.

Aidan struggled to hit them all. Even fat marshmallows were still tiny targets. Meanwhile, Goodbarrel ate all the ones he didn't hit.

My class of first-years even made progress with their riding. Half of them had mastered mounting bareback, and the other half were shaky. But they could all get on their horses after no more than two tries.

It probably helped that I'd threatened to "go all fire witch" on them if they failed three times. None of them knew what that meant, and I didn't exactly, either, but the mystery of not-knowing seemed to be even more effective.

Sometimes it paid to be evil.

I'd hardly seen Eva in a week, she'd been so busy with preparations for the ball. That evening when I came back, she wasn't in the dorm; she'd probably long ago left to set up.

But Loki was there, sleeping on my bed. A rift had developed between us ever since I'd missed the last mission, and it was on me to mend it.

I came to sit by him. "Hey, cat. Let's make a deal."

He cracked one eye. "I don't generally deal with my inferiors."

"You be my date to the ball, and I'll get Vickery to conjure up your favorite fish."

He sat up with a yawn. "She does that every time she sees me, anyway."

"How about you just be my date, then?"

"Eh..."

"I won't make you wear a bowtie."

"Fine. I am in the mood for salmon."

I showered, dressed in work-casual guardian clothes: a long-sleeved shirt, my jacket, riding pants and boots. Then Loki and I made our way toward the meadow, where ethereal music echoed through the trees.

When we arrived, we found ourselves standing at the entrance to a grand portal, lights set up in a circle from the ground to twenty feet in the air. Inside, the ballroom shimmered with courtly elegance—golden tables with woven iron legs, vines with white flowers draping from the trellises that ran high up to create a curving ceiling. At the far end of the room, a chorus of angelic female voices sang in synchrony as what sounded like a harp was strummed.

The ball was entirely changed from last year. More... otherworldly.

"This is different," I said as we stood in front of the grandeur.

"It's supposed to be the fae portal." Loki's tail feathered against my leg. "Shall we pass through?"

Through the portal, I found the entire student body had transformed into fae.

I stared as a couple whom I could have sworn were Maise and Torsten passed me by with fae wings attached to their backs. Then two of the first-years from my riding class. Finally, Aidan and Saoirse, one of the first-years from my riding class.

I couldn't wait to tease him about it.

When Fi Waters came by with iridescent green wings, I stopped her. "All right, explain."

She shrugged, lifting her drink at me. "I'm off-duty, Guardian."

"Not that." I flicked one of her wings, which shuddered in a strange way. "This."

She glanced over her shoulder. "Oh. The theme's 'Through the Portal.' Didn't you get the memo?"

At my feet, Loki scoffed. "Of course not. So embarrassing."

I glanced down at him. "I can still find wings for you. Don't doubt my tenacity."

"Gods no." He slipped through the crowd, disappearing toward the food table.

Fi remained in front of me. "I meant to thank you, Clementine." She nodded at my jacket and boots. "It can't be fun dressing for work tonight."

I shrugged; if only she knew how little I minded. "At least no one will ask me to dance."

She smiled, always demure and understated. "We'll remember this. The sacrifice you and Liara are making."

The music shifted to a new song, one just as ethereal, but with more of a lively tune. At the head of the room, the instrumentalists had shifted to a fiddler and a single singer who looked just like Professor Fernwhirl.

I squinted. It was Fernwhirl.

Akelan appeared at Fi's side with an elaborate bow, requesting a dance. He was as big as Torsten, with the same stolid movements of an earth mage. Except now he had a pair of dwarfed blue wings clinging for dear life to his back.

Fi glanced back at me, her glass of mead extending my way.

I took it. "I'll take care of this. No use wasting a good drink."

Off they went, and the second I'd begun to finish off Fi's mead, Eva landed before me in a rush of wings and white elbow-length gloves and lace.

She enfolded me in a hug. "You're here."

"I swore I would be." I backed up to eye her. "You look like you're smuggling a giant cupcake under that skirt."

She blushed into her shoulder. "It's ridiculous, isn't it?"

"No. You look beautiful."

She swept a hand around. "I mean, the whole thing. The wings. The portal."

"It's an excellent approximation," a voice said from beside us.

Ora Frostwish approached, one hand wrapped across her waist and the other holding a thin-stemmed flute of golden drink. She wore a navy silk sheath, her body almost breakably slender beneath it. Her cropped blue hair held such a perfect edge it could definitely cut skin.

Eva clasped both hands. "You think so?"

"I do think so." Frostwish managed a small smile at her. "I think someone's looking for you, Hostess."

Eva spun to where a hand waved from beside the tiny orchestra. "Oh! I'm needed for the next song." She threw a glance back at me. "If my singing's terrible, I won't be offended if you plug your ears."

Frostwish leaned toward me as Eva departed through the crowd. "Lovely girl. A shame she lacks in confidence."

I kept watching Eva as she mounted the small stage to stand with two other actual fae. "She's humble."

Frostwish took a sip of her drink. "Two sides of the same coin."

I resisted lashing her with more than my tongue. It was clear she knew nothing about Eva. But it was better to say less to Ora Frostwish; I wanted her to know me as little as possible.

Before us, the trio of singers stood in a line with Eva at the center, and as they began their song, their arms lifted in synchrony, rising above their heads. They moved with sinuous elegance, stepping and sliding in amongst each other as their arms waved like boneless lengths of silk.

"This is an ancient fae song," Frostwish whispered to me. "Do you know it?"

I shook my head, transfixed. As was the rest of the room; everyone had stopped to watch. Students, professors, even Vickery and Loki over at the food table.

The three of them moved as though they were parts of the same whole, their mouths open to reveal white teeth as they sang a melody that didn't sound of this world.

As it turned out, Eva was humble. She had a beautiful voice, but it wasn't like anything I'd heard from a human. It was the ocean in a conch shell. It was exquisite, enchanting. Maybe Odysseus had mistaken fae for sirens.

The three hooked arms, each of them taking flight to spin like a flywheel above the room, their heads dropping back, one foot set atop the opposite knee. When they came spiraling back down, their arms remained interlaced. The song crescendoed, and they patterned their arms together in various braids, shifting seamlessly between one and the next.

As the song finished, they went angular, bending their elbows to form a braid of limbs before the crowd.

Clapping began around me, but I only stood rigid, staring at the fae as they remained in their final pose, chests heaving.

The symbol they had made with their arms...

I knew it.

Three interlocking triangles.

"What did you say this song was called?" I said to Frostwish.

"I didn't." She leaned closer. "This is called the 'Trickster's Triad.' It's the story of how the fae portal was closed during the Battle of the Ages."

My head jerked, and I stared at her. "What was that symbol they made with their arms at the end?"

Frostwish turned lidded eyes on me. "Curious you would notice that. The trefoil knot is quite obscure."

The trefoil knot.

I set my glass down on a nearby table, backed away. Frostwish said something else, but I was already headed back through the portal of lights and into the darkness of the meadow.

I finally had a name for it.

CHAPTER TWENTY-SIX

Before bed, I waited for Eva to return. Meanwhile, I studied the symbol Rathmore had written on the page he'd ripped out from *Jane Eyre*.

It wasn't the first time. It wasn't even the tenth. I found it had a strangely calming effect, to stare at something so small, so simple.

Three interlocking triangles, all overlapped and perfectly spaced.

Early into the summer I'd memorized the symbol so my brain could work on deciphering it while I did other things. I'd shown it to Aidan, who had no idea what it was. But I hadn't yet asked Eva.

When she finally arrived after midnight with a sleeping Loki in her arms, I stood from my bed.

She was flushed, dewy with sweat. One hand went to her chest when she saw me. "Oh, Clem."

I came forward. "Can you look at this symbol?"

She pulled off her gloves one by one. "Now?"

"If you don't mind."

"Of course." She sat at her desk, accepted the sheet of paper, examining it. "What is this, anyway?"

"It's a page from *Jane Eyre*. Don't ask. Look at the symbol in the corner."

She brought the page closer. "Oh. This is the symbol for a famous fae-run place."

I sat beside her. "It is?"

"Yes." She set a finger to it. "Some sort of club, or bar..." Then, reaching into her bag, she pulled out her phone and set it before the symbol.

"What are you doing?"

"Taking a picture, obviously." She snapped the image, and beneath it, an internet search of similar images appeared. Including the bold green-and-white signage off the side of a building.

I pointed. "It's that."

"The Hrungnir Inn. Very old, very fancy." She handed the page back to me, thumbing her phone screen. "Says it's in Novi Sad."

"Where's that?"

She scrolled on her phone. "Serbia, apparently."

I stared at the symbol on the page. There was no question the interlocking triangles were the same as the inn's sign. "That dance you did at the ball, the Trickster's Triad. At the end, you made a symbol with your arms."

Her eyes widened on mine. "My gods, Clem. I didn't even make the connection."

"Frostwish told me it's called the trefoil knot."

Eva's brow furrowed. "I've never heard of it."

"Apparently it's pretty obscure." I folded the page. The message was clear: I had to go to Hrungnir Inn.

But when?

I flipped the page over, studying both sides for clues.

"Why is the trefoil knot drawn on that ripped-out page?" Eva asked, watching me.

"This was in the letter you gave me last spring. It was a message from Callum Rathmore."

She gasped. "I knew there was something between you two."

My eyes flicked up to her. "You did?"

"Well, I never said anything because I didn't want to embarrass you. But after I saw you dance with him at the Winter Solstice Ball..."

So even she, from across a room, had sensed what I had felt.

"You have to go, Clementine." She set a hand on my arm. "You have to go to the inn."

"Even if I were to go, he's not going to be there every day of the year. You gave me this last May. Besides, I'm on duty."

She leveled me with her eyes. "If it's for true love, I insist you take one of your days off."

My insides constricted, and I laughed, nodded at Loki. "Keep your voice down. He'll never let me hear the end of talk like that."

She slipped the page from my hands. "Rathmore wouldn't draw this symbol without it mattering. You have to go anyway. And I'm coming with you."

When winter recess began, I asked Fi if I could take a floating day. It would be my first day off since I'd become a guardian.

Fi agreed to give me the day before Christmas, and by then, Aidan knew about the plan to go to Novi Sad. He had insisted on coming instead of returning home right away.

When I'd asked Eva if the inn would even be open on Christmas Eve, she'd laughed. "Of course," she said. "We're fae. It'll be the liveliest night of the year."

Now, as she, Aidan, Loki, and I stepped through the veil and into the wintry nighttime street in Novi Sad, I wondered if we would even be able to enter the inn. The liveliest night of the year sounded crowded.

The city certainly was. It bustled with activity and laughter and young people.

Entering this festive place, another part of me almost didn't mind the inn being full. For the first time in over three months, I felt airy and light. I had zero responsibilities. The horn could sound and I didn't have to pay it any mind.

As soon as we'd all come through the veil, we stood gawking up at an enormous old cathedral in the square before us. Its spires wanted to pierce the sky.

"Don't suppose that's the Hrungnir Inn," Aidan said from beside me.

Eva laughed. "No, but these old cathedrals do take their influence from fae architecture. Those spires? They're an imitation of the classical fae period."

Loki shivered beside me, and I picked him up and held him close. "And when was that?" I asked.

"The start and end dates aren't so clear." She pulled her white peacoat tight, the gold buttons gleaming in the lights off the buildings as she began leading us down the street. "Much isn't clear before the Battle of the Ages and the fire that decimated so much history."

"To my grandmother's lifelong chagrin," Aidan said as we walked.

"Whatever gives your grandmother chagrin, I take pleasure in." I wrapped my free arm around Aidan. "No offense to the other Norths."

"Novi Sad's lovely, isn't it?" Eva gave a spin, one finger twirling above her head toward the Christmas lights strung between the buildings. "So romantic."

"Romantic," Loki said in my arm, "and cold as my castrated balls."

I snorted so loud, the other two looked over. "Loki's just—" I waved a hand. "He's just being himself."

"Yes, myself minus my balls," Loki said. "Which were quite large and fuzzy before that Dutch family had them removed, if you want to know."

"If we're on this touchy subject," I murmured as Aidan and Eva walked ahead, "that must mean you're feeling vulnerable with me. It must mean you trust me again."

"You provide me warmth and transportation." He climbed his way up the inside of my cloak to my shoulder, where he leaned against my neck. "And food, I hope, in exchange for coming all the way out here."

"When have I ever let you down?"

"Well, let's start with when you were twelve, and you tried spraying my litter box with glitter perfume. And then when you were thirteen, and you tried to paint my nails orange—"

I was really, really glad Eva and Aidan couldn't understand him. "When it comes to *feeding* you."

"You never have."

"In addition to which, I'd like to note that I didn't have enough money to feed myself sometimes."

He shuddered. "Gods, so many times I wished you could just conjure some chicken. Now you make nothing but bread and sugar."

Finally, I knew what I needed to do to get back in his favor. "For you, Overlord, I'm going to learn to conjure salmon."

That was when he began to purr. I was back in his good graces.

"Clem!" Eva said from ahead of us. "We're here. Now, what I need you to do is to come here and close your eyes and imagine—"

I pointed at the signage hanging out over the street ahead of us. I could have sworn the word *Hrungnir* was written on it. Plus, the trefoil knot had been etched into the wood. "Isn't that the inn, right there?"

Laughter and clinking emanated from inside the frosted windows, and the sounds of that fae fiddle I'd first heard at the Winter Solstice Ball.

Eva's hand went to her chest. "You see it?"

"And hear it."

She grinned as she came over to me, tucked my hair behind my ear. "You've come a long way from the fae market in our first year."

For a moment, I remembered standing outside the barren park in Vienna. I remembered Eva's hands over my eyes, all the sights and sounds she'd told me to envision.

Only when I'd dedicated my whole self to it had the market appeared.

And here in Novi Sad, I'd come upon the inn without realizing it was magical. It had just presented itself like any other bar I would have snuck my way into when I was underage.

Except this one contained mostly fae, a race who didn't align themselves with the formalists. That set my heart a little at ease.

And, of course, the thought that Rathmore had wanted me to come here.

We came to the door, and Aidan opened it to usher us in. Eva passed through first, and Loki and me second.

She hadn't been wrong; the inn was practically shoulder-to-shoulder full.

Inside, warmth and the spicy smell of liquor washed over me. Low lights illuminated fae wings all around, set so much else into gauzy relief. Some people laughed and spoke in English, and some sang in Faerish to the fiddler's playing.

I spied a bar at the back, manned by a fae conjuring goblets as fast as he could. Around us, most of the tables were occupied. On my right, a whole cluster of people danced together as they had at the ball to the fae songs.

Aidan came to my side. "You want a drink?"

"Of course." I nodded to Loki on my shoulder. "And something for a cat to eat."

Aidan passed Eva, murmured something to her, and threaded his way to the bar. Meanwhile, Eva found my hand and led me toward an empty table in one corner.

When we sat, she sloughed off her coat and her wings came free. Her gray eyes were alight like I'd never seen, her hands steepling as her elbows came to rest on the table. "Welcome," she said, "to a fae solstice celebration."

CHAPTER TWENTY-SEVEN

"Funny." I glanced around us. "A fae solstice celebration looks a lot like what happens when humans get drunk."

Aidan set a goblet in front of her, and Eva managed to lift the enormous thing with grace. She grinned. "And from whom do you think that stemmed?"

I picked up the goblet set in front of me as Aidan sat down. "So you mean to tell me everything in our world is just derivative of the fae. I find that hard to swallow." I took a sip of my drink. "No offense."

Whatever I'd drunk exploded like a firework as it passed down my throat. I started coughing, and Eva laughed while Aidan patted my back.

"That"—Eva pointed at my goblet—"is a weak fae brew. We prefer ninety percent alcohol."

Meanwhile, Loki hopped off my shoulder, sat away from me with his tail curling around his legs like he didn't want to be associated with the lightweight.

"What *is* the concentration, then?" I asked once I'd gotten air. "It tastes like pure alcohol." And it had a glittery aftertaste.

"Eighty-five percent." Eva took a long, easy sip and set her goblet down. "Are you all right?"

I pounded my chest a few times with a fist. "Oh, sure. If my esophagus still works, I might have some more."

Aidan took a small sip. "Loki's food is on the way."

Loki slow-blinked at him. "Tell the human I appreciate his gesture, and won't forget it."

"Tell him yourself." I nodded toward Aidan. "He understands cat affection."

Loki sniffed, looked away toward the crowd now thumping to a bar song. "I'm already overstimulated."

As we talked, I kept searching the place for any sign of one of two things:

First, the trefoil knot.

Second, Callum Rathmore.

But I hadn't spotted either, except that I knew this was the place from the sign outside and the knot etched into the wood.

"This must be it." I pulled out the page from *Jane Eyre*, unfolded it on the table between all of us. "Do any of you see this symbol anywhere in here?"

"I've been looking, actually." Eva had already finished half her drink. "From the moment we entered."

Aidan nodded. "Same."

"Where's my food?" Loki groused.

As if she'd heard him, a fae with a long, unkempt turquoise braid swept up to our table, caught a glimpse of two humans, and said in English, "Who's ordered the chicken platter for two?"

Loki stood and meowed.

Aidan raised a hand. "Here, please."

My eyebrows went up as the elaborate platter landed on the table, and I yanked the page out of the way before it was doused in grease. "For two, huh?"

Aidan lifted a drumstick. "I'm hungry, too."

Eva leaned across the table toward me as the other two ate. "There must be something we're missing. Maybe it's not the symbol at all we're looking for."

"What do you mean?"

                    S.W. CLARKE

"Suppose the symbol was only meant to lead us here. What would be next?"

My eyes flicked down to the page in my hand. Maybe he hadn't just meant to share a line from *Jane Eyre*.

Maybe the page held more significance than that.

I glanced back up at Eva. "What does Hrungnir mean, anyway?"

"I actually looked it up before we came," Aidan said through a mouthful. "He was a jotunn."

"A jo-what?" Eva said.

"A giant from Norse mythology." Aidan went on eating like he was starved as Loki did the same. "He was killed by Thor."

I sat back. Long ago, this inn had been named after a giant from Norse mythology. What was the significance of that?

Eva drained the rest of her glass. "I'm going to get another. Who wants to walk me to the bar as my winglesswoman?"

I raised my hand. "Since Aidan and Loki are both disqualified on that count."

She smiled at me, and we stood together, threaded our way toward the crowded bar where the harried fae went on making drinks as fast as his hands could move and his wings could carry him.

We came to one end and idled, waiting to catch his eye.

"You know," I said, "you could easily get his attention, if you wanted."

She nudged me. "So could you."

"Fair enough. Here's my best trick." I stepped up to the weathered wooden counter, began to trace a finger over it. No man, human or fae, could resist a woman touching something like she was lonely and arou—

My finger hit grooves. Lettering, carved into the wood itself by an elegant, careful hand.

I stared down at it. The lettering wasn't in English. "Eva, can you read this?"

She came to my side, examined it. "It's Faerish. It runs the whole length of the counter, so I can only make out the first few—"

"What is it?" I looked up at her. "Why'd you pause?"

She stared closely. "It begins with the words 'Hrungnir had a heart.'" Her eyes traveled right. "But the rest is blocked by all the goblets and elbows."

"I lied before." I stepped up to the nearest fae who was standing at the counter. "Now I'll show you my best trick."

When I said excuse me to the half-drunk fae, he turned to me at once. I had, after all, used my *Buy me a drink?* voice.

It'd been a while since I'd used that one, but it seemed it hadn't lost its potency.

Except when he turned around, I said (with a smile), "Please move."

And, with wide, confused eyes, he did. I wasn't proud to be using my feminine wiles like this, but I had no patience to wait for the inebriated fae to drift off. Not tonight.

I gestured for Eva to keep reading.

"Wow." She stepped closer, eyes on the words. "That was impressive."

"Directness with a smile. It works a charm. Now what's it say?"

"'Hrungnir had a heart that was famous. It was made of hard stone...'"

"And?"

She glanced up at me, then at the other patrons blocking the bar. "Can't read beyond that. Elbow in the way."

I sighed. Went over to the next fae and did my trick again. I had to do it three more times—and it did, in fact, work a charm every time—until we'd read the whole inscription.

Which was this:

Hrungnir had a heart that was famous. It was made of hard stone with three sharp-pointed corners just like the carved symbol hrungnishjarta.

When we'd finally read the whole thing, Eva and I turned to look at one another.

"Three sharp-pointed corners," I said.

"A symbol," she said.

Hrungnir's heart was a trefoil knot.

An hour and a few drinks later, we came out of the inn and into the night to clear our heads. Around us, a light snow had begun to fall, and Loki's feet made tiny paw prints as he walked beside me. The whole time, he kept mumbling about how good the chicken had been.

Meanwhile, the three of us were dumbfounded.

We'd asked the bartender about the inscription on the counter. He had told us the line in Faerish was from a thirteenth-century book called *Skáldskaparmál*. We had circled the wagons and spent the next hour discussing it while Aidan did intermittent research on his phone.

"I still don't understand," Eva said as she buttoned her jacket against the cold. "Let's say I agree that the giant's heart was in the shape of the trefoil. Where does that get us?"

"It has to do with the symbol Rathmore drew." I stared into windows as we walked down the street, still vibrant with pedestrians and people out for the holiday. "He knew about the prophecy. He studied it, and it's possible he's trying to help me."

"Really?" Aidan walked with his hands deep in his jacket pockets to keep warm. "If that's the case, why wouldn't he just... tell you in person?"

That was a question I couldn't answer. All I knew was Rathmore had to leave, and if he'd kept away, it was for a good reason. He'd helped me become a better witch. He'd wanted me to know myself— my real self, and not who I was when the Spitfire emerged.

I trusted his choices. And that was a rare thing.

"I don't know," I said. "But I know the Hrungnir Inn matters. I know what we read in there matters. We just have to piece it together."

"Isn't it obvious?" Loki stopped, sat to lick his paw and clean his face even though his butt was planted in the snow. "You saw the dance Eva partook in at the ball. The one where three fae formed the knot."

I stopped with Loki, a memory surfacing. Frostwish had told me the name of the dance, but I couldn't remember it while my head was swimming with fae alcohol. "Eva, what was the dance called?"

She stopped, turned as the snow dotted her lavender hair. It had begun to fall harder, collecting on the windowsills and roofs. "The Trickster's Triad."

The Trickster's Triad.

Three interlocking triangles.

"Why is it called that?" Aidan asked, his voice uncommonly slurred. "The dance, I mean."

Eva stepped closer. "I've forgotten now. It was something to do with fae lore and magic. The Battle of the Ages?"

My brain wouldn't work right, and Aidan and I exchanged an unsteady glance. Even through the haze, I recognized that look. It was the one we always shared when we knew we would have to do some research. We needed to know more about this dance; it would bring us closer to an answer.

But, watching him stand uncertainly on his feet, I sensed this was as far as we would get tonight.

Which meant I had exactly three hours left before my day off was done. Three hours of freedom.

And I was still half-drunk.

"Let's keep walking." Eva turned on her heels. "There's a sweet shop ahead I want to duck into before they close. Mama and Papa will be—"

I'd already crossed over to one of the windowsills, gathered up a bundle of snow into my hands. "Say, Whitewillow, have you ever taken part in this human tradition?"

The moment Eva turned, I hurled snow at her.

She shrieked, shielding herself with both upraised arms. "What was that for?"

Aidan burst into laughter, immediately bent down to gather snow himself. He nearly fell in the process.

Meanwhile, Loki pressed himself against the side of a building. "Uncouth plebeians."

Soon enough, Eva was packing and hurling snow. The three of us wailed on each other for a good thirty seconds before a passing group of young men joined in.

Two minutes later, we'd initiated a full-on snowball fight in the middle of downtown Novi Sad. I was pelted from every side, and eventually I had to stagger out of the thick of it. My hands had gone fully numb.

When I emerged out the other side of the throng, Loki slipped along the buildings toward me. He leapt two feet off the ground to avoid an errant snowball before he reached me.

I rubbed my hands together, blew into them. "Nice dodge."

He came to my feet, scrabbled up my cloak. "This is all your fault."

"Yeah." We stood on the other side of the laughter and flying snow, watching. In the middle of it, Eva's hair lifted from her head as she spun, her tinkling laughter echoing off the buildings. "I'm happy to say it is."

He came close to my neck. "It's almost midnight, you know."

I rolled my eyes. "Do you have to remind me, Fairy Godmother?"

"I never thought I'd be the one saying this, but you shouldn't be drunk on the job."

"I'll sober up by the time we get back."

He went silent, but I could tell he was judging me from the way he wasn't fully leaned into my neck. It would be fine, anyway—I would chug water as soon as I got back, sleep off the hangover and be in perfect shape by morning.

We hadn't had a rescue in months. Chances were it wouldn't happen in the next eight hours.

Twenty minutes later, Aidan and Eva finally emerged from the fight. They were both drenched, her hair hanging in purple icicles. Both of them had red cheeks.

Eva pointed at me, then at the battle. "Look what you started."

I raised an eyebrow. "But you're grinning."

Aidan rubbed one eye. "I think I have snow-induced retinal damage."

"Gods." Eva shook her hair out. "That was the most fun I've had in ages. Forget the sweet shop—they wouldn't let me in now, anyway."

So we struck through the streets back toward the leyline by the cathedral. When we passed through, it was just before midnight. We departed to our dorms, cold and wet and sleepy.

I forgot to drink water. I just stripped, showered, and collapsed into bed.

It felt like I'd been asleep for a whole sixty seconds when I heard it. My eyes snapped open in the darkness.

The low sound of the horn. For the first time in over two months, the guardians' horn had come to life.

CHAPTER TWENTY-EIGHT

I sat up in bed, my head pounding. "Loki."

"I'm up," his voice said from somewhere nearby. A thump sounded as he landed on the floor. "Meet you at the veil."

What time was it? I threw my covers off and opened the door for him to slip out, struggled to pull on my clothes in the sliver of light cast by the ajar front door. First my pants, then my thermal shirt, then my riding boots.

By the time I'd gone for my cloak, the horn had crescendoed.

And now Eva was up. "Clem?"

"I have to go."

I heard her get out of bed, move into the bathroom. "Did you drink water before we went to sleep?"

I swept my cloak around my neck, fastened it. "I can't remember."

She emerged with her sleek metal canteen, handed it to me. "You need this."

"I don't have time—"

"Drink it as you walk." She forced it into my hand. "Trust me."

With canteen in hand, I passed onto the landing and started down the steps toward the grounds as fast as my unsteady feet would take me.

This hangover was a bitch.

When my feet touched the frozen ground, I uncorked the canteen and upturned it as I made for the stables. Voices sounded in the night around me, and I glimpsed shadows above.

"Move it, Cole," Circe called, a blue streak past me. "At this rate the whole thing'll be done before you've gotten through the veil."

Easy for her to say; she didn't need to retrieve a horse.

I sprinted for the stables. Quartermistress Farrow was already there, leading Siren out into the aisleway.

When she spotted me, she nodded toward Noir's stall. "He's raring to go."

When I approached the half-door, he nearly knocked me over as his head surged out. He snorted, knocked the door with his knee.

Farrow wasn't kidding.

"Been too long, huh?" I unlatched the door, guided him out just as Fi arrived. At least I was faster than someone.

Farrow and Fi set to work saddling Siren.

I brought Noir out into the back paddock, mounted him. Farrow had already opened the gate into the night, which Noir had noticed. The moment I was on his back, he started for it. He seemed even more anxious to be off than me.

We galloped for the leyline; I hardly had to direct him this time. He seemed already to know exactly where to go.

As we came into the forest, I slowed him when I heard a meow ahead. Green eyes glittered in the pale moonlight.

I leaned halfway down, throwing my cloak to the side for Loki to climb up like a rope ladder. He climbed quick as Circe's shadow, and when I straightened, he was already on my shoulder.

Umbra's voice entered my head. *Bucharest. One boy, sixteen.* A vision of a street materialized in my head. Nearby, a block of old Soviet-style apartments, gray and geometric, rose ten stories high.

That was where we would arrive.

Bucharest. That wasn't far from us.

Which meant it was the witching hour *here*. It was three in the morning.

"What are you waiting for?" Loki snapped.

"Yes, Lord." I pressed my thighs into Noir's side, and we galloped toward the leyline, where I found Fi standing beside her horse with the veil parted to seven feet in the air.

She nodded at me. "Saw it?"

"I saw it." Hooves thundered behind us. When I glanced back, Akelan and Mishka were on their way. "Are the fae through?"

"They're through," Fi said. "When you get to the other side you'll see them."

I ducked as I urged Noir through the veil. We stepped from the frozen forest floor onto asphalt, and the air warmed as the city's residual heat enveloped us.

The city lay quiet and sprawling, the neighborhood street almost soundless except for the far-off rumble of cars.

Once upon a time I'd dreamed of traveling to Europe, cities like Bucharest. This wasn't how I'd expected to experience Romania's capital.

Fi came through after me, Siren's hooves clattering. "We're all here." She walked Siren forward a few paces toward the apartment complex closest to us. "What's the status?"

Above us, a voice called down, "Two of them heading east on the cross-street. They're moving as one tight unit."

I glanced up, spotted the vague, gray outline of a fae standing on top of a four-story apartment complex. It sounded like Elijah or Isaiah.

"Right. They're avoiding the leyline because they know we'll be coming this way." Fi turned Siren in a circle. "Fae, track them. I'll follow on the parallel street to keep them boxed in."

Noir stamped with a resounding noise, and Fi glanced in our direction and then up. "Liara?"

"Here," came Liara's voice from above us.

"When you've got a good shot, take it. Elijah, Isaiah, whistle if you've got line of sight and you need Clementine for a coordinated attack." She started Siren toward the nearest cross-street. "Let's not waste any more time. I'll be nearby."

"Clementine," came one of the twins from above, "let's go."

"I can smell them," Loki said as I started Noir into a canter down the street. We took a right at the first cross-street, fae wings flying above and to the side of us. "Keep going this way."

As we came onto the next road, more apartments greeted us, tall and gray and austere at either side of the street. Small cars lined the sides, narrowing our course. Fortunately for us, the roads weren't trafficked at this time of night, so we didn't have to skip onto the sidewalk or deal with headlights.

"I can see them," Liara called down. "Three blocks ahead of us and moving fast to the outskirts of the city."

"Toward what?" I called back.

"There's hills all over," one of the twins said. "Could be headed for a lesser point of power. We're closing on them, though."

I leaned forward, staring ahead.

In the same moment, Loki's claws dug into my shirt. "Clementine."

"What is it?"

"I smell them to the left."

"But they're ahead of us."

"I know that," he growled. "But they're *also* to the left of us."

<hr>

I glanced left as we passed through an intersection, caught a glimpse of Fi's horse keeping pace with me. "Where?" I said.

"Left, behind us." I felt Loki shifting on my shoulder. "They're following."

"These ones are the Shade's army, too?"

He paused, sniffing the air. "The scent is of dark magic. It's very nearly the same."

I hadn't been prepared for this circumstance. In every scenario, we did the chasing. And there was always one group of them for us to pursue.

But tonight, they had split up.

The monsters were following us.

"Watchers," I called up as we cantered, "Loki says there's more of them following us. Southwest."

One of the fae said something to the others, and I saw one of them break off and fly over the street, disappearing behind a building in that direction.

"Elijah's gone to check it out, and Liara's going for the chase on the main group," Isaiah called down. "Clem, be ready for a fight if she hits her target."

I kept Noir at a canter, passing down the road without sapping his energy too much. My eyes were fixed ahead, waiting, waiting—

Then it happened. Lightning zig-zagged through the air toward the ground with a crackle, illuminating everything in its path. Including the creature.

The light disappeared just as quickly, and I was left with a searing spot in my vision. "Did she get it?" I whispered to Loki.

"Can't tell." Loki leaned forward. "But the smell is getting closer... Dodge!"

I swerved Noir, and we passed around a strange dark spot and the smell of burning in the center of the road.

"She got one," Isaiah said down to us. "Not the one carrying the boy."

Still, that was a victory. We had one less enemy to worry about.

"The other one took a hard left," Isaiah said. "Take this cross-street, Clem."

When I got to the corner, I veered Noir down the street, found Fi also turning ahead of me. She raced along on Siren, slowing to allow me to catch up so we could move together.

"Did you hear?" I said. "Loki scented a second group of them."

"Elijah told me." Fi was focused ahead. "I'll keep them away as best I can. You stay with Liara and Isaiah. Wait for your moment."

I nodded as Fi slowed Siren at the next corner, turned, and struck off down the cross-street.

Another bolt of lightning surged through the air ahead, shooting toward the ground. It sizzled when it hit the road, but this time it didn't illuminate anything.

She had missed.

"Clem," Isaiah said, "Liara needs a breather. We've got to coordinate."

Even as he said it, I spotted Liara falling back, slowing to keep pace with us.

"Got it." I sent Noir into a gallop as Isaiah flew ahead, leading the way. As long as I kept one eye on him, he'd show me which way to chase. And, most importantly, he'd give the cue for our attack.

"You're gaining on it," Loki said from his tight press against my neck. "I can see the creature up ahead, carrying the boy."

I leaned closer to Noir's neck, giving him less resistance. I had to be close enough on the creature's flanks that I could strike it with fire without hitting the boy.

And, too, I had to time it right. In practice, Isaiah and I weren't perfectly compatible. He always fired off his attack at about the same time as he yelled for me to go in, which led to mistiming.

But after a few tries, I'd gotten the hang of his ways. Isaiah always dive-bombed to within about twenty feet as he attacked. So all I had to do was keep an eye out for the swooping fae, and then I'd know to go in before he yelled for me.

Ahead, a car's headlights washed over the street as it passed through the intersection. For a moment, the creature was illuminated—and then it leapt up onto the car's hood and then onto the street on the far side.

Had the driver even noticed?

If so, they hadn't swerved, hadn't honked, hadn't braked. I was reminded of Fi's explanation: regular humans don't see or hear the creatures. They might as well be wraiths.

Noir and I galloped through the intersection. If a car had been coming, one of the watchers would have warned me. The benefit of working with fae.

Now I could see the boy in gray scale, about a block ahead. His head bobbed, arms dangling as he lay over the creature's shoulder.

"There he is."

Loki snorted. "Your eyes are terrible."

"I make up for it in other ways." I gripped Noir's mane tighter with my left hand, loosened my right hand. I would need the full use of it for my attack. "Help me time it, Loki."

"You need to get about twenty feet closer."

I pushed Noir as hard as he would go, until I sensed the stallion galloping at full tilt. This was as fast as we'd ever ridden, maybe even faster than in the first guardian trial.

He was like a goddamned bullet train.

My right hand came up, eyes flicking between Isaiah and the creature, now in full view. Fire sprang to life on my fingertips.

"Not yet," Loki said.

I rode with one hand aflame, my whole body tense, eyes alternately on the sky and the earth. Isaiah hadn't gone in for his attack yet.

When he did, Loki sensed it before me. His claws dug in. "Now."

I rose half-upright as we came to an intersection, right arm curling back.

On my left, a careening scream echoed down the street. "Clem!" Fi cried.

I only had time to look left. When I did, one of the Shade's creatures leapt from all fours, launching himself at me.

Bitter cold enveloped me, and then the sensation of falling. And finally—inevitably—the unforgiving, brutal asphalt rising to meet me.

CHAPTER TWENTY-NINE

Something in my body broke when I hit the road. Under the adrenaline, I didn't feel the pain—but I did feel a bone snap as I landed on my side. My cloak fell on top of me in a heap, obscuring my vision.

Beneath the shock, I heard noises. Noir's hooves clattering down the road away from me. Loki hissing. Someone yelling my name.

But beyond everything, I felt the cold.

Cold like I'd experienced only once before in my life wrapped around my ankle, began pulling me across the hard asphalt. Cold clawed its way up my leg, sapping all my energy as it reached my core and seeped through my arms and head as fast as I could recognize it.

One of the creatures had me in its grip.

Loki's hiss turned into a growl, and then a scream like only a cat could produce. "Wake up, wake up, wake up!" His scream crescendoed, and the enveloping cold fell away. Loki had saved me. "Goddamnit, Clem. Fight."

I'd begun to feel the pain now. It bloomed from my right shoulder, and my arm didn't seem to be responding. Of course—I'd had to go and break my dominant arm.

As soon as the creature let go of me, my will came surging back.

I threw the cloak off, and the lamplit street came into view. I jerked up, spotted the thing in front of me: pure darkness, pressing away light. Just as they had looked that night they'd taken me.

It was like staring into a void. The depths of nothingness with the outline of a human being.

I also discovered that Loki had attached himself to the creature's arm and was attempting to bleed him out with his back legs.

But I doubted these creatures even had blood. At least he'd gotten it to let go of me.

The creature reached again for my ankle, and I jerked away.

It wanted me.

Hooves barreled over asphalt, nearing us from the cross-street. A moment later, the road splintered in a straight line, knocking the creature off-balance as Siren—with Fi atop her—galloped by.

"Three more are behind me," she yelled as she passed. "Two coming from behind you, Clementine."

On my left, three of them bounded on all fours toward me. When I glanced over my shoulder, two ran upright.

They were all converging on me.

Where were the fae? I didn't hear them, didn't see them in the sky. Probably they were still on the chase.

There wasn't time to worry about them. We were being ambushed.

My right hand made to lift, but something was so broken in there it couldn't even rise. I shifted my weight to my left side, pushed up to a crouch.

The creature that had knocked me off Noir had dropped again to all fours, preparing to leap.

I didn't have time to make plans. Didn't have time to deliberate on the best direction to run.

I only had one option.

The Spitfire.

The last time I'd fought these monsters at the gates of Hell, the Spitfire had burned a dozen of them to ash. It was my only real chance.

But when I tried to summon the fire, it wouldn't come. Only the cold—which began at my ankle and sent chills through my limbs—allowed itself to be known, as though it had doused my heat.

I crouched, frozen, in a new sort of shock. I'd never needed the Spitfire and not been able to access it.

Loki leapt to my side, back arched and tail bushy. "Light the fuckers up."

"I... can't."

The fingers on my left hand twitched like a tweaker jonesing for a hit, and I couldn't tell if I was shaking from the creature's residual touch or my own adrenaline.

Maybe both.

And still they neared.

Siren's hooves clattered behind me as a rumble started along the street. Just before the creatures reached me, the cement shot upward, forming sudden mountain peaks six feet high in a circle around me.

Fi's magic.

Siren skirted the destruction, Fi yelling something before one of the creatures leapt onto the back of the mare, attached itself to her. She screamed as it threw her off. She disappeared behind the rubble as Siren went on galloping away.

I pushed myself to my feet with a yell. Maybe her name, or maybe just frustration; it was hard to say if words had come out.

One of the creatures leapt atop the rubble to my left, perched there as it spotted me. Another appeared to my right, landing six feet up like the outline of a gargoyle.

Out of sight, Fi groaned.

"Clementine!" Loki yelled.

I squeezed my eyes shut, fist clenching past the cold. My breathing came so hard my head felt light, dizzy. That old feeling had returned: pure, unadulterated fury.

But the Spitfire didn't raise its head.

Still, my anger was enough to ignite. Fire sparked on my left fingertips, and when my eyes opened, a small, uncertain flame grew there. I flicked a spark of it to Loki; it landed on his back and spread across his body.

It wasn't the full force of my fire, but it was something.

Six creatures watched me. They seemed to be coordinating, waiting for the moment to pounce.

With gritted teeth, I forced the fire to encompass my left forearm. The right went on dangling uselessly. "What are you waiting for?" I yelled, throwing my good arm out.

A wave of flame swept through the air to my left, and the creatures on that side easily dodged it.

That seemed to be the trigger.

All at once, they came at me. And what was scarier than yells and war cries was the sound they did make. Which was nothing at all.

I punched flame at the two creatures on my left. The flames left my knuckles, shot through the air, and powered through a creature's chest. I could see the street through the smoking hole I'd created in his sternum.

And yet the creature simply ignored it, kept running toward me.

This was why you needed two forms of magic.

The Spitfire had been enough at the gates of Hell, but I didn't have the Spitfire right now. I only had what little fire I could summon, and it wasn't enough.

I kept fighting, and so did Loki. I threw my arm long, sent an arc of flame around as Loki leapt at one on my right, landing on its arm and racing toward its neck to lodge his teeth in.

My flame cut through half the creatures, who seemed to slide around it and reform on the other side.

That was when two of them grabbed me. One took hold of my left arm at the wrist, and on my other side, a hand fell on my shoulder. I knew I would have felt pain if the cold didn't numb me out.

I yelled as my will began to sap away. Maybe I said names—Fi, Liara, Elijah, Isaiah—or maybe I just made a guttural noise.

Where the hell were the fae?

Somewhere out of my view, a blade whistled through the air, and I spotted silver gleaming in the lamplight as a massive form dropped into the center of the rubble, metal armor rattling. But I'd lost all will; I couldn't even shift my gaze to look to my left.

But I could still hear.

The blade whistled again as it cleaved through one of the creatures. I saw half of one of the monsters slide to the ground in a heap of blackness, dissipating into nothing as it died. More destruction as the armor shifted, metal clinking against metal as the blade did its work.

One by one, the creatures fell away.

Finally, a gloved hand slid around my waist, yanked me free of the last creature's grasp and lifted me six feet to the rubble's peak.

And with a final shove, I went tumbling down to the unbroken road. I came to a stop near Fi, who had blood smeared across her head and blinked at me as she touched at it while propped on her elbow.

As sensation and willpower returned, I pushed myself up, staring back at the rubble.

The blade's edge rose once more, shining long and tall, before it cleaved down out of view. And finally, all went still.

Fi and I breathed hard, both watching in silence, as a figure climbed atop the asphalt and stood with sword in hand staring down at us.

I recognized that sword, as long as my own leg. I recognized that armor, a gleaming ebony.

"Who is that?" Fi whispered.

It was Lucian the prince.

I scrabbled backward, boots sliding over the street. "Fi," I managed in a hoarse breath, "run."

A black streak appeared in my periphery; Loki, leaping out of the rubble. He raced toward me. "We have to go."

Before us, the demon prince remained where he was, his chest moving under his armor but nothing else. His sword gleamed in the shadows of the moths dancing under the nearby lamp.

He stared at us.

I found my feet, pushing myself upright with my good arm. I reached out for Fi, who took my hand.

Just before I pulled her up, the prince's armor shifted as he lifted one hand. Ten other creatures had appeared around him, eager to come for me—

But they were stayed by the demon prince.

I helped Fi up, keeping an eye on him. I couldn't see his eyes behind his helmet, or his mouth. Two metal horns curled from it, and I caught the faint outline of his lips. They parted to speak, but a horse's whinny cut them off.

Behind us stood Noir, tail flicking and head jerking. He looked like he'd run for days; froth clung to his lips, his eyes wild with arousal and exertion.

So he'd come back for me after all.

I grabbed Fi's hand, spun toward the horse. "Come on."

Loki ran ahead, still aflame and leading the way toward my horse. When we reached his side, my familiar waited for me to mount Noir before he leapt onto the hem of my cloak and climbed up.

I reached down for Fi, who looked woozy. Blood trailed down her face and neck. "Get on."

"Siren," she murmured.

"No time." When I glanced up, the prince had disappeared, as had the creatures with him. Which meant they could be anywhere. "We have to leave."

She took my hand, and with a jump and my help, she managed to get up onto the horse behind me. Her hands went around my waist. "Where did they all go?"

"Doesn't matter. What matters is this mission's a botch." I grabbed Noir's mane with my working hand, swung him around. "We're headed home."

Lucian still stood there, staring, his sword touching the broken asphalt. He shrugged off one of his gloves, a human hand appearing. And in the moment before I looked away, two of his fingers folded.

Then we were off.

We started into a canter back toward the leyline. We hadn't gone three blocks when a gray creature barreled through the cross-street ahead of us.

Siren.

I swerved Noir to follow her, and we caught up to her by the next block. She was a mare, and inclined to follow a stallion like my horse. It was easy enough for her to fall into line with him, and soon enough I was herding her in the right direction.

A minute later, wings sounded above me.

I glanced up. "Where the hell have you been?"

"I was chasing," Liara shot back. "We weren't able to get the boy before he was taken. Is Fi bleeding? And why isn't she on Siren?"

I ignored her questions. "Where are Elijah and Isaiah? We need to get back."

"I don't know. I'll shoot a flare." As soon as she'd said it, she directed a bolt of her lightning into the sky.

Soon enough, the other two were with us. They both fell into a litany of questions, but I ignored them. I rode hard, eyes ahead.

We needed to get to safety before we talked. The game had changed entirely, and we were no longer the hunters. We were the hunted.

CHAPTER THIRTY

We made it safely back through the leyline. By the time we came out the other side and into the forest outside the academy, Fi was practically draped on my shoulder.

I rode us straight for the infirmary at a canter, Siren following behind.

Liara flew alongside me. "Your arm is broken, isn't it?"

"Seems that way."

She cursed. "What happened out there?"

The adrenaline had started to wear off, and pain was setting in. "I'll tell you once I don't feel like screaming."

When we reached the infirmary, Elijah and Isaiah took the horses as Fi and I staggered inside.

Nurse Neverwink wasn't on duty. Of course; it was just after four in the morning.

Liara went off to get her while Fi and I collapsed onto two of the beds. The pain in my arm had gotten to be excruciating, and I fell into a delirious haze for a time. It seemed like moments had passed before Neverwink's anxious face appeared.

She set to work on me, cleaning me up and spoon-feeding me a strange-tasting liquid and resetting the bone in a way that made me grit through a yell. Fi must not have gotten it as bad, because I didn't hear her at all.

At the end of the ordeal, Neverwink patted my arm. "You'll be good as new by morning. A bit sore. Rest now."

And, still hungover and injured, it didn't take me more than a few seconds to do exactly that.

When I woke, it was daytime. I jerked upright, still in a strange residual fight-or-flight frenzy. Loki slid off my chest with a grumble.

Fi was gone. The room was empty.

"How long have I been out?"

He stretched, his back arching. "Not long enough. I was at the height of REM sleep."

I tested my right arm, found it exactly as Neverwink had promised: sore, but working perfectly. Thank god for magic, or else I wouldn't have the use of any of my limbs anymore.

And somehow, a still-warm cup of tea and cookies sat on the small table next to me. I polished them off before Loki and I came into the waiting room, where Neverwink sat reading a fae romance.

She glanced at me overtop her book. "Better?"

"Much." I showed off my range of motion with my right arm. "You might be my favorite person at the academy."

She laughed, gestured me off. "They all say that once they're well. Bring me treats and then I'll consider whether you mean it."

I snapped my fingers, and a plate of perfect steaming fae rolls appeared on the table before her.

Her eyebrows rose, and we exchanged a small, secret smile.

"There's more where those came from." I came over and set a hand on her shoulder. "And you know I'll be back soon enough, anyway."

"Don't I, though." She shook her head as she plucked off one of the rolls, went back to reading.

When we left the infirmary, I glanced down at Loki. "I'm going to see the other guardians. You can head home if you want."

He remained tight by my side. "As much as I'd prefer darkness and quiet over all your whiny voices, I'm a guardian as much as you are."

He was right; the two of us went straight to where I knew the other guardians would be.

We came into the common room, and I found Mishka sitting in an overstuffed armchair before the fireplace. She had another plate of conjured baklava next to her and a big book in her lap. As soon as she saw me, she closed it up with a clap. "We've been waiting for you."

We started up the stairs together. "How long was I out?"

"A good twelve hours."

I winced. I didn't like being out that long.

When we came up to the third story, I found the rest of them up there. Elijah and Isaiah were playing chess, Fi was staring at the globe, Keene and Circe were arguing in one corner, Akelan paced the circular landing, and Liara sat at the meeting table facing away from me, her arms folded.

Akelan stopped. "She's here."

Fi stepped away from the globe. "All to the table."

Everyone stopped what they'd been doing—which I sensed all amounted to passing time, waiting for me—and filtered toward the table Liara was already seated at.

Mishka and I both sat down at the table, and Loki hopped up on the table before me, sat with his tail curled neatly around him.

Fi stood at the head. The blood had been cleaned from her face, and no wound was visible. She looked exactly as she had the day before, only she wore a gray weariness around her eyes that Neverwink's healing magic couldn't erase.

I wondered if she'd slept.

She tented both hands atop the table, leaning forward. "We need to talk about last night."

"You mean that clusterfuck," Isaiah said.

"Yes," Fi said. "That."

Liara straightened. "I was chasing the target, and then the team wasn't with me anymore. Elijah was gone, Isaiah peeled off, I couldn't hear Clem's horse…"

"We were ambushed," Fi said. "There were at least twenty of them out last night. They came at me from the side, and then they went for Clem."

"Isaiah and I went off chasing a couple of them," Elijah said. "But they led us away from the main group. Diversions, I think."

I chewed on my cheek, listening.

"Diversions?" Mishka said. "But that's impossible. They don't divert."

"They did last night," Isaiah said.

Keene glanced at me, then at Fi. "They 'went for' Clem?"

"Yes," I said. "One broadsided me on my horse, and six of them surrounded me in an intersection."

Everyone stared at me. Apparently this was entirely outside their typical behavior.

"I came to help Clem," Fi said, "and one pulled me off my horse. After that, Clem and Loki managed to fight them off. We both got on Noir, and then we regrouped and headed for the leyline. It was a total failure."

"Hold on," I said. "We didn't fight them off."

"Of course you did. Who else would have?"

Loki and I exchanged a look. It was clear he remembered the whole thing as well as me.

"Fi, do you remember the man?" I said. "With the sword and the armor?"

Her mouth opened, and she stood up straight. "I thought he wasn't real. I had a concussion, and there was so much blood in my eyes…"

"You may have had a concussion, but you didn't imagine him." I set a hand on Loki's back. "We were saved last night by the demon prince."

Around me, no one spoke.

Finally, Circe said, "He's real?"

———

"He's real." I nodded at Loki. "My familiar and I have seen him twice."

"Ho-ly shit," Elijah offered with folded arms.

"And he aided you," Circe said. "Why would he even be there?"

He knew I was there, I thought at once.

Umbra had once told me he could track anyone anywhere in the world if he'd touched them once. Now I knew he and I must have touched on that night so long ago, when I'd stood in front of the gates of Hell.

Which meant he could track me anywhere.

"I don't believe it," Keene said. "The *demon prince*—the Shade's right-hand man—helped you."

I pointed at Loki. "Want to ask the cat? He doesn't lie."

Loki gave an unmistakably loud, decisive meow.

"Gods," Fi said. "Why would he help us?"

My conversation with Umbra entered my mind. She had suspected the demon prince might be helping me, but she hadn't speculated as to why.

"I have no idea," I said. "But what I do know is everything has changed. We can't operate the way guardians did for however long you've been in operation."

Fi finally sat down, looking woozy. "We need Umbra in here."

"For more reasons than you think," Liara said. "She needs to teach us how to cast that telepathy spell."

Elijah pointed at Circe. "I do *not* want you in my head."

Circe set a hand to her chest. "Just me? What did I do?"

"Everything." He eyed her meaningfully.

"We need better communication," I said overtop the two of them. "Yelling to each other isn't going to cut it. If we can learn the telepathy spell, we'll be at a huge advantage."

"And if they're ambushing us," Liara said, "then we need to operate differently. We can't just be watchers and guards and chasers anymore."

She was right. This wasn't just a hunt—it was a battle.

Keene went to find Umbra, and a half-hour later she stood in front of us. We told her everything that had happened.

"Well," she said. "It seems the Shade's army is no longer composed of halfwits."

Akelan snorted. "What does that mean?"

"It means," Umbra said, "that she has gained more intricate control over her creatures once they've left the underworld. She can control them to not simply steal and run, but to coordinate elegant attacks as they did last night."

"She's grown in power," I murmured.

"Yes." Umbra nodded at me. "As we had expected, though not nearly so fast. And as a result, we will have to grow in power and cunning as well."

Mishka sat forward. "Where do we begin?"

"We begin with the suggestion Clementine put forth." She raised her thumb. "I'll teach you all how to seamlessly communicate with one another."

Liara crossed her legs. "My head's already too crowded."

"A fine point." Umbra crossed to Fi, mimed setting her thumb to her forehead. "Except none of you will be proficient enough to stick in one another's heads for long. The beauty of your own inefficiency is this: you must touch your thumb to another guardian's forehead to initiate the connection. Given your inexperience, it won't last more than a few hours."

Akelan tapped his fingers on the table. "It sounds like air magic."

Umbra lowered her hand. "For those who use air magic, it will be. But for those who use earth magic, it will be an earth spell. The connection is between your magic."

It seemed like the best option. So we agreed.

Next came battle strategy.

Umbra sat while Fi went to the chalkboard, drew a map of the fight that had taken place the night before. How I'd been knocked off my horse and surrounded. How she'd been taken down. How we'd survived.

Umbra glanced at me. "The demon prince helped you."

Loki's tail flicked. "He certainly wasn't hurting her."

"Yes," I said. "And without him, I wouldn't be here. I couldn't fully use my magic after the creatures got ahold of me."

Fi turned to us. "You didn't mention that."

"I didn't think of it until now." I rubbed at my hands in memory of last night. "It was harder to access my magic after they touched me."

Umbra let out a long, contemplative breath. "This, too, was to be expected. The underworld is the realm of the dead, and the creatures the Shade controls are of death itself."

"Of death?" I repeated. "So she's dead."

"Oh no." A vague, sad smile appeared on Umbra's face. "She is very much alive. But when surrounded by an army of death, you deal in the hand you're given."

Death. Their touch was death.

This was a new wrinkle: I absolutely could not let the creatures touch me. If they did, I wouldn't be able to summon the Spitfire properly. I wouldn't be able to defend myself.

And I wouldn't always have the demon prince to protect me.

The strategy session went on around me while I took this all in. Now that a mission had occurred, the two teams would become one again—ten of us (including Loki) on the missions. Except, after much deliberation, it was decided the floating day benefit would remain.

Each of us would keep two floating days a month, for our sanity.

Fi argued for a tight ship on missions. We would stick close together, no one straying more than a block away. The guards wouldn't just focus on corralling the creatures ahead of us—they would also focus on keeping the core team protected. And two of the watchers would keep an eye on our flanks.

The goal: never allow ourselves to be ambushed.

More chalk drawings appeared on the board, like we were members of a football team. Elijah and Isaiah got heavily involved, suggesting a playbook.

Meanwhile, a vision of the demon prince appeared in my mind. And I focused on one small detail I had forgotten until this moment.

His bare hand, two fingers folding. Which left three straightened fingers.

Three fingers.

It was a message, but I didn't know what it meant.

CHAPTER THIRTY-ONE

Two hours later, we broke for a meal. We had to return in an hour; Umbra would begin teaching us how to use the telepathy spell. And we couldn't afford to go on another rescue without knowing it.

Loki and I came out into the afternoon sunlight, and instead of darting straight for the dining hall, he passed in front of me as I walked.

"Woah." With a hop-skip, I managed to avoid plowing right into him. "Rude much?"

He trotted toward the meadow, tail upright. "This way. We need to talk."

This was unlike my cat. He never used the "we need to talk" line, which made our walk a little terrifying.

When we had arrived in the meadow, he crossed to my favorite tree on the far edge. A flight class was in session on the other side, and he sat on the frozen ground and observed them as he waited for me to arrive.

I stood behind him. "Don't keep me in suspense, now."

He glanced back. "You'll want to sit. Neverwink will hate me if you fall over and injure yourself already."

Could he make this any more foreboding?

I took a seat against the tree, ignoring the cold emanating up through my cloak and skirt. "What is it?"

Loki went on observing the class. "I need to tell you something, but you won't be happy to hear it."

"You can leave the happy part up to me."

"The demon prince." He paused. I had never heard him so serious. "I smelled his scent last night."

"And he smelled like death?"

"No." He gave a long sigh, turned around to face me. "He smelled like someone we know, Clem."

My eyebrows went up as a bird took flight in my chest, batting against my rib cage. "Oh? Don't tell me Lucian is Goodbarrel in disguise."

He didn't even snort. His green eyes glittered in a rarely beautiful way as the sun hit them at a slant. "He bore the same scent as Callum Rathmore."

My eyes closed the moment that name entered the air between us.

It sounded ridiculous, but it also sounded right.

"He couldn't possibly be," I whispered.

"Couldn't he?"

"Callum Rathmore isn't a demon."

"And how can you be sure?"

My eyes opened. "His mother was a witch. Can a witch sire a demon?"

"I don't know, Clementine. But I know what I smelled."

The two parts of me contended for rational dominance.

It was ridiculous. He'd been here at the academy for a whole year, teaching us how to use fire magic. He'd taught me how to control the Spitfire and to fire ride. His father was a professor at a Scottish university. Callum was the center spread in a magazine, a mini-celebrity.

He was too high-profile. And he was too... good.

Yes, he had problems. His mother had been killed. He clearly had a troubled relationship with his father and the government he lived under. But looking back, he'd had my best interests in mind. He'd been harsh but fair. He'd made me the witch I was today.

Hell, he'd even told me he believed *he* was supposed to fulfill the prophecy to defeat the Shade. If Callum Rathmore believed that of himself, how could he possibly be the demon prince?

The other part of me knew it sounded right.

That night outside the gates of Hell, I had seen a man. That man looked like Callum Rathmore, and that was why I'd been terrified of him the first moment I'd seen him outside the academy. My instincts had been right—he was one and the same.

It was how he'd known where to find me when Noir had spooked and taken me outside the academy grounds. Callum had touched me once already, and he could sense where I was.

He could track me anywhere in the world.

In the end, I was still conflicted. Neither side dominated, because I couldn't bring myself to believe that he was a demon. That he would serve such evil. That he was my enemy.

"You look like you've witnessed a death," Loki said. "A gruesome one."

"Maybe I have." The death of who I thought Callum Rathmore was.

"Do you believe me?"

"I don't know." I leaned my head against the tree trunk, already knowing how I felt. "I need to think about it."

His ears twitched as one of the first-years yelled from the far side of the meadow. "You saw what happened when he took off his glove last night."

"Three fingers." I held them up myself, only my index and thumb pulled together.

"He's helping us." Loki licked twice at a paw, as though it was an uncontrollable urge. "But I have no idea what it meant."

"Let's say he is Callum Rathmore." I pulled the page from *Jane Eyre* out of my skirt pocket and unfolded it. "What do three fingers have to do with the trefoil knot?"

Loki stared at the tiny symbol. "Three triangles. Three fingers."

"Umbra suspected Lucian was helping me." I paused. "And she was right. She thought he was the one who infused the leyline with magic back in August, who sent us to Siberia."

Loki straightened. "And?"

"If it was Callum who sent us, then it's another clue related to the trefoil knot." I studied him. "Loki, how fresh does a magical scent have to be for you to sniff it out?"

"Fairly fresh." His tail flicked. "But the amount of magic it would have taken to affect the leyline in that way would be simply massive. It would leave the strongest trace of all." He knew exactly what I was thinking.

I ran a hand over his head, under his jaw, and started scratching. "We need to go back there."

His eyes closed in pleasure as his chin stretched out. "We need to be back in the common room in an hour."

"As if I would skip telepathy training." I stood. "We go after."

"No," he said, eyes opening. "*I* go after. You stay here, on the grounds."

Loki made good on his promise.

I sat in the guardians' common room and practiced Umbra's spell as she had taught it to us. Meanwhile, he went back to London to investigate the spot in the leyline where Aidan and I had encountered the strange magic back in August.

I had just pressed my thumb to Keene's forehead for the third time —unsuccessfully—when Loki entered.

He and I exchanged a look, and I stood. "Be right back," I said to Keene.

"It's my receding hairline, isn't it?" Keene swept a hand over his head, mussing his hair into an unpleasant disarray.

"No, it really isn't."

Loki and I passed into the empty upstairs kitchen. He hopped on the counter as I leaned against it. "Well, I found a faint scent."

My eyebrows went up.

"It was the same." His tail swept across the countertop, back and forth in agitation. "It was the same scent, Clem. It was Rathmore."

I leaned hard against the counter, staring at the kettle on the burner across from me. "You're certain."

"It was him who sent us to Siberia."

"Okay." I tapped my fingers on the counter behind me, all the possible meanings spooling out in my head. "I need to talk to Aidan and Eva."

"Aren't you telepathic yet, fire witch?"

I shot him a look. "Not even close. Liara seems to be getting it, though."

"No surprises there."

"Yeah." She was, after all, just like Umbra in that sense: they both channeled lightning. And she was another person I could trust with this information.

I pushed away from the counter. "Let's go."

We spent another hour at work on the spell, and by the end of it, only Liara and the other fae seemed to have any real sense of it. Despite what Umbra had said about it being a universal spell, evidence proved otherwise.

Except I had an ace up my sleeve: Liara was teaching me things. No doubt I could cajole her into teaching me this, too.

The next morning, I was on my way to the library to meet with Aidan and Eva when I was stopped in the clearing by Ora Frostwish.

"Clementine." She stepped into my path. "How have you been?"

Of course she didn't want to know; she'd only asked it to pretend she had. I knew why she was standing in front of me.

"I've missed your class," I said. "I know. I'm sorry."

One imperious eyebrow rose. "Eight times. You haven't returned to class since winter recess."

I grimaced. "Ah, you know. Guardian things."

"Guardian things." She nodded. "And yet I've heard from others in House Whisper that you've been training with Liara at night."

"More guardian things. She is one, you know."

"Of course. So the two of you practice air magic together under the moonlight."

"Right." I sidestepped her. "I'm meeting someone in the library, and I'm late."

She stepped with me. "I was also notified by my librarian friend that you and Miss Youngblood visited the Kowloon Library in Singapore."

I went rigid. "You know Rosewort?"

"Of course." Her head tilted, blue-black hair gleaming in the early morning light. "It's the largest fae library in the world, and they have books on hexes. For a time it was a second home to me."

"Of course." I pulled my satchel tighter over my shoulder. I wasn't about to explain myself to her. "I really do have to go."

This time, she let me pass. But once I was beyond her, she called out my name with saccharine sweetness.

I glanced over my shoulder.

"If you miss class again this afternoon," she said, "I'll have no choice but to fail you. I'm sure you can understand."

"Sure." I kept walking. "I'll be there."

When I sat down across from Aidan and Eva in the library, I groaned. "I'm going to fail Hexes."

Eva looked up with a cup of tea in hand. "But aren't you training with Liara?"

"Yeah. That's the problem." I set my satchel down with a thud. "She's the only one I can trust. And I've skipped Frostwish's class so much she's grown highly suspicious."

"So just go to class." Aidan pushed the plate of biscuits toward me. "Go to class and let her paralyze you and pretend like you suck."

I picked up a biscuit. "Anyway, it's the least of my worries. I've got news."

They both sat forward, setting down their respective mugs.

I bit into my biscuit, chewed as I contemplated how to deliver this. I decided to be straightforward. To start, I told them about the absolute failure of our last guardian mission—the ambush, the attack, the injuries.

And at the end, I said, "Lucian the prince showed up."

Eva's eyes went wide as grapes. "How did you escape?"

"It was because of him I escaped." I set the remainder of my biscuit down on my plate. "He saved me. And Loki got a good whiff of him as he did. According to him, the demon prince smelled... like Callum Rathmore."

The shock of that one took a while to get over. The two of them peppered me with questions until I finally raised a hand. "There's more. Loki went back to the spot in London where we felt the tremor in the leyline—remnants of Rathmore's magical scent were there, too." I stared at Aidan. "He was the one who sent us to Siberia."

Aidan sat back. "Ho-ly crow."

"Now we need to figure out why." I pulled out the page from *Jane Eyre*. "And what that has to do with the trefoil knot he drew here, and this giant Hrungnir."

Aidan set a finger to his temple, eyes flitting over the page as he considered it all.

"You have the coordinates, don't you?" Eva asked.

He nodded. "But there's nothing out there."

And then it hit me.

"There is one thing we know is out there," I whispered, and pushed my chair back. "But it's not visible to the average eye."

CHAPTER THIRTY-TWO

I found my answer in the globe.

As I stood in front of the massive turning globe in the guardians' tree, I turned it to Siberia and pointed my finger over the coordinates Aidan had given me.

Of course. It had been here all along.

I had noticed during my first visit that the leylines didn't run in straight lines—but I hadn't looked at Siberia.

There, the leylines almost bent at angles around the spot where we'd stood in the tundra. And if you looked at it a certain way, their overlapping seemed to form a triangle.

A leyline triangle.

And at the center of that triangle was where my finger pointed: right at the center of a lake.

Something was out there, and if it was Callum Rathmore who'd sent us to that spot, then he'd been trying to tell me all along.

But couldn't he have just told me in person?

No.

"He has to stay away from me," I whispered.

My finger lowered, eyes unfocusing. When he'd left at the end of the school year, it had been for a reason. Something had changed, or maybe that had been the plan all along—to come to the academy, to leave at the prescribed time.

Why?

If he had given me this many clues—hell, if he'd saved my life—then he was doing everything he could.

He wasn't evil. I couldn't believe he was.

My fingers touched the folded page in my skirt pocket. *Remember yourself.*

What if that had been as much for him as it had been for me? Maybe he was trying to tell me a truth about himself all along.

All I wanted was to step onto that tundra, to figure out the answer to that mystery, but I had to get to Goodbarrel's class. In the midst of everything, I had to be a student.

I left the spinning globe and the trefoil knot of leylines with the knowledge that we would have to return to Siberia. We would have to figure out what was out there.

I suspected I knew exactly what we would find.

When I hit all ten targets on my first try in the Spark common room later that morning, Goodbarrel clapped his hands with a roar. "Oh, well done, Clementine!"

Despite myself, I grinned at his enthusiasm. "Well done even if I'm the last in the class to get it?"

He leaned toward me like we were conspirators, red-blond eyebrows rising. "Which makes it an even larger accomplishment. What we struggle most to achieve is what builds the greatest character in us." He nodded toward the targets. "Now hit them again with your eyes shut."

I set my fingertips alight again, closed my eyes, and flicked my fingers toward the targets. Two hit, eight missed.

He winked at me. "Keep at it."

Meanwhile, Aidan had mastered his marshmallow target practice before winter recess. At the start of the semester he had migrated to a corner of the room, where he sat with folded legs, his birthmark glowing red as he concentrated.

When Goodbarrel went over to him, they had a conversation I

couldn't make out over the sounds of students chattering and practicing. After they'd spoken, Aidan's eyes closed once more.

And for the first time, I saw blue flames burst into life along the outline of his birthmark.

His grandmother had called the everflame a rare gift. Now I knew the birthmark was where the gift emanated from.

I waited until the end of class to approach him, wiping sweat from my brow. "Hey, North."

He blinked his eyes open, the birthmark fading. "Hey."

"I've figured it out."

"You mean Siberia?"

I nodded, crouched in front of him. "The leylines there are angled into the shape of a trefoil knot."

His eyes danced. "How did you discover that?"

"The globe in the guardians' room. Every leyline in the world is depicted there."

He slapped his thigh. "So that's what it was. Every book I looked at was so primitive in its understanding of leylines, every single depiction of them had them in straight, unbroken lines."

I tilted my head. "And what do you suppose is at the center of our trefoil knot?"

"We'll have to find out, won't we?"

"I've got two floating days I can use at the start of the month."

"Two weeks?" He groaned and stood. "Why'd you become a bloody guardian, anyway?"

I stood with him, hauling my satchel over my shoulder. "Oh, you know. The perks of getting to skip class on demand." I waved. "Siberia. Count on it. Until then, my students await."

Twenty minutes later, I sat atop Noir in front of my class of first-years, including the lovely Saoirse, whom I eyed like Aidan's best friend would.

I still wasn't sure if they were a thing. But given the way she'd adored me at the start of the year and now seemed bashful after the Winter Solstice Ball, I had a feeling.

"All right, mortals." I swung Noir around toward the adjoining field.

"Now that you can all get on your horses, it's time to master your gaits."

"We're leaving the paddock?" one of them asked with unmistakable concern.

"We all have to leave the paddock"—I walked Noir through the ajar gate—"if we want to reach the meadow."

"Is this safe?" another asked.

I glanced over my shoulder. "It's safer out here. If you come into the meadow, you may fall off and break a bone. If you don't come to the meadow, I'll stick you in an oven."

They all complied, and I grinned as I turned back around.

It was in that moment I realized I was becoming the fire witch equivalent of Goodbarrel. Not quite so jovial, with a much higher frequency of burn-you-to-cinders jokes. But I was surprised to discover I liked seeing their progress.

I didn't hate teaching. Who'd have thought?

Saoirse rode up alongside me on Siren as we passed into the field. "Professor."

"I'm no professor." I patted Noir's neck. "I'm just your teacher."

"What should I call you, then?"

I glanced at her. "Clementine. That was how I introduced myself when we met, wasn't it?"

She reddened. "Clementine—I know you're friends with Aidan."

So here it was.

"Most of the time. Except when he disappears for days into the Room of the Ancients."

She barreled on. "He and I are…"

"Dating?"

"Not exactly." She paused. "We've been on one date."

"What's your question, Saoirse? I can practically smell it burning the tip of your tongue."

She glanced around to make sure we were out of earshot of the others. "He's not like other guys I've dated. He's harder to read."

"He's not like many people." I paused. "You want to know if he's into you?"

She turned her face away, and I knew I had hit the nail on the head.

"I'll ask him." I smirked at her. "If you can canter on Siren bareback today."

She spun around, mouth open. "But..."

I urged Noir into a canter, pulling away. "Show me how bad you want it, Saoirse!"

Turned out, she really wanted it. That girl was cantering bareback for the first time within ten minutes.

A week later, I tore the rind off an orange as Aidan and I sat on a log, watching Eva practice her dueling with Loki under the afternoon sun.

After an hour of dueling her myself, I was exhausted, and yet Eva had wanted to carry on. She was hellbent on passing the guardian trials, and she was convinced the second trial—the duel—would get her.

To appease her, I had infused Loki with a little fire, and now a flaming cat leapt at her in the glittering white meadow.

Eva threw herself out of the way, wings fluttering as she sent out a blast of air magic to strafe. She was brilliant.

Meanwhile, Aidan had just come as moral support. He'd mostly sat on the log and read a book and watched us.

I offered him a wedge of orange. "Citrus?"

His nose scrunched. "I'll get sticky. No one wants sticky mittens."

I laughed, popped the wedge into my mouth. "You know, I haven't thought about wearing mittens since I found out I was a witch. Nice perk, huh?"

"Yeah, when you can use your flames at will." He sighed, glanced back down at his book. He always found safety in staring at whatever page he was reading.

"So, the everflame." I hesitated, careful with my words. "Any time you use it, you could just... lose control?"

"Yeah."

"But that hasn't happened since we went to see your lovely grandmother."

"That's because I've spent a lot of years getting it under control." He paused. "A lot."

"But you don't fully trust yourself still."

He smoothed the page, another tic of his. "I guess not."

"Which is why you wear mittens instead of using your magic to heat your fingers."

"I guess so." He glanced up at me. "Shouldn't you be off on a guardian mission or something?"

The very thought of the horn—which hadn't sounded since our last disastrous mission—sent chills up me which were entirely unrelated to the weather. "Don't jinx me."

"The rescues are getting farther apart," he said. "That's strange."

"I'm not complaining. And neither are the mages who aren't being kidnapped."

"But everything indicates the Shade is growing in power."

On this beautiful day in the meadow, the last thing I wanted to talk about was the Shade. "So, Saoirse Connelly."

Even at the edges of his scarf, I could see the pink patches as blood rushed to the surface of his neck. "What about her?" he asked too quickly, eyes fixed on me.

"She digs you." My eyebrows went up. "A lot."

He let out a breath, fogging the air between us. "How do you know?"

"She told me. I'm her teacher, after all."

Silence fell, during which I stared at Aidan, waiting for him to spill his guts. And he didn't.

Finally, I elbowed him. "Dish, North."

He shied away like I'd hurt him. "Dish what?"

"Do you like her?"

"Sure. She's very smart." He rubbed at his arm. "But... it doesn't matter."

I sighed. "Do I need to tell you how special and worthy you are?"

"It's not that." His eyes found mine, strangely lidded and shy. "It's the everflame. Surely you can understand."

All at once, the memory of the time I'd lost control in his parents' garden came back to me. The fear in his eyes. The anger I'd felt. How hard it had been to rein the Spitfire in.

I glanced away, toward Eva and Loki, still dueling. "Yeah. I guess that's why the only person I've let myself like since I arrived at this place is completely unattainable."

Aidan gave a small laugh. "Rathmore."

I didn't deny it, but I also didn't confirm it. No point in doing either.

I eyed him. "Going to wear those mittens on our trip to Siberia next week?"

"And why not?" He held both hands out, brown mittens on display. "My mother made them. They're warm. They match my outfit."

"I suppose their dorkiness doesn't bother you."

He flapped a hand. "I'm focused on this prophecy, Clem. Not being attractive, and not Saoirse Connelly. There'll be time for stylish gloves after the Shade's dead."

I sat forward, gripping my knees as I watched Eva. "Let's hope."

CHAPTER THIRTY-THREE

A week later, in the chill of March, we stepped out onto the tundra.

Our boots crunched over snowpack, the air strangely stifling around me. A blinding, clear-as-day sun glared down on us, and Aidan shielded his eyes as he came through the veil. The sun still reflected white-gold off his glasses.

Eva pulled her cloak tight against the cold. Which was, despite that we had come at midday, still biting. "Oh," she said, turning a half-circle. "It's beautiful, isn't it?"

"If you like snow." Aidan folded his arms tight. "And wind."

Loki stepped daintily through, lifting his nose to the air. His whiskers twitched.

"Smell anything?" I asked him.

He turned his face up to me, fur glittering in the sunlight. "Nothing."

I'd asked that question as a bit of a long shot, but it still put a pit in my stomach to hear his answer. The place was beautiful and eerily devoid.

Which made it a good spot to hide the third piece of a dangerous weapon.

"Aidan," I said, "are you sure these are the right coordinates?"

"This is the spot." He gestured ahead of us. "There's the lake we saw."

He was right. This was the exact spot.

So this was where the leylines bent to form the trefoil knot—we stood right in the middle of it. But that still gave us a vast swath to cover; we had to find the location of the chain in a tundra, which seemed to me much harder than a needle in a haystack. You could knock the haystack down. Pull it apart. Shake it until the needle hit the ground.

Out here, you could spend the rest of your life digging and still never find what you sought. I kicked at the snow, testing its hardness. My boot scuffed just a little off the top, but the rest remained hard.

We had to know the exact spot.

I slid the deceiver's rod out of its pocket in my skirt. If we came near, the orichalcum in the rod and key should illuminate. "How do you all feel about an afternoon walk?"

Loki groaned.

I pointed at him. "Don't answer that, you."

Eva bent and swept him up into her arms. "Let's keep each other warm."

I smiled as I turned away, the sound of Loki's purring amplified in the relative silence around us.

We walked toward the lake. When we reached its edge, we found the entirety of it frozen. I tested it with the toe of my boot, pressing down.

Firm. Totally firm.

And before us, it spread glittery and frozen for as far as our eyes could see, until it reached a straight cliff that rose to a tall bluff.

I pointed. "That's a better vantage."

Aidan squinted. "It'll be a long hike."

I stepped out onto the ice. "Not if we head straight for it. I think I see a switchback path up the far side."

"Have you lost your mind?" Aidan said from the bank. "It could break. You could fall right through. You'd freeze before we could get you out."

I stopped, glanced over my shoulder. "I'm a fire witch. You really think, of all the ways I could die, it'll be by freezing?"

"First you'll drown," he went on soberly, "and *then* you'll freeze."

Eva laughed, struck out across the ice with Loki in her arms. "It's quite solid. It isn't even above freezing out here, Aidan."

Aidan hovered on the bank, wringing his mittened hands. His birthmark had reddened, and I realized this was touching a deeper chord for him.

I turned fully around to face him. "Something happened to you as a child, didn't it?"

He began walking alongside the bank, which was his indication he didn't want to talk about it.

"Nearly drowned in the tub?" I called out. "Got dunked too long in the swimming pool by the local bully?"

He shouldered against the wind. "I'll walk around. Meet you both there."

Eva and I exchanged a look, and she shrugged. "He seems pretty set in his decision."

"What do you think happened to him?"

"It wasn't getting dunked." Eva stared after him. "I suspect it was worse. One time we went out to the pond on the academy grounds, and he strayed too close to the water and tripped in. He flailed, screaming murder."

I avoided laughing. "That bad, huh?"

"That bad."

We began walking across the lake together, and the farther we got, the more beautiful it became. An incredible dark blue stretched around us, old cracks in the ice zig-zagging deep into the lake.

But the rod didn't illuminate.

When we had reached the middle, I raised my eyes to the bluff. Shielded them. "Eva, do you see a person there?"

She stopped. "I... see something."

We remained where we stood, and the figure at the edge of the bluff didn't move. It was too far away to tell properly if it was just a rock, but we humans were so good at finding ourselves in everything. Our brains saw faces everywhere.

Eva petted Loki. "Whatever it is, it's still not moving."

"Probably a rock." We kept on, and when we reached the far side of the lake, I found I was right: a path switchbacked all the way up the side of the bluff.

Well, someone had been here at some point.

I replaced the rod, which hadn't ever lit up, back in my skirt in preparation for a hike.

"I'll fly ahead." Eva set Loki down beside me. "Check out up top."

Loki and I stared up the side of the cliff as Eva removed her cloak, exposing her wings, and took off straight up.

Then he swatted at me. "Why couldn't you have wings?"

I stepped to the edge of the path. "Because then I'd be perfect in every way. That wouldn't be fair."

He groaned, walking behind me.

When we'd gotten partway up, Eva's voice called out over the bluff's edge. I stared up and saw her lavender hair hanging down like a curtain over her face. "You won't believe it!" she said. "Come on. Faster."

"Way to keep me in suspense, Whitewillow." I gritted my teeth, thighs already burning as I forged my way up the bluff.

When we reached the top, I paused for breath. Loki streamed past me, a black spot in my vision before he disappeared.

Eva took hold of my arm. "Look. It *is* a human." She turned me.

There, at the edge of the bluff, stood an enormous figure carved from rock. A massive stone horse stood beside him, and together they stared out over the lake.

One of his arms was permanently lifted, his index finger pointing straight out.

Aidan was still crossing around the far side of the lake, a small speck along the bank. It would be at least twenty minutes before he got to us.

I circled around the statue. It was old, weather-beaten, but once upon a time someone had carved it with incredible precision.

When I came to the front, I discovered I was not even half its height. The man and his horse stood twelve feet tall, staring out and past me. He had a long beard, a sword sheathed at his hip. He didn't wear a shirt, but he covered his parts with a belt and cloth.

Who was he?

Loki padded with me, sat by my feet. "There's an inscription here."

I crouched. Down at the base, someone had carved lettering I couldn't read into the stone. "Eva?"

She came around, refastening her cloak at her neck. The wind pushed it out toward the lake; here on the bluff, we were totally exposed to the elements. "This thing is so old, some of the horse's tail hair has worn smooth."

I squinted up at her. "How old, you think?"

"I couldn't say. Maybe Aidan would know."

"If he ever gets here." I nodded at the base. "Can you read this?"

She came and stooped beside me. "Not a word."

Well, there went my Faerish theory.

"Clem"—Loki turned to stare over the lake—"what do you suppose he's pointing at?"

I stood, turning with him. "He's pointing to the horizon."

"I know your eyes are far weaker and more myopic than mine, so I'll help you out." Loki upturned his face to the arm casting a shadow over us. "He's pointing at an angle."

From where we stood, I couldn't properly make out anything about the angle of the statue's arm. I had to back up a good twenty feet before I could see what he was talking about.

And he was goddamned right. The arm wasn't horizontal.

The statue was pointing at something *below*.

I came back to the edge of the bluff, where Loki and Eva still stood. "He's pointing at the lake."

Now it was obvious. The finger angled downward.

"Why"—Aidan sounded completely defeated and breathless—"would someone put this thing all the way up here?"

"Welcome to the party." I gestured him over. "We need your translation services."

Aidan trudged over, his cheeks red. He looked more irritated than

I'd ever seen him—until he finally turned around to observe the statue. "Ho-ly hell." His historian's fascination had engaged. All annoyance evaporated.

"He's pointing toward the lake." I nodded at my cat. "Credit goes to Loki."

Aidan stepped toward the statue, raised a hand and set it to the thigh. "The lake, huh?"

"And there's an inscription at the base." Eva pointed. "Not in Faerish."

Aidan made a circuit around the statue before coming to the inscription. He adjusted his glasses, knelt in the snow, and stared at it for a long time. He kept mumbling things, his finger trailing along the letters.

"Well?" I said finally. "Can you read it?"

"Yes," he said. "Barely."

Eva came close. "What language is it?"

"It's the mages' language." He stood. "A dead language that hasn't been used since before the Battle of the Ages."

"The mages' language?" I repeated.

When he turned to me, I caught a glint of something in his eyes. "It's like our equivalent of Latin. My grandmother taught it to me as a boy to help read some old texts."

"And what does it say?"

His breath crystallized as he let it go. "'On this lake is where Hrungnir battled Odin—and died. And—'"

I pointed. "That's Hrungnir?"

"And his horse."

This was no coincidence. Except the inscription was so dull, so devoid of hints.

"But"—I gestured to his face—"look at that expression. He's totally full of secrets. There's way more here."

Aidan shot me a look. "I hadn't finished." He turned to me in full. "Someone defaced the statue. They added a second inscription beneath the original." The tenor of Aidan's voice had changed. A nervous quaver had entered, which told me what he was about to say was the most important part of all.

This time I waited.

He closed his eyes a moment, opened them as though to bolster himself. "'The chain cannot move. It cannot see. But as the summer solstice nears, the world becomes light.'"

I stood frozen. Then my eyes lifted to the arm, following it out toward the hand. And then I followed the index finger's angle down toward the lake.

When I stepped out to the edge of the bluff, Aidan and Eva stepped up beside me.

The chain couldn't move because it was frozen in place.

It couldn't see because it was buried at the bottom of the lake.

And when the summer solstice came, the ice would melt away. The world would become light.

"So it's in the lake." My hands itched to make fire, to begin burning. "It's down there."

"It's down there," Aidan said. "And whoever commissioned this statue knew about the prophecy."

Eva peered over. "How deep is the lake?"

Loki peered with her. "Deep."

"We have to wait until summer." My hands went on itching. I was tempted to burn straight through the ice. "We have to wait until the lake unfreezes."

Aidan surprised me by asking, "But why not use your fire?"

That made my fingers twitch. "Because if all it took was fire, it would be too easy. You remember what the prophecy said: 'a hex will tether the cursed chain.'"

Aidan snapped his fingers. "Three."

We all glanced over at him. "Three?" Eva said.

"This is an incredible point of power." He pointed around us. "Three leylines surround us. Do you know how hard it is to cast a spell with this much power in the air?"

I made a face at him. "Should it be easier?"

"You'd think." He looked almost giddy. "But past a certain point, the power becomes stifling. Three of them surrounding this place means their power is pressing against each other. It's a massive amount of natural magic that your average spell won't be able to penetrate. Think of it like a cloud."

Now I got it.

Three interlocking triangles formed the trefoil knot. The demon prince had shown me three fingers.

No simple hex would bring out the chain. It had to be massively powerful. It had to be from three sides to press back the cloud of magic.

"I don't just have to cast the likeness deception to retrieve the chain." I stared down at the ice. "I have to summon *two more* of myself to cast it."

I didn't know if that was even possible. But if it were, I knew exactly who I needed to teach it to me.

CHAPTER THIRTY-FOUR

"Two deceptions?" Liara folded her arms under the moonlight. Beside us, a frog croaked out over the academy's pond with rhythmic consistency. "I don't even know if that's possible."

"If one, why not two?" I removed the deceiver's rod, held it up. "Especially since I have this."

Liara eyed the rod. "You said it allowed you to cast the hex before you even knew what you were doing."

"That's right." I gave it an irreverent twirl. "So what if I cast the hex while holding the rod?"

She shrugged, unfolded her arms. "It's worth trying. And we're out of time to think up other solutions."

That was putting it lightly.

I pointed the rod at her. "I always knew I liked you, Youngblood. Even when you tried to bully me."

She scoffed, eyes glinting. "I wasn't bullying you. I was protecting the world from an evil witch."

"You did a shit job of it, didn't you?"

"Yeah, especially when those wisps came out to attack me." She paused. "I never did understand why."

Oh, that.

I twirled the rod again, which I now realized meant I was a little nervous. "Rathmore told me the wisps were servants of the Shade. They contain the lobotomized souls of evil mages from centuries past."

Her eyebrows went up. "But they saved *you*."

"She was a fire witch. I'm a fire witch. They couldn't tell the difference."

She nodded slowly. "Which is why they gave you the key. But... if they protected you once, why don't they protect you now?"

"I don't know. Because Umbra keeps them in her office and the library?"

"You should be able to control them, shouldn't you?"

I had never thought about that. But now wasn't the time to be adding another job to the list; we only had a few weeks left.

I straightened. "It's double-hex time."

Liara swept a hand out. "I'm waiting."

"*Mealladh coltas*," I murmured, closing my eyes and clenching the rod tight. When I opened my eyes, only one of myself stood before me.

Maybe I had to say it twice.

I said the phrase again, but still only one apparition stood staring back at me.

Past my likeness, Liara tilted her head to meet eyes. "Your pronunciation's gotten better."

"But there's still a problem." I stared at the illusion, who stared back at me with a wide-open, innocent face. "She won't double."

"It might not be possible," Liara offered. "You're in uncharted territory, Clem. Or at least unrecorded."

Unrecorded was the key word. Who knew what Raven Murkwood —if she were the Shade—had accomplished? Much of it was lost to history, but you didn't rule the world without immense power.

I had a feeling about this.

If the hex needed to be delivered from three sides of the rod, only one person could do that. It had to be a fire witch, but how could you ever bring three fire witches together?

I was the last witch, of fire or air. The others were gone from the world. Which meant I needed the likeness deception to duplicate. I needed it twice.

Maybe that was the idea. Maybe the mage who'd sundered the weapon and buried its pieces set these requirements for their unearthing in the hope they would be nearly impossible. Then no one would ever reassemble the Backbiter, and the world would be free of its gargantuan magic.

Still, the feeling remained as I slid my thumb over the deceiver's rod. Given everything else that had happened to me to obtain the key and the rod, this was possible.

But I had no idea how, and the more I stood here deliberating on it, the more frustrated I became.

That was always what preceded my decisions to screw around. Frustration.

I silently encouraged my likeness to turn around and face Liara, which she did. Then to extend her arms, hands dangling from wrists, and to say, "Fae brains are *delicious*."

Liara rolled her eyes. "Zombies don't make syllables."

I made my apparition groan and shamble, which had no effect on the fae except to annoy her. A moment later my likeness walked right through Liara, fell forward into the lake, and disappeared as she hit the water.

Liara glanced behind her. "I'll say this in your favor: that's more control than I read was possible."

I brushed invisible dust off one shoulder. "Wait until you see my vampire impression. I'm a straight-up Christopher Lee."

She turned back around, eyebrows raising. "Clem."

"What, you don't like old vampires? What about sparkly ones?"

She scrunched her face, batted my question away. "Who cares about vampires? Resummon the likeness."

I bobbed the rod like a wizard's wand and said the fae phrase. As I did, my likeness appeared next to Liara with similarly folded arms and a scowl on her face.

Liara glanced left. "Cute."

"You have to admit I do a pretty good impression of you. Pay me five bucks, and I'll have her follow you around giving you praise whenever you snap your fingers."

She stepped away from the apparition, and I tried not to laugh; she was so easy to goad. "Tell it to say the phrase."

"Tell it to..." Then, as the implications processed, I nearly dropped the rod. Blinked wide at her.

Liara Youngblood was a true genius.

But instead of giving her the satisfaction of saying that aloud, I closed my eyes and imagined my likeness speaking the hex. My lips even moved, the words coming silently as I did so.

And as I did, I heard my own voice from six feet away, the murmured fae words coming back to me in real sound.

"Clem," Liara whispered, "open your eyes."

When I did, two of me gazed back at me. One was much fainter than the other, nearly transparent. She was a faint simulacrum, but she was better than nothing at all.

But now I knew it was possible. My likeness had summoned another likeness.

And I knew what I had to do. As long as the horn didn't sound, I had to prepare myself to retrieve the chain.

Time began to move quickly after that.

Nights I trained in the likeness deception with Liara, and in the daytime I pretended to struggle to learn the paralysis hex with Frostwish. She paralyzed me so often I had begun to resist it sometimes, which made her deliciously upset.

All the while, the horn remained silent again, and I focused on what I could control.

The prophecy. The chain. My own power.

CHAPTER THIRTY-FIVE

Three weeks later, I was called on again.

Winter had broken, and we were in the early days of spring. I stood in the meadow with Ora Frostwish, who—after I'd resisted her paralysis hex a second time in a row—insisted I attempt the likeness deception.

"But, Professor..." I began in a perfect-pitch whine.

"No more excuses." Her eyes had gone flinty. "You've been training with Liara Youngblood—gods know how she learned hexes. I suppose it all began in the Kowloon Library when you two broke in."

She was onto me. She was a fae I couldn't trust, and she had seen me with the Shade's weapon. Now she was calling my bluff.

I *knew* I had sensed someone in the trees the other night when Liara and I were training.

I didn't speak. Times like this, I knew speaking would only incriminate me. And I knew she wasn't going to let up, so I finally acquiesced.

When I closed my eyes, the meadow was filled with the low blast of the horn. It sounded over the grounds, raising every hair along my spine straight up to my scalp.

My eyes opened.

I had been saved. In the worst way, but still.

When I turned to Frostwish, her lips had fallen into a frown. "No rest for the weary." I backed my way through the meadow. "I'll be back as soon as I can."

"You won't be back within the hour." She waved me on. "Return tomorrow."

I turned away.

"Clementine," she called out.

When I glanced over my shoulder, she hadn't moved.

"Gods' speed to you, and safety." She paused. "It's an old Faerish saying."

I stared at her a second longer before I fell into a jog back toward the stables. Her wish for my well-being had been delivered in about the same way I'd tell someone to die in a fire.

And I would know—I had said it a few times.

I put her out of mind. Nothing mattered more in this moment than getting on Noir's back and making for the leyline outside the grounds.

As I came to the clearing, a small black form with tail upright crossed paths with me, began jogging alongside.

"Good timing," I said down to him.

Loki huffed. "The worst timing. I was woken from my afternoon nap."

Oahu. One boy, thirteen, Umbra's voice murmured into my mind, followed by the brief image of a long tree-lined road, leaves swaying, a moon half-obscured by clouds.

In the next second, the image was gone. "Saw it, Loki?"

"Yeah. We're going someplace warm." He leapt onto the half-door of the stables. "Finally." Then he disappeared inside.

When I opened the door, Fi and Mishka were already inside.

Once again, those two had beaten me to the punch. Someday I would be as quick as them.

The moment I entered, Mishka came forward, pressed her thumb to my forehead. I felt a brief moisture from her water magic, and then the connection.

The tiniest smile appeared on her face as she spoke into my mind. *Don't burn me.*

I pressed my own thumb to her forehead, incanting the spell in my mind with a pale flicker of flame. And then she was gone, headed to her horse's stall.

I found Fi saddling Siren. She came to the stall door, and we pressed our thumbs to one another's heads. After several weeks of practice, none of us had to attempt it twice any longer.

Loki sat on Noir's stall door, watching me. His eyes flicked to Akelan as he came into the stables, and the two of us came at each other with raised thumbs. When we touched, I felt a strange, electric synchronicity in the stables; three other minds were capable of speaking into mine.

Siren's hooves came out over the aisle, followed by Fi's voice in my head. *The fae will come to you.*

I brought Noir out, mounting him as Akelan and Mishka went on saddling in their stalls. A second later, Loki leapt from the stall door, landing on my shoulder.

We rode out after Fi, turning sharply in the paddock and leaving through the gate toward the clearing. As we passed through the grounds, Keene appeared ahead of me, flying straight at us.

He slowed enough to keep pace with Noir's canter, flying backward, his thumb going out to my forehead. I did the same with him, and a moment later, the two of us were connected.

As we rode out, the other fae flew by—Circe, Isaiah, Elijah, Liara—and each of their thumbs had touched my forehead by the time we arrived at the leyline.

Fi was already there. *We're starting in diamond formation.*

The diamond formation. That put Mishka and me—the two ground chasers—in the center, Fi and Akelan at each side, and the fae at fore and aft above us.

I nodded.

Once everyone had arrived, Liara darted forward and parted the veil for all of us. Elijah and Isaiah, the forward point of the diamond, went through first. Then Mishka and me, followed by the others.

We came into a balmy night on the exact road Umbra had shown us, the horses' hooves clattering over asphalt. A soft, fragrant breeze pressed my hair back, and in a heady moment I realized I had fulfilled one of my sister's dreams.

Tamzin had a childhood dream of going to Hawaii. She'd wanted to surf.

If only she had known she was a witch like me, she would have been able to travel here with a simple slice of the hand.

I squeezed my eyes shut, blocking out the old pain. When I opened them, I was surrounded by the other guardians. It was time to rescue a mage.

"Clem," Loki said, claws digging in.

"What is it?"

"The Shade's creatures are not far ahead of us." His nose sniffed the air. He turned on my shoulder, back arching. "And not far behind us."

I shouted one word into everyone's head: *Move.*

I urged Noir into a canter down the road, and the others followed. Soon enough Fi and Akelan were at either side of Mishka and me, the fae in front of and behind us.

Clem, what is it? Fi asked.

I pushed Noir into a gallop. *Loki says we're followed.*

Circe, with me, Fi said at once. *We'll hold them off. The rest of you forge ahead.*

I glanced over my shoulder. Fi and Circe dropped back, and as they did, I spotted the creatures.

Two of them on all fours, running along the road not a hundred feet behind us. As though they'd planted themselves at the leyline. As though they'd known we would come.

Fi's open hand shot out behind her, and she raised a wall of earth. A moment later, the creatures climbed over it. One was knocked away by Circe's blast of air, but their attack hadn't been coordinated enough to stop either one of them.

But it wasn't my job to interfere with their protection.

I had to chase.

I leaned close to Noir's neck, squinting down the length of road until it curved around a tall, tree-covered slope. When we passed around the curve, three came into view ahead, two of them on all fours and the one in the middle running like a bipedal creature.

And as I stared, I saw why.

It carried a person. I could see his white shirt flapping in the breeze.

Spotted them, Liara's voice said into my head. *Three. Middle one's carrying the boy.*

Go for it, Fi said. *Mishka and Clem, if she misses, be ready.*

Liara raced ahead, a streak over the road in the moonlight. She half-disappeared for ten agonizing seconds, and then a bolt of her lightning illuminated the road and the creatures, nearly blinding me.

And it hit a tree, setting it on fire.

She'd missed.

They're headed to the ocean, Liara said. *Clem, Mishka, you've got maybe a minute.*

We won't make it, Mishka said. *Not with two of them chasing us.*

As if a testament, the earth rumbled behind us, and I looked back just in time to see Fi attempt to entrap one of the creatures by grabbing its leg with the earth. It leapt over the reaching ground, throwing itself at Siren.

The horse shied, whinnying as it skirted sideways, nearly throwing Fi. She managed to keep on the horse, but now she was the one being chased.

Defend Fi, Elijah said, slowing above me. *Fall back.*

No.

I wasn't going to fail again. Not with the little boy still in sight, his white shirt like a beacon in the night.

"What do you think, Loki?" I whispered. "Turn back?"

"No." He pressed close to my neck. "We can save him."

I knew there was a reason I loved that cat.

Mishka, I said. *Keep with me.*

No, Clem. She was already slowing Minibar. *You heard Elijah. Fall back.*

She disappeared behind me, and then it was just me, Loki, and Noir galloping toward the ocean-bound road. If it was just me and my fire magic, then I couldn't kill the creatures. But maybe I could knock the middle one off his feet, get the boy free of them long enough to save him—

Faster, fire witch, a voice said into my head.

My eyes lifted, and above me, Liara flew alongside. Lightning crackled along her fingertips. *Are we doing this or what?*

Of anyone, I'd never have thought it would be Liara Youngblood who'd be by my side on this Hawaiian road. But life never gave you the people you expected, or even wanted. It gave you the people you needed.

My mouth set, and my fingers tightened in Noir's mane. We were closing on the creatures. *I've got an idea. Wait for my call.*

Better be brilliant. She kept pace with me. *You've got thirty seconds.*

When you see me standing in the road, I said, *blast the middle one.*

I could feel her staring at me as she flew beside us. I knew if I looked up, confusion would be written across her face. But I didn't have time to explain.

I reached one hand out, slipping it into the tangibly manipulated space inside my cloak. When I retrieved the deceiver's rod and held it in my hand, I knew I could pull this off.

We'd practiced, and I was ready.

For the first time in goddamn years, we weren't going to let them take a life.

My eyes went lidded as I spoke the words for the deception, just as I had hundreds of times by the pond.

And up ahead, my likeness appeared in the center of the road. She faced back at the creatures. When I lifted my own arm, pointing the rod, she raised her arm, pointing.

Flames lit on my fingers, and flames lit on her fingers.

Liara gasped, and the creatures ahead of us slowed. Not a lot, but enough.

Now, I shouted to Liara. *Don't miss.*

In the same moment, three spears of magic shot toward the center creature.

The flames from my hand.

My likenesses's fake flames from the front.

Liara's crackling lightning.

They converged on the middle creature, striking him in the back. I couldn't tell if we'd hit the boy—god, that would make this all for nothing—but as the flames dissipated, Liara raced ahead.

The boy's alone in the road, she said.

Meanwhile, my eyes were still seared. I slowed Noir until we spotted the white shirt in the road. We came to a stuttering halt next to him and Liara, who knelt by him.

She looked up at me, eyes glassy. "He's alive."

My hand began to shake, my fingers still tight around the rod, emotion tightening my chest. After a year of this—of preparation and failure and practice and more failure and exhaustion and grief—we had done it.

We'd saved a life.

CHAPTER THIRTY-SIX

The next day during our celebrations, a drunk Circe swayed toward me in the guardians' common room. She raised her fluted glass, waiting for me to clink mine with hers. When I did, a smile graced her face. "Clementine Cole. No offense, but I never thought it would be a fire witch who'd bring us our first successful rescue in years."

Around us, the other guardians laughed, chattered, all of them either buzzed or on the other side of inebriated. Mishka dug into a plate of baklava as she and Loki meowed at each other. Elijah and Isaiah horsed around in front of the fireplace.

I half-smiled into my drink, taking a sip. "Neither did I."

After we'd managed to take down the creatures who had kidnapped the boy in Hawaii, we were able to circle back around for the ones chasing us. In all, we'd taken down five of them last night.

And still nobody except Liara and Loki fully understood how we'd managed to save him. They were the only ones who'd witnessed the likeness deception.

That was fine. I didn't want anyone else knowing what I was capable of, and I especially didn't want it getting back to Ora Frostwish.

When Liara approached me later, she tilted her head with a small smirk. "You know what that rescue meant, don't you?"

In front of us, Loki rolled onto his back in front of the magical fire, all four paws in the air. "Our job is done?"

She ticked a finger. "Higher expectations. Now that we've had one success, nobody will be happy until we've had more."

"So be it. We were never happy about our failures."

"But we had grown accustomed to them." Her fingernails tapped on her glass. "And now we won't be. You can't use a hex every time, either. Not unless you want the whole academy to know."

I dropped into an armchair. "You really know how to suck all the air right out of a warm, cozy room, don't you, Youngblood?"

She swigged the last of her mead, set her glass on the end table beside me. "Air is my specialty." She turned away, paused to glance back. "Tonight, the pond. We're training."

I leaned my head back, keeping her in view. "No rest for the fire witch."

"Not until you're dead, or she is."

Liara was right: one of us would die. The Shade, or me.

So I showed up at the pond that night, and the night after, and the night after that. I trained in the hexes we knew: paralysis and the likeness deception. I repeated the words so many times they became like a childhood jingle, popping into my head at totally unrelated times.

Liara tried them herself, but found she couldn't manage either. And for a prodigal fae, that sent her into a few hilarious tantrums. Balled fists, pulling at hair, stomping around.

I needed the humor, so I just watched and laughed until she remembered the urgency of what we did.

We had until the summer solstice to perfect my grasp of hexes. It wasn't long at all.

The horn sounded three more times during April, and twice in May. Nearly once a week, and I rode out for every rescue. We got good at defending ourselves from the creatures, but Liara and I were never alone again during a chase, and I couldn't use the likeness deception.

We failed four times. Four lives lost.

But on the fifth time, Liara and I managed to coordinate our magic just right. We saved a teenage girl in Fushan, and suddenly we had become heroes to the entire student body.

It was the last thing I wanted. All the first-years in my riding class became shy around me, afraid to mess up for different reasons. Not because I would bake them in an oven, but because I was a minor celebrity. People looked at me again—not because I was a witch, but because I was a guardian who successfully guarded.

I'd rather be distrusted. It was all I knew.

"Clem," Eva said the night before the first guardian trial in late-May, "do you have a second?"

I'd been sitting in bed reading *Fae Customs and Culture*. I was about to ask her about the "fae rite of goodness," which was some sort of ancient pact. Apparently if a fae swore on the rite, they would be cast aside from the path of goodness for breaking their oath. The author described it as a "death knell" for fae.

When I looked up, Eva's eyes were wide with fear and anxiety. She'd been picking at her face, and she hadn't healed it. A particularly brutal, bloody spot shone under the overhead lamplight.

"I wonder," she said, "if someone like me could become someone like you."

She'd trained for years for this. Ever since she'd come to Shadow's End Academy she'd wanted to be a guardian. And here she was, the fae who'd sacrificed her chances in the first trial last May so I could pass, wondering if she could be like me.

I hardly knew what to say. I had to do this right.

I closed my book. "You do not want to be like me. Do you know how hard it is to get a brush through this frizz?"

She gave a soft laugh as she ran both hands through her unkempt hair, pushing it back. "I don't know if I should enter the trials."

I slipped my feet onto the floor, turning to face her. Set one hand on Loki's back. "My very wise familiar thinks that would be a terrible idea. Know why? Because you're going to pass all three trials. God knows you've trained your tiny tush off."

Loki grumbled in his sleep.

She stared at the floor. "Do you know how many times you've come back with injuries? Bloody and bruised?"

I took a quick mental survey. "Enough for you to notice, I guess."

"Twenty-two times." Her gray eyes met mine. "You've been too busy this year to blink, but I've counted."

Twenty-two times. I hadn't even realized. I sat forward. "This job will bust your ass, Eva. You know that better than me—your parents are guardians. Is that what you're worried about?"

A muscle in her jaw twitched. "I'm afraid, Clem. I'm afraid I'll fail you when you need me. Whether it's on a mission, or when we go to get the chain..."

"The cursed chain? Eva, that's one risk I'm not expecting you to take."

She made a face. "I'm going with you. Unless you'd prefer Liara."

Ah. So even the very best of us were susceptible to jealousy.

I stood, went to sit next to her. My arm went around her shoulders. "If you never do another thing I tell you, do this: enter the first trial tomorrow. You're going to astonish them. And when we go on our first mission as fourth-years, you know what I'll say to Liara?"

"What?"

I jerked one thumb over my shoulder. "You fly back there. Evanora's my sidecar fae."

She burst into melodic laughter. "What does that even mean?"

"You know what it means." I kissed the side of her head, mussed her hair as I stood. "Now sleep, or else Professor Fernwhirl will destroy you in the first trial."

***

The next morning, I rode Noir out into the meadow and met up with the other eight guardians and a group of professors. Loki wasn't allowed to ride with me; it would have been too easy for him to sniff out the other students, giving us an unfair advantage.

So it was just me.

Today I was a hunter, and twenty-nine other students were my prey.

The makeshift stands were full to the brim with students, including Aidan and Loki together. A few of my first-years called out my name as

I passed by. I shot them the evil eye with a pointed finger, and they pretended to be afraid.

I was losing my edge.

When I reached the corner of the meadow, I wasn't at all shocked to discover who was leading the group of hunters.

"If it isn't the uncatchable witch." Fernwhirl stood in the middle of the group with folded arms and a wry expression. "Good of you to join us, Clementine."

I stopped Noir among the others. Mishka, Akelan, and Fi sat atop their horses, and the fae guardians hung together in a cluster. Also present were Frostwish, Goodbarrel on a big bay horse, Quartermistress Farrow atop Minibar, and a professor from House Crest who swirled a globe of water in his hand, his fingers curling around it like a stress ball.

I patted Noir, winked at Fernwhirl. "We wouldn't miss a chance to outrace you again."

Circe snorted behind her hand.

The fae professor seemed to grind her teeth with something like ire or competitiveness. No doubt she remembered well how many times I'd evaded her last May.

Fernwhirl turned to the group. "Remember, all of you: you're forbidden from hunting down anyone you have good feeling toward. Professors, if you see one of your students, alert someone else to do the tagging. Guardians, don't hunt your friends. You'll never catch them."

"And why's that?" I asked.

Fernwhirl glanced at me. "You'll inevitably let them get away. I know Whitewillow's entered the trials, and the gods know you'd never run her down like you need to."

Well, she wasn't wrong.

"Beyond that," Fernwhirl said, "you're welcome to catch the students as you see fit. Ride or fly alone or in groups—it's your choice. But give it your all, for we only want the most capable of our students to join the guardian ranks."

Behind us, voices sounded. Out in the center of the meadow, the trial entrants had gathered around Umbra. She was explaining the rules to them, her hands moving as she described the intricacies of the trial. Even now I remembered it all with skin-prickling clarity.

There was one real rule: Don't be caught.

Among the group, I spotted Saoirse bareback on one of the mares. So *that* was why Aidan was here to watch. I leaned toward Circe, pointed. "See the bareback rider? That's my girl."

"From your class of first-years?"

"That's right. Bareback's the new saddled."

I also saw Eva.

Her lavender hair had been pulled into a tight braid, which she'd wrapped and pinned to her head. She wore dark colors to blend in with the world around her. As she'd dressed this morning, I'd wished I could have done more to help her. I wished I could have picked out places for her to hide, as she and I had done together last year.

But I couldn't. I was forbidden from helping her any more than I had already done.

Faintly, I heard Fernwhirl telling us to scatter into the trees, to prepare for the trial's start.

"Cole," a voice said. When I turned back, Liara hovered in the air in front of me. "Want to do some hunting?" Her lips curled.

I patted Noir's neck. "Sure you can keep up?"

"In the trees, or out in the meadow?" She one-shoulder shrugged. "Either way, we both know who's faster."

"Sure, Youngblood." I started Noir into a trot toward the tree line, and Liara flew alongside. "In fact, how do you feel about a little competition?"

"If you can hope to provide any."

We came into the shade of the trees, passed far enough through them that we weren't visible from the meadow before I turned Noir back around. "We press our thumbs to each other's foreheads. Every time we tag someone, we call it out. If I win, you have to flash Frostwish in the Whisper common room. And I don't mean with your lightning."

She snorted. "So banal." Then, "If *I* win, then the moment before you kill the Shade, you have to say, 'Liara Youngblood sends her regards, bitch.'"

I nodded slowly, impressed. "You do know how to play the long game."

Her eyes darkened with intent. "So you agree to my terms?"

"If you agree to mine."

"Fine." She flew to my side, lifted her thumb. When she pressed it to my forehead, she whispered into my head, *Prepare to lose.*

I pressed my own thumb to her forehead. *You forget I've got one advantage.*

And what's that?

As Umbra drove her staff into the center of the meadow and lightning cracked from the sky straight down, I pressed my heels into Noir's side. *This horse.*

We burst from the tree line at a gallop, so many juicy targets scattering. Horses and fae rushed in every direction. I caught a glimpse of Eva darting southward.

Fly, fae, fly.

We raced on another vector, toward the nearest cluster of horses and fae. As soon as they saw me, panic laced the air, and I let out a manic cackle. The meadow was my purview.

One hand went up, fire sprouting on the tips of five fingers, and I flung it at the departing backs of two riders and three fae.

Three of my shots missed, but I did get one rider and one fae. The rider's shirt caught on fire, and he scrambled to pat the sleeve out as he slowed his horse to a walk.

The headmistress's harsh reprimand echoed through the meadow, "No fire, Clementine!"

I called out an apology; in my glee, I'd forgotten my fire burned right through Umbra's enchantments.

Two, I said to Liara.

You're kidding. There hasn't even been time to tag two.

Maybe for you. I was already galloping Noir toward the eastern tree line, where I had seen three juicy targets disappear amongst the trunks and foliage.

I could do this every day.

CHAPTER THIRTY-SEVEN

At the end of the hour, I rode a tired Noir into the meadow when Umbra's lightning cracked, sounding the trial's finish.

I'd tagged five students—four riders, one fae. And during the whole hour, I never saw Eva or Saoirse. All the better; I didn't want to.

Those who remained came from all sides. The guardians, the professors, and the students who'd passed, all headed toward Umbra.

I counted eight students who'd survived.

And among them was Evanora Whitewillow.

Her hair had been pulled loose, her braid hanging long and strangely more elegant down her back. Her cheeks were pink with the blood that still ran hard through her veins, and her chest moved as though she was still out of breath.

When I rode up next to her, her face jerked up as though she hadn't expected to see me. Then she blinked, her eyes soft, her brows drawing together.

I leaned down, reached out my hand. When we clasped fingers, I squeezed. We didn't need to say anything.

Liara and I met eyes as I straightened atop Noir. *Five. Can you top that, Youngblood?* I said into her head.

She wiped invisible dust off her shoulder. *Eleven.*

I stared at her, mouth open. Of twenty-nine entrants, she'd been responsible for eliminating *eleven* of them.

Umbra began naming the students who'd passed; Liara hid her grin behind the back of her hand. When she had finished, a voice called out from across the meadow, "One more!"

It was Goodbarrel, riding his big draft horse alongside a bareback Saoirse Connelly. She had a twig stuck in her ponytail and her horse's head hung low, but Goodbarrel wore an absolutely delighted grin. "A first-year made it through," he bellowed.

From where she sat atop Minibar, Farrow nodded at me. I'd known her long enough now to read everything that look was saying: *You've done good, Clementine.*

Of course, it wasn't the bareback riding. It wasn't that she was my student.

It was Saoirse.

I didn't know at what point I'd begun to believe that a person's capabilities were determined by their own grit and persistence, but I knew now as Saoirse rode up that I would never take any credit for another person's accomplishment.

This was hers and hers alone.

When Umbra had finished speaking to those who had passed the trial, I rode over to Saoirse. "Well, a first-year passed the first trial."

Her cheeks reddened. "It was a fluke."

"No." I jerked my thumb at Liara, who was leaving with the other guardians. "If you weren't better, she would have caught you. Trust me."

Saoirse glanced her way. Back to me. "I just wanted to thank you. I rode better bareback. My horse was faster, and—"

I raised a hand. "What kind of mage are you, Sor?"

Her face lightened at my nickname. "Earth."

"An earth mage." Noir stamped a foot under me, shifted his weight. "You know, one of our earth guardians is graduating tomorrow. We'll be down to just one." I turned Noir away, looking at her over my shoulder. "Hope you're as good off a horse as you are on one."

"Clementine?" she called.

I brought Noir into a trot, turning him in a circle. "Yeah?"

"Did you talk to him?"

Aidan. She meant Aidan.

"Not that it should matter to you right now"—I brought Noir around to the end of the circle—"but yes. He likes you. He's just got issues. Magical ones."

I left it at that. If she liked him enough, she'd ask the questions she needed to. It was up to him as to whether he'd get over his hangups about the everflame.

That night, Eva, Aidan, Loki and I attended the graduation ceremony in the amphitheater. Most of the student body had shown up, all dressed in their fine school robes. Everyone's house color hung on a sash over their shoulders, including mine—a blood red, of course.

This was my first time. I'd been too preoccupied with my own disdain for ceremonies for the past two years to even consider attending.

Clementine of two years ago had been such a drag.

"Why didn't I tangibly manipulate these," I said as I tripped over my robes and narrowly avoided falling down the amphitheater steps, "to be shorter?"

Loki hopped up onto the stone bench seat as we filed into the row, walking down it with his tail upright. "Because you clearly have a secret death wish by falling."

Eva patted my shoulder as we sat. "It's because you're not wearing heels."

I lifted one foot, observed my boot. "Oh. Right." Set one finger to my mouth for her to keep that hush-hush as I tucked my foot back in under my robes.

That night, Fi Waters and Circe Petalfleck were graduating. I came in support of them, because after all, they were my friends. We'd been guardians together, but they'd also protected me. Fi had once saved my life on a mission.

As the students passed across the stage down below, Umbra tipped her staff, touching them on each shoulder and once on the forehead like a knighting. To each student, she said, "And now, graduate, you pass into the world with a promise to bring the shadows to their end."

To bring the shadows to their end.

So that was the reason for the academy's name. It was a command, an imperative. We had to heed the call.

Eva leaned close to me. "Which guardian do you suppose I'll duel tomorrow?"

I half-shrugged. I was already envisioning the goblet of mead I would drink at the after-party. "Not me. Conflict of interest."

"Thank the gods." She gave a great sigh as the ceremony ended and we fell into clapping. "As long as it's not Liara, I'll be happy."

Eva had to duel Liara.

I returned to the amphitheater the next day for the second trial, this time in jeans and a T-shirt. The school year was over, and I wouldn't wear that skirt and jacket until the clock struck midnight on the first day of classes next August.

I had managed to pass all my classes. Even Hexes with Frostwish, who'd downgraded her expectations of me as the year went on. At the end, she'd told me I could pass if I managed to cast the paralysis hex on her just once.

And when I'd done it, she had given me a begrudging pass. I had managed to evade all her scrutiny, and now I was free of her.

I sat with Eva, Loki, and Aidan as the duels began. Frostwish was overseeing by picking names from the pot, selecting the duelists. Nearby in the amphitheater, Fi and Circe had stuck around for a last hurrah in case they were selected to duel—and in fact, Fi's name was picked from the pot for the first duel of all.

She was to fight Saoirse.

"Earth mage against earth mage," Aidan murmured. "Interesting."

I gave a soft laugh. "That stage'll be a shipwreck by the time they're done."

And it was. The whole thing was splintered, boards split and littering the ground after just a minute. Saoirse put up an admirable fight; she lasted a full minute and a half against Fi, which shocked just about everyone.

But eventually, Fi had caught both Saoirse's legs and knocked her off the stage with an upraised board before Saoirse could react.

I crossed my arms. "She's gonna be one to watch next year."

On my left, Eva's legs jiggled up and down. She was an anxious mess, and I doubted she'd even heard me.

On my right, Aidan had been watching Saoirse the whole time. He kept watching her as she stood, his hands bunching his pants as they had been throughout her duel.

I doubted either of them had heard me, for entirely different reasons.

I scratched Loki under the chin. "You're the only one who pays attention to me."

His eyes closed as his face lifted in pleasure. "Whatever you say. Just keep itching that spot."

Two more duels passed. First Mishka fought a fae—and left her drenched and unable to fly—and then Elijah was placed against a fire mage, whom he clobbered off the stage with brute force.

Then Eva's name was called. And with it, Liara's.

Eva's hand went to my kneecap, and she squeezed with so much force it actually hurt. "Did she say my name?"

I extricated her clamped hand from my knee. "Yes. You'll be fine."

She turned eyes like dinner plates on me. "She'll incinerate me."

I turned to her in full, set both hands on her shoulders. "Evanora, believe in me who believes in you."

She blinked. "What?"

I shoved her upright as Frostwish called her name for a second time. "Go kick her ass. Literally—get behind her, and kick. Tell her it's courtesy of the fire witch."

A dumbfounded Eva threaded her way through the row and down toward the stage where Liara stood already waiting.

Meanwhile, Frostwish had launched into a small monologue in the silence. "Soon, students, summer's height will be upon us. And it will bring the longest days of the year. In some parts of the world, the sun will never set..."

Never set. The sun will never set.

That was when I stopped listening. As Aidan scooted closer to me, a gear in my brain began clicking.

In some parts of the world, the sun would never set.

There would be no witching hour.

And if there was no witching hour during the summer solstice in Siberia, I couldn't retrieve the chain.

As Eva flew onto the stage, I grabbed Aidan's arm and pulled him upright. We moved down our row, started up the steps to leave the amphitheater. All the while, he whisper-complained and asked me if I was crazy.

Loki trotted behind, tail upright, not saying anything—he was used to this kind of behavior.

"Clem," Aidan was saying as we got out into the clearing, "Eva's about to fight…"

When we were alone, I dropped Aidan's arm and turned to him. "Tell me there's a witching hour during the summer solstice at the coordinates you gave me."

Aidan shook his head. "Why does this matter right now? This is Eva's moment."

"Because the riddle may not tell us what we think it tells us." I stepped closer. "And we may be running out of time."

Loki lolled in the grass between us. "Always out of time. Try being a magical cat who's been alive more than three times as long as you—you'll never care about time again."

Aidan sighed, pulled out his phone. After a moment's research, he turned the phone toward me. "It's near the Arctic Circle. There's only daylight in the middle of summer, Clem."

As I stared, I saw he was right. Pure daylight.

I looked up at him. "The riddle's a warning."

"What?"

"We need a witching hour to get the chain. We have just three weeks until the solstice, and every night that passes grows shorter."

Aidan glanced down at the phone as though for confirmation, then back up at me. "I think you may be getting smarter than me, Cole."

"No." I walked slowly back toward the entrance to the amphitheater, gazing down into it. On the stage, Eva and Liara were duking it out. Lightning crackled, and the whole place gusted like the moments before a storm. "I just couldn't stop turning it over in my head."

Two minutes later, Eva won her duel. She evaded Liara's lightning, swept under her arm, swung around behind her, and with one raised boot kicked her straight off the stage.

And then, breathing hard and half-keeled over, her gray eyes lifted. She didn't see me as she looked out over the cheering crowd. I hoped, for the first time, she saw herself.

I hoped she saw herself as I saw her—as she really was.

She was Evanora Whitewillow, and she was destined to become a guardian.

CHAPTER THIRTY-EIGHT

That night, it was agreed: after Eva passed the third trial—which she *would* pass—we would set out to Siberia to retrieve the chain. We would go the following night before the daylight took over as the solstice drew near.

Even then, I was nervous about how much darkness we'd have.

After the second trial, everyone had gathered in the dining hall for a last hurrah. All the remaining professors and students and guardians, everyone chattering about the trials and graduation and what they would do over the summer.

I hadn't even given my summer plans a single moment's thought.

I wanted to leave tonight. But the others—Aidan, Eva, even Loki—insisted I wait, and Eva had been most vociferous of all.

As we sat at a table and discussed the plans, Eva, with an enormous brownie in one hand and a finger pointed at me, said, "You are not going to Russia without me. Promise."

I swilled my goblet. "I'll take you along if you pass the third trial. Fair?"

She took an angry bite of brownie. "Absolutely not, but since I know you won't give me any other choice, I agree to your terms." Then, as she chewed, "This is delicious."

"I know," Liara said as she came by with folded arms, a purple drink in one hand. "I conjured them. What's this about taking Eva with you?"

In a whisper, I explained our plans to Liara, at the end of which she glanced around at all of us and said, as though it were the most obvious thing in the world, "Well, I'm coming."

Before I could respond, Loki, who sat on Aidan's lap at the table, gave a loud meow. Which translated to, "And why don't you people ever conjure me anything?" He really was obsessed with food.

I pointed at my cat. "He's interrupted our very important conversation to let us know he wants milk."

Eva did the honors, conjuring him a metal plate of crisp-looking milk. As I watched him lap at it, I screwed up my mouth. "Liara, are you sure?"

"That's a stupid question. If I wasn't sure about walking into certain danger before I offered to do it, then I would be pretty damn disingenuous, wouldn't I?" Liara's abrasiveness sometimes chafed like sandpaper, and sometimes it was the most endearing thing about her.

At least she said what she meant.

"So be it."

"Now," Eva said to me, "if you don't relax for one night, I'm going to be very cross with you."

My eyebrows went up. "I can't even imagine what that would look like."

She leaned close with unbroken eye contact. "You don't want to know."

So I relaxed. Or attempted to.

I said my goodbyes to Circe, who was off to her home in New Zealand, where she planned to start an organic fae farm. As to what that entailed, she shrugged. "I'll be the first, if you'd believe it. Who knows what goodies will grow from fae magic?"

When Circe left our table, I discovered someone had conjured Loki his favorite food: grilled salmon. I pointed at it. "Now that I think about it, can mages conjure... other things? Non-edibles?"

"Sure," Aidan said, "if you take the conjuration class. It's only offered to fourth- and fifth-years."

"As an elective," Eva added. "But even then it's only offered every other year, because most don't pass Milonakis's entry exam."

"Milonakis and another exam?" I made a face. "Count me out."

"Oh, you'll regret that." Aidan drew his finger over the table. "If you're halfway decent at tangible manipulations, you can combine your conjuration skills with it to craft all sorts of helpful things from the veil."

"Craft them?" Now I was just a little intrigued.

"Sort of like a 3D printer," Aidan said. "But with magic."

That did sound halfway appealing. I tapped my goblet with my fingers. "And what about Umbra's enchantments?"

"What about them?" Liara asked.

"Can they be learned by us plebeians?"

Liara snorted. "If you can get Umbra to teach a class, I'll bow down and call you queen."

"Deal."

Ever since I'd been a girl, I'd had a recurring dream of strange men trying to break into my home. For years I'd been having it, and as a result, I fantasized often about safety. About closing doors between me and people who wanted to hurt me. About wrapping myself in invisibility cloaks. About creating salt circles evil couldn't penetrate.

Umbra's enchantments seemed pretty appealing to twelve-year-old Clementine.

And I also knew when I started fantasizing about safety, I was feeling insecure. I knew exactly what was behind that feeling.

The cursed chain.

I was still antsy, even as all the other students around us were half-drunk and giddy with the year's end. Nothing I'd done this year would matter if I didn't get that chain.

So I did what I could to stave off the nerves, and I downed my whole goblet at once.

"Does that even burn on the way down when you're a fire witch?"

When I lowered my goblet, blonde-haired Fi stood in front of me with a soft smile.

I stared into the empty bottom. "Not a bit. I never even realized why that was until I found out I was a witch."

"Dangerous stuff, then." Her head tilted. "Without the burn to slow you down."

"What are you going to do?" I said. "After this."

"Well, I suppose I'm going to join the non-academy guardians." She paused. "Funny thing, but I never did enjoy the missions. They always made me as anxious as I could be. All the same, I can't see any other path for myself. Do you know what I mean?"

"I think I do." I surveyed the room, the other guardians. "Who'll lead us without Fi Waters, anyway?"

"Hm." She eyed me. "I was thinking you or Liara. Depending on who's willing to fight harder for it."

My chin lowered. "Not one of the upcoming fifth-years?"

"They'd be fine." She gestured at me with her drink. "You two would be brilliant."

"How's it even decided?"

"A vote."

I snorted. "In that case, I'm definitely out."

"You'd be surprised. I was voted in for my cool head. But you and Liara..."

"We're hotheads?"

She smiled in confirmation. "You care. You don't give up. And you've been responsible for the only two proper rescues we've managed in years. The others have noticed."

I wondered if she knew what most often drove me: the persistent, gnawing sense of guilt, and sometimes—in my less proud moments—to prove to myself and others I wasn't that coal-dark seed sitting in the center of me.

If I did good things, I could be good.

My eyes found Liara, who was in the middle of a long conversation with Loki, punctuated by his meows, and I wondered if that was what drove her, too.

***

The next night, Eva entered the third trial along with five other students who had earned the right to step into the Boundless

Labyrinth. She went into the maze in the deep of night, while the rest of us slept, and when I woke up, there she stood in the middle of our dorm room.

She had dirt on her face, her hair was wild, and she was crying.

I threw off my covers, jostling Loki off my chest. "You didn't pass?"

She didn't respond. Her face went into her hand, and she wiped the tears away. "No." Then looked up at me, and a jagged set of emotions appeared on her face. I recognized relief, joy, shock. "People don't always cry when they're unhappy, Clem."

I stood, fully a wreck. "So you passed."

Her smile grew. "I was the first one to escape."

For a moment, I wasn't Clementine at all. I became a girl who wasn't afraid to share her emotions, to let them encourage me to throw my arms around her and haul her off her feet. She screamed, and the two of us danced around a bleary-eyed Loki.

When I set her down, I said, "Welcome to never getting a good night's sleep again, constant grief, and the very, very occasional but muted feeling of success."

She laughed. "Gods, you're dark."

"Better get used to it. It's all I know."

It was strange, but I felt happier for Eva passing than I had when I'd gotten through the trials. I suppose because it had been a different thing entirely for me—I'd retrieved the deceiver's rod, gotten through by cheating—and Eva had done it all by the book.

She deserved it. And now I would have a fae I could trust with my life out there in the night with me.

She sat on her bed. "I've never seen you this…"

"Insane?" Loki offered.

"Happy," Eva finished.

I turned to her, surprised by the words that came to my mouth. "I am happy for you, Eva." And then, in true form, "Or maybe it's just the manic happiness you feel right before you have to go on a life-or-death mission."

Her eyebrows lowered. "We still have to get the chain. For a time, I'd forgotten."

I wished I could have forgotten. Just for one day. For one minute.

But I couldn't.

I dropped onto my own bed, my heart still beating hard. "If you're coming tonight, you should sleep. I'll need you rested."

"If?" She kicked off her shoes. "*When*, Clem. I may have spent my whole life wanting to be a guardian, but do you know why?"

"Because both your parents are guardians and it's the only example that's been set for you, and subconsciously you think if you don't manage it then you'll never live up to familial expectations?"

She half-smiled. "Okay, too real. And maybe. But *consciously*, I did it to protect those I love from the Shade. I wouldn't be any sort of guardian if I wasn't protecting you as you fulfill that prophecy."

I felt that. I felt it right at the center of my chest.

Loki hopped onto my bed, curled back up. "I'm going to drown in sap before I even have a chance to die in the Siberian tundra."

CHAPTER THIRTY-NINE

When Aidan, Loki, and I arrived at the stables that night, a figure stood inside, the aisleway light still on.

"Who..." Aidan began as we opened the half-door, but I already knew.

As we stepped inside, the quartermistress came out of the tack room, wiping her hands.

If anyone would be here at ten in the evening, it would be Quartermistress Farrow.

She eyed the two of us. "Late night."

"Same for you." I started toward Noir's stall. "We need two horses. Aidan, which one do you usually ride?"

"Siren." Farrow remained where she was in the aisle. "I'm glad to help you saddle her, as long as you tell me why you're taking my horse out at night."

I stopped at Noir's half-door. His head came out as he snorted hot air over me.

Aidan met my eyes as he stood in the aisle. The look was obvious: *Should we tell her?*

"It's... complicated," I said to her. "And we don't have much time."

"I'm a quick study." Farrow's arms folded, and she went to stand casually in front of Siren's door. "Give it to me in broad strokes."

Aidan remained silent. He would leave the choice to me.

I turned away from Noir, toward Farrow. Of all the professors here, she was the one I was closest to. The one I trusted. The only one who invited me to her home just because.

But she and Umbra were also close friends, and had been for some decades. They probably told each other most everything.

I had to make a quick decision.

And the fact that floated to mind—the decider—was this: Farrow's best friend as a girl had been a witch.

She was a good woman. She would understand... I hoped.

I took a quick breath. "There's a prophecy."

"A five-hundred-year-old prophecy," Aidan added, now that the choice was made. "Delivered not long after the Shade's banishment."

Farrow's eyebrows rose as she glanced between us. "This really is going to be complicated."

I told her about the prophecy, reciting it, and how I'd come into possession of the liar's key, the deceiver's rod, and now, how Aidan and Liara and Eva and I were going to Siberia to retrieve the cursed chain. Because, I explained, I was going to finish reassembling the weapon, descend into Hell, and kill the Shade.

Farrow took all this in with an unreadable, calm face. At the end, she said, "Do you have any proof?"

I nearly laughed. Of all things, I hadn't expected her to say that. All the same, it was a fair question.

I brought out the rod from my cloak and held it under the light. "Will this do?"

Farrow came forward with slow steps, her eyes on the rod. She glanced up at me. "May I touch it?"

They always asked that. I nodded once.

When Farrow's fingers connected with the rod, she held them there for a moment. Her eyes closed, and she nodded slowly. "I can feel the power in it. Greater than any object I've touched in my long life. Orichalcum?"

"Yes." Aidan stepped forward. "How did you know?"

"The greatest weapons in history are forged from orichalcum." A wry smile appeared. "I know a thing or two about the world beyond these stables."

I gripped the rod, lowering it by my side. "Eva and Liara are waiting for us at the leyline. We have to go now if we're going to get the chain."

"And where is this chain?"

"We believe it's buried under a lake," Aidan said. "And Clem has to raise it."

"Raise it how?" Farrow asked.

"A hex," I said. "One called the likeness deception."

"Hm." She took a contemplative breath. "Siberia, you say. A cold place, even in the summer." She started into the tack room, disappearing from sight.

Aidan and I exchanged a look.

"Does that mean you're letting us take Siren?" I called.

"Saddle the mare, but leave the two horses in their stalls for a moment," Farrow's voice called back. "I'll be out straightaway."

I had no idea what that meant. Neither did Aidan, from the look on his face, but neither of us hesitated. He went straight to the tack room to get Siren's gear. I went into Noir's stall, running a hand over his face, speaking to him in a low voice until Farrow's boots sounded in the aisle.

Her shadow appeared in front of the stall door, and then she was opening it, something clutched in her hand. "Lift his hooves one at a time for me."

I stood by his shoulder, slid my hand down his leg until I reached the hoof. He lifted it automatically. "Is this important?"

"Maybe not, but if you happen to encounter ice, you'll be thanking me for your life." In the half-light, Farrow crouched, hammering something into his shoes. She applied four to the first hoof in under a minute, then we moved on to the next one.

"What are they?" I asked.

"Corks." She didn't look up, just kept working. "But tougher than regular ones. These are magical little things, designed to keep your horse from slipping no matter the terrain."

My chest got tight as I looked down at her. She hadn't even thought twice about helping us. "Farrow…"

She ignored me; she knew I was going to botch an awkward attempt at gratitude. "Clementine, remember what I told you about fire riding."

"Which part?"

"Your hatred." She hammered in the corks on the last hoof, then stood to look at me. "It's not for any faint-hearted witch. It's a dark art, but you may very well need it. If not tonight, then soon. And you know what you need to do."

I had to inhabit my hatred. I had to let the Spitfire consume me.

"Yes."

"Good." She set a hand to my shoulder as she passed toward the stall door. "I hope you'll never need it. But if you do, I have no doubt you'll surpass even Rathmore."

Then she was in the aisle, calling out for Aidan to get Siren's hooves up for the corks.

In the half-light, I wiped a hand over my eyes. I wouldn't forget what Farrow had done for us tonight.

When Farrow was finished, we mounted and headed toward the leyline to meet up with the fae.

Before we passed through the veil, I halted Noir, swung him around toward the group.

Liara and Eva stood next to one another, their wings silver-tipped in the moonlight. Their hair had been pulled tight, wrapped into traditional fae knots at the backs of their heads. They both wore fitted black from chest to toes, like slips in the night. Only Eva's bright hair would give her away.

Beside them, Siren stood tall and straight, Aidan on her back. His cloak lay over her hind end, his glasses reflecting the moonlight. If I could have seen his birthmark, I imagined it would have been a bright red.

"None of you have to be present for this," I said. "You don't have to risk your lives."

A moment passed, and then—

"I don't have to do anything," Eva said, flying a foot into the air as though to punctuate her sentence. "I choose to."

Aidan tightened his grip on Siren's reins. "I'm not letting you go out there alone."

And, finally, "Part the veil, Cole." Liara sounded disdainful. "It's three in the morning, and I'd like to get this chain and be back in bed by no later than four."

So be it.

I dismounted, leaving Loki atop Noir's back. When I crossed to Aidan, I indicated for him to lean down. My thumb went to his forehead, creating the connection between us.

Meanwhile, Liara did the same to Eva. The two of us went around, ensuring a connection between our minds and Eva's and Aidan's.

Finally, Liara and I came to each other. As one, we pressed our thumbs to each other's foreheads, and in the moment she connected with me, I saw her magic floating in the air, a light blue in the moonlight.

Good luck, guardian, I thought into her head.

She didn't speak back. But she nodded at me before she turned away.

I crossed toward the leyline, reached up as high as I could, flattening my fingers until my entire hand made a knife, cutting it down toward the ground.

I didn't dare part it. Not until I was mounted.

When I'd pulled myself onto his back, Eva was already at the veil. "I'll go through first."

Liara moved her aside. "I'm the fastest here. Whatever we find on the other side, I'll deal with it first."

"Can the fae quit bickering so we can just pass through?" Loki asked, climbing onto my shoulder.

Without waiting, Liara tugged the veil aside, her wings starting into motion. She slipped through silently, and Eva caught the veil, holding it open for me and Aidan.

I went through first, from darkness into a strange, silvery light, Noir's hooves crunching over snow.

Snow. There was still snow here, even in June.

Before us, the land spread white to the lake, which reflected the full moon with perfect likeness.

"The lake's still frozen," I whispered.

"Unlucky," Aidan said, riding up beside me.

I flashed him a look. "What do you mean?"

"I mean we got unlucky. It's a cold summer here."

Noir stamped. "So the coldness is a fluke," I said. "We just happened to pick the wrong June solstice."

If the lake was frozen, I couldn't raise the chain. What then?

Liara's voice came into my head: *We're not alone.*

I stiffened atop Noir, eyes immediately drawn over the land surrounding us. The moon afforded a good view, but I only saw open tundra and trees—

Look up, Liara instructed.

My eyes rose, and I saw them standing on the bluff.

A dozen? No, dozens of creatures, looking back down at us, surrounding Hrungnir's statue and speckling the bluff at either side.

The moment I'd spotted them, they began filtering their way down toward the lake, some of them taking the switchback path down toward us.

How had they known?

Somehow, they'd known we would be here. They'd been waiting for us.

And now the truth of the situation was this: the lake was frozen, the Shade's creatures were here, we were outnumbered, and we had failed.

After a whole year preparing for this moment, we had failed before we'd even begun.

We should leave, Liara said into my head. *If they touch us—*

If they touched us, they would sap our power. I knew. I knew how dangerous it was, and yet a deep, ferocious anger had kindled in me. After everything, we couldn't end it this way.

I didn't have another year to waste. I couldn't come for the chain the following summer, not when the Shade's army had grown so quickly in power. By then it would be too late.

Frustration simmered in my gut at a broil, lashing at my insides, and the Spitfire raised its head.

The Spitfire.

"Clem," Aidan was saying from beside me, "do you see, across the lake..."

Eva was talking, too. Loki whispered something into my ear.

I didn't hear any of them. A plan was forming in my mind. Reckless. Dangerous. Explosive. But god, if I wasn't those things, was I even a fire witch at all?

"Aidan," I whispered, "what's the temperature?"

He paused. "What?"

"Tell me the temperature."

"I don't know exactly."

"Guess."

"I'd say... negative three."

"Goddamnit, I only know Fahrenheit. Is it well below freezing?"

"Yes."

My grip on Noir's mane tightened. *I'm going*, I said into all their heads. *Don't follow me.*

"What?" Aidan said, his voice rising. "Clem, don't be ridiculous. There must be twenty of them..."

But I had already squeezed my thighs against Noir's rib cage. The impulse had rocketed from my brain down to my muscles, sent them into motion. The snow cracked under his hooves as he leapt straight into a canter, taking us straight toward the lake.

We hit a gallop not five seconds later, and soon the wind whistled by as I leaned close to Noir's neck.

Someone flew up next to me. Liara.

"What are you doing?" she said aloud.

"I'm getting the chain."

"Clem—"

"I can do it," I said. "If anyone has prepared for this, I have."

She hung by my side a second longer, her wings in terrific motion, before she finally said, "Just remember, you can't die until you kill the Shade."

It was her way of saying *good luck*.

Then she dropped away, leaving me and Noir and Loki alone and racing toward the frozen water.

I wasn't sure if she even understood my plan. I suspected she trusted me either way.

The creatures moved fast. Some had already reached the lake, pure darkness racing on all fours across the ice.

"The ice may not hold us," Loki said in a frantic voice, perched close to my neck. "It may be too thin."

"Jump off, then. Save yourself."

His claws dug in. "If you drown, I'm drowning with my idiot of a human."

I almost laughed. Almost.

But we were about to hit the ice, and then we would find out how thick it really was.

CHAPTER FORTY

oir didn't hesitate. He leapt when he reached the bank's edge, landed on the ice with a clatter of hooves. For a moment we slid, and then he dug in, those corks punching into the ice. He pulled us straight toward the Shade's creatures.

His hooves on the frozen lake sounded like four shots at a go ringing out over the landscape, echoing into nothingness a mile away.

Despite it all, the ice held. It didn't break under our weight.

Loki clung to my shoulder. "What the hell are you doing?"

I kept my eyes on the nearest creatures as they bounded closer. "I'm taunting them."

"Oh, you're taunting them." He let out a wild, careening laugh. "Wonderful."

One of my hands left Noir's mane, and I upturned the palm, a flame coming to life in the center of it. I knew what this must look like to anyone with eyes: a beacon in the night. And I knew now those creatures had eyes somewhere in their heads.

All of them came at us now. Every single one.

We rushed toward the opposite side of the lake, the bluff approaching so fast my breath seemed to freeze in my chest.

We couldn't be touched. I couldn't let them near me.

We flew past two of the creatures, who slid across the ice as they tried—and failed—to pursue us.

As we neared the bluff, I turned Noir at a long, careful angle, taking us along its face as the creatures dropped down all around us, too slow and too ungainly on the ice to properly pursue.

Come on, I thought as I passed them up. *Just a little farther.*

I needed them all behind me. This wouldn't work if I didn't have them on my tail.

As we cleared the bluff, I glanced over my shoulder. The whole group was in pursuit, every last four-legged bastard.

I swallowed, straightening. "Here I come, Rathmore."

My thighs tightened around Noir's rib cage as my left hand lifted away from his mane. I felt the fire in my belly, the rage waiting there as it always had, just beneath the surface of my calm.

I dug down into it, dredging up everything.

My mother and sister, gone.

Six years in the foster system. Unwanted.

My foster father who'd hurt me.

Maury at Corner Grocery Market, his hand on my thigh.

Every person who'd ever hurt me. Who'd betrayed me. Who'd gotten my blood up. They were all there, waiting, a ghostly line of their faces as clear as anything in my mind's eye. I despised them all, even now, even here on the other side of the world.

It wasn't hard to access. It wasn't faint, and I didn't feel the peace I thought I might about the pain in my past—

A wreath of nettles still sat in the center of my chest, piercing me every day. It hurt me so well and often, I could often forget it was there. But it always had been. It had never left me.

When the Spitfire raised its head, I knew the calm I sometimes felt wasn't real. Rational Clem wasn't real. Only the Spitfire existed, and it was all-consuming.

The fire claimed my hands, licked its way up my arms and toward my chest. It consumed me, veiling my vision in blue-white heat as it slid over Loki and on down to my legs.

I was the Spitfire. The Spitfire was me.

Last of all, it touched Noir. And when it hit his black coat, it took like a wildfire. Encompassed him, made us one. He lit up in the course of a single moment, head to tail, and we were a single creature of flame on the ice, unquenchable and mad with heat.

The Spitfire had control. I gave it over willingly.

Behind us, the ice cracked and crashed. It fell away, following our path, every hoofprint a scalding iron, our flames flowing out and down —undeniable, a furnace of heat.

The lake's cold was nothing. We were the dominant element on this tundra.

And, beneath the fury, I recognized how natural this was. How easy it was to sit atop the horse as he galloped, for the two of us to become one, to set the whole world on fire.

And we did. By the time we'd come back around to where we first leapt onto the ice, half of it had crashed away into the lake. The Shade's creatures had fallen with it, disappearing beneath the black water, never raising their heads.

It wasn't enough.

We took a straight course through the middle, our flames demolishing the ice in our path. And only then, cresting the other bank, did I finally find the wherewithal to lower my hands back to the horse's mane.

No, not wherewithal.

I was exhausted.

The flame sputtered, and I half-collapsed against him, Loki rebalancing himself on my shoulder and griping at me all the while.

Noir came to a stuttering halt, breathing hard and hacking, his head lowering.

The Spitfire receded, and Rational Clem—weak and tired and full of normal human concerns—returned.

From the far bank, small voices called. I couldn't make out the words.

I didn't know how long it took before I lifted my head, but Liara was already on the bank next to me by the time I did.

I cracked an eye, and she stood beside me with folded arms. "That was the stupidest thing I've ever seen anyone do."

I found my voice, but words felt strange and foreign. "Are they all gone?"

"Oh, they're gone." She swept a hand out. "And so is everything else."

When I looked out over the lake, I glimpsed Eva flying across it toward us. Aidan rode around on the bank, Siren a speck in the distance.

And in the center, floes of ice bobbed and floated, the smell of burning everywhere. Smoke hung over the lake like a late-summer fog.

I let out a breath, pushing myself upright.

It was time to tether the chain.

Eva landed next to me in a blitz of wings. "Clem, that was incredible."

The anger and heat still tingled in my fingers. "I live to entertain."

Aidan rode up at a gallop, stopping Siren hard. "More will be coming. We have to get out of here."

I shook my head. "We're not done."

Eva rose into the air. "You can't possibly intend to get the chain now. You're exhausted."

I sat up as best I could. "I do intend. This will only take a minute." I hoped.

Liara stared out over the lake. "How will you raise it? There's nowhere for you to stand."

I nodded up the bluff. "From above. Let's hope that's close enough."

Noir climbed the bluff with admirable determination, Loki silently bobbing on my shoulder as Siren followed. The two fae had flown ahead, Eva landing on the horse statue's back, and Liara on Hrungnir's head.

When we crested the bluff, Noir let out a massive, hacking cough, and I slid off his back. One hand slid down his hot, sweaty neck. "Eva, can you heal him?"

She flew down, landed beside Noir. "What about you?"

"I'll be fine. He's the one who did all the work."

She raised her hand. "If he'll accept it."

"He will." My fingers ran over his mane. "He's a different horse than he was."

Eva set one hand to his neck and one to his shoulder. I caught a glimpse of her yellow magic for the first time as I started toward the bluff's edge. It swirled around her and the horse, poppy-yellow on the stark tundra.

Aidan dismounted, came to stand beside me as I stared down at the lake. "We won't have much time."

I glanced over at him. "If they come before I'm finished, will you hold them off?"

"As best I can." He half-smiled at me. "I've perfected the Five-Finger Flick."

I snorted. "You still need to rename that."

Liara landed on my other side. "Remember, you need two of them."

"I remember." I slid my hand into the secret pocket in my cloak, lifted out the deceiver's rod. Its power was palpable under my fingers. "Hex, and hex again."

"That's the gist of it." She slapped me on the back. "Now go. Fast."

I stepped up to the edge, beneath Hrungnir's pointed finger. Closed my eyes. I could feel the magic pressing in from the leylines, a triangulated power squeezing out my own magic.

I pointed the rod down toward the lake. "*Mealladh coltas*," I whispered.

"Louder," Liara said.

"*Mealladh coltas*," I repeated, casting my voice into the air.

When I opened my eyes, my likeness had appeared on my left, staring back at me. I couldn't even see through her.

"It's good," Liara said. "A strong one."

The trick was to do it twice. It was also the challenge.

I closed my eyes again, imagined my likeness speaking the hex.

Nothing happened. She didn't speak.

I had to be louder.

So I imagined her projecting her voice across the tundra. Louder.

Still nothing.

"Clem?" Aidan said.

I raised my free hand for silence. Squeezed my eyes shut harder, my fingers tightening around the rod. I funneled what power I had into it, pressing back against the stifling magic around me.

This time, I imagined my likeness screaming the words.

That worked. She yelled them over the bluff, her voice carrying so far she reached a geographical barrier somewhere far off and echoed back.

My eyes opened. A second likeness stood on my right, also gazing back at me. She wasn't as strong as the first—her semi-transparent form allowed me a view of the lake and tundra beyond—but she should be enough.

Eva's wings sounded behind me as she landed. "Wow. This is what you've been doing all year?"

She had never seen the likeness deception before. Not like this.

"Wait until I raise the chain." I took a long breath. "Then you can be impressed."

"You need to imagine them both saying it as you say it," Liara said. "All three at once. It must be three together."

"Right." I knew what I had to do, and I knew our time was limited. I lifted the rod, pointing it straight down to the center of the lake. Both of my likenesses turned as well, their right hands going out, index fingers pointing at the spot.

I imagined myself as me and as them. All three of us were one.

"*Mealladh coltas*," I yelled out over the lake.

My likenesses yelled the same, but their voices came as an echo of mine, a half-second out of sync.

And nothing happened.

"I expect you need to speak together," Aidan said. "All at once."

Liara nodded. "North is correct."

Behind us, Noir stamped. He often did that when he was anxious to move—or when he sensed something. Or someone.

I swallowed. All three of us had to speak it together.

This time I took a step closer, until the likenesses and I shared space. My left arm ran straight through the torso of the likeness on my left, and my right shoulder touched the other's.

We were joined. I imagined myself as three and one at the same time.

And this time we called out the hex together. We weren't a single beat out of step.

I stared down at the lake, which remained a black, unmoving pool. Not a wave, not a bubble, not a tremor.

"It didn't work," Liara spat. "Why didn't it work?"

A voice sounded from above us, and our faces lifted to discover a fae hovering twenty feet above the bluff.

Blue-black hair. A lithe, feline body. The last person I'd expected to see.

"Because you're still a novice at hexes," Ora Frostwish purred down, "even with half of the Shade's weapon in your possession."

CHAPTER FORTY-ONE

"You followed us," I called out to Frostwish.

Frostwish floated down to our level, still floating over the lake. "Maeve Umbra isn't the only mage powerful enough to sense a ripple of magic. And you, fire witch, created a massive one."

Of course. I had fire ridden across the lake.

"More creatures are converging on this place," Frostwish said. "Many more, and soon."

"If you sensed the ripple," Eva said, "then the headmistress and the guardians should be on the way, too."

Frostwish shook her head. "I told Umbra I would personally come, to spare the guardians their lives. You see, the magic of the leyline is so potent here, they would be practically useless. It's a miracle you managed to summon those two likenesses, Clementine." She paused. "But they won't be enough to raise the chain."

So she knows about the prophecy.

More were coming, and soon. I felt the urgency of that, but I also had questions that needed answering.

"Tell me how you know about the chain."

"One cannot become fascinated by hexes without learning of the Shade—the originator of them." Frostwish tilted her head. "I knew of the weapon and the prophecy before you were born. I read *The Witching World* before you drew breath."

I went stiff; now I was free to finally ask what I'd suspected. "Raven Murkwood. She's..."

"Yes," Frostwish said. "She was the witch who became the Shade."

I'd spent so long half-certain Murkwood was the Shade, but the knowledge practically knocked me over. I had read the Shade's book on witching almost as soon as I'd arrived at the academy. I had memorized long passages of it.

The Shade had taught me how to be a witch.

I pushed my shock aside. Frostwish was speaking again.

"You have one chance to extract the chain," she was saying. "I will imbue your likenesses with my magic, and it will be enough to press back the leylines' power. But we must do it now."

I focused on her. "You'll help us."

Rathmore's words sprang to mind: *Don't trust Ora Frostwish.*

I didn't trust her. I felt even less confidence in her now than I ever had.

"Yes." Her hands clasped at her waist as she hovered before us. "I will."

"Why?"

"I serve the light, as you do. I wish to see the Shade eradicated from the world, and I would help you fulfill the prophecy."

"You spent an entire year teaching me hexes," I said. "And now here we are, needing a hex to raise the chain. That's a stunning coincidence, Frostwish."

Her head tilted. "And why do you suppose I taught you them?"

"So you saw the rod in the forest that day."

"Of course I did. And I knew long before, back when I saw you duel Mariella during the second guardian trial. Your magic was too potent, too powerful, and I knew you had the liar's key."

I finally understood. "So you requested that Umbra allow you to teach me hexes. That was why."

"That was why. Little good it did, with how obstinate you were." She glanced at Liara. "Though it seems you trust a Youngblood more highly. At least she's done you some favor."

I glanced at Liara and Eva, her two protégés in House Whisper.

Liara stared on at Frostwish, scrutinizing her. Meanwhile, Eva met my eyes. She looked uncertain.

Liara? I said into her head.

She paused. *I don't know. I can't read her, but what other choice do we have?*

Then it hit me. We had a guarantee.

I pointed at Frostwish. "Swear your intentions on the fae rite of goodness."

Aidan shot me a look, clearly baffled. *He* was supposed to be the one who knew about things like this.

Frostwish's eyebrows rose. "Oh, little historian. Well done."

I said into my friends' heads: *It's a rite all fae must abide by. If they swear on the rite, they will be cast aside from the path of goodness if they break their oath. It's the worst fate for a fae.*

Smart thinking, Liara said. *For a human.*

"No matter." Frostwish thumped one closed fist over her chest. "I swear my intentions to aid you on the rite of goodness."

I could practically feel our window closing, and it was getting harder to maintain my likenesses. "Good enough for me. Let's get this goddamn chain and go."

Frostwish swept a hand out. "I'll follow your lead."

I took a quick breath, pointing the rod toward the lake. As one, my likenesses did the same with their empty hands.

From where she hovered, Frostwish flicked both hands out, a wave of purple magic flowing toward us. The moment it swept over me and the likenesses, I felt the whole world open up.

Finally, I could breathe. It was as though blankets had been lifted, and the magic flowed as easily as it did when I trained with Liara beside the pond at the academy.

This time, it would work.

"Scream it," Frostwish instructed. "As loud as you can. Give it everything and nothing less, and then you may be worthy of the chain."

I brought as much air as I could into my lungs, filling them until my throat caught. And then I poured out everything I had, leaning forward to yell the words out over the lake, my likenesses doing the same.

As one, all three of us as one.

The hex rushed from the bluff out over the water, carrying through the tundra and disappearing in amongst the trees.

Above us, a cloud passed over the moon, obscuring the brightness of the night. And below us, the lake remained placid and still.

It hadn't worked. It hadn't—

"Wait." Eva rushed to the edge. "Did you see that?"

Aidan and Liara came to either side of her, staring out.

I came last of all, my likenesses disappearing. And when I arrived, the water's surface trembled, rumbled, the center of the lake bubbling.

The bubbling seemed to go on for ages, until finally, as the cloud moved past and the moon's light rushed back over the world, something emerged.

A metal link glinted in the night, the edge of it rising straight up out of the water. Link by link, inch by inch. Up and up it went until ten feet of it hovered above the lake in a vertical line.

The cursed chain.

"Beckon it," Frostwish said. "The chain will come."

I extended the rod out, and the orichalcum chain sensed the nearness of its element. It rose toward me in a swift arc—

And was caught by Frostwish.

The chain went limp the moment her hand wrapped around its middle, hanging long from her grip. As it did, the stifling sensation returned around me, pressing in.

The power of the leylines was back in full force.

I stared at her. "Bring it to me."

She shook her head slowly, side to side. "No."

"But the rite—" Aidan began.

The truth descended on me even as Liara voiced it.

"She's already left the path of goodness," Liara said in a whisper. "She left it long ago. She lied."

Frostwish lifted one end of the chain, her fingers running along it. "Do you know which is the most powerful piece of the weapon, fire witch?"

I gripped the rod hard. "Whichever I'm holding."

"Wrong." She snapped the chain out, and the rod slipped from my grasp with a whistle, rushing toward Frostwish. "It's the largest one."

The rod raced through the air, the chain's end slipping through it and seating itself at the far end—in Frostwish's hand. I heard a mechanism clank into place, and I knew now the chain could not be separated from the rest of the weapon unless it were sundered again by a great mage. And the great mage who'd originally separated the pieces had died five hundred years ago.

Frostwish had taken the chain from me, just like Rathmore had once taken the liar's key. This was different than when Umbra had taken the key, which had returned to me when I'd moved more than six feet away from it. Both Frostwish and Rathmore had overridden the weapon's bind to me.

And I suspected I knew why.

"You serve her," I said. "You serve the Shade."

Frostwish tested the weapon, racing forward and snapping the chain out toward Liara, who ducked away just in time. "Serve? I wouldn't use that word. But she and I are in agreement: this world thrived best under one queen's rule. Her name was Raven Murkwood."

In the distance, I heard the sounds of scuffling over the tundra. When I glanced back, I saw them.

The Shade's creatures. Hundreds of them, rushing from every side.

I raised a hand, expecting it to ignite. But nothing happened.

"You're exhausted, fire witch." She flicked the chain back toward her, hovering closer. "No one—not even a witch—fire rides and burns a fae in the same hour."

I stepped toward Noir. "Aidan, get on Siren."

Behind me, I heard Frostwish whispering. Her words sounded vaguely familiar, but I didn't have time to focus on them.

No response from Aidan.

When I glanced at him, he was frozen on the spot, his face a rictus of grim horror.

The paralysis hex.

I spun. "Eva—"

Her scream ricocheted through the tundra as I spoke, and she dropped to her knees, her wings stretching wide with agony. But there were no wounds on her, nothing obviously wrong...

"It's the agony hex." Liara swept by me, rushing at Frostwish. "She knows them all."

The *agony* hex?

Liara's lightning illuminated the night, a jagged streak that brought Frostwish into relief the moment before the metal links of the chain swung around—faster than any lightning—and slammed into Liara.

"Foolish fae." The chain swung back around, whistling through the air. "If you interfere again, you will die. And I had not wished for that."

My vision had been seared by Liara's lightning, but I still saw her drop. The moment the chain had made contact with her body, she'd fallen like a rock onto the bluff.

Frostwish had hexed her in midair.

Now she writhed. Now she screamed just like Eva.

The agony hex. With the chain, Frostwish could hex three people at once. Maybe more.

I didn't exactly know the power of the chain, but I was beginning to understand. It was cursed, and so it cursed whoever touched it.

In the darkness, I heard the chain come back around. It was making another revolution, and I knew I was next.

A small form landed on my shoulder. Loki. "Mount Noir."

But Eva and Aidan and Liara...

"Get on the horse." His voice was more intense than I had ever heard it. "Get out of the knot. She'll follow."

Then I understood: out of the knot. We had to be outside the leylines' trefoil knot of interference to fight Frostwish and the creatures.

Without the weapon, it was my only chance.

I grabbed Noir's mane, swung myself up onto his back. My thighs squeezed his rib cage, and he started into motion down the bluff, the chain slamming over the ice right behind us.

She had missed.

She believed there was only room for one fire witch in the world. The Shade. Frostwish had taught me hexes so I could raise the cursed chain from the lake, and so she could return it to her mistress.

"She didn't hex me," I breathed.

"Because you're a witch, Clementine," Loki said. "You're a witch who knows the art."

Of course. The more you practiced certain hexes, the greater your resistance to them.

But that didn't mean she couldn't kill me by other means.

"How far does the knot extend?" I said to Loki.

"Let's hope not far."

Ahead of us, the creatures rushed up the bluff. I knew I couldn't fire ride without the weapon, not while we were still inside the knot. Which meant I would have to use old-fashioned means.

I leaned close to Noir's neck, urging him into an all-out gallop as we reached level ground. "Hold on."

"If I held on any tighter, you'd have permanent scars. Now light them up, Clementine."

I was about to object, to tell him I was exhausted, but with him beside me I had the odd sense I wasn't as exhausted as I'd thought.

I lifted one hand as we came closer to the first throng of creatures. Five points of fire appearing on my fingertips on the first try. *Thank you, Goodbarrel.*

I squinted into the darkness, waiting for the right moment. When I flicked my hand, five sparks flew through the air, met the creatures ahead of us, and ignited. It wouldn't kill them, but it knocked them wide of our path.

We swept by the first five creatures, their bodies aflame, and rode deeper into the tundra.

CHAPTER FORTY-TWO

We left a trail of flaming creatures in our wake, Noir weaving and dodging, snorting with the dime-stop movements and exertion.

This was just like Farrow's barrel training, except the barrels would kill us.

"Eleven o'clock," Loki called out.

"I see it." This time my left hand rose as though I carried an invisible spear, and the flames illuminated in my grip as my arm jerked and threw it at the four-legged monster.

It pierced straight through his head, left a flaming hole where his head had been.

It threw him, but didn't stop him. Only two elements together would stop them.

"Is she chasing?" I asked Loki; I didn't dare look over my shoulder.

Ora Frostwish's throat-shredding yell sounded some fifty feet behind me, words spoken in a language I didn't understand. But I got the gist of it.

"Yeah," Loki said. "She's still on you."

We galloped toward a thicket of trees, burst into them so suddenly

I hardly ducked before the pine needles slashed my face. Noir navigated between the trunks as I sat low to his neck.

Loki had crawled inside the neck of my cloak, sat nestled close to me as Noir found his way through the mess of trees. If we survived this, I would never complain about him sleeping on my face again.

If we survived.

In the darkness of the thicket, I saw flashes of the horrific scenes I'd left behind. Liara, Eva, Aidan. The agony hex. Frostwish's feral face. Now, more than ever before, the darkness scared me. I didn't know how I could possibly defeat Frostwish and the Shade's army.

But as we emerged from the thicket and the white tundra came back into view, I knew I only had one choice: to fight. To fight and die, or fight and live.

That was my mother's legacy, too; she hadn't been a wilting flower of a woman. My eyes lifted to the moon in a silent moment of gratitude to the witch who'd raised me before Loki's voice rang through the night.

"Clem, on your left!"

I knew what that meant. Our enemy was close.

When my eyes flicked left, the creature—seething darkness, pressing away light—was already leaping. It was on course to knock me straight off Noir's back.

Fool me twice...

My reaction was automatic. I gripped Noir's neck, slid my weight right with my thighs tight to his rib cage, one foot hooked over his spine as I hung off his side. Loki would hold on because he was a cat. And as the creature launched itself overtop us, a streak through the sky, I heard my cat's yowl as I clung to the galloping horse.

The creature landed on the other side in a tumble, all its momentum in the wrong direction. Noir left him behind in a flurry of churned snowpack.

The moment before I pulled myself up, I glanced back.

Frostwish had emerged from the trees, her arms swept behind her, the rod in one hand and the chain floating through the air in her wake, waiting for her command.

She was so fast. Maybe faster than Liara.

Behind her, a whole legion of the creatures leapt from the trees, a personal army of darkness. She truly belonged to the Shade.

With a grunt, I hauled myself upright, ignoring Loki's claws digging in through my shirt.

"Unho-ly hell," he breathed the moment we were back up. "Clem, she's coming."

"I saw." We had come onto a wide, flat plain—Noir's specialty. "And we're going to lose her."

I ran a hand down Noir's neck in the second before I did something I had never done before: I jabbed my heels into his sides.

Sorry, my man.

He'd felt it. His head jerked, and with a snort, all four legs left the ground in a leap. When we hit the ground, he was moving so fast the wind numbed my cheeks. As fast as during the first guardian trial—

No, faster.

His hooves hardly touched the ground anymore. We moved like air across the plain, his head and neck and spine and tail all a level line, carrying our three souls as fast and far as we could go.

That is, until Frostwish's scream careened into my ears.

"Fire witch!"

My heart burst into a bird's frenzy; I'd heard the malice in those words. When I glanced over my shoulder, Frostwish was a shrinking dot on the plain. She'd stopped, hovering ten feet in the air.

And beneath her, I recognized three forms carried over the shoulders of the Shade's creatures.

Eva, Aidan, and Liara.

"I will kill them," she yelled. "If you don't stop, they'll die tonight. And not fast."

Ahead of me, the plain went on and on, promising safety.

Behind me, the only non-feline friends I'd ever had.

I closed my eyes, fighting back the profoundly human desire to take that path to safety. I wanted it so badly I could taste it like sugar on my tongue, willing me to find the edge of the trefoil knot and escape beyond it.

But my body had already made the choice. I wasn't a creature of instinct anymore—not like I had been for so many years.

I was a guardian. I had sworn to protect them.

I straightened, providing resistance, slowing Noir's gallop.

"Clementine…" Loki said.

Noir dropped to a canter, and then a trot as I swung him around. The moment we reached the farthest point in our arc around, I felt it.

Clear, crisp air. The edge of the knot.

We had made it.

Noir breathed like a bellows as I stopped him on the border of the leyline.

Now that I knew where we had to go, a plan began to outline itself in frenzied flashes in my head. It was a desperate one, but I was good at desperate. It made me hungry.

"Did you feel the edge of the knot, Loki?" I asked as we turned back around.

He sighed. "I suppose not crossing it means you're feeling bold."

"If you want safety, you can have it. It's ten feet behind us."

"You forget one thing," he said as we faced down Frostwish, "I'm a guardian, too."

I trotted Noir forward, his head upright.

"Frostwish," I called out. "Meet me here. Just you and me."

Her laugh broke like ice across the plain. "At the edge of the trefoil knot? I don't think so, fire witch."

My fingers tightened in Noir's mane. So she knew where the knot ended. Of course she did—she'd probably known the chain lay out here for a lot longer than I had. I'd put money on her knowing the lay of the entire land.

Well, there went my plan. Now I would have to improvise.

I took quick stock of what I had at my disposal. My horse, my familiar, my dampened fire magic, and my hexes.

But I also had something else. My connection to Eva, Aidan, and Liara's minds.

I'm coming, I said into Aidan's head. *I'm coming for you. Be ready with your everflame.*

I started Noir forward, toward Frostwish and her small legion of the Shade's creatures. We fell into a trot, his head low in his state of semi-exhaustion. I wouldn't push him harder than he could go—just enough.

I'm coming, I said into Liara's head next. *Be ready with your magic.*

And finally, I said the same to Eva.

None of them responded; none of them could, captive as they were. But I knew they'd heard me.

"Loki," I whispered as we approached, "I need you to do something for me."

"Say it already."

"I need you to create a distraction."

"That means I have to get off and walk, doesn't it?"

"I'm afraid so. I'll need you to keep as many of them occupied as you can."

"Give me your fire, then."

I raised one hand, snapped my thumb and middle finger together. A small flame flickered to life, and I set it under Loki's chin. "Keep your tail on, all right?"

"I'll be exactly as reckless as my witch."

Well, that didn't comfort me any.

Before I sent Noir into a canter, I leaned off his side, allowing Loki down to the ground. He hit the tundra at a run, flames racing along his body, already doubling his size in fire.

When I straightened, I patted Noir's shoulder. "One more time. Then you'll get a long, long rest."

I squeezed his rib cage, and he shifted to a canter. And then, as we neared Frostwish—who remained hovering, the weapon in her grasp, watching me—a gallop.

I removed my hands from his mane as Loki broke away with a growl, leaping toward the nearest creatures.

It was time to test how good I really was at the art of hexing... sans any magic weapon.

I spread my hands out as we galloped, feeling the air over my palms, and called on the Spitfire deep inside me. It was stifled, pressed down, but still there. And as my eyes flicked over my captive friends, its head raised.

That's right. Be angry. Give me your power.

My chest filled with a soft heat, and I knew this was as good as it would get inside the trefoil knot. I spoke the fae words for the likeness deception.

"Mealladh coltas."

Beside me, a flash of red hair appeared atop a galloping black horse. I couldn't even see through her; she appeared as real as me. So that was what I looked like while riding; not half bad.

Together, we rode toward the enemy.

"Well done, my little witch," Frostwish cackled, sweeping the rod and chain out. "But you'll have to do better than that."

With one flick of her free hand, a massive wall of her silver air magic rushed toward me. She was massively empowered by the weapon.

I jerked Noir left, and at the same moment, my likeness jerked right. The two of us crossed paths, and I narrowly avoided Frostwish's magic. Meanwhile, my likeness passed right through it unharmed.

Somewhere to my right, I heard Loki's snarling. Good. As long as he was making a cacophony of noise, I knew he was alive.

Another wall of air magic came at me. My likeness and I crossed paths again as I avoided it, and I could see Eva, Aidan, and Liara clearly now. The creatures held them over their shoulders off to the left of Frostwish, standing in wait.

I made straight for them as my likeness headed for Frostwish. The chain swung out, and when I took a peek over my shoulder, I spotted it swing through my likeness's body. *I guess that means I aced her class.*

Frostwish cursed, spun toward me. But it was too late.

This part I'd have to time just right...

I raised my right hand, flames appearing on three fingertips. I took aim at the creatures—Just like target practice in the common room, Clem—and flicked off three arrows of flame even as I spoke the fae words.

"Pairilis síoraí."

The flames hit the three creatures in the chest, knocking two of them back. The third went rigid with the paralysis hex and collapsed.

In the process, it dropped Liara.

The fae landed on her stomach. One arm wrenched out from beneath her as she half-lifted her face, and a small bolt of her lightning shot out from her fingertips, incinerating the paralyzed creature. It dissipated into nothing, scattering across the snow.

Liara shot a second bolt at the other two creatures, and it passed through one creature's body and into the second one. The creatures, already aflame, staggered and melted into the tundra, leaving only Aidan and Eva on the ground.

I rode to a hard stop next to Aidan, leaned down with a hand out. "Get on."

He gazed up at me, full of exhaustion from his sapped energy.

"Come on, North," Liara called out, pressing up to her knees. "Put your back into it."

He managed to reach one hand out, clasping mine. I yanked him up, and he had enough wherewithal to climb onto Noir's back behind me.

By now Eva was staggering upright, and I turned Noir toward Frostwish and the legion. In the distance, Loki's flame ducked and weaved as he fought on, still distracting at least six of them.

But the bulk—at least thirty—now rushed us.

"Aidan," I began.

He was clutching me for dear life. "Everflame. I know." One hand left my waist, and blue flames appeared in his hand. He shot a blast toward Frostwish, a blue ball racing through the air on course with her pretty head—

And it passed right through her.

"It's a perfect likeness deception," I whispered in the moment before a strange weight pressed in on my skull, and then my body was wracked with excruciating, unending pain.

CHAPTER FORTY-THREE

Pain. A thousand volts of pain, every nerve lighting up from toes to fingertips. I dropped from Noir's back, hit the frozen tundra in a heap. Above me, I saw the chain wrap around Aidan's neck. Blue fire erupted from his hands in a wild spray as he was yanked off Noir's back.

The horse screamed, leapt. Raced forward and disappeared from my small window of sight. I couldn't move to watch him go, couldn't even shift my eyes.

The pain was all-consuming.

Somewhere in me, the part that could form words knew I was under the effects of the agony hex. So this was Frostwish's power with the weapon in her possession, and I had developed no resistance to the agony hex.

It was gargantuan. Heart-stopping. Rage-inducing.

Not just the pain, but what accompanied the pain.

The helplessness, what she'd done to my friends, the knowledge that everything—all I had worked for—would end ingloriously out here in the middle of Siberia.

And I would die in pain.

I could feel it working its tendrils into the deepest parts of me, seeking its way up the ventricles of my heart until it could clamp down on the electric impulse that kept that most crucial organ beating.

It was a sad irony that the last witch in the world would die to a hex cast by a fae. And I would go out on my back, staring up into a strange sky.

I heard my name—Loki had come to my side, pressing against my body, yowling. Somewhere, Aidan screamed; the agony hex again. I couldn't hear Liara or Eva, and the fact that I couldn't hear them was worse.

The chain rattled across the ground, and Frostwish's face appeared above me, her petite frame wracked with adrenaline. I could see it in the fast movement of her chest, in the red in both cheeks. But she also held delight in those dark eyes.

In my periphery, I sensed the Shade's creatures looming. Watching.

"It's the end for you, I'm afraid. I'd hoped you would be sturdier." The chain clinked, and her hand moved to draw the weapon aloft. "And you never even knew what you were. Well, so few of us ever find out the truth about ourselves."

I couldn't even respond. The pain wracked my body until I was as gnarled as an old tree.

I hadn't expected in my last few moments I would hear a drumbeat. Soft, sure, rhythmic. That I would feel its vibrations under me, rumbling through the ground.

Maybe this was my body's way of hallucinating something comforting to distract me from what was to come.

Except Frostwish heard it, too.

Her face jerked up, eyes searching the plain. Her lips parted, and the drumbeat grew. It grew and grew until I understood it wasn't an instrument at all, but a gait.

A horse's gait.

Soon it thundered, filling my ears, and Frostwish turned fully toward the oncoming animal.

"Well, you've come a bit late, haven't you?" she called out. "The party's already ended. I had to do all the—"

Her words ended in a yell. But even that was cut off, because she was forced back by the horse—a black streak in the night—galloping right through the spot where she'd been standing.

The hooves came to a hard stop some twenty feet beyond me. And in the same moment, the pain ended. Frostwish's concentration had been broken.

Aidan stopped screaming, and the world went briefly quiet.

I sucked in air, able to move for myself again. Residual pain shuddered through my body, but I was so grateful to have the use of my hands, I dug my fingers right into the ground and pressed myself up to see something besides the sky.

Frostwish had taken to the sky. Aidan slumped to the ground, fresh out of his own strangulating pain. Eva and Liara were free of their paralysis hexes, and they were staring...

At the horse. A black horse like Noir, but not Noir. This one was bulkier with muscle, taller even than my horse.

A massive man in armor sat on its back, now dismounting. The Shade's creatures had fallen back from him, and when his boots touched the ground, I could swear the layer of frost cracked under him.

Lucian the prince.

"Leave, Clementine," he said, and I knew that voice. It was exactly the voice I'd been wanting to hear for a year.

He pulled off his helmet, black hair coming free, and even in this pale light I recognized those features. The set of that jaw. Those dark eyes and brow.

The demon prince was, and always had been, Callum Rathmore.

In a moment Rathmore's sword sang from its sheath, and he stalked toward Frostwish, still hovering above us.

It was then I became truly aware of my own anger.

Ora Frostwish had hurt me. I'd heard kidney stones were bad, giving birth was bad, but Frostwish's agony hex? I didn't know if I'd ever stop feeling the phantom pain of that minute.

It was like being dismembered one molecule at a time.

I found my feet, swayed on them, kept upright by my fury.

Rathmore was already standing beneath Frostwish, weapon ready. When they fought, everything happened quickly: she slashed out at him with the chain, and he parried. Metal clanged against metal, flashed in the night. She sent a vortex of air at him, and he dispelled it with his fire.

Frostwish had kicked up a terrible wind, and Rathmore laced it with his fire.

When she swung out again, the chain wrapped around the blade. Instead of tugging it from his hands, he yanked *her* toward the ground with one massive roar.

She hit the ground in a heap of wings, the chain clinking as it fell around her.

He brought the two-handed blade up, swung it down as though to split her like a fruit down the center.

But with wild speed, Frostwish's wings were in motion. She pressed off the snow, flew out from under the blow. The Backbiter remained on the ground.

He shifted the swing, clipped her with the flat of his blade in the back. She flew off course, spinning around, pointing at him. "Betrayer. Your father was right about you."

That set off the Shade's creatures. They started into motion toward Rathmore, who set one hand to his sword and ignited the entire length of it with fire. Then he began hacking, the flames flaring in the night as he brought the blade down and down again.

And I?

"Clem—" Eva had flown over to me, her hand going to my arm.

I ignored her. The Spitfire's wrath was in me.

Loki raced beside me, still on fire. "Clementine."

I ignored him, too, started toward the Backbiter still in the snow. When my fingers touched the cold rod, it heated at once, my anger and its power fusing. The chain rattled as I lifted it, and I turned toward the battle. Toward Frostwish, whose magic whipped through the air to fend off Rathmore.

The weapon was what I had come for. Before I left with it, I would make Ora Frostwish feel what she'd done to me.

Liara understood. I sensed her fall in beside me, and a moment later, she said, "I'll keep them off you. Get her."

I kept on toward Frostwish as a bolt of Liara's lightning jetted through the night, disintegrating one of the oncoming creatures.

What I didn't expect was Aidan's everflame. It blasted by me so large and loud, I felt some of my arm hairs singe off. It found its target in a cluster of the creatures, destroying three of them at once.

Apparently subjecting a mage to the pain hex twice in one night makes him mad. Even when he's as anti-violence as Aidan North.

Frostwish lifted into the air as I neared, her eyes lighting on me. "Come on then, fire witch."

Rathmore spun toward me, his blade a whip of flame. "I told you to go!"

He had told Clementine to go.

Not the Spitfire.

Nobody had control over the Spitfire. Not even me.

It was in the moment I fell into a run toward her that I felt it take control for the second time tonight. My chest burst with flame, extending down my arms and legs and right into the weapon in my hand.

Creatures streamed into my path. I flicked the rod, sending the chain aloft and snapping it down. It tore into their bodies like a knife into butter, cleaving them with fire.

They wilted, didn't get back up.

That pressure pushed on my skull again, and this time I knew it for what it was: Frostwish's agony hex. The pain was back.

The Spitfire powered on, pain or no. I staggered forward anyway.

A wave of Frostwish's air magic blasted over me, sending my loose hair back, but I pressed straight through it, bringing the rod around for my next strike. I found wielding it to be as simple as holding a pen.

It felt right in my hand. Especially in the midst of my rage.

I wasn't just mad at Ora Frostwish. I hated her. The blue-black bob cut, the perfect slender neck, those dark, cruel eyes. After what she had done to me, to Eva, to Aidan, to Liara.

She deserved to die.

I passed through a second wave of her magic; it rushed like a breeze over me, didn't even douse the flames a little. God, the Spitfire pulsed with power, and I would use it.

My hand came up, bringing the rod overhead even as Frostwish made to fly from my reach. She was fast—she'd always been fast, ever since I'd seen her rush into Eva during the first guardian trial.

But she wasn't fast enough to evade the chain.

It snaked out, bit her leg in a moment of cruel contact. And I felt the power of the chain, understood what it could do: it hexed what it touched.

Frostwish went as still as a statue, her wings frozen in the paralysis hex. She slipped to the ground, landed with a thump.

I didn't have another thought. The Spitfire lifted my arm again, the chain flashed in the moonlight, and it dragged a line across Frostwish's upturned face. She didn't scream, but I knew if she weren't paralyzed, she would have expressed that pain until her throat went hoarse.

I'd shown her a little bit of what I'd felt.

Now I would show her the full extent of it.

A pair of armored arms wrapped around me, trapping mine against my body, pinned by shaped metal. "No, Clementine."

The Spitfire thrashed, raged. Then I was spun around, found myself staring up at Callum Rathmore, the flames off my body creating shadows over his face. Those tragic, dark eyes stared back at me.

"Remember yourself," he said. "Don't kill her."

Remember myself. The words sounded like another language, odd and pathetic and full of the kind of softness I didn't—couldn't—feel.

And then he was whispering more words—"I am not an angel, and I will not be one till I die"—and the more he spoke, the harder it was not to remember that these were *my* language. That even tonight, I had been someone besides the Spitfire.

His fingers squeezed. "I will be myself."

I will be myself.

I was Clementine Cole, a fire witch, but never a killer.

CHAPTER FORTY-FOUR

As my flames died away, it was just me left. Me and Callum Rathmore, his arms around me in the snow, the two of us breathing in a post-battle rhythmic cadence. The adrenaline was like a drug.

My hands began to shake, the chain tinkling in the night, as I looked up at him. "I was right about you." My voice sounded like it had been pressed through a tiny hole and barely emerged out the other side.

The faintest smile touched his lips. "Which part?"

"You're a demon."

His eyes tracked between mine, an inexpressible and obvious tenderness there I'd never seen before, and coupled with it the absolute enormity of saying all the things he needed to say. Where did he even start?

I read all that in the moment of silence that fell, and then, before he could speak, Aidan appeared next to me, breathless and glowing with blue fire. "We're still surrounded, Cole."

I couldn't break away. So Rathmore did it for me, his hands falling away. "I can't keep them steady long. Maybe a few minutes' more before Frostwish rises."

I didn't know what that meant, but I got the idea.

Around us, the creatures had fallen again into stillness. They watched, stared, some of them as close as ten feet away.

With Frostwish on the ground, Lucian the prince had command.

I turned slowly, found her where I'd left her. She was still under the effects of the paralysis hex, though I hadn't concentrated on it at all. And a massive red gash ran down her cheek, her blood glinting on its way down toward the earth.

It was the chain.

The chain was maintaining the hex. For how long? I couldn't say. I would have removed it if I could have, because in this moment I didn't hate Ora Frostwish. I didn't want her dead. Not like the Spitfire.

I was Rational Clem.

"Frostwish?" I said to him.

"She'll live." He gave her one hard look. "She'll always carry that scar, but she'll live. And she'll slander you. Be prepared for that."

I'd dealt with worse than slander.

Nearby, Eva and Liara leaned on one another, walked over to us. One had a limp—I couldn't tell who, though I'd never seen Liara's face so contorted with pain.

She'd been hurt. Badly.

And yet as she focused on Rathmore, her eyes narrowed with a strange recognition. "You."

He ignored her, sheathing his sword. "She'll send more." *She* was the Shade—that was obvious. His sword scraped along the ground as he retrieved it. "You have to leave now. Get on your horse and ride."

My horse. Noir.

As if he'd heard, I spotted him trotting toward me over the plain. He came to my hand, pressing his nose into my free palm, searching for oats.

Still, I didn't move right away. I just stared at Rathmore, who straightened and turned back to me. His helmet hung from his other hand. "What now?" I said. "You've betrayed her."

"I betrayed her long before tonight." He slid his helmet over his head. "It's your life that matters. You still have one more piece to retrieve."

In a moment, my mind traced all the annals of its knowledge and remembered the name of it: the thief's blade.

"But she'll kill you."

He shook his head. "Not quite yet."

I stepped up to Noir's side, even as Rathmore came to my side, his hands going around my waist as they had the first time we'd met. He lifted me onto the horse's back, and though he hadn't asked, I didn't object.

He looked up at me through the slits in his helmet. "You'll find it in one of the closes in Edinburgh."

"The closes," I echoed as I reached out for Aidan, helping him onto Noir's back.

At the same time, Loki leapt onto my cloak, climbing up onto my shoulder. "Let's go. You can eat cookies and deliberate in the library *later*."

Eva helped Liara onto Siren, who stood not far off, and the two of them mounted. "Clem," Liara said, my name a reprimand from her mouth.

Rathmore set one hand on my forearm; I couldn't tell if it scalded because of his magic, or because it was him. "When you go, you'll find your mother and sister there. Be prepared." And then he took one step toward Noir's hindquarters, gave a bellow so loud the stallion nearly reared as he took off into a canter.

My mother and sister.

He'd said my *mother and sister*.

I swung Noir around toward the wide plain and the end of the trefoil knot I knew lay on the other side. We could pass through the veil there. But my eyes were still on Rathmore as Liara brought Siren around to follow. "They're alive?" I called. "My mother and Tamzin?"

Rathmore didn't answer. He only raised one hand, pointing in the direction of the bluff and the lake.

There, a swarm of creatures poured down the white hill toward us.

He'd been right: the Shade had sent more. Many more.

Around us, the nearest creatures seemed aroused by the arrival of reinforcements. They began to move toward us, sliding past Rathmore. As they did, his sword came free once more to send them back to hell.

I pressed Noir into a gallop in the opposite direction, gesturing to Liara. "This way."

She followed on Siren, and the two horses moved like light across the plain. Soon we were near the edge of the knot, and I gestured ahead. "Liara, can you part it?"

She nodded, lifting herself to a crouch atop Siren's back as Eva slid forward to grip the horse's mane. A moment later, the dark-haired fae launched herself into the air, took off with wings blurring as she raced ahead of us.

She half-disappeared in the darkness ahead, and I squinted to make her out. Behind us, I could see them giving chase, pouring around Rathmore's flaming sword and following us.

Careful, demon prince.

What would happen to him if he was overwhelmed by the Shade's creatures?

Death. I didn't even know what that meant for him.

The pang of that last thought pressed like an iron into my chest, and I kept my eyes on his receding figure just a second longer than I should have.

No, I told myself. *This can't be the last time.*

Even if that was a delusion, I had to believe it or I wouldn't have been able to ride away.

I turned back around, one hand squeezing Aidan's fingers at my waist. "Almost there, North."

Come on, Liara. Part the damn thing.

Then I saw it—blue air magic illuminating the tundra as Liara's hand cut straight down through the veil. She'd started eight feet in the air, and just seconds later, a straight line of blue magic etched its way down to the ground.

She always had been the best at that, but this speed...

"Fast, right?" she called as she turned, waving us forward. She'd pulled the veil aside for the two horses.

We galloped past the edge of the knot, and all at once air came into my lungs, the magic's pressure relieved as Noir raced a second later through the veil and into the darkness of the forest outside the academy.

I brought him to a skidding halt on the grass, turning him in time to see Siren pass through with Eva atop her and Liara flying through last of all.

The moment she was through, she reseamed the veil, closing off the tundra before the creatures could pile through.

And just like that, we were alone in the quiet of the forest.

We all breathed hard, the silence almost ringing in my ears. Liara crouched low to the ground, staring at the earth, and Aidan slumped against my back.

Somehow, we'd survived.

"It still burns," Aidan murmured. "Everywhere."

I knew what he meant. If I paid it any attention, I could feel my nerves burning like they were on fire—my hands, my arms, legs, feet. Everywhere.

That was the power of Frostwish's agony hex. Or maybe it was the Spitfire. Probably it was both.

"You all right, Loki?" I whispered to the cat still on my shoulder.

"Don't mind me," he said. "Though I may have wet myself. And you, by extension."

Then Eva and I met eyes.

"Stables, then infirmary," she said in a weary, hoarse voice. She wasn't in good shape.

As Eva helped Liara onto Siren's back and they began riding toward the grounds, I lifted the rod in the spotty moonlight through the canopy. The chain tinkled as I did.

My own professor had tried to kill me for this, and the demon prince had sacrificed himself so I could keep it.

The Backbiter certainly did feel cursed.

Nurse Neverwink wasn't yet awake when we came into the infirmary. She stumbled down the stairs from her home into the infirmary's waiting room a few minutes after we'd all piled in.

Her tired eyes shifted to alarmed the moment she took in the four of us, and Loki standing at my feet. Then, to me, "What have you done now?"

"Me?" I struggled to set one mock-offended hand to my chest, but found my left arm screaming as I did so. Where should I even start? It didn't even matter, really. "Fire witch stuff, basically," I said. "Do you have treatment for hexes?"

I had never seen Neverwink so shocked. "*Hexes?*"

"The agony hex, specifically." I nodded to Aidan, who I was helping to walk with one arm under him. "Everyone got hexed, but I think he got it the worst."

"Hexes!" Neverwink threw her hands up. She started toward the medicine pantry, then stopped and pointed. "Take a bed, each of you."

Twenty minutes later, Loki was drinking from a bowl of catnip-laced milk in the corner and those of us who had been agony hexed had been given a poultice to drink. It tasted like mushrooms with the texture of slug slime, but Neverwink watched me until I'd downed the whole thing.

Afterward, she plucked the cup from me. "The burning should subside within the hour."

"The hour?" I took a deep, bolstering breath.

She clucked at me. "Do you know how long it's been since I've had to brew a remedy for a hex? *Twenty years*. You should be glad I even know how, Clementine Cole."

I knew what that meant.

Neverwink hadn't had to deal with the after-effects of hexes for so long, she thought maybe she was done with them. Twenty years was a long time, after all—long enough to feel like another lifetime.

And then a fire witch had shown up and brought those hexes roaring back.

When Neverwink left, I glanced over at Liara in the bed next to me. "Hey, fae," I whispered, low enough that Aidan and Eva couldn't hear from their beds on the opposite side of the room.

Her eyes tracked toward me. "Hey, fire witch."

"I know tonight wasn't what you expected." I paused. "It wasn't what I expected, either. I..."

She snorted. "Do I hear a half-assed apology coming?"

"Maybe."

"Save it." She placed one hand over her chest, eyes on the ceiling. "Life never goes how you expect it to go. That's why expectations are useless."

I wondered if she was thinking of her family. I was certainly thinking of mine. Who might still be alive, in Edinburgh.

"Fair enough." My eyes stayed on her. "But I won't rope you into anything else. Whatever indebtedness you felt toward me, it was paid long ago."

"I know." Now her face turned to me, dark eyes hard in the dim lamplight on the bedside table between us. "So we're even. Everything I do from this point on is because I want to."

My eyebrows went up. "From this point?"

"You heard Rathmore." A strange look crossed her face, somewhere between anger and resoluteness. "Edinburgh is where we need to go. Well, aside from hell."

We.

She'd said we.

A face appeared at the end of our beds. Eva, who looked somehow good as new. Except she wore a grimness around her mouth. "Did I hear someone say Edinburgh?"

I raised a finger to my lips, glanced to where Neverwink was puttering around in the other room.

Eva gave a half-smile. "Don't tell her this, but Neverwink's hearing isn't great."

Liara flicked a hand up and down Eva's body. "How do you look so... good?"

"Healing magic." Eva shrugged one effortless shoulder. "You probably won't be surprised to know I'm aces when casting it on myself. Do you want...?"

"No," Liara said at once.

"I hear a conversation happening without me," Aidan's voice called from across the room. "And I have a feeling I want in on it."

"Yeah." With a silent leap, Loki came floating onto the end of my bed the way cats do. He wavered with enormous pupils. "I hear *three* conversations, actually. Gods, I've got to get into Neverwink's catnip stash."

Even Liara laughed at that.

Aidan limped over, closing the curtain around our beds, and took a seat at the end of Liara's bed. He still wore pain on his face and in his slump, but he didn't complain. That wasn't his way.

In fact, no one was complaining.

"What do you think's happened to Frostwish?" Eva asked. "Will she come back?"

I shook my head. "Rathmore said she'd slander me." I didn't think she was dead, but she wouldn't be returning to the academy. "But I doubt she'll be returning here."

Not after I told Umbra about where her allegiances lay. In fact, after my last conversation with Umbra about Lucian the prince, I had a feeling things between us had changed.

She was willing to tell me more truths, and I was willing to do the same with her.

I had a feeling she knew more answers to my questions than she'd ever let on.

"And Rathmore?" Eva whispered.

Pain lanced my chest when I heard his name. I still didn't know what had become of him.

Liara shifted on the bed with a sigh. "Like he said: his life isn't important. It's getting Clementine to the thief's blade in Edinburgh that matters."

I tried to ignore that first part. "He mentioned a 'close.'"

"Which close?" Aidan's palms went out. "There are loads."

"What even *is* a close?" Liara asked, then glanced around at us. "I'm from Singapore."

"Old roads under the city proper," Eva said. "Edinburgh was built atop itself over the centuries, and the ancient city lies under the present-day one."

I sat up in bed. "So we have to go under the city."

"At night," Aidan said. "During the witching hour."

"And you have to figure out how to summon the thief's blade," Liara said. "While avoiding the formalists and the Shade's army."

And facing whatever I may find there. Including my mother and sister.

Finally, I met eyes with Loki.

"Let's not burn the whole place down, shall we?" he teased.

At that, Rathmore appeared in my mind, his words in my ear—

Remember yourself.

No matter what came, I couldn't let the Spitfire consume me. For everyone's sake.

Of all of us, I was the last to leave the infirmary. Neverwink had insisted I stay because I was in the worst shape, it seemed. And so I'd urged the others to go on without me, that I would find them that afternoon.

But when I came out of the infirmary with Loki later that day, it was Maeve Umbra who stood in the clearing.

She turned toward me, sorrow written all over her features. Someone had told her what had happened. But it was more than that.

Umbra was worried.

CHAPTER FORTY-FIVE

Outside the train window, the Romanian countryside swept by, all hills and sun-kissed trees. And amongst them sat my faint reflection, so much red hair and freckles.

"Have you ever been on a train?" Maeve Umbra asked from the seat across from me. Her robes draped proud and regal over the seat, her staff propped against the empty one next to her like a second passenger.

I met her gaze. "Only the metro back home, and that was mostly underground." Then, "Why didn't we just take the leyline?"

She gave a long, satisfied sigh. "When you've parted veils for as long as I have, you begin to relish traditional means of travel. I find, when I have nothing else to do and nowhere to be, I can think better."

It's more than that. But I knew this was as much as I would get from her.

We were otherwise in agreement on travel, except for one part: trains meant I was in motion. As a teenager, I'd preferred to be in motion, to be moving away from things. To never be caught.

Beside me, Loki slept. A pot of tea and cookies sat on the tray between us, and I wished I had asked if Eva could come along.

When Maeve Umbra had approached me in the clearing earlier

that day, she had invited Loki and me to stay with her for the summer at her family's home in Zurich. When I'd found Eva in our dorm to talk to her about it, she had said to me, "You don't turn down an offer like that from the headmistress."

So I didn't. I'd said my goodbyes for the summer and I had gone with the headmistress.

And not just because of protocol; I had a feeling she had a specific reason for inviting me along besides being oh so fond of me.

"Now that we're alone," she said into the otherwise empty car, "I have wondered for some time now: how do you hide it?"

I straightened. "Uh, hide what? My latent self-loathing? I don't."

"The weapon." Her violet eyes fixed on me. "The Shade's weapon."

Both Loki and I started at the same time. His head rose in the seat beside mine, and my hands went over my armrests. "I don't..." I began.

"You obtained the key two years ago," she said almost dully. "You retrieved the rod from the labyrinth last year. And I assume, given the time of year, your injuries, and the fact that Ora Frostwish has left the academy with some suddenness, that you've raised the chain from the lake."

I shook my head, fully astonished. "But you hid the key. You locked it away because it was too powerful."

"And it was gone from the safe that very afternoon." She raised her teacup from the tray next to her, took a sip as though we were gossiping about her next-door neighbor. "Apparently you've learned well how to harness that power."

Umbra had known about the key all along. She had known and allowed me to keep it.

I stared. I didn't know what to say.

"If you don't want to tell me," she said into the silence, "you're welcome to keep your secret, of course."

As I considered the past three years in terms of her role, a strange constellation began to emerge in my mind.

It was her who had taken me to the maze. Had she known the rod was there? She must have. Which meant she'd been... helping me? She had, after all, suggested Lucian had sent me to Siberia. And she had been right.

If she knew the chain was buried in the lake, then she also knew about the prophecy.

I met eyes with Loki.

"She hasn't killed you yet," he offered.

He was right. Of course, she could be taking me away to Switzerland to kill me away from any witnesses.

Umbra set down the teacup, some real gravity finally entering her expression. "I understand your hesitation, child. The reason I ask about the weapon is because now more than ever, you'll need to keep it close to you."

But my mind was still stuck on Umbra's involvement in all this. "Did you know about Ora Frostwish? Is that why you had her teach me hexes?"

"I knew her allegiances were historically... uncertain." She sighed. "I'm sorry for what you must have endured. I had hoped she would be your defender in what is to come."

"'What is to come?'"

Her gaze shifted out the window. "The Shade's power grows faster than I had ever anticipated. A second battle comes, Clementine, and soon. She draws allies to her each day, and from places you wouldn't expect."

I swallowed. "Callum Rathmore is Lucian the prince. But I guess you knew that."

She gave a slow nod. "I suspected so, though I wasn't certain if he had taken up the mantle from his father."

His father. The mantle.

"Tristan Rathmore?" I whispered.

"Yes," she said. "The Rathmore line has served the Shade since the Battle of the Ages. Lucian the prince has been many mortal men over the centuries, the most recent of whom is Callum. Though I have a feeling he's the most noble-hearted of any of them."

"Is that why you brought him to the academy as a professor?"

"Yes," she said, eyes piercing mine. "After he had been estranged from his father for years. You can imagine the kind of allies Rathmore and Frostwish would have been. I suppose Rathmore is still in question, isn't he?"

I closed my eyes, sighed. She knew it all, so there was no real point in lying about what had happened. "He saved me. He was the reason I was able to escape Frostwish."

She gave a slow nod. "Well done, Callum. So perhaps one of them has been saved. No doubt Frostwish will return to Tristan Rathmore's side and curse your name far and wide. She does not take defeat lightly."

I set a hand on Loki. My rock, my comfort. "Why are you taking me to Zurich? And don't tell me it's to see your family."

The faintest mirth touched Umbra's face, but was just as quickly replaced by a furrowed brow. "To keep you by my side, to keep you safe, while I train you."

"In what?"

Those violet eyes glinted in the light from the window. "In everything I know. You still have one piece of the weapon yet to retrieve, and procuring it will be your greatest trial yet."

EPILOGUE

I sat cross-legged in the grass, staring at the far-off mountains and meadows. Switzerland was as idyllic as a picture, even here in the middle of it.

Behind me, the faint scent of baking bread wafted through the window. The headmistress's forty-something daughter hummed a song I didn't know, but it was as pleasant as her two rosy-cheeked children, whom I could hear playing in the toy room.

And I could hear Maeve Umbra playing with them.

She was pretending to be a bear, growling and stamping. She roared, the children shrieked and ran and laughed. I had never heard her like this, so easy and carefree.

Turned out, Maeve Umbra wasn't just a headmistress—she was a human being like the rest of us.

Beside me, Loki lolled, paws up in the air. When I tried to stroke his belly, all four sets of claws latched onto my hand. "How dare you." He fixed me with dilating green eyes.

I winced, tried to disentangle my hand. Like a Chinese finger trap, that only made him hold on harder. "I have regrets," I said.

He disengaged his claws and rolled onto his belly. "You're supposed to be focusing, anyway."

I groaned, readjusted my seat. "I have been—for hours. A normal human's attention span is only twenty minutes, and I'm so not a normal human."

All I wanted to do was go back and reread that snippet from the latest *Witches & Wizards*—in which Frostwish had declared she'd been scarred by the fire witch. Before, I had been a fugitive of the formalists with no record of evil-doing. Now, I was a deserved fugitive.

"That you are not." Loki's tail flicked as he stared out at the road weaving through the meadow below us. "Here's a hint: Umbra's magic is an earth color."

The first step to casting Umbra's enchantments was seeing her enchantments. They were air magic, and while I could see Eva's and Liara's and Frostwish's magic, I couldn't see Maeve Umbra's.

And I didn't know why.

"How can *you* see it?" I groused. "I had to work for months at it, and you..."

"I'm just a cat?" He glanced back at me, and I could have sworn he smirked. "What does that say about you, then?"

I sighed, refocused. It would take as long as it would take, and I had the rest of the summer.

The sun had fallen behind the mountains, and Loki had retreated into the house by the time Umbra came out, her staff tapping on the stone walkway to announce her arrival. She came to stand beside me. "Dinner's served."

"I know," I said. "I can smell it."

She set a hand on my shoulder. "Be patient, child. You cannot possibly hope to see the world properly without sustenance."

I looked up at her. "Why did we take the train here? Really."

She winced in the half-light. "I suspected you wouldn't be put off."

My eyebrows went up.

She gestured with her staff out at the pristine meadows and valleys. "This looks quite beautiful, but you cannot yet see what I can see. Before the summer ends, you will."

"And what can you see?"

"The leylines." Her eyes tracked across the skyline. "Some have begun to darken with the Shade's magic."

"Darken," I echoed.

"Yes," she murmured. "She has begun to corrupt them as she did five hundred years ago."

END OF BOOK 3

BOOK 4: *"Thief" isn't the worst thing I've been called.* Clementine's adventure as a fire witch continues in her fourth year at Shadow's End. ***Good Witches Don't Steal*** is available to read on Amazon.

FREE SHORT STORY: Liara Youngblood and Lucian the demon prince clash in the prequel story *The Fae and the Demon.*

Join S.W. Clarke's reader newsletter and get *The Fae and the Demon* for FREE only at subscribepage.com/swclarke.

AFTERWORD

Hi friend,

In her third year, Clem begins to appreciate the "consistent, unsexy effort" people put into their lives. She respects it almost more than anything else.

And the older I get, the more I find I agree with her.

Of the people I've known in my life, I've had a special, unique admiration for the people whose consistent, unsexy efforts I've been witness to.

My father, who never missed a day of work at his exhausting sales job to support his family.

That writer I went to school with, whom everyone knew would succeed because she wrote every day. (And she has.)

Five years ago, I first read *A Tree Grows in Brooklyn.* Of all the characters, I was most heartbroken and changed by the main character's mother. She was an Irish immigrant, and she spent her life washing the floors of wealthy homes to keep her children from dying of poverty.

I'm fortunate I haven't had to get on my knees. Which is why I'll never underestimate the beauty of even the workmanlike days of writing a novel. In the end, nothing is sexy all the time—but consistent effort put toward the things that matter will grow you.

As promised, here's the soundtrack to *Good Witches Don't Curse:* https://open.spotify.com/playlist/oM1WPky2NPNGk19GlVjMmo?si= 5cvIjPmQQQOv8bvkpTYn7Q.

Until next time—

Shavonne

ABOUT THE AUTHOR

S.W. Clarke is a fantasy romance and urban fantasy author. She lives in a magical tree (well, we all have dreams, don't we?) with her partner and two identical, unrelated cats. She writes to inhabit the lives of the smartest, bravest women her brain can conjure.

Want to be notified of her latest releases? Join her reader newsletter!

facebook.com/authorswclarke

instagram.com/authorswclarke